SHIELD AND CROCUS

By Michael R. Underwood

Ree Reyes novels

Geekomancy

Celebromancy

Attack the Geek (novella)

Shield and Crocus

SHIELD AND CROCUS

Michael R. Underwood

47NORTH

Text copyright © 2014 Michael R. Underwood
All rights reserved.

Published by 47North, Seattle

www.apub.com

Amazon, the Amazon logo, and 47North are trademarks of Amazon.com, Inc., or its affiliates.

ISBN-13: 9781477823903
ISBN-10: 1477823905

Cover design by Jason Gurley
Illustrated by Stephan Martiniere

Library of Congress Control Number: 2014931179

Printed in the United States of America

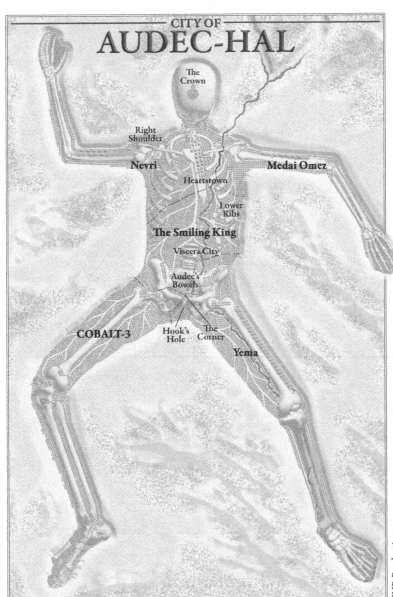

CITY OF
AUDEC-HAL

The Crown

Right Shoulder

Nevri

Medai Omez

Heartstown

Lower Ribs

The Smiling King

Viscera City

Audec's Bowels

COBALT-3

Hook's Hole

The Corner

Yema

For the instructors, students, and staff of Clarion West 2007,
the original Shield-bearers

Chapter One

First Sentinel

Wonlar's apartment was a carefully constructed ruse. The floor was spotted with yard-high stacks of books and carpeted by papers, schematics, and yet more papers. Delicate arrangements of spare parts and sealed bottles of reagents formed mounds outside lanes of traffic. Bookshelves filled the walls from floor to ceiling along three sides of the apartment, broken only by a closet, the hall to the bedrooms, and the opening to the kitchen.

Over the last twenty years, the apartment had settled into Wonlar's image: scholarly, brilliant, and scattered. That was the intent.

His neighbors wouldn't expect that Wonlar Gonyu Pacsa, absent-minded artificer and handyman, could also be First Sentinel, leader of the Shields of Audec-Hal, the only major force standing against the rule of the oligarchs. If they thought he was barely organized enough to keep track of whose oven he had to fix by Monday and mumbled incoherently when pressed with small talk, then they wouldn't ask questions about why he was up at all hours and never seemed to be around for parties.

Wonlar stood above a table, squinting to focus on the job at hand. He was approaching his seventy-first birthday, but he looked no older than any other Ikanollo. He had the same square jaw, the same high forehead, sun-yellow skin, and dark brown hair. For other races, speech patterns, clothes, and personality were most of what set Ikanollo apart, since each man looked like every other, each woman a perfect copy of another in features and build. Living side by side with the other races, Ikanollo had learned to differentiate themselves intentionally. For Wonlar, it became just another part of his cover.

Favoring his left leg, Wonlar stepped over a short pile of books about rare reagents. He'd cracked his hip a year ago in a skirmish with the Smiling King, and it still took three cups of *dounmo* tea to push back the pain. Wonlar sipped from his third cup of the day, taking a break from mixing the unguent that would refresh the enchantment on the Shields' pendants.

The oligarchs had stepped up their patrols in preparation for the upcoming summit, especially in COBALT-3's territory, and Sapphire had nearly been caught in Bluetown while on her way back home. *So how do I make them last longer?* Wonlar asked himself, holding the formula in his head. He'd been enchanting the pendants for fifty years, protecting the Shields from the Ikanollo birthright of reading threads.

Any Ikanollo could see the emotional threads that connected a person's heart to the people and world around them; whether it was the stark yellow of fear, the brilliant emerald of compassion, or the blood-red of rage, each thread stood out to his people, thicker where the emotion was strong, thin where it was tenuous. Without the amulets to conceal their threads, any Ikanollo servant of the oligarchs could identify his or any Shield's threads and bring the tyrant's wrath. And Wonlar had no desire to see the oligarchs' servants knocking down his door or setting his building ablaze. His amulets gave them all false threads, ready-made identities that would lead Ikanollo anywhere but to the truth.

The alarm bracer on his left arm whooped. He looked down at the six gems to see the ruby was pulsing with light. *That's Blurred Fists'. Must be something on his patrol,* Wonlar thought. He looked at the amulets, then to the window, and sighed. He gulped down the rest of his tea and stomped over to his bedroom, crumpling papers as he went. Where the living room was shabby, his bedroom was spotless, everything in its place. Wonlar threw open the closet and pulled down his longcoat, one of the raiment suits, a pair of boots, and his belt.

As fast as he could, Wonlar donned the raiment that marked him as First Sentinel, leader of the Shields of Audec-Hal. He pulled on a black shirt emblazoned with a watchful yellow eye and a turret on the chest, the symbol he'd chosen not long after the tyrants had claimed his city. He slipped into his black linen pants and then snapped on his belt. The product of decades of work, his belt contained smoke bombs, enspelled wands, throwing knives, and a handful of specialized artifacts for the Shields' most powerful foes.

He wasn't as young as he used to be, but as the saying goes, old age and trickery beat out youth and speed every time. *At least, so far.* Wonlar threw on the longcoat, then opened his window and jumped up onto the railing. He produced his grapple gun and dove off-the balcony, firing. The hook caught on a worn gargoyle across the street, and First Sentinel began swinging his way across the city.

Even taking the high road over roofs and towers, swinging whenever possible, it would take almost a half hour to reach the district of Audec's Bowels in the south-center of the city, where Blurred Fists was scheduled to patrol that morning.

We can't be everywhere, not with so few of us and the city so large. The Shields lived spread out between the five domains, to minimize the delay in their response, but when a Spark-storm erupted, they were often too late. When the storms came and went before the Shields could respond, all they could do was clear the rubble and prevent the terrified citizens from lashing out at the new Spark-touched.

First Sentinel followed the red light in Blurred Fists' gem, which glowed the brightest in the direction of Wonlar's friend, like a magical compass leading First Sentinel to his fellow Shield's location. As he swung down the refuse-filled alley between two ruined buildings, to avoid a group of sentries, Wonlar heard Sarii's voice in his mind, rehashing an old argument.

"Why do we even bother, Wonlar? We'll never win, we're always too late. How many people do we really help? More than you've gotten killed in your crusade?"

The memory of her words stung as he hurried through alleyways and streets, ran over buildings, dodged laundry lines, and avoided COBALT-3's patrols.

The ribs rose above the horizon as he swung north, crosshatching the sky to form a net of shadows. *I've been fighting for fifty years, Sarii; I'm not going to change my mind now. Getting old means I've earned the right to commit to my bad decisions.*

Without Selweh, he might have lost hope. The boy was First Sentinel's compass. In the cold of night, when his joints ached and the guilt from fifty years of failure snuck into his mind, his son's optimism was more valuable than a legion of soldiers. *While he's alive, while the Aegis continues to return to us, I have hope.*

Soaring over the outskirts of The Corner, the district to the south of Audec's Bowels, he approached the boundary between COBALT-3's domain and that of the Smiling King. Two blocks from the border, he swung down from a high office building toward a clock tower. COBALT-3 had posted two guards at a landing just below the clock, looking west and east, with two more level with the massive clock face, watching north and south.

The sentries were her basic model: no taller than First Sentinel and about as sturdy as a jury-rigged bicycle. They were piles of brass and copper riveted together and run on an electric battery, but they were skilled enough to hold a crossbow and hit people that didn't know how to dodge.

But First Sentinel had been dodging crossbow bolts since before COBALT-3 was built. He swung wide as the south-facing automaton opened fire. Then he hauled on the grapple line, pulling himself out of the way of the bolt. Using the boost in speed, he swung into the automata and kicked it through the clock face.

The sound of shattering glass echoed throughout the neighborhood, drawing the attention of every automaton for several blocks. Alarms rang out as metallic voices blared COBALT-3's standard warning:

"Alert: Dangerous insurrectionist activity reported. Please return to your homes and allow security forces to protect you. Reassurance: COBALT-3 is watching."

She hasn't bothered updating that recording in years. COBALT-3 had more of a personal touch than her creator, but only just.

The alarm was all part of First Sentinel's plan. Make a scene at the tower and draw attention there, maybe let some people sneak through the crowd.

First Sentinel gave the guards more to focus on as he dove back out of the tower. He fell a hundred feet before he caught his grapple line on a roof just inside the Smiling King's territory. Several crossbow bolts cut through the sky in his wake, but none of them came close. First Sentinel smiled as he swung onward. *One hurdle crossed; now for the real threat.*

This method of travel was dangerous, but with it came freedom of movement. Most of the populace of Audec-Hal couldn't swing over the district walls or fight their way through the bone pathways. They had to present their papers, pay the toll, and pray that they weren't selected randomly for additional inspection.

For fifty years, the people of Audec-Hal had been searched, detained, and taken as "volunteers" for the tyrants' experiments. Everyone in Audec-Hal has lost someone in the tyrant's reign.

The Shields had staged dozens of raids on the gates between the domains, trying to stop the abductions as they happened.

Even if all six of us did nothing but hassle the guards at the gates between the districts, it wouldn't be enough, he thought as he swung up toward the ribs.

First Sentinel swung up to a graystone apartment building, a tall warehouse, and finally an ostentatious gargoyle atop an office building. *City Mother be praised for roof gargoyles.*

At the apex of his swing, he kicked out and released the grapple, sailing just barely into range of one of the ribs.

He shot out his grapple line, which embedded into the bleached bone of a huge rib. First Sentinel pressed the switch to scale up to the ribs. Audec's skeleton was massive, twenty miles long from head to toes. From this spot, walking along the ribcage, he could walk nearly a third of the way across the city as long as he kept his footing and avoided the aerial patrols.

Beneath him, the city of Audec-Hal stretched out in every direction. Today only Audec's bones remained, but when he first fell to the earth, the titan's body had carved out a deep valley in his shape. First Sentinel's ancestors built their city in and around the titan's remains, towers with bone foundations, the streets like his long-atrophied veins, and thousands of homes standing in the shadow of the titan's immense skeleton.

Back toward Hook's Hole and the south of the city, Audec's hips crested high, pointing down to the legs, where countless thousands huddled in honeycombed tenements. Directly below First Sentinel, the districts in Audec's trunk were home to trade and industry, keeping the money flowing; materials and food coming in; and weapons, textiles, and machines going out through the river that flowed into the left shoulder, wound through the city, and then flowed underground from Audec's foot.

Past the ribs stood Heartstown, a bustling city-in-a-city that was the home to the city's upper class—people who'd made their bed working with the tyrants but weren't yet rich enough to live in the Head. Only the wealthiest collaborators could afford the mansions and villas inside and atop Audec's skull.

First Sentinel saw millions of faint threads connecting the people of the city, his Ikanollo birthright revealing the emotional ties that bound heart to heart. Burgundy domination and yellow fear were the most common, arcing out from the tower of the City Mother. She used to protect the people, bring them together. Now she was the tyrants' greatest weapon against the people.

Amidst the threads, First Sentinel saw the source of Blurred Fists' alarm: a Spark-storm in full fury, warping the edge of the neighborhood. Impossible colors stood out from the drab grays and browns of the streets and buildings. The storm didn't seem to be moving, but regardless, the streets at the edge were filled with waves of thousands, desperate to escape. This was the seventh storm this year by First Sentinel's count, and it wasn't even the middle of spring. They used to strike just two to four times a year. *Why so many, and why now?*

Scanning the buildings and feeling the wind, First Sentinel plotted out a path back down into the city toward the storm. He could head directly into the storm, try to start pulling people out of danger. But the crowd was on the verge of breaking into a stampede.

Sometimes, on long nights when sleep refused to come, he didn't see the city as home anymore, just an unending series of fires to fight. First things first. If he couldn't clear the crowd at the edge, there'd be nowhere to send people trapped in the middle.

The wind tore at his face as he dropped, and the shock of his line going taut set his shoulder on fire, igniting another old injury. First Sentinel grit his teeth as he landed on a low roof.

He cupped his hands, calling to the volatile crowd.

"Please be calm! You are already outside the storm's range. Keep moving and you will be fine."

His words broke on the crowd and dissolved in the sea of yellow threads. And yet, dozens turned to face him, scrambling for any chance of help. If he just left them, someone would likely get trampled to death. But hundreds could be dying inside the storm.

Some days First Sentinel longed for the time when his idea of a hard decision was which artificer's academy to attend or what flowers to buy his beloved Aria for the equinox. *The privileges of youth,* he thought, a wave of nostalgia breaking over the beach of his worry.

"First Sentinel, save me!" called a Pronai woman, her red form a blur as she rushed over to the base of the building where First Sentinel stood. With her birthright of speed, she could run out of the neighborhood—dodge around the crowd without trouble—if she'd just calm down.

An Ikanollo woman raised a screaming toddler, "Take my daughter!" *If I took the child, then I'd have to spend another half hour finding the mother again to return her safely.*

"Don't let me become a monster!" cried a man, another Ikanollo. First Sentinel pursed his lips, torn between the people's needs. *Keep yourself together, old man. They need you to be strong, patient, kind.*

On another day, these people might have thrown rocks at him or tipped off one of the Smiling King's guards to get an extra loaf of bread. He didn't blame them. The City Mother's power—twisted by the tyrants—kept them cowed, so only the most passionate could tame the fear and rebel. Afraid and desperate, they did what they had to do to survive. *And today, I'm their best hope.*

But these people aren't the ones in real danger, Wonlar. You have to keep your head on, can't stop for every scared mother. If you stop now, how many will die in the storm?

These people on the edge—they were already safe, but didn't know it. The ones that really needed help were the ones in the storm, unaware inside their homes, those who didn't know they were in danger or were too infirm to get out, or too stubborn.

First Sentinel tried to direct traffic, shouting over the crowd, calling for order. After a minute of failed attempts to calm the crowd, Wonlar cursed under his breath and raised his grapple gun. He was needed elsewhere.

"Keep moving, and keep your neighbors safe." He swung away, ashamed, watching the shuffling crowd covered by the long shadow of a rib. He hoped he'd done enough for them.

As he got closer to the storm, First Sentinel saw the reality of the damage. Buildings had been stretched thin like taffy, then toppled under their own weight. Several attenuated graystones had fallen already, rubble warped like candy left out in the sun, melted and re-formed.

The air around was filled with brief, ungrounded sounds— chirping birds, buzzing saws, and ecstatic screams. The phantom noises mixed with the real shouts for help, tearful prayers to the gods, and the cracking, shifting, organ-twisting sounds of the Spark wreaking havoc on reality.

First Sentinel had seen hundreds of Spark-storms, but each time they froze him for a moment as a needle of fear stabbed into the back of his neck. The Spark-storms tore away the city bit by bit, replacing his home and neighbors with strangers and unfamiliar landmarks.

The street was lined with dozens of new Spark-touched. The recently transformed lay sprawled or ran spasmodic in the streets, still in the throes of metamorphosis. An Ikanollo man banged his head against a wall, screaming in pain. With each blow, his head bloated and hardened, shifting into an armored shell with lacerating spikes. He slammed his head through the wall, still screaming. His voice dropped an octave, then another, until it was too low to be heard.

First Sentinel had seen countless transformations, each stranger than the last, but they never got easier to watch. Each one reminded him of his first Spark-storm, the one that had changed his life and set him on the path of losing Aria. *But without the Spark, could I have saved her at all, or would I have been widowed that much sooner, with no son to keep me from despair?*

The peoples' threads raged like another storm, colored ties between brothers, lovers, and friends. Each person's threads stretched from their heart to the emotion's source. The street was filled with yellow threads of fear connecting citizens and their freshly changed neighbors.

He couldn't see Blurred Fists' telltale red haze of speed moving amidst the storm.

The cobblestones of the street had become volcanic rock, uneven mounds of jagged stone with striations in red, gray, and brown.

First Sentinel landed at the edge of the storm to start pulling people out. The Spark-touched man's head had grown to three times its normal size, too heavy for First Sentinel to haul over his shoulder. Instead, the Shield held him around the middle and dragged his stone-crushing skull across the rough ground. First Sentinel winced in sympathetic pain as the man's head skipped across the rocks, but the exoskeleton didn't yield blood.

The storm stopped after he'd plucked another dozen victims from the center. First Sentinel didn't fear the Spark's effects. He'd been touched once, and the Spark did not touch those it had already twisted.

The Spark left a mangled neighborhood in its wake, lying dormant until the next storm. It could be that night, the following week, or a year later. Given the recent pattern, it'd be within a month.

The district of Audec's Bowels was under the control of the Smiling King, a madman who had appeared after the Senate fire and carved out a kingdom with his Spark-touched thralls.

There would be no municipal assistance for this disaster or its victims. Instead, the Smiling King would send in his Spark-touched servants to claim their new comrades, cart them off, and lock them in dank cages that they would soon call home. Once the Smiling King had his new pets, he let the horror of their change boil over into madness, until only he could soothe their pain, using his power over the Spark. Eventually, they all joined his "family."

First Sentinel had seen friends taken by the Spark and then found them across a battlefield, their faces familiar but distant, crazed.

Once inducted into the Spark-touched family, they could not be deprogrammed. He'd tried everything, even having Ghost Hands bring him into their minds to talk through the pain. He'd spent a year visiting Red Vixen like that, until Ghost Hands forced him to step away and leave the former Shield with her madness.

But this time, there would be no recruits. *He'll have to come through me to claim them.* But he couldn't shield them all, not from the Smiling King, and not from their neighbors.

Always too many to save and too few Shields for the task.

A red shape settled into focus beside First Sentinel. Blurred Fists was thin, but heavily muscled, a lifelong athlete. Beneath his mask, his hair was receding—or would be if he hadn't taken to shaving his head the year before.

To any but another of the red-skinned Pronai, Blurred Fists' movements would be twitchy, spastic. Their race's metabolism put all others to shame. They matured faster, moved and reacted more quickly, and died sooner. But despite his incredible speed, Wenlizerachi was one of the most reserved men First Sentinel knew. The Pronai had learned at a young age to slow down for the other races, talk at their pace so he could be understood, and even more, so he would be taken seriously.

Blurred Fists' raiment was a tight, red running suit with a painted pattern of a black fist on a red background on his chest.

A red mask hid his identity, his features distinct, unlike First Sentinel's.

The Pronai nodded to his old friend. "You made it."

"Where are we needed most?" First Sentinel asked.

Blurred Fists shifted through five poses in an instant, pondering. "The school. It's alive; the doors are mouths. It's already digesting them."

Children. City Mother, spare them. The City Mother was hidden away in the tower on The Crown, her ears and eyes shut to the voices of the people. For decades, she'd heard and obeyed only the oligarchs. Once, she'd spread compassion and maternal love. Under their power, the City Mother kept people afraid, placated. First Sentinel doubted that she'd heard him since the tyrants bound her, but still he prayed.

"Take me there." Blurred Fists dashed to the corner and waited for First Sentinel, who followed in a run, aching as he went. The *dounmo* was wearing off. He'd left in too much of a rush to make the elixir he drank before missions, so his collection of injuries were making their presence known, old companions he couldn't be rid of and never liked.

Some of the unchanged were helping the new Spark-touched; others took up clubs and knives to drive them out. First Sentinel had learned long ago that he couldn't help everyone, but it didn't stop the guilt. These days, guilt was all that was left to him. And rage. *Without Selweh to put it to good use, I'd burn out in a year and take the Shields with me.*

When they reached the school, it was chewing on something that First Sentinel prayed was a chair. Pointed teeth burst from a crimson mouth, its lips as long as a full-grown Ikanollo was tall. The building itself had turned a sickly shade of green, square walls replaced with a bulbous mass of mottled skin, oozing sores, and random scales.

The school walls sported more mouths down the street, similarly arrayed with leg-length teeth. The walls of the school rose and fell as it breathed through wheezy nostrils where the windows had been. Youthful cries for help echoed from inside, along with the sound of mastication.

First Sentinel turned to Blurred Fists. "Get inside and start pulling the students out. I'll try to break some of these mouths open to provide exits."

"Good luck." By the time First Sentinel felt the slap on the shoulder, Blurred Fists had disappeared into the maw of the school.

I should be used to that by now. First Sentinel had fought alongside four generations of Shields from Blurred Fists' family, ever since he met Blurred Fists' great-grandmother during a food riot.

First Sentinel drew his fighting staves from his belt and stepped forward to study the door. It spat out a pile of bones and licked its lips as he approached. First Sentinel took a step back, recoiling at the stench.

The teeth were large, the enamel thick and tough. The sticks wouldn't do anything, shock gloves barely more. The maw opened to reveal three rows of teeth, ingrown on one another, covered in grime despite being less than an hour old.

The mouth distended out from the fleshy wall and took a bite at him. First Sentinel jumped back, the teeth tearing off one corner of his longcoat as it billowed under him. *Dammit. I just mended that last month.*

First Sentinel reached into his belt and grabbed two stone spheres, each the size of a small lime. He pressed a small button on each stone and then tossed the bombs into the mouth. He shuffled back as fast as he could, favoring his hip.

The teeth closed on the enchanted stones. A second later, they detonated with a muffled boom, sending shards of bone and teeth flying across the street. First Sentinel ducked under his longcoat, feeling blunted cuts as the shards clattered on the street and bit into doors and walls opposite the school. When he looked up, the mouth lay slack and open, teeth shattered and mouth bloodied. A quick glance around the street told him that no one else had been caught in the explosion.

Much better.

The stench of the school's interior sagged in the air, worse than the breath of a dog who feasted in the sewers. First Sentinel wore a re-breather, usually saved for poison gas, as he walked down the hall. The youthful wails continued from the hall way and to the left. The school was nearly empty, tiled floors now mottled soft tissue. With each step, First Sentinel's boots sank nearly to the ankle.

A red streak settled into the form of Blurred Fists at the corner. "Up here. They're stuck in the teeth."

First Sentinel pushed down the hall, pulling his feet out of the suction of the floor. Blurred Fists waited for him at the door to the classroom, no marks on the floor from his footfalls. First Sentinel huffed to himself, wishing not for the first time that he'd been born a Pronai. Their gift of speed he'd take, but that power was not worth their short lifespan. As a Pronai, he'd have died barely after the tyrant's rise, might've never had a chance to serve as a Shield.

15

As the two Shields stepped inside, the stench hit First Sentinel like a wet slap to the face. It was nearly unbearable, even with a re-breather.

The classroom was a dentist's nightmare. The chairs were rows of jagged teeth over a yard tall. A spotted red carpet stretched the length of the room, rolled over on one end. Several folded-over clusters of ingrown molars trapped the dozen children left moving.

First Sentinel's mind raced, trying to sort out how to save the children without hurting them—and fast. They'd need to crack the enamel, delicate work with them squirming and crying. It would take time, but it shouldn't be too dangerous. A boy of no more than seven cried out for his mother, and sympathetic pain arced down First Sentinel's spine. *He sounds just like Selweh did at that age.*

First Sentinel dashed forward to the children, but two steps in, the floor rolled underneath him. What First Sentinel had taken for carpet licked up at the two men from the far wall, lashing out like a thick tongue.

Fantastic. First Sentinel rolled off to the side, glanced off a stand of teeth, and rose to his knees. He stuffed the staves back into his belt and pulled out two alchemically sharpened knives. He held one in reverse grip, high by his face, for defense, and the other out in front to slash and stab. He stepped between the children and the tongue, trying to read its movement.

The tongue lolled at First Sentinel. He dodged back and buried his forward blade in the thing as it crashed down on him. Ignoring its wound, the tongue slammed First Sentinel into a cluster of teeth, the sharp enamel glancing off his magically hardened longcoat.

A wave of light red flashed in front of First Sentinel as Blurred Fists pushed the abomination back with a barrage of punches. The

Pronai raced around to the other side of the tongue. First Sentinel pressed forward, spinning his knives in an advancing figure eight. He cut gashes out of the frenulum at the tongue's base while behind the tongue, Blurred Fists' gloves made the sound of a boxer pounding frozen carcasses.

Dodging the spastic swings of the tongue, First Sentinel landed several more blows, the tongue now seeping bright red blood. After the last slash, the tongue twitched, dropping to the floor.

First Sentinel sighed.

Now to put this thing out for good and get back to the children.

Instead, the tongue twisted end over end and lashed out at First Sentinel as he stepped forward. Reacting with decades of experience, First Sentinel leapt into a forward flip, digging the knives into the tip of the tongue, riding the cut down the other side. He removed one knife and stabbed again, fresh blood seeping down his arms as the tongue slammed into the ceiling.

The impact squeezed the air out of his lungs like a bellows. First Sentinel rolled to the floor, gasping. Blurred Fists appeared above him, hammering away at their foe. After a few moments, the tongue twitched again, started to rise toward the ceiling, and then dropped to the floor, lifeless.

First Sentinel wheezed for a few seconds as Blurred Fists pummeled the tongue a few more times for good measure.

Sitting up, First Sentinel caught his breath, looking to the children. Several had massive bruises where the pressure of the teeth had started to crush their arms, legs, and sides, and a few more had cuts from the edges of the teeth. *Please be all right. City Mother protect them, keep them safe.*

Pulling out a hammer and chisel, First Sentinel took his time, searching for a place to start.

"You're going to be fine," he said to the children. "I'm First Sentinel, and this is Blurred Fists. We're going to get you out now, but I need you to be brave."

The Ikanollo boy whose cries sounded like Selweh's nodded. The child sighed, relaxing his trapped arm. The others winced and made small whimpers, but they did their best.

"Good. Just relax, and think of home. We'll have you back there soon." Whatever home was left to them after the storm.

He worked with care as Blurred Fists tended to their wounds. With luck, the only scars the children would have from the day would be psychological, for all the comfort that was worth.

Small blessings, Wonlar thought.

Chapter Two

Sapphire

W *here is that screaming coming from?* Sapphire asked herself, locking on to one sound amidst the din. A little girl's voice rang through the street. She sounded no more than eight years old, and terrified.

The street was a broken maelstrom. Phantom sounds assaulted Sapphire's ears, pulling her attention from the real shouts for help or the footfalls of citizens driven mad by the Spark. *Is that even a real voice?* Sapphire wondered.

Scanning the street, Sapphire towered over everyone in sight. She was the only Freithin there, and even among her people, she was one of the largest, more than eight feet tall and still growing. It gave her as clear a view of the street as could be had amidst the chaos.

Sapphire hauled a quivering piece of animate slate off a Millrej woman and hurled it to an empty expanse of volcanic street. The stone floundered like a fish on the shore.

The street pummeled her senses with impossibility. On her left: buildings that started two stories up without any foundation, stretches of street that ramped up into the sky to become a pile of stinking fish. To her right: new Spark-touched reeling in horror at their transformation. At any moment, she could become one of them, but after more than a dozen Spark-storms, she'd never been affected. First Sentinel was immune due to previous exposure, but Sapphire and the other Shields took their lives into their hands every time they charged into a Spark-storm instead of fleeing from it.

First Sentinel maintained that the greater a person's emotional and physical fortitude, the less likely they were to be affected by the Spark-storm, but even he admitted it was just a theory.

It's not something you can fight, Sapphire admitted, worry crackling down her spine. The Spark-storms came without warning, struck without logic.

The first few times, she'd been terrified. Each time it got a little easier, but whenever she saw someone change, she wondered if she would be next. The fear never went away, but she was a Shield of Audec-Hal, and she had to be greater than her fear. And if not for First Sentinel and the Shields, she'd be in Omez's cages still, or she'd have been put down when she got too large to control.

Instead, she had friends, a home, and life. Her brother had a family. Her people had their freedom because of the Shields. It was a debt too huge for one woman to repay. But she tried anyway.

Sapphire took wide steps to land between jagged scraps of refuse and the sinkholes in the street, weaving her way through the storm.

The smoky-sweet smell of burning flesh hovered over the sensory mishmash. A hundred Shields wouldn't be enough for disaster relief. There were at best six on-site, if all of them answered Blurred Fists' summons—and Aegis hadn't make his last check-in. They were too few—and too late for many.

But they aren't here. It's just me and the chaos.

She ripped an awning off a ruined storefront and stopped for a moment to lay it over a pile of bodies to give them at least a shred of dignity. Undertaker had become a very profitable profession since the tyrants' reign had begun.

Several people thrashed in an alleyway, arms moving between thick leaves and plant stalks. *What is happening in there?*

She ran up a storm-made mound in the street, leapt from the peak, and landed soft, her bare feet sinking into what had looked like solid ground. She waded through the liquid stone, slogging her way toward the alley.

The narrow alley was shaded by a nest of trees growing out of the roofs and up from the concrete between the buildings. They made a canopy over the gap between the buildings and a jungle in the alley.

Screams for help echoed from within.

Sapphire cupped her hands around her mouth. "Hold on! I'm coming!"

The alley was barely five feet wide, designed for Ikanollo and the smaller races, not the statuesque Freithin. She turned to shuffle sideways, tearing up roots and breaking branches. *Don't bring the building down on yourself, Rova. Be careful.* Wildlife she couldn't name scrambled and flapped through the sliver of misplaced jungle. She breathed shallowly, trying to weave through the thick stalks and broad leaves.

She found a wounded Pronai clutching his arm beneath a huge flytrap plant. The man scrabbled on his back, trying to push through the thick brush to escape the carnivorous plant. Its spiny, bristled mouth gnashed hungrily, stretching toward Sapphire's hands.

"Stay down," she said, stepping over the Pronai to bat the mouth aside. When it snapped back at her, she slammed it into

21

the side wall. The crushing vegetation made a satisfying crunch. She reached around to the stem and pulled, tearing it off at the head. *Sounds just like the one serving of vegetables we got back in Omez's pens. We only had to be healthy enough for labor, not healthy enough to keep our teeth.* The sound was just as rewarding now as it had been then.

Sapphire tore off one of the broad leaves and used it to make a tourniquet, then carried the man out of the alley and left him on a stoop. All the while, more pained voices called to her from the alley.

She snapped a sapling in half and ripped it from its cobblestone roots to clear her way. Sunlight from the far street started to break through the dense cover as she cut through the alley. Sapphire picked out two more people from the alley jungle: a young Qava girl whom she found huddled in a ball inside the trunk of a tree and an Ikanollo man who was being pecked at by a swarm of brightly feathered birds that were no larger than his thumb.

After dressing the Ikanollo's wounds and making sure the others were stable, Sapphire pushed back into the alley, crashing through small trees and knocking another barbed flytrap from its stem with an uppercut. After working her way through the entire alley, Sapphire leapt out of the brush into the far street. Like the others, it was littered with debris, both organic and artificial. The air popped with a dazzling array of colors. But still no girl.

A half-dozen citizens on the street stopped to watch Sapphire. It seemed the Spark hadn't touched anyone on this side of the street, and no one looked injured. Most of the locals were doubtless huddled inside their homes, hoping that the buildings would shield them.

They'd go back to their routines and live on a street where the cobblestones were purple, the sidewalks a swamp, and their buildings made of chitin. Over the years, many neighborhoods had been abandoned after Spark-storms, but some continued on, residents adapting to their new environs.

It's amazing what people can get used to in fifty years.

Sapphire pulled a dying ten-foot-long cockroach out of the street, legs still twitching despite a missing head. She shook her head in befuddlement, and then saw a flash of movement at the edge of her vision.

Sapphire narrowed her eyes and followed the motion—a cloaked figure hauling something behind it. She lumbered up to a run as the cloaked figure disappeared behind a lamp and several wrecked motor trikes. The cloak looked familiar, but just as out of place as the cockroach. *Is that a warlock? Here?*

Sapphire bounded over the trikes and cut off the cloaked figure. It was a Warlock Guard—one of Magister Yema's bound slaves. The Warlock Guard came from all of the city's races, but they dressed in the same ragged brown robes and hoods. This warlock was far outside his master's domain—there had to be a reason for his presence. *Something to bring to the group. Maybe First Sentinel will have an idea.*

The warlock dragged a child behind him, thick red curls bouncing along as she strained to keep up. Her dress was actually a green shirt that fell below her knees. *It probably belongs to her father or older brother.* She thought of her own brother, and wished a quick prayer for his safety to the City Mother.

Sapphire drew up to her full height and filled the street with her booming voice. "Let her go!"

Instead, he ran. *Really?* she wondered, overtaking the warlock after three quick strides. She grabbed his arm, breaking the warlock's grip on the girl. Sapphire closed her fist and felt the cracking of bones. The warlock cried out in wordless pain.

The girl dropped to the street and then scurried away with a whimper. The warlock produced a wand from his cloak and spat a curse at her. A blast of force from the wand hit her full in the chest. She staggered back a step, but only just. A shot like that would crack an Ikanollo's ribs, but to her it was no worse than a stiff punch.

Sapphire lifted the warlock over her head with both arms. His fingers danced in arcane patterns, but she interrupted his spell by slamming him into the loose rocks of the street. He raised the wand once again, so she snapped it in half between her fingers.

"None of that," she said. "What are you doing here?"

Instead of answering, the warlock began to foam at the mouth. Damn. The warlock grew hot to the touch, and she kicked him across the street. The warlock's skin bubbled under the cloak, and she watched as the suicide spell Magister Yema put on each warlock dissolved the man into a boiling puddle.

Sapphire shuddered, looking away. Medai Omez had been a cruel master, but he'd never had that much control over the Freithin. *Praise be to the City Mother.*

She scanned the bodies, looking for movement or scraps of the dress. A moment later, she saw the girl hiding behind a cart made of fresh-baked bread that had doubtless been made of wood before the storm. The girl's eyes were covered by wild hair, the kind that took hours of brushing to tame. Sapphire's hair had been that long once, when she lived in the pens, and she had made a brush out of loose bits of wire and a broken broom shaft.

Sapphire approached and held out a hand the size of the girl's head. "It's all right. I won't hurt you, honey. You're safe." The girl didn't take much comfort from Sapphire's approach. *Understandable.* She didn't see a caring hero, just a huge muscled woman five times her size. *I'd be scared of me too.* Instead of reaching out to take Sapphire's hand, the girl sobbed.

Kneeling, Sapphire tried to catch the girl's gaze. "Please, don't be afraid." The child was unresponsive, curled up into herself, crying.

The Shield took a step back, let the girl be by herself for a moment. Yema's territory ended miles to the southeast, and the Smiling King had never been known to allow the servants of other tyrants into his territory without some ridiculous and specific price: a perfectly round pebble, the three smallest toes of a foot, and so on.

The other tyrants were more consistent with their rules. Nevri just charged a toll, as did Medai Omez. COBALT-3 kept her domain under a strict curfew, visitors and residents both. When relations between the oligarchs were better, travel was easier. But tensions were high, the tyrants wary of one another, even as rumors of a summit made the rounds.

So why her? Sapphire wondered. Looking closer at the girl, she saw the furry ears, the hair. At first, she took the girl to be a Spark-touched, freshly changed.

But no, she was Millrej—a vulpine-kin. All Millrej were born with features of their family's animal, a cold nose for the canines, a fluffy tail for the felines, tiny scales for reptiles, and so on. Only a tiny percentage manifested as Full-bloods, taking on the features of their animal patrons over the course of adolescence. Full-bloods were rare, but they made powerful warriors.

Red Vixen, one of the Shields who'd freed Sapphire from the slave pens, had been a Full-blood vulpine-kin, and she'd been nearly as fast as a Pronai and twice as ferocious. But this child was years from manifesting. Perhaps Yema was planning ahead, kidnapping Millrej children and hoping to bind an army of Full-bloods to his service before they matured.

There were others to be saved, but Sapphire looked at the girl again and saw in her the fear she'd seen in her people all those years ago, when Wonlar and the Shields freed the Freithin from Medai Omez. Fear mixed with desperation, fledgling hope looking for purchase.

She'd stay.

Sapphire used her calmest tone of voice, the one she'd learned after being freed. She'd once gotten fifty lashes when she halted the working line to help her brother after he'd collapsed due to malnourishment. She still bore the scars from the warden's blows. "My name is Sapphire. Can you tell me your name?"

The girl's voice was as light as a ghost. "Fahra."

Sapphire smiled. *Thank you, City Mother.* "Hello, Fahra. We should get you home. Where do you live?"

Fahra looked around, up and down the transformed street with its speckled colors, transmuted cobblestone street, and Spark-touched. "Not here."

"What neighborhood, Fahra?" Sapphire asked.

"High Thigh."

Sapphire nodded, standing. She extended her hand again. "Let's get you home, all right?"

"They're dead." Fahra pointed at the unconscious warlock. "He did it."

Her heart sank. "Your family?"

She nodded.

"Where do you want to go, Fahra? Is there anyone who can look after you?" *Please let there be someone left, City Mother. Audec-Hal has too many orphans already.*

The girl stood and clamped herself around Sapphire's muscled leg. Fahra's hands barely touched around the Shield's thigh. Sapphire chuckled nervously. *Better than being terrified by me.*

The Shields' nearest safehouse was the coffeeshop basement in Viscera City. At least they could feed her well there.

"Fahra, would you like to go with me? We can visit some friends of mine; they're very nice. And we can have cookies." Another squeeze. *Everyone loved cookies.* The first time Rova had eaten a cookie, she'd nearly died of amazement. After gruel and one handful of rotten vegetables a week, anything would have been heaven, but ever since, the big Shield had a soft spot for sweets.

"It'll be okay, Fahra. You're safe with me."

The girl nuzzled Sapphire's leg, holding tight. The Shield cradled the girl in one arm as she made her way through the uncanny street and out of the storm.

Chapter Three

First Sentinel

After the storm had passed, First Sentinel and Blurred Fists spent two hours clearing rubble, performing first aid, calming panicked Spark-touched, and returning children from the school to their families. Several locals had opened up their homes to make an impromptu hospital, since the nearest real hospital was half a district away and was not worth the gamble. Per the Smiling King's orders, his Spark-touched guard dismembered every tenth patient at random.

Stopping every half block to respond to another plea for help, it took First Sentinel most of an hour to make it to the nearest safehouse. By his orders, the Shields gathered after every Sparkstorm to compare notes, gather the injured, and learn everything they could to fight smarter the next time.

From the outside, Douk's Daily was a friendly neighborhood coffeeshop, well placed on a corner in a decent part of Viscera City, in COBALT-3's domain, surrounded by shops and offices. It was owned by Douk Tager and his wife, Xera, pillars of the underground resistance arts community. The Tagers gathered dissident artists in secret meetings at night, where they shared paintings, poems, whatever forbidden art they could find from the handful of people willful enough to resist the tyrant-corrupted threads of the City Mother.

Xera was nearly a magician with her baking and song, bringing in musicians from around the city; Douk had contacts from the docks to Heartstown and a ready smile for everyone. They were also old friends of Wonlar's and long-time Shield-bearers. The Shields' supporters came and went over the years; some burned out, some went bankrupt, some were taken by the tyrant's guards. *Without people like Douk and Xera, we'd have lost the war decades ago,* First Sentinel thought to himself.

First Sentinel swung past the front entrance and dropped onto the roof, watching to make sure no one had him in their sights. This neighborhood was fairly pro-Shield, which meant that people didn't go running for guards when they saw one of the group. But it only took one informant to compromise a safehouse. First Sentinel opened the hatch on the roof and climbed down three flights of stairs to a basement hall that joined up with the loading cellar.

He rapped on the door in the Shield's code: three short knocks, two long, and then five syncopated with both hands. A moment later, the door clicked and opened.

"Hello, old friend." Douk's well-trimmed beard outlined his chin like an exaggerated smile. First Sentinel had known Douk since he was a fresh-faced dissident, still in university and looking for a way to fight back against the tyrants' regime.

There aren't many whose passion was strong enough to overcome the City Mother's controls. Anyone with the will to join the Shields' fight was a hero in their own right, and Douk had shown his devotion a hundred times over.

The basement was laid out for storage more than service. Douk offered up his cellar to the Shields as a bolt-hole and staging ground, mixing in weapons and supplies with his dry goods. The Shields did their best to stay out of the way of his business, but over the years Douk's Daily had developed an underground reputation as a haven for Shield sympathizers.

Several lamps stood at the edges of shelves and at the walls, filling the room with a cross-hatching of shadows and light. The décor was a mix of storage basement, war room, and chic hangout. Douk had done his best to make it comfortable without giving the cellar away as anything more than a storage room with extra tables, should the wrong person find their way down the stairs and past the locks. The room was a perfect reflection of Douk's contradictions—he insisted that they be comfortable but also tried to protect them through stealth. Douk was a good man, but he lacked the makings of a spy.

Wenlizerachi reclined on a couch, his Blurred Fists raiment discarded in a heap at his feet. He had three plates of food balanced on his lap, chest, and legs, and his hands flickered from plate to plate, to mouth, and back to plate.

Bira Qano and Sarii Gebb were sitting at one of the old glass-top tables, a game board set up between them.

Bira was still wearing her Ghost Hands raiment, mahogany robes that flowed and billowed when her powers were unleashed. Ghost Hands' legs were crossed, hovering several inches off her seat. Ghost Hands was First Sentinel's oldest friend and steadfast ally. They'd joined the Shields on the same day, when the first Aegis had found them during a Spark-storm.

Like all Qava, she had no eyes, nose, or mouth, no orifices or features. Many found it unnerving, but after five decades of friendship, First Sentinel had long gotten used to it, and learned to read her small movements. She had the strongest talents in tele-kinesis and telepathy that First Sentinel had ever seen in a Qava.

Bira had confided to First Sentinel years ago that she won-dered if her power was Spark-touched, but the Smiling King had never reached out to enthrall her, and her abilities had grown gradually over the years. Like Wenlizerachi or Sarii, she was a nat-ural talent honed by years of pushing herself harder and harder.

In contrast to her wife, Bira, Sarii wore her emotions carved into her slate-gray face. In her Shield guise, she was Sabreslate, mistress of stone. She balanced Ghost Hands' reasonable opti-mism with staunch skepticism, questioning every plan as a matter of course. But even though she tried his patience, First Sentinel knew that their plans were always better because of her. Sabreslate sipped *dounmo* tea from a thrown clay mug almost the same gray as her skin. She wore her raiment of woven stone, the hood pulled back from her face.

Several steps into the room, Douk set a hand on First Sentinel's shoulder. "Can I get you something to eat, a drink? Maybe send down a musician? They can be trusted."

First Sentinel restrained a sigh. *What would they play? A rous-ing dirge for our pyrrhic victory against the insanity of the Spark?* "No, Douk. Thank you again."

He wasn't in the mood. Dozens dead, hundreds more homeless, and the only real relief would come from the few neighbors whose compassion outweighed their fear. The Shields would help where they could, but with the summit coming up, it would not be much.

Blurred Fists raised a glass in salute as First Sentinel walked over to the group—a warrior's salute, not that of a celebrant.

The mood was somber, despite Douk's eternal cheeriness. They had few things to celebrate most days, and this was no exception. The storms had been getting more and more common, but why?

First Sentinel took a seat with Ghost Hands and Sabreslate, lowering himself gingerly onto a crate filled with coffee beans. First Sentinel managed a small smile of greeting even though the images of the monstrous school and the Spark-blasted streets hovered in his mind.

Ghost Hands floated the teapot and a mug from atop another crate. The cup settled into his cupped hand, and the teapot tipped in the air, pouring him a drink. The teapot returned to its perch, and he lifted the cup to Ghost Hands in thanks. She nodded her featureless head.

Ghost Hands spoke directly to First Sentinel's mind, reaching out with her birthright. Her voice echoed as if through a cave, distant but clear.

[You should take it easy, Wonlar. You'll run yourself ragged.]

Sabreslate jumped in as well. "We have bigger matters to attend to," referring to the summit. "When is the meeting?" *Sabreslate, bastion of empathy.*

"It was an emergency. We were needed. The day we ignore the people's troubles is the day we become just like the tyrants," First Sentinel said, not meaning the words to sound as preachy as they came out.

Even if we can't help them all. First Sentinel wondered if anyone had died in the flight from the storm.

"Bad day, eh?" Sabreslate asked. Her carved features had gotten harder along the years—the chipping around her eyes showed her age.

We're all getting old, the first of us Shields who remain. How many generations will it take? Will Aegis' grandchildren fight for the city's freedom during the one hundredth year of the oligarchs' reign?

If we can't turn the tide against the tyrants, chances are none of us will live to have grandchildren anyway.

First Sentinel sipped the tea. It was crisp, strong, and had clear notes of cinnamon, blackberry, and clove. Douk didn't skimp. He'd bankrupt himself for their sake if they let him. Douk had claimed the Shields as family, and he was the kind of host that would give you the robe off his own back.

"Next meeting is tomorrow, my apartment, noon. Can't do it now. I need everyone to bring plans and maps, especially of any district north of The Rack."

Ghost Hands sighed in his mind. *[Have you heard from Selweh/Aegis?]* She thought both names at the same time, the private and public faces of his adopted son.

First Sentinel leaned back against the shelf, shaking his head. "He's gathering information on the summit. He said he'd be back before the meeting, even if he missed the check-in." *Please come home safe, Selweh.*

Sabreslate gestured with her empty cup, pushing it out toward First Sentinel. "That boy will get himself killed one of these days. You'd think that growing up with you for a father, he'd have learned some caution."

I wish. First Sentinel leveled his gaze at Sabreslate, meeting her eyes, and then looked down. "He'll do what he wants now. And who knows what news he might bring back."

Another series of raps at the door. First Sentinel stood and drew a knife, only relaxing when the knocker finished the correct code. Douk opened the door and Rova hunched her way through, still in her raiment as Sapphire. *She wasn't even six feet tall when we first met,* Wonlar mused.

Sapphire had a little girl with her, a Millrej with red hair and tufted ears. She looked terrified—probably in shock.

First Sentinel set down his cup and walked over to them, wincing as pain flared in his hip. Rova drew herself up to her full height once inside, two heads taller than the elder Shield and twice as broad.

First Sentinel took hold of Rova's hands in the Freithin greeting between blood-kin. They nodded, and then First Sentinel knelt to look the girl in the eyes.

"And who is this?" he asked.

Rova swung the girl's arm gently for encouragement. "Fahra."

"Hello, Fahra. I'm Wonlar."

She hid behind Rova's leg, hands tight on the woman's pants. First Sentinel rose to his feet, slowly, and looked to Sapphire. "Why is she here?" It was a huge risk bringing a stranger into a safehouse, no matter how young.

Rova leaned in, speaking softly. "She's an orphan. She was being taken by one of Yema's warlocks . . . in the Bowels."

"Ah." There was no way that could be good for anyone. "Any idea why Yema wanted her specifically?" Yema wouldn't send warlocks into the Smiling King's domain without good reason.

As Rova shrugged, the movement rippled muscles all the way to her elbow. "That's why I brought her here. She has nowhere to go, and we shouldn't let her out of our care until we know Yema's intentions."

First Sentinel turned and walked to Douk. "She'll need a hot bath, fresh clothes, and some warm milk to help her sleep." First Sentinel recalled the tricks he'd used to help a young Selweh get to sleep after returning from missions as First Sentinel. The boy had known his father's secret calling even before he could read. He would wait at the door, sobbing and willfully ignoring his babysitter's best efforts. Sometimes, it had taken Wonlar hours to calm the boy down enough to put him to bed.

Wonlar pulled back from nostalgia to hear Douk trading stories with Blurred Fists, who was working on his second round of plates.

First Sentinel mirrored Douk's gesture, putting a hand on the café owner's shoulder. "Douk, old friend, I have another favor to ask of you."

He perked up, head turning from his conversation. Douk loved being useful, drew a thrill from being close to exciting events. It was a dangerous impulse, but Douk was smart and a smooth talker, so he'd been safe so far. "Anything for you, Wonlar."

"Can you and Xera look after this little girl? She was targeted by Magister Yema three districts out of his domain—she needs to be kept safe."

Douk's eyes lit up. "Of course."

He and Fahra danced the dance of introductions, the poor child barraged by unfamiliar faces.

First Sentinel poured himself another cup of tea. They moved to brainstorming the possible reasons for Yema's move, the coincidence and correspondence with the Spark-storm.

Sarii suggested that it was likely a way to build an elite unit of full blooded Millrej. Rova thought it was something about the hybridity, the possibility that Yema was doing some kind of ritual that needed Millrej. Wenlizerachi speculated that the girl might not have been born Millrej but was instead made one by the storm, and that Yema wanted to use her to find a way to control the results of the Spark-storms.

Wonlar took in all of these ideas and set them together in the tumbler of his mind, trying to polish away the imperfections and arrive at finished theories.

As they talked, the threat of the Five-Tyrant Summit loomed large in his mind. *We have to break their alliance, whatever the reason for calling the summit. But if we push too hard, it will only strengthen their resolve.* First Sentinel took a long sip from his mug and returned to thought.

Chapter Four

First Sentinel

For once, the chaos of Wonlar's apartment was sincere. Stacks of maps and his journals made a mountain in one corner, with dozens more laid out, layered with thin parchment spread over them so he could take notes without marring the original maps. He'd been up most of the night thinking, only catching a few hours' sleep on the couch, too tired to walk to bed.

Wonlar spent the morning pouring over maps of the city, charting the year's Spark-storms, looking for a pattern. *Why this many, one after another?* They were spread around the city, more toward the center, and far more frequent in the last few months, but they never ranged outside the canyon that housed Audec-Hal.

Wonlar cleared off his long dinner table, where he held the Shields' meetings. He couldn't remember the last time he and Selweh had actually used it to entertain.

Maybe last fall, for the harvest days?

With preparations for the summit, Wonlar the artificer would have to take a break for a while; sour luck for Jull Jeenks down the street. First Sentinel could mark the months by the neighbor's calls for oven repairs.

Wonlar kept the shades drawn, the door locked and bolted, the windows shuttered save for the one above his balcony for a quick escape. First Sentinel took every precaution imaginable, preparing for the most important meeting they'd had in years.

Almost noon, and Selweh wasn't back yet. *Please come back safe, my boy. I made a promise.*

Someone knocked at the door—with the right code—and Wonlar rustled papers crossing the room to answer. Wenlizerachi shook Wonlar's hand and dashed inside to take a seat at the table. He was dressed casually in loose running clothes, a messenger's satchel over his shoulder. When he wasn't Blurred Fists, Shield of Audec-Hal, he was Wenlizerachi, freelance courier.

"Aegis?" he asked.

"Not yet." Wonlar tried to hide the fear in his voice, hoping that Wenlizerachi wouldn't notice.

"Kids." Aegis was actually older than Wenlizerachi, but for the fast-paced Pronai, fifteen was middle-aged. Wenlizerachi had only a few years left to him. His family had been Shields since the first years, passing the mantle of Blurred Fists down from his great-grandmother, just as Selweh was the fifth to serve Audec-Hal as Aegis.

When the shield had found his son two years ago, Wonlar wept, remembering the ones who had come before. He wept for Aria and the promise he would be hard pressed to keep. He wept for the other bearers of the Aegis that had come before—for his fallen mentor, the founder of the Shields, whose real name he never learned. After him came Zenari, the office-worker who had taken up the Aegis and led the Shields to destroy the first COBALT in a battle that played out atop the machine's great zeppelin. The brilliant and kind Aria Enyahi Gara, love of his life, was third; Aernah was fourth, a lifelong teacher who became a clever tactician and recruiter of Shield-bearers. And he wept for Selweh most of all, because no bearer had survived to pass on the shield of their own accord.

"Can I get you anything?" First Sentinel asked. Wenlizerachi waved Wonlar off and produced a flask from his belt.

Each time First Sentinel heard knocking at the door, he tensed up while they rapped out the pattern, but each time the code was correct, and he opened the door to reveal a friend. *Relax, old man,* he told himself, to no avail.

Twenty minutes later, everyone but Aegis had arrived. Bira and Sarii came together. Bira floated in with her cloak over her arms. Sarii strode in beside her, a piece of stone rolling and flowing through her fingers. Rova came last, drawing Wonlar into a powerful hug after stooping through the door. The other Shields were all retired or dead. Mostly dead.

Rova took up two spaces on her own, elbows on the table, forward and attentive. Bira sat tall, arms crossed. Sarii leaned back in her chair, doodling with the same piece of stone. It shifted between a horse, a tent, a clock, and a pacing woman to illustrate her boredom, her power showing the artist's career she could have had if the city were sane. The Spark had never touched Sarii, but her control over the Jalvai birthright of stone-shaping was powerful enough to spin stone into thread or raise a fortress in minutes.

Wenlizerachi just sat, drinking tea. For meetings, Wonlar had learned to just give the Pronai a whole pot and let him serve himself. He was Blurred Fists just as much when his hands moved over food and drink as when they pummeled the tyrants' guards.

Wonlar cleared his throat and sat down at the head of the table, an empty seat beside him. "Let's get started."

"What about Selweh?" Sarii asked.

Wonlar glanced over to the empty seat, a pit in his stomach. "He'll be along. We don't have time to waste."

"I hope he's alright." Rova laid her huge hand over Wonlar's. The touch settled Wonlar's stomach, but only a little.

"He'll be fine." Wonlar squeezed Rova's hand, then let go and stood to start walking around the table, thankfully free of the pain in his hip.

Pacing helped him think, as the worn circle around the table proved. "Our latest intelligence indicates that Nevri is close to getting all of the tyrants to agree to the summit. When Aegis comes back, we should have confirmation of the details."

Sarii huffed. "I'm surprised they're even agreeing to meet after what happened the last time." The last talks had been seven years ago. Those had ended with a civil war in the streets between Medai Omez and the Smiling King. Hundreds had died.

"Whatever it took, they're doing it, and that's our problem right now," Wonlar said.

[And if they come to terms now, it will be so they can be rid of us,] Bira said in the Shields' minds.

Wonlar nodded. "Perhaps. We've survived in between the cracks, playing off their antagonism. If the summit goes through, if the tyrants actually unite, behave like the oligarchy they pretend to be, our job becomes far more difficult."

"You mean they'll hunt us like dogs until they've killed every last one and put our heads up on pikes in Republic Square." Her stone became a coffin. *Sarii, always a ray of sunshine in the darkness.*

Wenlizerachi cracked his knuckles one by one, fast enough it sounded like one motion. "So what are we doing to screw it up?"

That was the challenge. First Sentinel stopped and put both hands on the table. "We need a plan we can pin on one of the other tyrants, turn them against each other, and get them to call off the summit before it can get underway."

Rova joined the conversation, her face-sized hand moving in broad sweeping moves as she thought. "A barracks. Attack their forces directly; leave the tools of another's soldiers."

Sarii shot her idea down. "Too obvious. We have to do something so big they'd dismiss it as anything but an attack by another oligarch."

I don't like where this is going. "What did you have in mind?"

Sarii said, "We need to think like they do, plan an attack as if we were the Smiling King or COBALT-3."

"You're talking about casualties," Rova said.

Sarii nodded. "It's the only way to make it believable. We have to be the monsters they paint us as and know we aren't." Save for the Smiling King, who only printed unintelligible pamphlets, the tyrants pumped out a constant stream of propaganda with their wholly owned newspapers. The Shields were "dangerous insurrectionists" and a "public menace." Many people were scared enough to believe them. And thousands more read the papers just to fit in.

A fist slammed on the table. Wonlar was surprised to realize it was his own. "No. We will not sink to their level. I won't allow it."

Sarii stood up across the table from him, her flint-cold eyes seeking his gaze. "What then, Wonlar? This could be easy. If you just used your real power, we could be done with this nightmare by the end of the year."

"For the hundredth time, no. I swore I would never use that power again."

Wenlizerachi spoke, slow and clear. "Just this once. It'd only take one time to bring down their whole regime. Wouldn't that be worth it?"

Wonlar's voice filled the room. "Yes, I could twist the threads, *make* them betray each other. Then you'd have me change more threads, *make* the people of the city fight for us, and *make* the City Mother serve us again, using a power I should never have been given and never should have used."

Aria has already paid the price for my hubris. "And I don't know if I'd have the strength to free the City Mother even if I tried."

First Sentinel stood up in a fit, knocking a chair away from the table. "You know what you'd have if I did all of that? You'd have a new tyrant, beloved by all, the master of the threads, an unchallenged hegemon. And any memory of the Republic of Audec-Hal would be buried for good. Is that what you want?"

For a moment, the room was silent, save for Wonlar's heavy breathing; his face flushed orange. Sarii threw up her hands in exasperation. "Yes! I want the fighting to be over. I want to go back to my life and for the people on the street to be able to get food when they're hungry, medicine when they're sick. I want a fire service that works, and a city ruled by a good man instead of monsters. I want to retire with Bira and live out our lives in peace!"

Not what I was looking for. Wonlar sat back onto his heels, looking to the other Shields for support or another counterargument to Sarii's stubbornness.

"That would make me no better than Yema, than Nevri. Just another tyrant using his power to make the city in his own image."

Sarii said, "You care more about this city than anyone, Wonlar. Why would it be so terrible?"

Wonlar turned and walked away from the table. Rova's heavy steps followed him. Her hand cupped his shoulder, holding him back. He turned, but couldn't meet her gaze. *I've failed too many times to trust myself with that much pressure. I can't risk repeating what happened to Aria.*

"We'll find another way," she said, her voice soft. "What is your plan?"

Wonlar faced the table again and took a breath, searching for his calm center. He grabbed a well-worn map from the floor beside his seat at the table and unrolled it on the table. Next he produced five statuettes that Sarii had sculpted for him years ago. Wonlar placed the slim-suited figure of Nevri over the head of the body, then the icon of Medai Omez in his hundred priceless scarves at the left shoulder. The bald, robed figure of Magister Yema went on the left leg, matched by the intricately carved statuette of the mechanical COBALT-3 on the right. Lastly, he placed the Smiling King's figure just below the ribs.

Wonlar looked at the figures on the map, marking their territories. He'd done this hundreds of times before, trying to hold the whole city in his mind. Districts and their populations, their industries, skirmishes fought, and civilians saved.

It had all started with Nevri, a gangster who'd bought herself a Senate seat fifty-three years ago. Six months after she took office, a "mysterious" fire collapsed the Senate building, killing all within. Nevri was absent that day. Nearly everyone accepted her guilt as truth, but it had never been proven. She ruled her domain with an iron fist, but she protected her citizens, provided public services, and enforced gender equality across the board. Rapists were hung in public; men who beat their partners were whipped in public. She was, after all, Nevri the Lash.

She was soon joined by Magister Yema, the most powerful sorcerer the city had ever seen. He'd made pacts with entities Wonlar had never heard of, but their power was all too real. His elite Warlock Guard were normal citizens whose hearts were removed with a ritual, kept alive through the spell, with their minds and bodies bound to his will. Yema kept the hearts locked away somewhere in the city, another mystery Wonlar had never solved.

When Medai Omez arrived, he'd brought spawning pits and birthed hundreds of Freithin to be his personal slaves, working in factories to dominate industry. Omez had been weakened since the Shields freed Rova's people and had played close to the chest ever since. He was a lesser power, but not to be ignored.

The Smiling King was Medai's complete opposite: a raving lunatic who used his own madness to enrapture nearly anyone touched by the Spark-storms. The Smiling King had appeared around the same time as the Spark-storms, and Wonlar was mostly convinced that the tyrant was their ultimate source. The Smiling King called the Spark-touched his "family," but used them like any another gang. Life in his district was a circus, with constantly changing rules. Walking on the eastern side of a street would win a citizen a prize one day, but the next it might earn them a public execution.

And lastly, there was COBALT-3. COBALT had come to the city shortly after the tyrant's reign began and set up shop to conduct experiments on the citizens. The Shields had destroyed him (at the cost of the second Aegis), and later COBALT-2, his greatest invention, but not before COBALT-3 was made. The newest model took after her grand-creator, delving into experiments on the species of Audec-Hal, seeking to "improve" organic life.

Looking at the map, the memories piled up. Hundreds of battles, strengths and weaknesses, triumphs and failures. *My failures. If the tyrants come to an accord and work together to destroy us, the city will never be free.*

"We have to stop the summit," he said. "How?"

Rova leaned over the table, her shadow covering the map. She pushed the figures of Nevri and Medai together. "We strain the existing alliances and set them back to infighting."

Bira added to the thought. *[What if we steal the next drug shipment from Nevri to the Smiling King, find a way to fence them to Yema? We make it known that the goods are hot, say they come from the Smiling King. They're all suspicious of one another, more so now heading into the summit.]* The figure of Nevri slid to one side, Yema to another, leaving the Smiling King in the middle.

Wenlizerachi jumped in. "Then we let the information trail get back to Nevri through her network. Nevri thinks she's been betrayed by the Smiling King and Yema." He gestured to the Smiling King.

Rova nodded. "The man in the middle tries to deny it, but no one believes him because he's crazy to begin with. COBALT-3 sides with Yema, who provides him with subjects, and Omez throws in with Nevri—she's got the money." She moved COBALT-3's figure beside Yema and Medai Omez's next to Nevri, leaving the Smiling King alone at the center.

A broad smile bloomed on Wonlar's lips. This was his team, his family.

Rova gestured at the map. "They're split two and two against one, and the summit dissolves. Nevri will refuse to deal with the Smiling King and Yema, and we get some breathing room."

Sarii chuckled, likely enticed back to the plan by the promise of chaos. Sarii touched the bases of several of the figures and set them to acting out fistfights. "We fan the flames of their bickering. Exacerbate the damage done to their organizations, and when the dust settles, two, maybe three could be out of the picture."

[*But then the ones left have all the more power.*] Bira's words were heavy with doubt.

Wonlar shook his head. "Not immediately. They'd have to consolidate and rebuild, but we won't let them. We press the conflict—with only two left, each of them will see sole dominion of Audec-Hal within their grasp. And when the last battle erupts, we make sure neither of them walks away from it."

They were past the time for incremental change and small victories. *We need to topple their regime now.* Between the storms, the disappearances, and the aging population, it wouldn't be long before the Republic of Audec-Hal was lost to memory entirely. Most alive didn't remember the Republic, and every year that passed, fewer would know anything but the tyrants' reign.

"That could work." Rova held her chin with one huge hand, deep in concentration as she looked across the map at the stone figures.

Sarii molded the figures into moving stone flames.

Wonlar answered. "But how many citizens will burn in this blaze? The longer this conflict drags out, the more people will be hurt. We have to be fast, surgical."

"I know one way that we can end this faster . . . " *And now she flips, playing adversary.*

"We can't win this war if we pretend that we can overthrow the tyrants without people getting hurt." Wenlizerachi's voice sped up as he talked. He moved through a dozen poses in an instant, pausing to speak. "But Wonlar has made his stance clear. We all have lines we won't cross. No reason to have the same argument again."

"If the tyrants come together and we cannot, the city is lost." Wonlar waited a moment, then turned to Sarii, stalwart skeptic and frequent burr in his saddle. "What do you say?"

"If you just used your power . . . " she said.

Wonlar matched her stare, and the room was silent again. Sarii's eyes crinkled in the look he knew as frustration, with him or with the situation, he didn't know. Then she relaxed, looking away. The aging Shield took his seat again, and the others followed suit.

He released a long breath, glad to have one thing settled. *Now, where is Aegis?*

Another knock on the door startled Wonlar from his thought. The pattern was slow, three solid knocks in succession. It wasn't a Shield code, and it wasn't the pattern he told customers to use. But Jull was forgetful . . .

Wonlar's voice was soft. "It's probably just a customer. I'll send them away. Just in case, go to my room to wait."

Wenlizerachi was gone in an instant, his chair unmoved. Sarii simply stood, gathering up her figures and melding them back into her flowing stone cloak. Rova and Bira shuttled out of the room, headed for the bedroom. Bira used her telekinesis to fold up the map and pull it to her from across the room.

Grabbing a butcher's knife from the kitchen, Wonlar held the blade behind his back as he opened the door. *Better safe than dead.*

The woman in the doorway was small, her forehead coming up only to Wonlar's shoulder. She was Millrej, a Full-blood snake-kin with brown scaled skin and a forked tongue that flicked as she spoke. "Executor Nevri sends her greetings, First Sentinel."

Wonlar slammed the door on her as she spoke, then shouted to his back room. "Out! Now!"

He'd never learned her name, but he knew that woman; she was one of Nevri's lieutenants, a trusted servant of the Plutocrat.

Introductions were a luxury when you were fighting for your life. She was vicious with a pair of scimitars, but not the most dangerous of Nevri's thugs. Wonlar took her to be more bureau-crat than warrior.

Wonlar threw open the closet and pulled out his belt, coat, and grappling gun.

"Evacuate! Nevri's forces!"

Rova's voice boomed from Wonlar's room. "They've got the windows covered!"

Wonlar opened the door to the balcony and looked down to the street. Forty of Nevri's soldiers stood with crossbows trained on him and the window to his bedroom. *Not good, not good.* In the moment of stillness, when he was ready to dodge, ready to die, ready to explode in twenty directions at once, they didn't fire.

They're waiting.

Wonlar heard a click behind him and the creak of hinges swinging open. Wonlar turned as the Millrej slithered in, crum-pling papers and pushing aside books.

She raised a scaled and manicured hand and said, "I didn't come to fight." She let it sink in for a beat, and then added, "In fact, I have an offer from the Executor. Nevri would like to hire you for a job; she thinks the terms will be most agreeable."

This has to be a trap. "What?" Wonlar backed away from her as she advanced.

"Do not run. I am unarmed, but you see that the building is surrounded. If Nevri wanted you dead right now, you'd already be a pincushion."

Just because they hadn't fired yet didn't mean they would not fire at all. But even if he killed the Millrej right there, Nevri would have hundreds of troops standing by. The Executor wasn't above sacrificing a lieutenant to get what she needed; the bottom line was her only concern.

Nevri's 8,000 mark bounty on First Sentinel's head was enough to feed a district for a year. Wonlar took it as a badge of pride.

"Stop there," Wonlar said, still holding coat, belt, and grappling gun. She halted, sitting back on her tail.

Wonlar's four teammates emerged from his bedroom, each wearing their Shields' masks. They surrounded the Millrej, Rova in the back. She could take a half-dozen crossbow bolts without slowing down, but Wonlar hoped it wouldn't come to that. He didn't have to worry about being identified. The universal face of the Ikanollo would shield him as long as he was dressed in street clothes. When he put on a mask, it wasn't to protect his identity, but to send the message that the role of a Shield was bigger than any one person. There had been five Aegises, four Blurred Fists.

Wonlar latched the grappling gun to his belt and drew a fighting staff. *I haven't survived this long by being lax in my preparations.*

The Shields let Wonlar take the lead. Sapphire didn't like negotiating with enemies; Blurred Fists would talk around them and never accomplish anything; Ghost Hands was always taken for aloof; Sabreslate would incite them past any reasonable conversation. And Aegis was still unaccounted for.

"Talk," he said with the force of a command. She never broke eye contact, ignoring the other Shields.

[Can you get a read on Dlella?] Wonlar thought in Ghost Hands' direction.

[No. She's got something to block me] came Ghost Hands' answer. Not surprising, but they might as well try.

The Millrej woman's tail lapped back and forth behind her during a little slice of tense silence. Wonlar kept his ears open for the trap. "I am Dlella. She would like to contract your team for an acquisition project in two weeks' time. The pay is generous, and the results are in keeping with your mission."

Sabreslate snorted. "Do you think we're complete idiots?"

"Yes," said Dlella, cutting Sabreslate off. "But your priorities in this case make you a valuable asset. The Spark-storms. How many are there per year?"

What is she getting to? A day after a storm, they were on everyone's mind, but Wonlar couldn't look past the correlation. "Two, sometimes as many as four," he said.

"And how many so far this year?"

"Seven," Wonlar said.

"Nevri knows what's been causing the higher frequency. And she wants to help you stop them."

"Bullshit," Sabreslate said. "We know less about Spark-storms than we do about the fall of the titan."

"What do you know?" Sapphire asked.

Bira's voice echoed in First Sentinel's mind. *[Don't trust anything she says. Nevri's doubtless trying to trick us. But we can let this lackey run the course of the trick, and perhaps we will learn what Nevri really wants.]*

Dlella smiled, clearly enjoying knowing more than the Shields. "The Smiling King. He's found—or created, we don't know—an artifact that produces Spark-storms, that or it increases their frequency." The story was plausible; at least it sounded like something the Smiling King would do if he could. But First Sentinel had never taken him for an inventor.

[How did you find out?] Bira asked.

The snake-woman smiled again. She could keep out Bira's probing but didn't block the mind-speech.

Interesting that she has that much control. Spark-touched power? Or does she have an artifact?

"Everyone has a price," she said. "Nevri will provide you with the location of this device and sufficient means to destroy it. You will see that the Smiling King's artifact is eliminated and that its destruction cannot be traced back to Nevri. Its end will be a resounding victory in your insurrection, and Nevri will see one of her rivals greatly weakened."

If the offer was legitimate, it could be exactly what they were looking for. Which is why Wonlar couldn't see it as anything but a trap. He looked over his shoulder to make sure the soldiers hadn't scaled the walls, weren't sneaking up on them, the offer only a distraction.

"Why has she come to us?" Wonlar asked.

The rest of the Shields stood around him, still tense and ready to move. Blurred Fists was deathly still, waiting. Rova stretched, showing off her towering stature. Ghost Hands floated silently, and Sabreslate's raiment of stone undulated over her body like waves on a quiet shore.

"Your . . . cell has proven very adept at secretive operations, with a penchant for precise property damage. And with your stance on the welfare of the people, you have a moral prerogative."

Wonlar scoffed. "How do we know you won't just blow us up when we go to pick up the explosives?"

She reared up on her tail, her head nearly brushing the ceiling, and then settled back down. Wonlar was unimpressed. The thick tail was strong, but more lightly armored on the bottom. All she'd done was expose herself to attack.

He'd fought larger foes—Spark-touched Freithin the size of a house, driven mad by pain; Onyx, one of The Smiling King's lieutenants; and the shardlings. Dlella said, "Because Executor Nevri will deliver the explosives to you herself."

"Will she wrap them up in a bow made from the bones of the innocent she's killed?" Sarii asked. Wonlar refrained from cutting her off. Sarii frequently stepped in to the negotiations, fanning the flames of tension. But if Dlella was off balance, she might reveal a clue to Nevri's motives.

"I will wrap it with your skin if you continue this obstinance, Jalvai." She spoke the name of Sarii's race like something you'd say as you spat in the street.

"And what assurance do we have that this won't just be a death trap?" Wonlar asked.

Dlella's tongue flicked the outside of her mouth, lolling side to side. "Are you just going to leave the artifact in place? Do you need the Executor to hold your hand, bring you sweets?"

Wonlar shrugged, trying to look confident. "We could just blow it on our own."

She slithered up to him, drew her hood above his head. "You don't know where it is."

Wonlar smiled. "Doesn't mean we can't find out. Triangulate the location of the last four Spark-storms, cross-reference against residential quarters, troop patrols. I should be able to narrow the location down to a two-mile radius in, oh, a week."

A snarl crossed Dlella's face for an instant. She pushed it down and resumed her businesslike demeanor, sinking back down to eye level and pulling back. "If you do it Nevri's way, you get ten thousand marks and one ton of medical supplies." *That's more than my bounty, enough to start our own war. Another war, that is.*

The last one hadn't ended well.

Wonlar thought of Aria and smelled crocuses, even though they hadn't started to bloom.

But how many families did she tax to the brink of starvation for that money, how many children press-ganged into her distant wars over dwindling Ibje ore?

"Again—why not hire mercenaries? You could get a squad for a tenth that price."

Dlella slithered back and forth, stalking the group. "Your organization has the . . . skills required to get to the artifact. It is heavily guarded by the Smiling King's army of abominations—it is his most prized possession."

"Not his blankey?" Sarii asked, the stone in her hand folded over like a blanket.

"We need to confer before I can give an answer," First Sentinel said, running over Sarii's obstinance. Resources, information, and access to Nevri's plans. The offer was too good to refuse, which made it all the more dangerous.

Dlella nodded. "I will meet you—with a small escort, of course—at the Ruby Shackles in two days. Come at the moon's zenith with your answer."

That could be the real trap, waiting to get Aegis as well. Nevri was smart enough to give her employee a flexible plan.

Dlella bowed to them with mock courtesy and then slithered out the door. Wonlar followed her and checked the lock, wondering again how she'd found him. *A tip from a neighbor? Or have the amulets been running out even faster than I thought?*

A few seconds later, when the soldiers didn't fire on the apartment and no one burst in to kill them, he looked back to the others and asked, "What do you think?"

"Are you insane?" Sabreslate asked.

Wonlar put on more water for tea.

I've lived here for years, made friends, and learned all the best routes out of the neighborhood. Now on top of everything, we have to move. Dammit.

53

The next morning, Wonlar stood on the balcony of the Shield's Viscera City safehouse and faced the warm sunrise of approaching spring. This apartment was far smaller and had only the bare minimum supplies, none of the comforts of home. *And no Selweh.*

One solitary crocus stretched up toward the sun. He'd planted crocuses in every safehouse he could as a reminder to himself, a bit of stability. *Quite a sign. City Mother be praised.* He bent down slowly from the knees to protect his hip, and then wrapped his fingers around the flower as he savored its smell.

The smell sent him back to the Shield's failed revolution twenty years before.

Each year the crocuses retreated to wait out the cold winter, and each year they emerged, heralds of rebirth. The winter of the Oligarch's reign had held for fifty years in Audec-Hal, and Wonlar longed to see the spring.

Chapter Five

First Sentinel

Twenty Years Ago

*C*rocuses. It smelled of crocuses the day Aria died. My raiment was soaked through, gore layered over grime.

Around me, three armies and a rebellion raged through the streets. We thought the tyrant's infighting would be the spark that lit the fire of revolution, the time when we could wake the city from its nightmare.

We were wrong, and Aria paid the price. Huddled in an alley, she was bleeding out in my arms, and I was helpless to save her.

I'd pulled her into an alley and hid behind an overturned food cart. A sense-mask cube gave us privacy, but nothing in my belt of tricks could close that many wounds, replace that much blood. Wide gashes made orange cross-hatchings on her chest.

I cupped her face and watched as her threads frayed and snapped one by one, her ties to the world fading.

Emerald and jade were the last to go—the first line trailing up and away to the safehouse and her infant son—the other, a jade band that crossed the hand's span between us. It had taken years for that thread to regrow.

Aria's faltering fingers found my face, slipped underneath my mask. Her hands were so cold. I willed her to live. We were supposed to find each other again so she could to forgive me. We could be together again, the way we were supposed to.

"Don't leave me, love," I said.

"Watch my little Selweh. Guard him."

I should have been his father, not some dissident journalist. "Nothing will hurt him, I swear."

She coughed blood onto my jerkin, shaking her head. "Make a promise you can keep."

I held her close, the emerald thread hidden by the press of our bodies. "I'll guard him with my life."

Aria's last thread frayed and snapped as she nodded to my promise. I held her still form for a long moment.

The cube gave the telltale pop at the end of its charge. Not a moment later, a Freithin berserker saw me from the street. It turned to charge. I jumped to my knees and drew my staves as training took over. My bond to Selweh shifted, jade brightening to glittering emerald. I promise, Aria.

I dodged the berserker's charge and turned to fight. I channeled my own rage until the Freithin was a mass of bruises and broken bones on the alley floor. But it did nothing for Aria.

The next day it frosted, and the crocuses died.

Chapter Six

First Sentinel

Now that he was an old man, only a few things made Wonlar truly happy anymore: savoring a cup of strong tea, scoring a victory against the tyrants, and seeing the smile of a child.

Taking a break from storms and meetings, Wonlar held court in Rova's living room (at her insistence).

Nearly a dozen children sat, stood, and knelt around the room. They snuggled into couches, piled atop cushions, and splayed out on the brilliantly colored carpets that Rova's brother wove for a living. The house was far from lush, but it was large, with high ceilings and wide doors to accommodate the larger residents. The walls were painted a bright orange, the trim on the doors purple. The Freithin, so long denied anything of beauty in Omez's cages, embraced bright colors. Coming here made Wonlar feel small, like he was a child again, living in a world full of things built for giants.

It had been Rova's idea for him to begin with visiting Freithin children in Bluetown, to tell them stories of the city's history.

In truth, it was propaganda—proselytizing—but it was necessary. Years down the road, he might have to call on these children to lay down their lives for the city. It was essential that they know the truth of the tyrants' crimes. The guilt of what he was doing tore at him, but the Shields had been fighting for fifty years, and the tyrants still held power.

I've made worse sacrifices. The weight of each life lost to the tyrants hung about his neck and shoulders, a long chain wrought of friends, allies, and innocents. The tyrants had made the city into their personal playground, laboratory, or marketplace, depending on the whim of the day.

Taking a sip of the marvelous *dounmo* tea, he scanned the room, leaning in to grab the attention of the nine blue-skinned children so he could continue the story. Wonlar drew their attention up with his hands as he stood tall, stretched to his limit— which was less than it had been when he was young—and said:

"And then the titan Audec, wounded from a hundred blows, fell from the battle in the heavens. He hurtled through the sky for a week, cutting through clouds, carving the Razorback Mountains with swipes of his hand as he tried to slow his fall. But it didn't help, and so he crashed to the ground!" Wonlar dropped to the floor and slammed his hands on the carpet, making as much noise as he could and also breaking the force of impact. Their screams of delight and excitement spread a smile clear across his face.

They were alive, so full of the joy their parents gave them, kept away from the full reality of what it meant to live in Audec-Hal. They would have to learn to survive, but no one could keep him from enjoying the sound of their innocent laughter while it lasted. *Rova was right to invite me over today.*

"When Audec fell to earth, he was already dead, heartbroken by the war in the heavens. But when a titan dies, it's not like you or me . . . " Wonlar took a controlled fall, raising a small cloud of dust from the old rug. "You fall over and you bounce back up, little things made of rubber like you are." Wonlar sat up and stood, pausing on the way to tickle Rova's nephew Dom under the chin. He was rewarded with a gurgle of delight.

"But Audec was a titan, twenty miles tall from the top of his head to the tip of his toes." Wonlar touched the top of his head and then knelt down to touch his toes.

"Centuries later, people found his resting place: a crater twenty miles long, in the shape of a person." Wonlar sat down slowly, minding his back, and lay on the floor, aping the shape of the city crevasse. Several giggles bounced through the air at his clowning.

Being a father prepares you for so many things, most of which you'd never expect. "But all that was left of Audec were his bones."

Wonlar picked himself back up. The children had closed ranks, tightened in to listen, their eyes wide, though most had heard the story a dozen times. "The founders had heard the stories of the titans, knew the myth of Audec's fall. And so they built a city in that crater. They named it Audec-Hal, in honor of the titan whose bones are here to this very day."

Wonlar stood tall, puffing his chest out with exaggerated pride. "Audec-Hal was more prosperous than any city in the continent. We discovered new technologies faster than the Five Cities of Tanno to the north, even though they enslaved their scientists to make them work harder. We welcomed people of all races, not like the Pronai-only city of Wheel or the Jalvai matriarchy in Quall's Quarry." The parents nodded in agreement. Wonlar saw no reason to lie about this, even if he was unabashedly biased.

Wonlar paced up and down the room, turning his back on the children but raising his voice so they could hear. "Audec-Hal is the greatest, most wonderful city there is, ruled by a Senate that represents the people and protected by the benevolent City Mother, the spirit of the city itself." Wonlar stopped, turning his head over his shoulder and speaking in a stage whisper. "Or it was, until the tyrants came."

At this, the children hissed. They were a brilliant audience. They knew when to cheer, when to boo. Like all children, they loved to hear stories again and again. *I must have told Selweh the story of the first Aegis a thousand times by the time he was three.*

"When the tyrants came, they took the city hostage with their evil. First was Nevri, the gangster." Wonlar tugged at a make-believe tie and rubbed together two coins. "Next came Magister Yema, the sorcerer. He stole people's hearts and locked them away in a secret vault to make them slaves, his Warlock Guard." For Yema, he waved his fingers in the impression of a conjuring, and one of the children ducked behind his sister to hide.

"And then there was the Smiling King and the terrible Spark-storms." Several of the older children shuddered, as well as fully half of the parents. For Wonlar and the Shields, the storms were challenging, daunting, and dangerous. For an average citizen, they were chaos and certain death dealt out without reason, without warning. "Before long, there was COBALT, the devious automaton lord." For COBALT, Wonlar moved jerkily, mimicking the old automaton's spasmodic motions. "And last, the cruel slaver Medai Omez."

The children started another round of hisses. "Now, Medai's coming wasn't all bad. He is a tyrant, that is sure, but he also gave

Audec-Hal one of its greatest gifts. What do you think that was?" Wonlar asked.

Yara Speaks, a girl of three raised her wide hand, eager to please. *She's already sharper than my knives.*

Wonlar nodded, and she said, "Us!"

"That's right." Yara lit up at Wonlar's approval. "He was the one who brought the Freithin to Audec-Hal. He made your parents and grandparents as slaves to work in his factories, because the Freithin are the strongest people in the world."

Wonlar mimed flexing muscles. More laughter. "But the Shields made a machine that would break the spell that controlled the Freithin." Wonlar crossed the room with huge tiptoe steps. "They snuck into Medai's compound and freed the Freithin!"

Applause.

"And the strongest of them joined the Shields, becoming the mighty Sapphire." The children cheered, proud of their home-grown hero. Wonlar snuck a sideways look at Rova and saw her hide a blush. She always got shy when Wonlar or anyone else talked about her. Eight feet tall, able to take on any of the tyrant's beasts, thugs, and traps, but still she was shy. Save her brother and his family, no one there knew her second life as a Shield. To the rest, she was just Rova Remembers, and he was just Old Man Wonlar, the Ikanollo storyteller with the funny voices.

I wish I could spend this much time in each district, speak to every child in the city. Not just because I might need these children to become Shields one day, but because the sacrifices we have made deserve commemoration. If the Shields failed to stop the storms or halt the summit, these children might have to take up the fight, or at least pass on the tales so that others might do so.

"Who can tell me the name of another one of the Shields?" Wonlar asked.

"Blurry!" one of the children said.

Wonlar crossed and rubbed the boy's head. His parents had his hair kept short, shaved like Medai had ordered of the Slaves. Wonlar wondered why: *comfort for the coming summer, or are some of the habits from their slavery harder to shake than others?*

"That's right, Blurred Fists, the fastest of the Pronai. He can fight a hundred guards at once or cross a district in five minutes. But he wasn't the first Shield called Blurred Fists. There were three more before him." Wonlar paused for a moment and hung his head, remembering Wenlizerachi's mother, grandfather, and great-grandmother.

I'm honored to have known each of them, counted them as friends. They had each paid the greatest price for their devotion, and their children still picked up the mantle.

"Who knows another one?" Wonlar paced the room, holding his chin in mimed thoughtfulness. He watched the children think in that hilarious too transparent way of youth.

"Aegis!" said Pavi Protects, a young girl who had just started talking since his last visit. Wonlar grinned. *I'll have to tell Selweh that his name was one of her first words.* The happy thought was followed by a twinge of guilt and fear. His son still hadn't come home. Every hour without word made it more likely he'd been hurt, captured, or worse.

Be present, old man. They don't need to know about that, he told himself.

"Yes, Aegis, champion of the Shields. There have been five people to carry the Aegis, you know, starting with the first of Shields of Audec-Hal. No matter what happens, the shield always finds its way to another champion."

Wonlar knelt, putting his hand on the shoulder of a girl, a friend of Dom's. "I like to think that it's the City Mother, struggling against Yema's control and trying to help us however she can."

He rose, knees creaking. "Aegis trained two of the other Shields. Which two?"

Yara raised her hand again, but Wonlar waited to see if any of the others would answer. A beat passed, and he called on Yara.

"Ghost Hands."

"Of course, Ghost Hands! She's been with them since the beginning, reading the minds of guards with Qava telepathy and knocking bolts out of the air with her telekinesis."

"And who is the other one?" Wonlar asked.

"First Sentinel," said a boy with a strong jaw and light-brown hair. He held his squirming sister, ignoring her hand as she pawed at his face.

"First Sentinel, the mastermind. He fights with gadgets and potions, knives and staves." He waited a beat. "You know, some say that First Sentinel is strange because he doesn't seem a likely hero. He's not strong like Sapphire, fast like Blurred Fists, doesn't control stones like Sabreslate. He's just an Ikanollo like any other." That was a lie. He had a power, granted by the Spark. But it'd brought him more pain than anything in his life and was best forgotten.

"But others say he's the most dangerous of all, because he fights using the most powerful weapon we can have." Wonlar knocked the side of his head like a door. "He fights with his mind. It's a weapon you should all learn to use as well."

More laughter.

When he'd first started visiting the children, Wonlar had downplayed his own importance—it felt wrong to do otherwise.

Rova and Bira called him on his humility, asked him to turn it into a teaching opportunity. Ever since, he'd tried to throw in a bit of humor all the same. "Who here goes to school?"

Barely half of the children of age raised their hands, then a few more when prompted by siblings and parents. *Not nearly enough. I'll have to see if I can do something about that.*

"Not everyone can afford school, but Rova and I have some friends who want to make sure bright young children like you have the best chance at a good life. When I come back next week, maybe I'll have some good news." Wonlar moved to the door to pick up his coat, waiting to see if the children would protest.

"One more story!" called Yara.

Wonlar turned on his heels, hiding his pleasure. "Really? You're not tired of Old Man Wonlar?"

A large girl, no more than six summers old but already four feet tall, said, "Tell 'Red Vixen and the Winter Lady.'"

A boy named Arno Drives said, "No, tell 'Aegis and the Automata.'"

The room burst into pleasant chaos and chatter. More children called out for their favorite tales. Toddlers slipped out of sibling's arms and dashed across the floor. Parents shushed children and chased after squealing youths.

Wonlar drank it all in. He stored the hope and energy away in his heart as armor to protect him from the long nights, the defeats, and the despair. *Without days like these, the simple dinners with Selweh . . . I don't know what I'd do.*

Wonlar had been visiting Rova's once a month for three years and still hadn't run out of new stories to interject when the popular tales grew too familiar. He had fifty years of adventures to recount, not to mention the myths and legends of six races.

If I'd known I'd become a children's entertainer and recruiter for a revolution, I'd have taken better notes in Dr. Hansen's class back in the Academy.

Back then, he'd been more concerned with exotic reagents and reading all the philosophy books he could to impress Aria. It always seemed like she'd read everything before Wonlar even learned it existed, unless it was a book on artifice, the one science she'd never pursued.

The children settled on their request and Wonlar launched into "Aegis and the First Spark-Storm."

"It was less than a month after the Senate building burned down in a 'mysterious' fire." Wonlar layered on the sarcasm as he spoke the word "mysterious," since it was all but sure who was responsible.

"I was just a young man then, studying at the Academy of Artifice. The first storm hit Broken Rib late afternoon on a crisp spring day. People milled back and forth, trying to get their errands done and enjoy the weather without attracting attention from Nevri's guards." Another round of hisses filled the room.

Wonlar squatted down and lowered his voice. "It started with birds. Cawing, crying, songs, every kind of birdsong you've ever heard and more. It came down like a wind, sweeping through the neighborhood, and then the streets turned to mud. What color is mud?" Wonlar asked.

Pavi's brother, Eava, said, "Brown."

"Exactly. But do you know what color this mud was?"

Yara raised her hand, and Wonlar give her a wink. She'd heard this one before, so she launched right in. "It was green! Nasty snot green and it burned at the touch. The cobblestone streets turned into mud that might as well have been lava. People scrambled away from the burning mud, terrified."

Wonlar stood, striking a heroic pose. "But then, Aegis arrived." The children cheered. "He wore white and emerald, and he had with him the Aegis itself, a magical shield with incredible power. With it, he jumped in huge bounds, from windowsill to cart, staying off the street. He pulled people out of the mud, helped bandage the wounded, and led them to safety. And then, he went back in for more. The storm changed then, and everything went sideways."

Wonlar picked up a toy ball from the floor and held it at shoulder level. "Normally, when we drop things," he said, dropping the ball to the floor, "they fall down." Wonlar picked up the ball and held it out again. "But things started falling sideways, slamming into walls." Wonlar tossed the ball to the side, and it bounced off the bright orange wall leading to the kitchen.

"Aegis walked along the walls of buildings like they were floors, and rescued people hanging onto the roofs of their buildings. The sky opened up and it started raining purple cauliflower and spoiled milk." Several children wrinkled their noses, and Wonlar continued.

Wonlar left out the truly terrifying parts, where the citizens had been transformed into boneless amoebas and spiked half-beasts, and most of all, he skipped the half-dozen that had just melted into the green mud, even though he remembered their cries as well as if it had been yesterday. A terrible thought rose up in his mind: *How many people have I seen die?* He pushed it back as he'd pushed back so many thoughts. Each time he went there to tell stories, he mastered his ghosts just a little more, but they did not yield easily.

"The last two people he rescued from the storm were a young Qava and her and Ikanollo friend. The Qava woman was doing her best to save them both, levitating out of the district, but she'd been hit on the head by a sideways-falling bicycle.

[Thank you,] the Qava said, speaking in their minds. Wonlar held both sides of his head to signal the Qava telepathy.

"Then the Ikanollo asked, 'But who are you? Why do you carry that shield?'"

Wonlar aped the first Aegis' voice as best he could, calm and confident. "'Call me Aegis. Will you help me tend to the injured?' And so the Ikanollo and the Qava became First Sentinel and Ghost Hands, the first of the Shields of Audec-Hal."

"Another!" Yara shouted, clapping.

Wonlar considered which story to tell next, when the alarm bracelet vibrated on his wrist. When he was in public, he set it to shake rather than blare. Wonlar stood, gave a polite smile to the children, and then crossed the room. He looked to Rova, trying to catch her attention.

"Did yours go off?" he asked. She nodded. Pulling back his sleeve, Wonlar saw the emerald gem on his bracelet flash twice more and then go dim. No direction indicated. *What would interfere with the locator, but not the base alarm?*

Without the locator, all he knew was that Aegis was in fact in trouble. *City Mother protect him.* Wonlar gritted his teeth and looked to Sapphire. She shrugged, a tense look on her lips.

Sapphire turned to the crowd and said, "Mister Wonlar has to go. Everyone say thank-you."

There were several groans, but after a few seconds, the children said in half-unison, "Thank you, Mister Wonlar," prompted by siblings and parents. The younger ones waddled over for a round of hugs. Wonlar took a couple of precious moments to accept kisses on the cheek and give hugs to several of the older children, the ones who had been coming the whole time.

The farewells done, Wonlar leaned in to Rova, "I don't have my raiment here. Meet me at the safehouse as soon as you can." Rova nodded again and returned to the crowd, all smiles as Wonlar ducked out the back.

City Mother, let me find him in time. Please. I'd rather die than lose him.

Chapter Seven

First Sentinel

The night air was still and cool as Wonlar stood on the balcony, trying to figure out how to find his son.

I remember changing his diapers, and now he's working to rattle the cage wrought by men and women who could be his grandparents. When Wonlar had adopted him, Selweh was a tiny despot whose crying and cooing posed a challenge more harrying than that of any tyrant. Wonlar raised the boy as his own, taught him everything he could. The boy had his mother's sharp mind and curiosity.

Wonlar never intended to raise a hero, but neither did he shelter the boy from the reality of his and the Shields' lives, even as he tried to show the boy the city and its people at their best. Wonlar gave him all the training and preparation he could to keep his love's only son safe.

Selweh had been a Shield in earnest since he was fifteen, when he made his own crude raiment and followed Wonlar on a mission. He'd claimed the moniker Second Sentinel, using Wonlar's old artifacts and weapons. *If I'd forbade him from doing it again, it would have only make him try harder and might have gotten him killed.* Instead, Wonlar had accepted it and started to train the boy formally as his apprentice.

Four years later, the Aegis found him. If he had been any other Shield, Wonlar would have expected it, welcomed its return. But Selweh was Wonlar's son, and Wonlar had promised to protect the boy. And now Selweh was hurt, captured, or worse.

Wonlar heard Rova step onto the balcony, felt her hand on his shoulder.

"He told me he'd start in the Corner, but he was going around the city for leads. And that was nearly a day ago. The most troubling thing is that the alarm bracelet never went off, which means the magic's been cut off, or someone took it before he could activate it."

The skyline outside the window started low, building taller toward the sides of the crater and toward the Crown. Poorly maintained buildings crumbled day by day, slatestone gray the dominant color of the city, offset with red clay, black soot, and the delightfully gaudy colors that covered the poverty of neighborhoods like Bluetown. The rich painted their homes in austere tones, showing their wealth in subtle golds and silvers. But the poor painted boldly, refusing to let their city be an aesthetic void.

From Viscera City, Wonlar could see down to Hook's Hole and his abandoned apartment, over to Audec's Bowels, and north all the way to Headtown and The Crown, towering spires that climbed above the lip of the crater toward the sky above. Above it all, Wonlar saw the tower temple of the City Mother, always in sight but out of reach. Wonlar had three cabinets full of rescue plans to free her, all delayed until they had the resources or the opportunity.

They needed a moment when the tyrants were distracted and their forces weak enough to effectively divert and divide. The moment had never presented itself. *Not yet.*

For a moment, Wonlar let the weight of years pull him down, instead of straining to shrug them off. He flirted with despair, then pushed it away again. It was a gnat buzzing at the edge of his mind, waiting to be let back in to sing the same song they'd sung for years, recounting all his failings.

Wonlar felt Rova's hand on his shoulder, bringing him back to the moment. "You're too good at playing the worried parent. You trained him well; he can stay strong until we find him," she said.

"He learned how to throw a punch before he learned to read," said Wonlar. "And that was before I admitted to myself that I was raising him to fight, to lead. He wrote his first manifesto at five. Do you think he could have grown up to become a banker, a teacher? I never gave him a chance to have another life."

"He was born to be one of us."

"And he'll die one of us, never knowing another life." Wonlar shrugged her hand off. "He wasn't even alive during the Republic. He just believes that things were better—and can be better—without questioning it. Because I raised him to believe, never let him doubt."

"Because you're *right*."

"We should discuss Fahra." Wonlar prayed she would take the bait and let him put aside his worry once more.

Rova obliged. "What are we going to do with her? We can't force Douk and Xera to look after her forever."

"No. But once we know what Yema wants with her, we'll have a better idea of what we can do to keep her safe." Wonlar rattled off possibilities, the half-dozen ideas that they'd discussed after the storm. "I think it's mostly likely to do with her Millrej heritage. I just don't know how, or why." Where the Smiling King's plans were hard to crack because of his instability,

Yema's were harder still to predict, as he was always working on twenty things at once, agendas buried under layers of plots and redundancy plans.

"So what do we do?"

Wonlar circled the balcony, thinking. "I can follow his trail, see what comes up." Wonlar stopped, then leaned on the railing and looked up to Rova. "But first, I'm going to find my son." The threads that connected Wonlar's heart to that of his son were muted, lost. Someone had blocked the threads, hidden them from Wonlar. Otherwise, finding his son would be as simple as finding a dog hiding its head under a sofa.

Wonlar walked back into the safehouse and collected his things. *I need to feel the wind roll over rooftops, spend some time thinking with my fists.*

"I'm going out. See what I can learn over in the Magister's territory."

Rova brightened up, happy to see him active. "I'll come with you."

"Another time. I need to think, move at my own pace. If I get a real lead, I'll send out the call." Wonlar held up his arm, pulling down the coat to show the alarm bracelet.

Wonlar saw her disappointment but tried not to let it weigh on him. He'd make it up to her later. As powerful as she was, tonight he needed stealth more than power.

"I'll show myself out," she said. Once she was gone, Wonlar prepared his elixirs and donned his raiment. Checking the streets and alleys for spies, he hooked his grapple line to a roof across the street and swung out into the city, bearing east for Yema's domain.

In the right neighborhoods, you could see families gathering for dinner. People lived their lives as if their freedom wasn't an illusion. You could pretend that the city wasn't ruled by madmen and monsters.

The Corner was not one of those places. The Corner wrapped around a broken-off shard from Audec's hip, which gave the neighborhood its name. The Corner had always been dangerous, but since the fall of the Senate, the neighborhood had been split between the domains of Yema and COBALT-3, changing hands sometimes as often as several times a year. It was a ten-square-block rolling gang war, drug market, and everything-has-a-price bazaar.

First Sentinel stood on the stone wings of a gargoyle and watched the flow of movement during the small hours of the night, the dark neighborhood lit by his shimmercrab goggles, which painted the neighborhood in hues of red. The goggles differentiated the smallest variances in hue and magnified even trace amounts of light, turning night into sharply defined day. The first hotspot was the brothel alley, with men and women coming and going in jerky flows of lust. The bars were a steady stream of booze and bluster. From his perch, First Sentinel saw little outbreaks of low-level thievery, looting, mugging. *I could be here all night and barely make a dent.*

But a dent was still a dent. First Sentinel hooked his grapple line to the lip of a rooftop a block away and dove from his perch, swinging down into an alley where a quartet of thugs was trying to break into a warehouse. Their threads to one another were dull green, a partnership of convenience, probably not long woven, and certainly not strong enough to avoid ratting one another out. A corrugated metal awning gave them more cover, but one of them held an oil lamp, making himself a convenient target.

First Sentinel swung feet first into the lamp holder and kicked him into the middle of the alley. Squaring off against the others, First Sentinel clicked the button at the pommel to recoil his grappling hook. The two other robbers turned from the heavy wooden door and its complicated lock. Yellow threads of fear snapped into existence, swarming toward him. They knew enough to be scared.

First Sentinel smiled. "Who'd like to tell me about Magister Yema's latest plans?"

The woman at the door pulled the crowbar back and up, readying for an overhead swing.

Wonlar started thinking with his fists.

In the moment of fear granted by his reputation, First Sentinel landed a right hook on a Pronai with a goatee and slammed him into the door. The noise would attract more attention, but that just meant he'd get more sparring partners, more people to question.

The woman came in with a clumsy swing of the crowbar. First Sentinel took a diagonal step around her and pushed her into the lantern bearer, separating the criminals into two groups.

The fourth thug, a Qava, extended a hand toward First Sentinel and sent him sliding across the alley with her telekinesis. The Shield braced himself with a leg against the far wall as the pressure held. The thug's telekinesis wasn't anywhere near as strong as Ghost Hands'. *Good thing, or I'd be a crater in the wall.*

Wonlar pulled a thumb-sized coin from his belt and rubbed it three times clockwise with a finger, then pushed off the wall to charge the Qava robber. The coin was one of his oldest artifacts, made when he was back in academy. It allowed him to overcome the momentum of Qava telekinesis. It was only good for a couple of uses per day, though.

First Sentinel tackled the woman, and they rolled into the locked door. First Sentinel landed several blows to her kidneys, and she went limp.

As he stood to face the others, the crowbar thug took a horizontal swing at his shoulders. First Sentinel lunged forward and slammed into her side. The crowbar skipped off his coat, and for the hundredth time, he mentally thanked Professor Yensto for his lessons. His coat had absorbed at least a hundred killing blows and a thousand lesser strikes. *If only I could keep it clean.*

First Sentinel swept the crowbar-wielding thug's legs and stood back. "Start talking and the hurting stops."

They kept coming, and beneath his mask, First Sentinel smiled. The Pronai rushed him with a flurry of punches, and First Sentinel stepped back, giving himself just a bit more time to respond, read the pattern. He tucked in and took the first two blows on the coat and hard bone beneath. The third caught his shoulder, and the fourth pushed him back off his balance. By the fifth punch, First Sentinel had the Pronai's timing and grabbed the thug's arm mid-swing. First Sentinel turned his fall into a throw, making the Pronai a mallet and their unopened door the gong.

First Sentinel played with the thugs for another thirty seconds, blowing off some steam. When they were all tied up, he questioned them about Magister Yema, Aegis, and the summit.

They didn't know anything. They wanted into the warehouse to steal a printing press, use it for counterfeiting. He dragged them to their feet and walked them a few blocks through the street, hands tied behind their backs. The tyrants' police force in The Corner would rather have First Sentinel in chains than a hundred robbers, so the embarrassment of being beaten was the best punishment he could mete out without inflicting permanent injury.

That and a couple of broken bones. They were criminals, after all.

First Sentinel's night faded into a blur of fistfights, interrogations, and dead ends. Three disrupted muggings, two aborted arsons, and one rapist snatched out of a window and hung upsidedown from a ten-story apartment complex later. First Sentinel started to feel better. It was then that he got a lead.

Crouching on a gargoyle at the corner of a warehouse roof, crammed up against the shard of the titan's bone, First Sentinel stared down at the rapist. The criminal was just a kid, maybe a couple years younger than Selweh. In another world, they could have gone to school together. First Sentinel took a breath and stopped telling himself stories.

"What is Magister Yema planning?"

The boy craned his neck up, suspended upside down on a rope that First Sentinel had tied off to the gargoyle. The rapist's voice broke. "I heard some warlocks talking. Some plan. Magister's been sending them all over the city, snatching up kids, just random kids."

"Why?" First Sentinel growled, pouring it on. The blood was pooling in the kid's head. He flushed and flailed.

"I don't know! I just heard it, right? Please let me down. I'm afraid of heights."

"That's your problem. I'll let you down when you give me something more. And if you do it quick, I might not break your arm for what you tried to do to that girl."

Wind dropping off the edge of the titan's bone buffeted the boy into the building beneath. First Sentinel held a knife to the rope as the boy looked up, eyes wide.

"That's all I heard. I heard it, and then they left. Please let me down!" *Talk, boy. This is not the night to push me.*

The boy's threads supported his story. Bright yellow fear, gray frustration, and the remains of a dim coppery thread that bound him to his victim in the alley below. The only thread strong enough to indicate loyalty lead to a Qava woman who watched the whole scene from down the block, content to leave her pawn to swing on his own noose.

"I can let you down, but I don't think that's what you really want." He brandished the knife, hoping the boy would crack soon. He needed to get out of the exposed position. Another minute or two and he was sure to be seen by someone who could pose a threat.

"Please!" The boy coughed, sobbing. First Sentinel sighed. *If he knew any more, he'd be talking by now.*

The air moved above First Sentinel, and he tensed. *Spend fifty years at the top of the most wanted list and you develop a pretty keen sense for ambushes.*

But this time, the warning wasn't enough. First Sentinel leapt off the gargoyle, reaching for his grapple gun, but something snatched him out of the air and tossed him ungracefully onto the roof.

First Sentinel rolled to his feet and scanned the roof, eyes darting back and forth, his shimmercrab goggles casting the dark night in red-scale. He looked up and saw Black Wind, Yema's right-hand Qava.

Her yellow and burgundy bands of fear and servitude stretched across the sky to Yema's tower. She floated above his head, arms crossed, in a raven-black cloak. First Sentinel had no doubt that if she had a mouth, she'd be smirking. It was harder to tell whether Yema or Nevri had the larger share of arrogant henchmen.

[Where is the girl?] she said in his head. When Ghost Hands spoke in his head, it was comforting. Black Wind's voice was intrusive, an unwelcome guest ready to snap at any moment.

"You've caught me at a bad time. I'm currently busy having a pleasant conversation with one of your master's up-and-coming criminals."

First Sentinel's knot untied itself in an instant, and the boy screamed as he dropped. *[Sounds like you're free now. The only way you walk away from this is if you give up the girl.]*

Another life on my hands. I can't remember when I lost count.

Still holding a knife, First Sentinel reached for another throwing blade with his free hand. Black Wind picked him up with a tiny gesture, and he flew across the roof as if he'd been swung by the red thread of hatred that connected them. He lashed out with the knife as he passed her in mid-air, cutting her robe.

First Sentinel hit the ground, and hoped that the cracking sound was his armor and not his ribs. He was shielded from most invasive telepathy by an amulet, but the momentum coin was spent, so he'd have to deal with her telekinesis directly.

She let him stand. It took a little longer than it should. Something in his back felt torn. *Not good.*

"What do you want?" First Sentinel asked, thinking through the possibilities. He couldn't stay long, injured as he was, but Black Wind might be the only way for him to get real information about Aegis or Fahra.

[Magister Yema demands you return the girl.]

"And I request the Magister's head, but neither of us is going to be satisfied tonight." First Sentinel drew a flash stone and a smoke stone, tossing the pair to the roof and closing his eyes. One stone emitted a burst of light, the other a plume of smoke. These worked far better against anyone but Qava, but the smoke would momentarily throw off Black Wind's telekinetic sonar. With luck, it would give him cover enough to take the offensive.

First Sentinel threw two more knifes as he advanced on Black Wind, biting his lip and pushing through the pain. He jumped up to a chimney and pulled himself up, muscles spasming in his side. As the cloud cleared, he leapt off the chimney to grab the bottom of her cloak. He wrapped his arms around her leg, dragging her down with his weight.

Climbing up her body, he pinned a knife in her thigh. *Purchase for me, pain for her.* She swatted him off with her power, and the knife went with him, twisting on the way out. The mental scream would carry several blocks, but for First Sentinel, it was an instant, near crippling migraine. The amulet could only do so much.

I've dug too deep—time to vanish, fast.

Growling to keep the pain at bay, First Sentinel dove off the roof and fired his grappling gun across the intersection, trying to put as much distance between himself and Black Wind as possible. If he didn't get out of her range, she could pluck him out of the air like a fly.

How did she find me? he wondered.

[I know where Aegis is.] She called in his mind, her voice taunting.

Dammit. She couldn't be bluffing if she knows that Aegis is missing. Could she? But if he went back, he might not escape again.

The sight of Aria's dying body in his arms flashed across his vision, and his promise echoed through his mind.

First Sentinel rounded a corner and turned back. He pressed the emergency button on his wrist bracelet, knowing that help wouldn't arrive in time. If he was lucky, someone would be nearby. Stranger things had happened. First Sentinel saw the broken body of the rapist on the street floor, a random passerby thumbing through his wallet.

First Sentinel grappled onto the corner open window and swung up around an abutment. Changing his angle, First Sentinel hit the roof in a roll, his grapple gun recoiling.

Black Wind was gone. The Shield scanned the roof and the skies overhead, but he saw nothing. *Why leave? Was she just taunting me? Don't drop your guard yet, Wonlar.* He paced the roof, looking for anything left behind as a clue, half his attention turned skyward on watch.

He was bending over to look at a brown rag he hadn't noticed before, when a solid weight crashed down on him.

She's brought friends. Marvelous.

He looked up at the blue on black of a Freithin brute against the night sky. This one he didn't recognize. The Freithin had range and strength on him and was probably uninjured. *Well done, old man.*

The Freithin lifted and held him off the ground at arm's length while Black Wind appeared again to gloat.

[You wear your weaknesses too openly, even for an Ikanollo.]

The brute slammed him into the ground. First Sentinel felt a rib crack, the coat's protective enchantment spent.

First Sentinel screamed. He focused his rage, spitting his words at Black Wind. "So you don't know where Aegis is, then?" The Freithin's mouth twisted into a sadistic, toothy grin.

Black Wind floated down to the roof, holding a hand to her chin. *[Oh, we do. COBALT-3 is having so much fun with him, she couldn't keep her metal mouth shut.]*

First Sentinel winced as he spoke, even shallow breaths flashing pain across his chest. "He'll be fine. He's tougher than your friend here and smarter than Yema." *Bluff for time, make a plan.*

[So smart that he's leaving his mentor to die on a rooftop in The Corner for snooping into the affairs of his betters.]

Keep talking, Black Wind. First Sentinel swung his legs up to wrap around the Freithin's arm, then twisted the thug's elbow against the joint, breaking the hold. First Sentinel hit the roof and rolled, gaining distance between himself and the Freithin. The ache in his eyes and at his fingers told him he couldn't push himself much longer. *Oh, to be twenty-five again. Hell, I'd take forty.*

Dodging and weaving for position, First Sentinel tried to bait Black Wind with taunts. *Think about how much you dislike me instead of just crushing me.* He'd learned all he needed to that night. Without backup, staying would just get him killed.

He juked left then right, dodging away from the Freithin long enough to pull the last throwing knife from his boot. He prayed that he wasn't already hemorrhaging internally. The Freithin saw him move and grabbed him with both hands.

No good. The thug swung First Sentinel overhead and slammed him into the ground again. But the knife was already out, and First Sentinel tossed it as he fell, using the Freithin's body as cover. It was a long shot . . .

The Shield's vision swam, then went black.

First Sentinel snapped back to consciousness, pain arcing across his chest as he sat up with a gulp.

Ten yards away, the Freithin thug hunched over Black Wind. His knife had found its target, then. Decades of fighting alongside Ghost Hands had taught him that Qava's telekinetic sonar was more easily tricked if a projectile launched from behind cover. A split-second of surprise combined with the Qava's own arrogance was sometimes enough to sneak a blow in.

This Freithin must be Black Wind's bodyguard, choosing to go to her side instead of pound on the Ikanollo in front of him.

Distracted by his charge's wounds, the Freithin didn't notice as First Sentinel pulled himself toward the lip of the roof.

He drew his grapple gun and caught the hook on the lip of an adjacent roof. Climbing onto the lip of his building, First Sentinel then rolled off, holding on to the grapple gun with both hands. The arc swung him past his former conversation partner on the street, picked clean of everything save his patched pants.

First Sentinel heard Black Wind's mental shouts of frustration as his feet nearly brushed the cobblestone street.

Get out, old man. Another two blocks and he was out of range of Black Wind's telepathic trace. From there, he kept to the side streets and made for his bolt-hole.

As he swung across The Corner, First Sentinel thought about Nevri's offer, Aegis' captivity, and Yema's still unknown plans for Fahra. First Sentinel plotted a course out of the Corner and toward Dr. Acci to get his ribs checked out. And then, to assemble the team. If COBALT-3 had Aegis, the only question was where. Which lab?

I'm coming, my boy.

Chapter Eight

First Sentinel

The downpour outside was a constant buzz, fat droplets without end. Inside, the group sat around a bare limestone table. Without a tablecloth, the stone showed countless stains from spilled wine and food.

Altars were made for communion, for coming together. It was fitting.

Beyond the foyer, a lone priestess stood watch—their door guard.

"We need the help," Sarii said for the fifth time since the Shields had sat down to make a decision about Nevri's offer. The meeting was scheduled for that night. He'd spent all morning going over his notes about COBALT-3's territory, where she might be holding his son. But if they were going to take Nevri's offer, they had to decide and act on that first.

Wonlar paced around the table, weaving between the pillow-seats and the altar, incense still burning. *Some would say it's blasphemous to plan war in a temple of the City Mother. But dreams of freedom are the best kind of worship we can give her.*

Many of the temples had fallen into disrepair during the reign of the tyrants. Some still prayed to the goddess that kept them afraid, hoping for mercy, but most just stayed home. As First Sentinel, Wonlar had befriended the priestesses of several temples, women who remembered the Goddess' true purpose.

[I think we can do it on our own,] Bira said.

Wonlar knew the Shields could gather explosives, but they didn't have the location of the machine or any of the other information.

He said, "Even if we can triangulate, it'll take longer with trial and error, and we might not be able to move by the summit. Nevri is a monster, but she's a businesswoman; she plays by her own set of rules. The offer might be a trap, but if it isn't, then she'd be with us through the whole thing."

Sarii was unmoved. Bira was silent, considering. Time for a different approach. "Let's pretend it isn't a trap. Nevri's above-board, and this is a good chance. How do we do it?"

Wenlizerachi set aside the loaf of bread he'd been munching on and pulled himself up in his seat. "With the map, I could scout the place out, check sentries, rotations. Dlella said it's protected, so we'd need to find out how well."

Wonlar nodded. *Thank you, let's stay positive here.* "We have just after midnight to meet her. The sun outside is fading to the south, so we've maybe got five hours. The Smiling King will have at least one of his lieutenants stationed at the machine. Which one?"

"Protean would kill minions to keep herself entertained," Sarii said.

"Onyx is his heavy," Rova said. A fellow Freithin, Onyx was of a size comparable to Rova's and was casual with the lives of his foot soldiers.

"That'd be my bet," Wonlar said. "For Onyx, I have the drainer disks. We'll just need someone to hold him in place long enough.

And if that doesn't work, I have something special I've been meaning to try out."

Rova cracked her knuckles. "I can handle Onyx."

[We'll need Aegis,] Bira added.

The last time Sapphire and Onyx had fought, it had been a standstill. *Bira might be right.* Wonlar kept the thought to himself, not wanting to show his doubt.

Sarii leaned onto the heavy stone table, inlaid in emerald with the knot-work symbol of the City Goddess. "Shouldn't we talk about Aegis?"

First Sentinel waved a hand, dismissing the topic. "If we get started talking about him, I won't be able to stop until we find him, and we need to address this opportunity, so no, we shouldn't talk about Aegis."

"He'll come back. Don't worry." Although Rova looked calm, Wonlar imagined she was as worried as he was. A jade thread reached out from her heart into the indistinct distance. Still hidden, Aegis' threads were masked.

All six of them had threads hanging loose, their connections to Aegis a constant reminder of his absence. For most of his companions, the threads were the shimmering gold bond of brotherhood.

In addition, there had been a soft jade thread between Rova and Aegis for the better part of two years, but neither of them seemed to be willing to make a move. *Two of the strongest people in the city, but they're scared of their own feelings.*

"Why can't Nevri just do it herself?" Sarii asked. "Even if she needs to have it not be traceable to her, she could hire any number of mercenaries. Why us?"

"That might be the most important question," First Sentinel said. "She means to involve us in this, and not just to serve our purposes. By using us, she's getting something else. What?"

Rova answered. "We should be going after Aegis. We don't all have to go to meet Nevri, do we?"

"We don't, but we would need everyone to face COBALT-3. I don't imagine she'd let him out of her grasp without a fight," Blurred Fists said.

Sarii jumped in. "Here's what she gets—a win–win situation. We go and die, she wins. We go and succeed, she wins. And City Mother only knows what she'll do to us if we pull this off and are greedy enough to come calling for our reward." She twirled a stone noose around one finger.

"It's undoubtedly a trap," First Sentinel said. "But is the chance to keep close tabs on Nevri worth the danger?"

[Once we get the information tonight, we can case the location and then decide,] Bira said, her thoughts speaking directly to each of the Shields' minds.

"What if they hold back the location until the meet with Nevri?" Wonlar asked. "We don't get the explosive until the meet with Nevri anyway. Whatever it is, we want it. None of the bombs we have are big enough to take out a machine the size I imagine this Rebirth Engine would need to be. So unless we want to make Bira float a whole crate of explosives and even then take our chances, we need that explosive."

Wenlizerachi stood, took three quick laps around the table, and lit three more sticks of incense, repeating the ritual supplication for a blessing from the City Mother. "Even if we get in and can plant the explosive, we'll need an escape plan, different from the way we got in—the Smiling King's reinforcements would flood us by then."

Bira chuckled in the Shields' minds. *[I can just knock out the walls, if we really want to cause trouble.]*

"Why not?" Sarii asked. "Why are we always playing it soft with these monsters? We should be leaving behind stacks of corpses until they decide to pack it up and find another city to terrorize."

Wonlar leveled a gaze at Sarii. "They're the killers. Not us."

"Fifty years you've been saying that, and what have we got to show for it? I buried my naïveté with the dozen friends who gave their lives for your dreams of a free Audec-Hel, Wonlar. I won't bury another friend, but I'd happily dig graves for the tyrants myself."

Bira spoke again, her voice calm, but insistent. *[We're losing focus. It's time to make a decision.]*

Wonlar took a deep breath. "Let's vote. All for taking Nevri's bargain?"

Rova's hand went up. Bira locked Wonlar in her attention, and he felt her presence in his mind, watching and listening. Wonlar raised his hand, and the Qava mirrored him. Wonlar tried to shut away his doubt from Bira, but he felt her find it, acknowledge it, and move past it.

Wenlizerachi raised his hand. "I still think it's a trap."

"If I have to bury all of you by myself, I'm going to cave in the tomb and never look back." *Sarii at her most sentimental—in public at least.*

Wonlar unfolded a map of the district around Ruby Shackles. "Alright, here's my plan. If it is a trap, we won't be caught unawares. Dlella will have people placed here and here." Wonlar indicated the alley in front of the brothel and the street behind it. *If Nevri means to imply that we were prostitutes, at least she thought us high-class ones.*

"Wenlizerachi, I want you, Bira, and Sarii to stay back, watch the exits and keep our line of retreat open. Rova and I will go inside."

[And what about Selweh/Aegis?]

Wonlar didn't notice a reaction from anyone else. The message was only for him, coming back to the doubt he'd let slip through to the forefront of his thoughts.

[I swore an oath to do anything I could to protect him. But we have to take this opportunity,] Wonlar thought back to his old friend. *[He would kill me if we passed up this opportunity just for him.*

[As soon as we get back, we start crossing warehouses and laboratories off the list until we find the right one and take it by storm.]

City Mother, let this not be a trap.

Most brothels had a doorman, some tough—often a Freithin—who kept out the riffraff and waded in when trouble started.

Ruby Shackles had three, standing in a wide V-shape: a tall lanky Pronai who wore a white straw hat, a portly Freithin as wide as the double doors, and a Full-blood ox-kin Millrej with raven-black fur and a bronze nose ring.

The first trick was getting in. Audec-Hal's sex trade had a great deal of money invested in keeping the tyrants in power. Before the Republic fell, prostitution had been tightly controlled and limited. But under the tyrants, no perversion was out of bounds. Anything for the right price.

As Sapphire and First Sentinel approached the door in full raiment, the three bouncers stood shoulder to shoulder to bar their way.

The Pronai adjusted his hat. "Who do we have here?" He drew out the last word slowly, a big grin on his face.

First Sentinel sighed. *I don't have time to do my laundry, so I certainly don't have time for small men with big egos.*

"We're here to meet Dlella. We're expected," he said, striding forward, attempting to force them to move out of his way.

They didn't. First Sentinel pulled up short on his toes just before colliding with the Pronai.

The thin bouncer looked down his hawkish nose at First Sentinel. "Your kind is bad for business, okay? Why don't you just keep on walking?"

Sapphire flanked First Sentinel, squaring off against the portly Freithin. "We'll play nice—buy some rounds and keep out of the spotlight. You won't even know we're here."

"With those outfits?" the Millrej snorted.

Come on, flinch, First Sentinel thought. He found thrashing smart-asses to be very calming.

Instead, he stepped back and addressed the group.

"Well, if you want to get on Dlella's bad side." He looked to Sapphire, then back to the bouncers.

They could fight their way through, but he'd rather not raise anyone's ire and set himself up for even more of a trap in the brothel full of gangsters.

Sighing, First Sentinel slipped the Pronai a crisp bill. Likely as much as the guard would make in a night. Then he pulled out two more, for the Millrej and the Freithin.

Having stuffed the pockets of the bouncers, First Sentinel held his hands up and asked, "Are we done here?"

They parted, and the Shields walked inside.

Ruby Shackles was a monument to indulgence. Wall-to-wall crushed red velvet, polished mahogany fixtures, and expensive

Jalvai sculptures, all from the last great pre-oligarchy movement, defined by bold lines and self-assurance. The bar was polished steel, manned by a four-armed Spark-touched woman and a slight Pronai. Naked and mostly naked women and men were scattered around the room like furniture. One man even was furniture: a broad-backed Qava who lay on the floor, having finger food eaten off his back.

The air was thick with threads the flushed pink of lust, the orange of greed, and even a few dashes of fearful yellow.

A stocky man in a gray suit nodded at the Shields from the second floor, waving them up.

"I don't like this place," Sapphire said.

"Neither do I."

Dlella didn't want them to be comfortable—classic business tactics. Take your opponents out of their everyday routine, put them on guard. Create and exploit every advantage. Luckily, First Sentinel was too angry to be defensive. He headed for the stairs, the weight of eyes following both him and Sapphire.

The elder Shield crossed the room with a hand on his belt, ready for the trap that he'd all but convinced himself was waiting. At the top of the stairs, a Jalvai attendant ushered them into a sitting room with a low black-lacquered table and pillows for seats. Dlella was coiled into an upright sitting position, with four more guards in gray suits posted in the corners.

Dlella had set the stage well—no matter where the Shields stood, they would be flanked and outnumbered. If they stood at the door, they'd show their distrust and continue to draw attention from the main crowd, but if they made a display of courtesy and sat at the table, they'd have to turn their backs to two of the guards.

Dlella swayed side to side as they entered. She gave a slight nod. "Please sit." First Sentinel threw back his longcoat and took a seat, turning to keep the far corner guards in peripheral vision. Sapphire knelt into a crouch beside him, ready to spring up in a Pronai's heartbeat.

Eyes darted across the room, from the guards to Dlella, to Sapphire. For a long moment, the seven waited for someone to make a move.

First Sentinel chuckled, and the tension spilled over. "If you're going to jump us, all I ask is that you do it now, so we don't waste our time."

Dlella just looked at First Sentinel, still swaying back and forth. "Your paranoia may have kept you alive so far, but it's not terribly endearing. We're here for a deal, nothing more."

"Good. Where is the artifact?"

Dlella produced a map and spread it out on the table before them. A bright-eyed Pronai boy appeared beside the table in a simple suit.

"Can I interest anyone in a drink?" Dlella asked.

"No, thank you," First Sentinel said.

Dlella sighs. "We're not going to poison you."

"Not thirsty."

Sapphire ordered a *dounmo* tea. It wasn't that she was more trusting than First Sentinel. If Dlella had poison strong enough to disable a Freithin, the Shields were doomed regardless.

Dlella ordered blackberry liquor, and the serving boy disappeared in a flash of red. The Millrej then drew the Shields' attention to the map. "The artifact is called the Rebirth Engine. It's kept in a guarded facility on the north end of Audec's Bowels." *And that's all we need to know for Blurred Fists to case the location. If we can string this out and get the explosives and more about Nevri's hidden agendas, then all the better.*

She pointed with a scaled finger at a building located in the heart of the industrial district, an area with a high crime rate and no safehouses within an easy walk.

We'll have to stage out of the coffeehouse basement, or from The Rack; talk to Colni and her sisters. The Shields could move through the district undetected, but it wouldn't be easy.

"What else do you know?" First Sentinel asked.

"Onyx leads a contingent of fifty Spark-touched guards that rotate on three shifts, starting at noon, eight, and four. Nevri recommends that you strike at the shift change at eight—that's when Onyx takes his respite, after two shifts on."

The middle of the evening. It wouldn't even be true dark by then. It wasn't the Shields' usual operating hours—too exposed to patrols. But if they could gain an advantage on Onyx, catch him when he was fatigued, it might be worth it.

The boy arrived with the drinks. Sapphire saluted the boy, and Dlella raised a toast, which Sapphire slowly returned.

"What about the meet with Nevri? The explosives? Why can't we just use a crate full of dynamite?" First Sentinel asked. "And why not give them to us now? Every extra meeting is a chance for us to be spotted by agents of Yema, the Smiling King—anyone."

Dlella shook her head. "Conventional explosives will not suffice. The Rebirth Engine creates pure change—it is change. A special explosive will be required to destroy it. Luckily for you, the Executor is procuring such a device as we speak."

The Millrej continued. "One week from today, Nevri will meet you in Heart Station, at the platform for the Headtown vein. A train will be emptied for the meeting." She took a small, controlled sip. "Nevri requires that you conduct your operation a week afterward, on the night of the eighteenth of Crooked Elbow."

"Why wait? There could be another storm by then," First Sentinel asked. *It's nearly a guarantee, in fact.*

Dlella stood taller on her tail. "Nevri will be working to make sure that your mission is not interrupted. The preparations are not yet complete. And she imagined that your people would require some time for your own planning."

Worry pricked at the base of First Sentinel's skull. *Maybe we should just call it here, try to do it on our own.* He looked to Sapphire. She would feel his worry, since they shared the Freithin blood bond. She was wary, eyes drifting to the corners every few moments.

"Is there anything special about that date?" If she wanted to spring a trap, First Sentinel guessed Nevri might wait for the pickup, which is why he planned on leaving half of the team behind in reserve.

Dlella gestured with her drink, the blue-red liquid swirling in the clear crystal glass. "It's just a schedule, First Sentinel. I'm sure you understand how much Nevri values a well-kept schedule."

"If there's another storm before then, so help me . . . " First Sentinel clenched his fists, lips curled into a snarl.

Sapphire put a hand on First Sentinel's shoulder, and he relaxed. "What else do you know about the device?"

The more they got her talking, the better chance they had of catching a glimpse into Nevri's plan. Nevri never made fair bargains, and so far this seemed too good to be true.

Dlella sighed, casual. "Not much. From what we can tell, it's not the origin of the storms; it just makes them come more frequently and last longer. It's more catalyst and accelerant than creator."

"How?" Sapphire asked.

Dlella slid to the side and reset her coiled tail beneath her. "Sadly, we don't know that. The Smiling King's always had a connection to the Spark and those it touches. It might be an elaborate focus for his power, refining his power over the Spark-touched into power over the Spark itself."

"Might?" First Sentinel asked, wondering where Nevri had gotten that information and why she had just sat on it the whole time. Had she already tried to destroy it and failed? That might explain Dlella's confidence about how conventional explosives wouldn't work.

Sapphire asked, "Have you tried to destroy it before?"

"Executor Nevri only learned of the device recently and decided to go directly to you." Dlella smiled, as if trying to build rapport. "Anything else?" *How about Nevri's head on a pike? Or Aria back from the grave?*

After a moment, First Sentinel grinned. "The money?" Dlella matched his expression as best as she could with her thin lips.

"Executor Nevri has generously offered to pay half now and half upon confirmation of the mission."

That way she gets her dirty work done, and she can betray us afterward. Very tidy.

"Half now, one-quarter when we get the explosives, the rest after."

Dlella's smile faded. "The terms have already been given."

First Sentinel stood, and the guards flinched, taking a half-step forward. Dlella raised a hand and halted them.

He shook his head. He'd been married to an attorney; he knew his way around a contract. "The deal isn't sealed until we get the first payment. Negotiation of the details is still open. You know we want the device gone, so we'll go after it. But if we take it out on your date, you pay on our schedule. Otherwise, we walk and do it ourselves, and whatever Nevri has planned for the night of the mission gets ruined."

"Very well," Dlella answered.

First Sentinel offered his hand, and the two shook. A shiver rippled down First Sentinel's spine. He tried to tell himself it was just the coolness of Dlella's scaled hand.

Dlella pushed up to the ceiling and revealed a plain brown sack that had been covered by her tail. Using her tail, she pushed the sack to First Sentinel. He looked inside, checked the stack of bills. "Looks good."

First Sentinel nodded to the Millrej, keeping an eye on Sapphire. The big Freithin picked up the bag and slung it over her shoulder with ease.

No one jumped them as they walked out, much to First Sentinel's surprise. *Maybe fortune was turning after all. When things look like they're going our way, I spend all my time wondering when it's going to fall apart. But if we do this right, we save lives and put the screws to the Smiling King and Nevri both.*

First Sentinel rather preferred the consistency of tough luck and endless setbacks. It was more dependable.

And now, to find my son.

Chapter Nine

First Sentinel

Twenty Years Ago

*A*t first, I was lost with Selweh. What was a bachelor artificer and revolutionary to do with a toddler?

"Mommy!" It was the only thing he would say. I suspected he knew more, but he was too young to grieve properly.

Darkened circles rimmed my eyes. Patrols at night and sleepless days of interrupted work and attempts to learn parenting took a toll.

He squirmed in my arms as I tried to feed him. We lived among piles of boxes and laboratory equipment, and I had to be as vigilant keeping him from eating beakers as I did watching my back on the streets.

I had to retrain my voice for compassion, separate the gruff warrior out and learn a new way of talking, of living. "She's gone, Selweh. But she loved you very much. Now it's just you, me, and the Shields. I'm Wonlar, remember? Wonlar."

Selweh threw a handful of applesauce at my face. "Wonner."

I smiled as I wiped off the food.
It was a start.

Chapter Ten

Aegis

A egis strained against the chains that bound him to the examining table. They hadn't budged any of the last hundred times he tried, or the hundred before that, but still he pulled. The third link on his left arm seemed to be weakening under the pressure. Every time he strained, the chain shocked him. He was burned and exhausted, but one of the links was almost broken.

He'd been imprisoned for five days; he was sure of it. Thanks to his father's lessons, he could keep time in his mind without a clock, without the sun.

The room was cast in darkness while COBALT-3 was gone, the lamps doused, and no windows to speak of. *She's very big on efficiency and thoroughness. If she were on our side, I'd admire it.*

He pulled again, felt the pinching heat of the shock. The third link seemed to stretch a bit more. By morning, he could have it broken. But then COBALT-3 would come again and replace it.

"Try harder, Selweh".

His father's voice spoke in his head in response to his own thoughts. Selweh could almost see his father shaking his head, chiding but amused. *"Don't try harder. Try smarter."*

Selweh had never known his birth father. He'd been some lover of his mother's that Wonlar never spoke about and who disappeared before Selweh's birth.

All of Selweh's memories of a father came from the stern but loving man who had raised him on tales of a fallen republic and his mother's heroism. To hear Wonlar describe her, she was the perfect woman, loving, strong, intelligent, and driven. Wonlar had taken Selweh as his own, though a shadow passed over his father's face sometimes when the old hero looked at him.

Aegis took a breath, cleared his mind, and remembered his father's lessons, hearing Wonlar's voice again: *"Imagine the room as if it were lit, the items clear in your mind."*

He brought up a mental picture of the room, drawn precisely each day when the light was turned on. *If I break the chain, I can get a link out. What can I do with one link of chain and a free hand in this room that will get me out?*

The room was twenty feet to a side, square. The ceiling was twelve feet tall. The walls, floor, and ceiling were made of graystone, and the table he was tied to was forged from high-grade steel and angled thirty degrees from the floor. Gravity was on his side to pull against the chains; his weight had been hanging on them since he was put in the laboratory days ago. His wrists had the cuts and sores to prove it. There were three lamps—one at the door, one suspended overhead, one in the far corner on the desk. At the desk there were scalpels, medical tools, and pattern machines for computation.

And below the desk was the source box for the chains, cables running under the floor. *That's it.*

Aegis strained against the chain again, pushing against the table with his legs, one arm, and his back. The chain on his arm pulled up and away. Electricity coursed through his body, and he bit back a scream as he pulled. But the chain bent, then broke with a loud snap. The sound reverberated through the room, loud enough to echo into the hallway.

I don't care if you heard, guard, just give me one more minute, and I'll be ready for you. Aegis looped the few links still attached to the manacle around his wrist and took the broken chain in his hand.

A mechanical voice called, "Unknown Sound. Investigating." The lamp at the door flickered on, and through the door stepped one of COBALT-3's automata guards, all chrome and brass. It pointed a halberd at Aegis and said, "Stop."

"Too late, rusty." The light was just enough to illuminate the source box. Aegis hurled the broken chain-link like a knife, imbedding it straight into the device that electrified the chains. As the box sparked and the guard charged, Aegis burst the de-activated chains.

And now, the fun begins. Aegis reached out with his unchained hand and grabbed the haft of the halberd. He pulled the automata into a waiting fist, knocking the guard's head off the struts of its neck. The head clattered against the wall, and the automata fell to the ground in a heap of clangs. Grabbing the halberd as it fell, Aegis snatched the lantern off the table. He flipped on the lantern and adjusted to the light.

Without his father's shimmercrab goggles, he needed the electric light to navigate his way out of COBALT-3's labyrinthine compound. Aegis thanked the City Mother for the android's simplicity in design. *Why design automata that see in the dark when your lighting system is so efficient?*

Aegis had no clue where in the compound he was, or even which laboratory this was. It was probably the main facility in Bent Knee, but she could have laboratories even the Shields didn't know about.

But before anything else, he had to retrieve the Aegis. More than being the source of his powers, the shield was the symbol of the city's desire for freedom, their struggle against the oligarchs' control. *Plus, Wonlar would kill me if I lost it. He might* actually *kill me.*

Luckily, since he had been chosen, Selweh had always been able to find his way back to the shield.

He closed his eyes, shut out the sounds and sights, and reached outward with his mind, feeling the familiar presence some hundred feet away.

That made sense. COBALT-3 would want to keep close enough that she could tinker and play with it on her own. She'd been trying to unlock its power, learn how it might be wielded by someone other than the chosen bearer. Since it had appeared in the hands of the first Aegis fifty years ago, the Aegis and its power had been usable only by the champion of Audec-Hal.

The shield had appeared beside his bed one morning, without warning. *I never expected it would come to me. Why not Wonlar or Bira? They've been fighting for so long.*

But it had chosen, and he couldn't deny the call. Even if it meant he'd have an early grave, like every Aegis that had come before him. Like his mother.

Aegis followed the feeling down the hall, started near the lab, looking up and down the long antiseptic-white walls. The next door was six inches of thick steel and locked. Without the shield in hand, he couldn't force it, and he didn't want to attract more attention by trying.

Across the marbled hall, he tried another door as the feeling got stronger. This room was nearly identical to the one he'd left. The operating table was covered in the orange blood of an Ikanollo. Wher had they taken the patient? Was the patient dead, or had the experiment been a success? COBALT-3 had kidnapped City Mother only knew how many citizens for her lab rats over the years. *This has to stop now.*

With the shield, he could free the subjects and start a great uprising against COBALT-3. He saw himself leading the charge in front of a hundred weary but enraged test subjects, the compound in flames and the city one step closer to freedom.

Aegis chuckled at the fantasy. *Don't get ahead of yourself, Selweh. Shield first.*

He looked around the corner into the next hall, hoping that he'd be able to loop around to the shield, having exhausted the shortest routes. He saw no one, heard no telltale clattering of brass on marble. He turned the corner, crept down the hall, the feeling of closeness getting stronger all the while, then rounded another corner and tried the first door. As he stepped inside, he lit the door lantern.

City Mother be praised. Pale yellow light filled the room, and his eyes were immediately drawn to the Aegis, picking it out of a hundred objects set in the labeled shelves of artifacts. The heater shield reflected the lantern's pale light, intensifying it until the room was as bright as a summer afternoon. Green and white swirled on the face of the shield, silver trim tracing out thick knots, a design reminiscent of the City Mother's threads before the tyrants.

In the darkest times, Aegis swore he could hear the shield talking to him. When he'd asked Wonlar about the voices, his father had shrugged.

"I can't tell you if it's real, son. But if you believe it, if it gives you strength, then it's real." Wishful thinking or not, he liked to imagine the voices were his mother, guiding him from beyond. That way she was with him always.

He bounded across the room and snatched the shield from its resting place. He slipped his left hand and arm through the straps and set the Aegis in its proper place.

As he wrapped his hand around the steel handle, he felt the strength of Audec return, filling his blood and bones with familiar warmth. He took a long breath and scanned the shelves for his belt, filled with tools and artifacts made by his father.

He should race home, tell the others what he'd learned, the eavesdropping that had gotten him caught.

The summit was happening, and they'd be changing their meeting place every day to thwart the Shields. Based on the terms Nevri was offering, the picture her messenger had painted of what the summit would allow, they had to stop it before it could start. Nevri was practically bending backward to get the tyrants to come to the table.

But now, I'm going to free every single person here, he told himself, his blood stirring.

A familiar voice filled the room, cold and hollow. "Observation: That took longer than expected. Hypothesis: You are an inferior successor to the mantle of Aegis. Hypothesis must be tested. You will comply."

Of course it's a trap. Aegis sighed as he turned to see COBALT-3 filling the doorway. The android woman was as tall as a mature Freithin, but more elegant. Her limbs were supple tubes of interlocking rings, impossibly flexible. Her head drooped, cocked to the side like a doll held up by its strings.

"I'll comply, but I don't think you'll enjoy my experimental methods." Aegis dropped into a fighting stance, left leg forward beneath the shield, the lantern held off to the side to illuminate his opponent.

"Statement: Challenging COBALT-3 directly is mal-adaptive. With subject's fatigue and armament, a one-on-one engagement has only a 1.73 percent chance of success at this moment."

Aegis smiled. "That's more than I had guessed. Thanks for the encouragement." He leapt forward with a shield slash, and COBALT-3 raised an arm to defend. The clash of metal against metal produced a rain of sparks as the shield slid up her arm and deflected over her head. Aegis spun and stabbed an elbow into her metallic torso.

The lantern flapped wildly through the air as he held tight with his right hand, casting the room in shaky, jerking shadows. The elbow connected, but didn't dent her armor.

Aegis pulled in the shield and slammed his weight into her, trying to push his way out into the hallway.

She was right. He couldn't take her on his own. Not when she'd set the terms.

His slam failed to knock COBALT-3 off her feet, but it did move her. He slid through the opening and past the android. He took a kick to the kidney on his way, which knocked him into the wall on the far side, cracking the stone.

Bad trade. Can't breathe. Keep going—move it.

Aegis gasped for air as COBALT-3 advanced across the hall, but his lungs wouldn't expand. He scrambled on the floor, trying to find his feet. He heard COBALT-3 clanging behind him and turned, ducking behind the shield. The android's blow pushed him into the corner. His breath still hadn't returned. Aegis scrambled down the floor, pushing off the wall and rolling to his feet. His head felt light, empty.

Aegis backpedaled as COBALT-3 came at him again. He gasped again, and this time his lungs filled.

She advanced on him with slow, inexorable steps. "Assertion: It is in your best interest to surrender. Aegis Shield-selection protocol investigation holds a higher priority than field-test hypothesis investigation. Reinforcements will arrive in 17.4 seconds."

"You're so helpful, you know that?" Aegis smiled and rolled backward, turning as he found his feet. He jumped up and started running at a full sprint down the hall, taking deep breaths. Aegis knew he could outpace COBALT-3 in a dead run, but navigating would slow him down. Still, better a running battle than fighting cornered and overwhelmed.

After a few turns down nearly identical corridors, the alarm started blaring, red emergency lights flicking along the walls, drowning his soft lantern light. *Here they come.*

COBALT-3 was close behind him, pistons pumping as she stormed down the hall.

Aegis slid on the marble as he turned right at full speed, the tyrant close on his heels.

A trio of halberds rushed up on him as he faced the corridor. Aegis raised his shield and pushed aside the blade of the nearest automata. He leapt toward the wall, took three steps along the stone, and jumped, slamming shield first into the guard on the near side. Aegis tucked into a roll as the pair of them hit the ground. He found his feet again and kept running.

Aegis heard his father's voice again, urging him on. "*Keep going. Get two turns ahead and you can turn this into a cat-and-mouse.*" Behind him, COBALT-3 shouted at her soldiers. "Order: Open a pathway, pursue in flank position. All guards converge in laboratory wing, hallway seven. Subject Aegis bearing south in escape attempt."

And now I know where I am, Aegis thought. He turned at the next left and stared down the hall at green double doors. An industrial sign overhead said "FRONT WING" in bold script.

Brilliant. He ran in long, even strides down toward the broad green doors. The Front Wing doors were aged wood rather than the metal pervading the laboratory wing. COBALT had taken over universities and hospitals during the early years, building on existing infrastructure.

The double doors opened as he approached, revealing the lower halves of two giant automata.

Less brilliant.

Without any more time to react, Aegis dove, sliding his arm out of the straps and kneeling onto the shield, head down, hoping to slide under the automata. Instead, metallic fingers clamped around his ribs and lifted him into the room. The automata had a squished cubic head with two glass bulb eyes glowing red, set atop a ten-foot-wide, gray, cylindrical body.

The Thresher automata were COBALT-3's largest creations: One of them was usually enough to keep two Shields occupied. But two of them, with COBALT-3 and guards in tow?

I hope the next Aegis does a better job.

Not ready to give up, Aegis slammed his shield into the Thresher's wrist, tearing through the weaker articulated metal. The Thresher lifted Aegis high in fingers as wide as the Shield's bicep. The hand squeezed, threatening to collapse his lungs as its other hand moved in. The Thresher's exhaust pipes vented steam, which seared his eyes but flushed the spoiled hospital smell out of the air. *Small blessings.*

Aegis wrestled the shield free as the Thresher's crushing grip squeezed tighter. He filled his lungs as he strained against the hand. Then he let out all his breath and slid down through the hand before it could contract.

He grabbed the automata's smallest finger, turning his fall into a swinging kick to its face. The Thresher's grip closed again, crushing Aegis' ribs and shoulder.

He heard COBALT-3's voice again, gloating—as much as an emotionless psychopathic android could gloat. "Order: Do not struggle. You are endangering your validity as a test subject. Without your scientific merit, you are only useful as raw materials."

Was that supposed to be a joke? Aegis wondered.

"You say the nicest things." He lifted his legs and wrapped them around the automata's wrist. Pulling at the weakened hand, he heard the pained groan of tearing metal. Wires snapped apart as the hand broke at the joint, and the pressure vanished.

But the hand was still attached on one side. The Thresher swung its arm, hurling Aegis into a wall with a dull thud. The Shield slid down to the polished hardwood floor in a heap beside the metallic hand as COBALT-3 approached, looming over him. His ribs hurt. His arms hurt. He could barely breathe, and he had no time to recover.

Sorry, Dad.

At least now he'd get to see his mother.

A crash echoed across the hall. Aegis looked to the far side of the room and saw familiar silhouettes backlit by sunlight.

City Mother be praised.

His father's voice carried across the long hall, every bit as strong as it has always been. "Get away from him, you heartless monster!"

COBALT-3 straightened up, looking almost happy. "Opportunities: (1) Comparative analysis of the capabilities of racial paragons. (2) Possible obviation of necessity of upcoming summit."

The android tyrant pointed at the Shields. "Order: Subdue."

The Threshers turned to face the group, leaving COBALT-3 and her guards to surround Aegis. He threw the detached Thresher hand at COBALT-3 while he limped along the edge of the corridor to rejoin the team.

Ghost Hands flew over the heads of the Threshers, dodging out of the way of the construct's probing hands. Blasts of telekinesis forced the Thresher back, its shaky balance keeping it from being able to use its size. Steam vented as the Thresher changed calibration to deal with the threat.

Sapphire charged the other Thresher head-on, hurling herself into the cylindrical torso. The Thresher staggered back, and Aegis could feel the Freithin's joy.

Sabreslate used her Jalvai stone-shaping talents to shift a section of the concrete wall into daggers, then hurled them at the guards that had targeted her partner Ghost Hands.

Sapphire leapt at the Thresher again, landing on its chest. She pounded a hole in the metal, then tore it open to get to the machinery within.

Aegis was still humbled sometimes by their power, the casual ease with which they fought. At the sight of Sapphire, his throat caught, but he shook it off and focused.

A red blur crossed the corridor in an instant, passing Aegis to deal with the smaller automata. Always happy to dive into a mass combat, Blurred Fists merrily dispatched the guards, finding amusing ways to disable COBALT-3's endless army of automata.

With his grapple gun hooked to a chandelier, First Sentinel swung across the room and landed at Aegis' side.

"Get out, we'll follow you," his father said as he drew his fighting staves. First Sentinel twirled them in a defensive pattern and stepped forward to meet COBALT-3.

The android laughed her hollow laugh, a dispassionate mimicry of real emotion. It seemed she'd learned that this was an appropriate time for someone in her position to laugh, and so she did.

She'd never be quite real, despite COBALT-2's genius. Just a machine playing out its original design.

But then again, am I much more than a creation of the first Aegis, carrying on his crusade? Aegis pushed back the doubt and circled the tyrant, determined to help despite his injuries.

COBALT-3 spoke again. "Datum: I have defeated and seriously injured you in four out of six engagements. Datum: You continue to fight. Hypothesis: You are no longer capable of learning, given your decrepit age and foolhardy ideals."

First Sentinel lashed out with a kick to the knee as he threw her diction back at her. "Datum: You have failed to discover the secret of the Aegis. Datum: You have failed to kill any of us." With each line, the elder Shield threw another blow, forcing COBALT-3 to break off her assault on Aegis. "And datum: I am going to rip out your power core and use it to run my refrigerator."

He isn't usually funny unless he's really mad, Aegis thought. If we make it out of this, I'm in serious trouble.

COBALT-3 answered as if First Sentinel's comment hadn't been a joke. "Datum: My power core is incompatible with conventional electronics, given its tri-band vicite core."

First Sentinel chuckled as Aegis continued circling. Out of the android's reach, he swung the shield at COBALT-3's back. The blow caught her shoulder, pushing her off balance and spoiling her own strike.

"Get out, now!" his father said.

That was the frustrated parent voice. *This isn't the time for protectiveness, Father.*

"We leave together," Aegis said as he planted a foot on COBALT-3's back and kicked her into the wall, splintering the ancient wood.

"Correction: None of you will leave," COBALT-3 said.

First Sentinel pulled out one of his shock gloves, slipping it onto his left hand. "You're not welcome in this conversation. Why don't you go back to playing with your toys?"

A quick look over the shoulder showed Aegis that one Thresher was shattered, the other buried to its chest in the stone floor.

"We're clear!" Sapphire shouted from the other end of the hall.

First Sentinel landed an uppercut with the shock glove, grounding COBALT-3 with a charge of magical energy. Aegis broke off and ran for the exit.

COBALT-3 recovered quickly, chasing them the entire way. Reaching the exterior door, Sapphire kicked it open, and the Shields flooded through. As father and son ran through the doorway, First Sentinel drew a skeleton key from his belt, one of the seemingly endless artifacts he'd designed over the years. It could make one door impassable, but only for a minute.

Looking around outside, Aegis saw they'd exited onto an open-air veranda on the second floor. First Sentinel turned and snapped the key in the lock to seal it. He stepped back from the door, still at the ready. "Scatter and regroup at the safehouse."

The group split, each taking their own way out. Sapphire took a running start and leapt across the street to another rooftop; Ghost Hands took off and flew hundreds of feet above the street; First Sentinel fired his grappling gun and swung away; Blurred Fist ran over and then down the wall of the compound.

Aegis reached down for his own grapple gun, but his hip was bare, the device lost during his capture.

Sabreslate reached out a hand to Aegis. "Come with me." He nodded. He took the Jalvai's hand, and together they leapt off the roof and sank into the ground. They waded through the cobblestone and into the earth below as if it were water. Using Sabreslate's Jalvai stone shaping, they swam a block through the stone and then emerged so Aegis could breathe. The street was clear, and they submerged once more.

Safe. For now. Until we get home and Father bites my head off.

Chapter Eleven

First Sentinel

He's safe. I haven't failed Aria again. Not this time, not ever again.

When Wonlar arrived at the coffeeshop, Selweh was already there, sitting on one of Douk's plush couches. His son was tearing into a loaf of bread so fresh it released steam when his son ripped off a chunk. The boy stood as Wonlar walked in, and the two embraced. Wonlar did not let go for a long time.

"Don't you scare me like that ever again."

Selweh's tone was sarcastic. "I'm sorry, Dad. It's not like I knew I was going to get kidnapped and tortured."

Wonlar knew that sarcasm; it came from Selweh's mother. She'd never be done with a conversation until she'd gotten a clever jibe in. He was barraged by emotions from all sides: longing, regret, love, and relief.

"You can let go now," Selweh said.

"If I never let go, you can't run off and nearly get yourself killed again."

"How did you find me?"

"Black Wind taunted me with the fact that COBALT-3 had you when I went sniffing in The Corner. After that, it was a process of elimination. The lab with the biggest guard force was bound to be the one." Wonlar pulled back, hugged Selweh again, and then let him sit back down to eat.

"City Mother be praised," Selweh said.

"When you're rested, we have a lot to talk about."

Selweh nodded, and Wonlar's shoulders dropped, relaxing. He gave a silent prayer. *City Mother, thank you for your gift. Thank you for giving me back my son.*

Wonlar took a seat, and Douk appeared with *dounmo* and several pastries. Father and son talked for an hour. Wonlar filled his son in about their abandoned apartment and Nevri's offer. In turn, Selweh shared the information that had gotten him caught, about the lengths Nevri was going to in order to make the summit happen.

If she's pushing that hard, if she's the lynchpin, then what happens if we let slip that she arranged to have the Rebirth Engine destroyed? Smiling King pulls out, and the other tyrants wonder what she's got planned to weaken them. Instant chaos, and we get some breathing room.

In the corner of his eye, Wonlar saw Rova come in to visit with Fahra. They played hide-and-seek, and Rova joined the girl in drawing. Douk brought down more scones and held them captive for twenty minutes with his stories of hobnobbing and shoulder rubbing with the elite of the city, the rich and collaborating.

For a fraction of a day, stolen from the world and the rebellion and the coming summit, they were a family again. *Even the tyrants can't take that away from us. Not all the time.*

The next day, Wonlar was back in the safehouse, unpacking papers while Selweh digested the events of the week. Wonlar watched his son's mind racing as the young Shield sat in a chair, deep in thought.

"They didn't jump you at the brothel, which means she's at least in for a long con. And if she actually shows up for the pickup, that's a display of trust on her part. She'd have to bring an army to be confident that we couldn't take her then and there. But if she's telling the truth about the Rebirth Engine, we have to destroy it as soon as we can. How long has the Smiling King had this thing?"

Wonlar opened another box. "Since the end of last year, we think. I checked my records of the Spark-storms, and the frequency spiked not long after the new year." The box revealed more flatware, half of the pieces cracked. *I'll need to ask Sarii to help us with these.* For all her contrarian ways during meetings, she'd always been happy to help with crafting and mending.

Selweh sighed, scrunching his eyebrows in the manner Wonlar knew meant frustration. "So even if we eliminate the machine, the storms will continue."

Wonlar nodded. "Unless we have enough time to figure out how it works before destroying it."

"Not much chance of that happening, unless we eliminate Onyx and the majority of the guards before getting to the chamber with the device." Selweh stood and began pacing, counterclockwise to Wonlar's own path. Father and son passed each other as they orbited the dinner table, not bothering to turn to speak. They thought out loud, bouncing ideas back and forth.

"Can we bring anyone else in on this?" Selweh asked.

"Who's even left?"

"What about Jong?"

A longtime Shield-bearer and part-time Shield, Jong was committed to the cause, but Wonlar knew that the Ikanollo carpenter lacked the mettle to be a real Shield. *One day, maybe, but not yet.* The Shields' attrition rate was high, and recruitment was far from easy.

"We can't count on him for anything that major."

When they had started, the Shield of Audec-Hal had just been Aegis and a couple of idealistic kids who refused to let the city change around them without a fight.

Bira, Aria, and I knew nothing when we started. Without Aegis, we would have gotten killed within a week.

Shields had come and gone over the years, but they'd never had more than seven active at a time.

We will have to be enough.

"What about this Millrej girl?" Selweh asked.

In her time with the girl, Rova had discovered that Fahra had an incredible talent for drawing.

"I don't know. I think Rova may be putting more importance on her than is warranted. Yema isn't the sort to do things randomly, but I don't see the pattern. The child is talented, but how does an art prodigy fit into Yema's plans?"

"Good question. Depends on if she really does have a power. Until we can find out, it's a hanging thread. We need to concentrate on the Rebirth Engine, set the ball rolling to stop the summit."

Wonlar stopped in front of Selweh. Their eyes met and they nodded. "Agreed. How do we pin the destruction of the Rebirth Engine on one of the others?"

Selweh put a hand to his chin. "Hard to say. Nevri's always been the most concerned about the Spark-storms. That kind of chaos is bad for business"

"The lack of control scares her."

"She's not the only one." The Spark or the tyrants alone would be plague enough for a city.

"Who, then? Yema? COBALT-3?" Wonlar asked.

"Why pin it on anyone? As you said, if we expose Nevri, the tyrants will turn on one another just as fast, especially since Nevri's been moving mountains to make the summit happen."

"We just need to get a message to the tyrants and have them believe us."Wonlar scratched his stubbly beard. "We record the in-person meeting with Nevri and leak the recording to Magister Yema. That should do it."

"So, we just have pull off the Engine job. Will we be able to neutralize Onyx fast enough to pull this off?"

"I'm glad you asked." Wonlar crossed the room and picked up his belt. He searched through a pouch and pulled out a stone wrapped in walkerweb silk. Wonlar held it up so the light shimmered on the translucent silk. *This one took me two months of research and another three months of failed experiments to finalize.* "The new drainer disks are finally ready. Two or three of these should bring him down to a manageable level for you and Rova."

Selweh smiled. "And we can make sure he knows we got the explosive from Nevri. The Smiling King's insane, but he's too paranoid not to fly off the handle at Nevri. And if Yema has reason to suspect her too, all the better."

"And then the others will be pulled in on either side."

Selweh mimed an explosion with his hands. "Poof, no summit. What does Nevri have to gain from the whole thing, aside from the Rebirth Engine being gone, the Smiling King's power lessened?"

Wonlar poured a fresh mug of tea and handed it to his son. "That's what has me worried. We can't be sure what she's doing on the side, what opportunities it's creating that she'll be taking advantage of. But since we know not to trust her, I hope that what we're pulling on her outmatches whatever she can throw at us."

Selweh blew at the top of the mug, steam rolling away from his breath. "It's still a very fine line we're walking here."

"I've walked this line for fifty years. We can do it." Selweh turned to the desk, the papers, and the maps, and set the mug down beside him.

We can do it, Wonlar told himself. And for once, he believed it.

Chapter Twelve

First Sentinel

Heart Station was always clean, thanks to a small army of custodians on Nevri's payroll. It was an outward symbol of her control: efficient, tidy, and unquestionable. The trains stayed on schedule, and everyone got where they needed to go. Provided they could pay.

Bland, tasteless murals covered the walls, works commissioned by Nevri's ministry of the arts. Above the ticket office, there was a pastel picture of the city at peace, painted by selected orphans to show her compassion, under the instruction of loyalist artists who only had careers because she had decreed they would.

Every few weeks or so, there was a piece of graffiti, genuine emergent art, unsolicited and unasked for. Sometimes it was oppositional, sometimes just the work of a bold creator taking a stand for expression. The longest lived of those works was lucky to be visible for three hours.

The station was bustling with activity, workers returning from their daily drudge. They brushed by one another, shoulders pressed together as they moved through the three-tiered train station like a river flowing down into the delta of platforms. The smells of sweat, stale air, and the dampness of spring showers mixed with an impenetrable blanket of noise.

The idle mumblings, shuffling feet, the comings and goings of trains, and the eerily serene voice of the public address system calling out arrivals and departures, every sound was a reminder that his motion was structured, his paths laid out for him by the Plutocrat. Freedom of movement was available here, but only on Nevri's terms and in her paths. The trains were the city's, but the staff were all Nevri's.

There's a reason why I don't take the trains much anymore.

First Sentinel spotted Aegis in his vantage point higher up in the station, a still figure in the shifting mash of bodies. First Sentinel nodded to his son and continued on. He wore his coat closed, without a mask, allowing him to pass among the crowd unnoticed.

Moving with the throng, First Sentinel descended to the platform where the Headtown line would arrive in twelve minutes. As he crossed the lowest landing before the platform, First Sentinel saw an open circle on the platform, five paces across.

A suited woman stood at the center, perfectly still. Dapper thugs stood at the four cardinal points around her. Her face was the same as any one of thousands of other Ikanollo women, but her presence was unique.

Nevri the Plutocrat, tyrant of Audec-Hal. Before that, she was Senator Nevri. Before it all, she had been Nevri the Lash, overboss in the Viscera City Slicers. Slanted bangs dropped across her face, barely revealing her left eye. She locked onto First Sentinel as soon as he stepped into view.

The nearest guard stepped to one side, and First Sentinel saw a self-satisfied smile cross Nevri's immaculately preserved face.

Still severe and striking, she had to be almost a hundred years old, but she looked just as healthy as she had the day the Senate burned.

In one manicured hand, she held a jet-black briefcase—the explosives. First Sentinel didn't know how Nevri stayed healthy that late into life. The tyrant had to be almost a decade older than he was, judging by her years as a gangster before the Senate fire. Most Ikanollo could expect to live to eighty; many lived to ninety or beyond, but not in good health. *Maybe she made a bargain with Yema or has secret artifacts turned out by her wholly owned Academy of Artifice.*

First Sentinel watched with his peripheral vision as he closed, stepping into the dead zone of her guards. *Hide your fear, Wonlar. Don't let her see any weakness.* Ghost Hands and Sapphire followed, under cover of illusion.

As far as anyone in the crowd knew, First Sentinel and Nevri were just two Ikanollo talking in the train station, flanked by huge bodyguards. *Nothing suspicious about that.*

Stretching his back to draw spectator's eyes, he rubbed the stone in a pocket that activated the recording enchantment. It'd be good for five minutes.

"City Mother be with you," she said, throwing the formal greeting in his face. *She's ours, don't you forget,* her words said, reopening a fifty-year-old wound.

"The mother who protects us all," First Sentinel replied, putting his emphasis on the last word.

Around them, the traffic flowed as people shifted back and forth, waiting for the train. They stared at newspapers from beneath dull gray and brown caps, talking in small groups in conspiratorial tones.

"To be honest, I'm surprised you came," Nevri said.

The ground beneath him rumbled, signaling an oncoming train.

"Don't ever doubt my dedication." He'd fight her every breath he had, until one of them went to sleep with Audec.

"Not for a moment. But to ally yourself with me, you must be desperate." She produced a cigarillo and snapped her fingers. One of the thugs produced a small artifact and provided a light. The smoke wafted over First Sentinel's face, with hints of cloves and spearmint. He exhaled audibly to blow the smoke away.

While they waited, First Sentinel kept his calm firmly in hand, remembering that Ghost Hands and Sapphire were right behind him, cloaked by a pair of rings that had taken years to get right and only worked for ten minutes a month.

The whirring drone of steam and a high whistle were twin heralds to the blood-red train's arrival. Ancient magic dating to the founding of the city powered the trains that were the pumping blood of the city, connecting the districts across tyrants' domains. The train crawled to a stop, and hundreds disembarked. Two of Nevri's guards moved to the door, browbeating the first few commuters who tried to board the train car. The train idled as the crowd shifted and people boarded the other cars. Guards in other cars waved those citizens off, leaving the cars all but empty.

A pointless display of power. First Sentinel said, "If you confuse desperation with dedication, then your riches still haven't bought you any wisdom."

She responded only with a smile, the threat veiled by polished white teeth. "Let's not fight, old friend." She took a drag from the cigarillo and then put it out on a pillar. A custodian appeared from nowhere and started cleaning the spot.

Nevri raised a hand toward the empty train car. "Please, join me." With three full strides, she stepped onto the train and took a seat. First Sentinel followed, trusting Sapphire and Ghost Hands to board the train as his backup.

For a little while, First Sentinel entertained the notion of detonating the explosive on the train. He could give his life to claim hers, take the quickest, easiest victory and kick-start the revolution.

But he wouldn't fight the war that way. What scared him is that he'd had to count the number of people such a display would likely kill before deciding to scrap the plan.

Fifty years is a long time. I don't have much left in me.

If he retired soon, he might hope to live to ninety, but he couldn't stop working. Still, even fool's luck had to give out eventually—bodies broke down, failed. One day he wouldn't be fast enough. They'd bury him in the Hall of Fallen Shields, the cavern tomb secured by the first Aegis not long after the start of the resistance. *Would there be another First Sentinel? Who would be stupid enough to do it?*

First Sentinel sat across from Nevri. The cold metal seat sapped body heat even through his cloak. The doors closed, leaving him with Nevri and her four guards.

"Are those the explosives?" First Sentinel asked, pointing to the suitcase.

She nodded. "And the promised portion of the payment beneath it."

"What are you doing on the night of the bombing? What makes it so important that we act when you say?"

Nevri demurred, waving a hand through the air. "I have my schedules to keep, and the appointed time is the one most convenient."

"Why not let the summit convene, make the ties between the others, and then undermine them using the added trust? I don't see the angle," First Sentinel said. *Come on, spill something so I can see the trap coming.*

She smiled. "And that is why you skulk in shadows, settle for stinging the feet of giants. You don't see the big picture."

"I haven't settled for anything." *Easy there. She's trying to bait you.*

Nevri crossed her legs, knees tucked together just below her black pencil skirt. "I grow tired of my so-called colleagues. I'd much rather have you and your Shields to compete with than the madman and the machine, the sorcerer and the slaver."

"I'm flattered." *If we're playing, let's play.*

"Don't think too highly of yourself. You rely on hope; they play to fear. And hope is fifty years out of fashion in Audec-Hal."

Wonlar wondered what the math would be if he called for Sapphire and Ghost Hands to attack, if they tried to take out Nevri then and there, then hit the Rebirth Engine. Sapphire and Ghost Hands could handle the bodyguards, leaving Nevri for him. But he had no way of knowing what kind of contingency plans she had: concealed guards, hidden weapons and artifacts, personal enchantments. And until he could evaluate the explosive, learn how it worked if it was so special, he'd be throwing away one of the greatest potential advantages of the bargain.

No good. He wasn't in control of the situation—it was her territory, her plan. But for the briefest moment, First Sentinel imagined the feeling of her windpipe collapsing in his hands. The chance to get justice for thousands dead and the fall of Audec-Hal flickered through his mind. It was very tempting.

"Can I see the explosive?" First Sentinel asked.

Nevri shifted in her seat, rebalanced the suitcase, and then held out it to First Sentinel. He took the case, one hand on top and one on bottom. He turned it back toward Nevri in case it was trapped, and then opened the brass clasps.

Nothing happened, so he turned the case around to see the contents. Nestled in rich blue velvet, the explosive was the size of his fist. Pipes and gears and valves in brass and bronze covered a gray-black orb with marbled hues swirling throughout the surface. The make looked like one of COBALT-3's.

How far does this plan go? Is COBALT-3 in on the gambit, or is she the convenient scapegoat? It wouldn't be hard to paint her as envious of any grand device not of her own creation.

Every minute got them deeper in bed with the Plutocrat, and First Sentinel wondered if he'd know when he was getting in over his head. Just because they had a plan didn't mean that it was good enough.

"What do you think?" Nevri leaned forward, eyebrows up, as if asking his opinion about the fit of a dress at a store. *I'm not one of your lackeys, Nevri. Never forget that.*

He studied the device, working out the connections between the detonator, the pipes, and wires that plunged into the orb. The deep cobalt blue was consistent with enchantments for magical explosives, but COBALT-3's devices bore different signatures from traditional artifice, using electrical current rather than mechanical triggers as the physical binding for the magic. He'd need to study the device further.

But not here.

He checked the compartment under the explosive, thumbing through stacks of bills. Even if they were counterfeit, they were good enough to pass in Nevri's domain. Technically, all the money printed since the Senate fire was counterfeit, but that was all semantics.

First Sentinel replaced the money and picked up the explosive. It was heavier than it looked. "What did it take for COBALT-3 to give you this, and won't she suspect when she hears about the Engine's destruction?"

Nevri lit a fresh cigarillo. "COBALT-3 has no more love of the Spark-storms than I. They're things of chaos."

The train passed in and out of the tunnel lights, casting Nevri in flickering shadow. She reclined into the seat, tracing a finger along the glass window above her head. A moment later, the train surfaced and started to roll through Upper Rib.

No answer. First Sentinel pushed her again. "What do I need to know to operate it?"

Nevri nodded to one of her guards, who stepped forward and opened a hand toward First Sentinel. Watching the guard's whole body for a wrong move, he slowly placed the globe in the guard's hand and sat back.

The thug handed the explosive back to Nevri, who spun the orb, pulled back a lever, and tapped a finger on a red button built into a copper box. "Move the lever this way to disengage the safety. Press here and the device will detonate after five minutes. If you place it next to the Rebirth Engine, it should obliterate the whole building."

"What about collateral damage, the buildings nearby?"

Her smile was smug, self-satisfied. Another flash of violent thought crossed First Sentinel's mind, how satisfying it would be to cut down the guards and wipe the arrogance off Nevri's face.

"War demands sacrifices. But I'm told its range is only fifty meters, little bigger than the building itself." Nevri placed the orb in the guard's still-outstretched hand, and then stood. First Sentinel clicked the safety back when the guard returned the explosive. The train slowed to a stop in Upper Rib before looping back around on its journey toward Headtown.

Executor Nevri bowed her head to First Sentinel as the doors opened. "Evening, one week from tonight. Between eight and nine." She tapped her collar, and an illusion of an older Jalvai with thin hair and a less impressive suit washed over her. She walked out of the train car between her four bodyguards and vanished when the mass of people closed in behind her.

First Sentinel sighed, placing the artifact back in its case. He walked up the end of the train car, opened the door to the one behind him, and rapped on the side of the doorway, signaling Sapphire and Ghost Hands to follow.

He leaned his head out the back of the train car, felt the train move back and forth on its tracks as the wheels started turning again. First Sentinel listened to the metallic groans of the train answer the rolling roar of the unoiled wheels against aged tracks as they moved away from the station, the thugs, and Nevri. Weapon in hand, he was one step closer to seeing how far this deal would lead.

Chapter Thirteen

Sapphire

Rova sat in the back room of Douk's Daily, laughing at Fahra's imitations. They were alone, the Millrej girl and her rescuer, as Rova took a break from patrolling the streets. Blurred Fists was casing the location of the Rebirth Engine, and if all was well, they'd strike the following night rather than wait for Nevri's appointed time.

Rova had started coming by the café every day to see Fahra. First it had been just checking in, but it had become a habit, a break from errands and work and revolution.

The girl stood up and struck a pose that Rova recognized very well. Like the café's owner, she had her head forward, hand on her chin.

"Did something interesting happen? Please? Tell me, I have to know! I know lots of important people—it's very exciting!" Fahra walked around the table, mimicking Douk's little ticks, the rise and fall of his voice.

"And did I tell you who came in to the café yesterday! Zija Varn, the violinist, you know, who plays in the Orquestra Siena.

Her hair is phenomenal, you know. Some say it's because she's Spark-touched, one of the subtle ones. I think it's one of those ambergris-laced shampoos though." She was a talented mimic, though she was enjoying herself too much for a perfect imitation, stopping every few moments to stifle a giggle.

Fahra looked up at Rova, struck by curiosity. "What's ambergris?"

Rova laughed. "You remember all of that and just ask about the ambergris?"

Fahra turned up her lips. "But what is it?"

"It's made from a part of whales." Rova motioned Fahra over and gave the girl a hug. Fahra's curiosity reminded Rova of herself, when she'd gotten lashes for asking questions and wanting to know more about the world outside the pens.

Fahra hugged back, squeezing with her little arms, then ran over to one of Douk's desks to throw papers around the room. She grabbed one particular sheaf, waved it in the air, and hurried back over to Rova. The little Millrej girl sat the drawing on the desk in front of Rova.

The drawing was a clear portrait of Douk's café from the perspective of a person on the street looking in. Fahra had drawn the finely carved stone of the bricks Douk had used to rebuild the façade and the lovingly painted sign Xera had made herself, adorned with the inviting plumes of steam in subtle shades and a perfect curl.

Several scenes played out in the front room, an inviting look at the way people came to life in the café. Douk stood behind the counter, gesturing wide with his hands like he was telling a story. Xera and Fahra sat at a table, with the Shields at another table, talking and eating. Wonlar paced around the table, one hand on his chin and the other gesturing as he talked. Bira and Sarii were playing a board game, the Qava floating an inch above her seat. Fahra had captured Sarii in a rare smile, sitting in a chair she'd spun from the same stone as her cloak. Wenlizerachi reclined in his chair, a trio of plates with food piled high in front of him as he ate with both hands, a wide smile on his face.

Rova looked at the picture. That scene had never happened just so, but Fahra had captured the feeling of a Shields' meeting at Douk's perfectly.

"This is wonderful. How long did this take you?" Rova asked.

Fahra smiled wide. "I did it yesterday when it was raining."

This girl is amazing. Xera's a painter; maybe she could tutor her . . .

They talked for a while, away from the bustle of the café, interrupted only when Xera or Douk paced through quickly on the way to the cellar for supplies. The smell of fresh pastries and coffee wafted back into the room, and Rova had to keep Fahra from wandering back in to get more sweets. *One plate of cookies is enough for the both of us.*

Fahra added more sketches of buildings in the neighborhood to her growing stack. While she drew, she asked Rova questions about everything and anything: history, food, science, and the Shields. Rova marveled at the girl's mind as it flitted from subject to subject. *We need to find her a school, and fast. With a mind that sharp, she'll put First Sentinel to shame when she's grown.*

While getting more iced coffee from up front, Rova saw someone running down the street, a toddler in her arms.

Rova crossed the room in three long strides, looking out to see what had the woman spooked. Three blocks down the street, a carriage was pulling its horses, the wheels broken out into wooden claws clambering down the street, dragging terrified whinnying horses behind it.

"Spark-storm!" Rova yelled back into the café, trying to spot Douk. The patrons at the café scrambled, sending desks and chairs rolling and crashing across the room.

Douk appeared from the kitchen and waved people toward him. "Everyone, get downstairs!"

"Fahra, honey, go find Xera and stay put!" Rova shouted, reaching into her pants for her mask as she stepped outside. She hoped no one saw her putting it on. In Sapphire's experience, abject terror and panic weren't conducive to reliable memory.

Xera and Douk could handle the patrons, but dealing with a storm was Shield business. Rova lifted up her sleeve, then double-tapped the gem on her alarm bracelet.

Please let someone be nearby, she thought as she dashed into the street.

A block down, horses melted into swarms of centipedes, birds flew straight into the ground as if pulled by invisible string, and the people's screams melded into the unsettlingly familiar cacophony of the storm. Another wave of people passed her in the street, fleeing the chaos.

Sapphire took three quick steps to build up to a run, crossing the distance to the edge of the storm's effects in just a few seconds. On the north side of the street, the graystones were merely turning random colors and dripping water, but on the south side, the mortar between the bricks was melting and coursing down the side, leaving the walls to sag and tumble, doubtlessly with people inside.

Oh no. She could charge in and try to haul people out before the building collapsed on them, maybe be able to shrug off a few hard blows from falling stones, but even she had limits.

Then maybe today is the day to find out what they are. Sapphire scaled the front stairs in one bound and ripped open the door when she reached the top. "Spark-storm! Everyone in the hall—now! You have to get out of this building!"

Citizens trickled out of their apartments, families in bunches and others in ones and twos. Sapphire stood in the doorway to hold it up, and the interior walls held long enough to get the first floor out. The storm might catch them outside, but that was down to chance, and she was almost entirely sure that the building was going to come down.

She raised her voice as much as she could, yelling up the stairwell. "Get out, now!"

A quick check outside told her that the storm had reached her block and would hit the café soon if it hadn't already. *Too many people to save and not enough help.*

She weighed options as graystone bricks fell around her. Another half-dozen residents stumbled down the stairs and ducked under her to vacate the building. As the top of the door fell onto her shoulders, she checked the stairs again. Nothing.

Sapphire grunted, her arms trembling with the effort of holding the building up. She shifted, then sprang out the doorway and onto the street, the building crashing down behind her with a cloud of dust. But instead of landing hard on solid stone, she plunged into sand, her feet sinking into the granulated cobblestones.

Sapphire looked down the street away from the coffeehouse, then back toward Douk's. Fahra's laugh passed through her mind, and she started dashing back toward the café. Buildings all up and down the street had been warped, changed in color, texture, and even size. Already-dead plants grew out of the windows of one building, dropping rotten fruit that exploded into bugs that were nothing but heads on legs.

The walls of the building across the north–south vein from the café had been replaced by multicolored coral, with sounds of chittering coming from within. The building just beside the café had burst like a bubble, spilling itself out onto the street. Liquid graystone and wood flowed in streams through the cobblestones. One or two buildings on each block were untouched, oases of normalcy in the Spark-storm.

As Rova bounded back to Douk's, she saw a trio of women run out from a graystone apartment in chic clothes and impractical shoes, detoured from their fashionable day by the world ripping open around them. They dashed for the café, swatting at a swarm of the buzzing head-bugs from the fruit.

The woman in back paused for a second, frozen, then continued running, but heading in the other direction, as if she'd been flipped around in an instant. Another woman of the group turned to look back, seeing her friend. She froze in place, her skin petrifying. The third woman of the group made it into the store, seemingly unchanged.

In fact, the café was untouched. Sapphire slogged through the cobble-sand toward Douk's, and her feet found solid stone once more. She stopped and took a look around the café. Why had this place been spared? The storms were random, but they usually worked their way through walls and buildings without trouble.

A thunderclap of recognition struck in her mind. She took a step back and two to the side. From there, she saw Douk's café framed the same way it had been in Fahra's drawing. Every single thing in that view had been spared the storm—the café itself, the rest of the building above it, and the sidewalk around it for five paces in each direction, the same place where Fahra's sketch had ended.

I have to tell First Sentinel.

Three hours of rescues and aftermath management later, Sapphire was sure she was onto something. She addressed the Shields in Douk's back room.

Sapphire held up a handful of Fahra's drawings, and then laid them out on the table. "After the storm subsided, I walked around the neighborhood. Every single building and person that she drew was spared from the storm. This is why Magister Yema sent warlocks after her—it has to be."

First Sentinel leaned back in his chair, holding up the drawing of Douk's café. "If you're right, we need to put her to work immediately. District by district, building by building, with as many portraits as possible. She could single-handedly end the threat of the Spark-storms."

"You don't know it for sure, either of you," Sarii said.

[And it will not be easy to test.] No one wanted more Spark-storms. Except the Smiling King, of course.

"Of course we'll have to test, but we can't just lock her up with a ream of paper and some pencils," Sapphire said.

Sabreslate rolled her eyes. "Of course we can't. But this is too valuable an opportunity to pass up."

Sapphire took a seat, let the moment calm. "I'm not talking about passing anything up. I went straight from Medai's pens to these meetings. I want to be sure that Fahra still gets to be a child, make friends, go to school."

"Agreed. We'll find a balance." First Sentinel set the drawings back on the table. "If she agrees, we'll have our newest Shield-bearer. Let's hope you're right about this, Sapphire. If we destroy the Rebirth Engine and get her sketches in order, we could end the Spark-storms for good." First Sentinel had a smile on his face, all the more rare of late.

Sapphire grinned, watching the hopeful looks on her friends' faces. *This is more hope than we've had in years. Now to foster it, help it grow, and use it.*

Chapter Fourteen

First Sentinel

For the rest of the night and the following day, the Shields prepared, reviewed, and analyzed every scrap of information they could find.

First Sentinel ran COBALT-3's explosive through every test he could, but the differences between COBALT-3's style and his own made it impossible to draw a firm conclusion. He resolved to bring the dynamite, with the marble as a last resort.

Meanwhile, the other Shields were out in full force: Blurred Fists made several runs to the location of the Rebirth Engine to scout out the patrol schedule, Sabreslate and Ghost Hands tried to run down rumors and details about the composition of the Smiling King's security forces, and Aegis checked in with their local Shield-bearers, setting up escape routes and contingencies.

During their preparations, another Spark-storm hit. It started in Greasetown, on the opposite end of the city from the subjects of Fahra's drawings. The storm came and went before any of the Shields could get on-scene, so all that was left to them was the clean-up. The Shields comforted families and tended to the worst of the damage, scattering when Omez's forces arrived.

First Sentinel had watched the "relief forces" from a hidden spot atop a nearby graystone. The slavers' guards pushed their way through the neighborhood, barking orders and treating the survivors as if the Spark were a preventable result of some negligence instead of a force of nature (or the madness of the Smiling King, depending on whom you asked).

City Mother, grant I never have to see another Spark-storm plague my home.

The night of the raid.

It was almost eight as First Sentinel waited outside the warehouse in Audec's Bowels. Citizens passed by in ones and twos, bundled in coats as clouds of misted breath trailed their conversations on their walk home. Of late, spring had slid back to winter. The cold sank in when the sun set and didn't fade until nearly noon the next day.

Holding Nevri's suitcase in his left hand, First Sentinel stood just beyond the cone of light from a streetlamp. He watched the guards at the door, waiting for the shift change. Taking a page from Nevri's book, he stood with a lit cigarillo, pretending to be an impatient businessman waiting for a meeting.

The two Spark-touched guards leaned against the wall and the door, chatting softly enough that First Sentinel couldn't hear them. One had eyes the size of fists; the other had the lower body of a spider. First Sentinel hoped their replacements wouldn't hurry in taking their turn at the door. In a minute, it wouldn't matter either way.

During a lull in the traffic, First Sentinel saw no one up or down the street for a block. First Sentinel dropped his cigarillo and stamped it out with his boot, giving the signal. Ghost Hands relayed the message with a projected *[Go!]*.

By the time First Sentinel looked up from the cigarillo, Blurred Fists had already knocked out the guards at the door. The Pronai whisked the pair around the corner to where Sapphire waited with a blanket to cover the guards. First Sentinel saw no need to upset people on the street. If they pulled the mission off without a hitch, all the neighborhood would hear was the sound of the Rebirth Engine being destroyed.

As First Sentinel crossed the street, Ghost Hands, Sabreslate, and Aegis followed, the Qava floating the crate of dynamite along behind her just above ground level. Sapphire emerged from the alley to join them. Blurred Fists unlocked the door with the guard's keys, and the Shields entered.

First Sentinel stood by the door, scanning the street to check whether they'd been seen. Satisfied that they'd entered undetected, he closed and relocked the door.

The entrance was a long corridor of stained, cobweb-covered concrete and lanterns with dusty glass panels. The Smiling King was not known for his attention to safety.

Blurred Fists scouted ahead, darting back and forth to check out each room as they advanced. The halls had been restructured to be more labyrinthine and less accessible. First Sentinel thought it likely that the Smiling King had personally advised the renovation. Blurred Fists subdued most of the guards without trouble, relying upon his speed and the element of surprise. The Shields moved through half of the warehouse using that tactic, staying quiet as Blurred Fists did most of the work.

The Pronai came back from the door of the next room and held up his hands, signaling a halt. "The next room's the mess hall. Twenty armed Spark-touched, long tables, and alarm bells at each door, all with guards standing by." The Pronai's smile was visible through his mask. "Looks like the rest of you are going to get something to do."

"Did you see Onyx?" First Sentinel asked. *Once he's taken care of, this will all get easier.*

Blurred Fists shook his head.

Twenty Spark-touched. That's a lot of unknowns.

First Sentinel said, "Don't underestimate them. They know what we can do, and each of them is a mystery. Treat them all like real threats, and look for the vulnerabilities."

"This is where it gets complicated," Aegis' voice was hushed. First Sentinel nodded his agreement.

Aegis pursed his lips and then decided. "Ghost Hands, go high and control the air, engage any fliers or jumpers. Sapphire and I will take their powerhouses. Blurred Fists and First Sentinel, control the crowds. Sabreslate, I want you to be swing, go where you think you're needed, and take out leaders if you can."

That's my boy. First Sentinel smiled. "Take us in."

We need to make an impression, since they can't all be fighters, even if they're hardened by the Smiling King. These people were once bakers and messengers, grocers and secretaries and grandparents, before the Spark.

Deep down, they're still civilians. And we're soldiers.

When the Shields reached the room, Sapphire charged the door shoulder first, breaking it off its hinges. As the door crashed to the floor, the Shields took the room in force.

The Shields caught them flat-footed. Blurred Fists dropped two before the door hit the ground, becoming a whirlwind of punches, kicks, and throws. Ghost Hands soared to the top of the thirty-foot-tall room to gain aerial superiority. She pinned three Spark-touched against a wall with a table, including one of the door guards, whom she pushed away from the alarm. Sapphire picked up the table nearest their entrance and used it to swat at more Spark-touched. First Sentinel drew a handful of throwing knives and targeted the guard closest to the other alarms, pinning sleeves to walls and hands to tables. Blurred Fists made the rounds to clear the Spark-touched away from the exits.

But then the Smiling King's forces returned fire. Arcs of electricity leapt from eel-like tentacle arms; others fired crossbows, and one Spark-touched vomited up foot-tall simulacra of herself, which began scurrying across the floor. Another Spark-touched took a breath in and expanded like a puffer-fish to three times his size, waddling toward Sapphire. Each power was stranger than the next. They knew the Shields' powers and tried to target the heroes accordingly, threatening each hero where they were vulnerable. A rail-thin Qava shoved a wall of force at Blurred Fists, knocking the Pronai tumbling, along with chairs, a table, and two other Spark-touched.

An arc of electricity caught one of First Sentinel's knives just as he released, and the shock raced through his arm down his whole body.

First Sentinel dropped to the floor, smelling his own roasted skin and burning leather. He rolled across the floor to smother the flames and gained his feet only to look up, way up, to the doughy Spark-touched giant. It raised a three-foot-long mud-spattered book to stomp down on First Sentinel's head.

The foot hung in the air for a moment, then wavered and fell backward as Aegis tackled the Spark-touched with a shield-first dive. The blow drove the Spark-touched back, crashing down onto a table.

Aria, are you watching him? That's our son.

First Sentinel pulled himself to his feet and returned to the fray. Smells crossed in the air as the fight continued: ozone and burned flesh, mucus and magic. Ghost Hands continued to dominate the air, and Sabreslate trapped a trio of guards in the wall by the far door. Aegis bounded fifteen feet into the air and clobbered the doughy Spark-touched with a shield bash to the head. The giant wavered in the air, so Aegis punched him in the base of the neck, targeting the nerve cluster. He rode the Spark-touched down, and the floor shuddered with the impact. *There goes all pretense of stealth*, First Sentinel thought. Blurred Fists finished off the crowd with a few quick blows, and the room fell silent.

Aegis stood victorious on the fallen giant. "Good work, everyone. Make sure the guards are secured before we move on." Sabreslate sunk through the floor, then emerged a moment later and beckoned her teammates.

"There's a sewer line down here. Bring them to me, and I'll stow the group." She ferried the guards down in groups of five, as much mass as she could comfortably move at once through stone, using her birthright. The other Shields stood watch over the demolished room, broken tables, and scorched walls. Blurred Fists and Sabreslate doused the small fires; Ghost Hands levitated the explosives up to the door from their resting place in the previous hall; and First Sentinel prepared for the next push.

Aegis walked up to First Sentinel. The older Shield felt his son's unease.

"Something's off," Aegis said.

Out of habit, First Sentinel checked over his shoulder. "Keep your eyes open. I doubt Nevri and the Smiling King went in on a trap, but . . . "

"All done," Sabreslate said, rising out of the ground.

Blurred Fists moved to the door, and First Sentinel gave him the go-ahead. Sapphire piled up several tables and chairs to cover the doorway they'd come in through as the rest of the Shields waited by the far door.

Whether the door would hold depended entirely on who was doing the pursuing. If it was a Spark-touched with gigantic ears or twenty fingers, they'd have some time. If it was Onyx, the barricade wouldn't last three seconds.

First Sentinel looked back from the barred door to see Blurred Fists settle back into sight. His excitement overtook his discipline as he slipped back into Pronai-speed speech.

"We're almost there. The Rebirth Engine's in the next bigroom."

Aegis gathered the group, speaking in low tones. "Everyone keep your heads. We stick to the plan, and this goes our way. Not Nevri's way, not the Smiling King's way. By tomorrow, the people of Audec-Hal will not have to face a storm every other week, and we'll have set into motion the toppling of the tyrants that made this city a living hell."

Sapphire held open the door, and they entered as quietly as possible. They crossed the last corridor in hushed paces, closing in on the artifact.

Chapter Fifteen

First Sentinel

First Sentinel stood in front of the black door that led to the Rebirth Engine. One hand holding the suitcase, he closed his other glove around the tarnished copper doorknob and looked to Aegis, standing at the ready. Aegis nodded, and First Sentinel threw open the door.

The room was mostly empty of furniture, save for a few tables along the outskirts and the Rebirth Engine in the middle. It was a towering contraption of gears, flesh, and valves. A ripple of energy arced between the jagged-bone peaks of two fleshy towers; a simmering Spark-storm just waiting to be unleashed. First Sentinel couldn't help but wonder if there was a person at the heart of it, or several people. He watched fleshy sacs rise and fall in a shallow rhythm within the body of the machine, gears spinning all the while.

And below the artifact stood fifty Spark-touched, with Onyx at their head.

Onyx's gem-black skin glistened in the full light of a hundred lanterns. The Spark-touched Freithin turned to face the Shields, smashing a ready fist into a waiting hand. He looked perfectly rested. *Nevri, you lying bitch.*

"Finally, some excitement." Onyx lumbered forward into a run. Sapphire stepped up to match him, with Aegis flanking her. They took his charge together, hitting hard and rolling toward a wall.

"The storms stop now, Onyx," Aegis said in between blows.

First Sentinel recalculated, a new plan spinning out in his head. He wove the thought into a net and used it to hold back his own worry.

[Play crowd control and don't let anyone get out,] he thought, commands passing through Ghost Hands to the group. The suitcase hung by a strap inside the back of his longcoat. He hoped that would be enough to protect the device and keep it from being activated by all the fighting. He didn't want to risk leaving it with the dynamite, for fear they'd accidentally wipe themselves off the map.

First Sentinel fit his left hand into a shock glove and drew a fighting staff with the other. A Spark-touched Ikanollo woman with five overly muscled arms closed in on him. First Sentinel circled back and away from her three-armed side.

With arms like that, she could wrap me up in a bow and present me to the Smiling King, he thought. The Spark-touched woman jumped at him. He wrapped a fighting stick around one of her arms, then pivoted on one leg. Leverage swung her past and away from him. As she passed, he hit her across the face with a right cross. Electricity discharged into her face and she went down like a felled tree. *Praise be to the City Mother for glass-jawed thugs.*

The elder Shield found himself the calm at the center of the storm. Shields and Spark-touched circled, swooped, and clashed throughout the room while the machine that had brought them here bristled with a growing storm.

He kicked, punched, and dodged his way through three more Spark-touched, making his way to the Rebirth Engine. Across the room, Aegis and Sapphire were tag-teaming Onyx, using hammer and anvil tactics to press the Spark-touched Freithin from all sides.

Blurred Fists was fighting off a pink swarm of starling-sized sharks. He dodged instinctively under a reptile–bird hybrid with two wings, four legs, and a yard-long tail.

Looking back, First Sentinel saw a Spark-touched forming a foot-wide snake's maw just feet from his head.

A metamorph. Wonderful. It pounced on him with one, two, three quick bites. He scrambled back, trying to keep the staff between him and the Spark-touched. The metamorph grew a set of claws on its body, which lashed out on spindly limbs.

The Spark-touched creature bit him in the back, but its teeth were unable to pierce the longcoat's enchantment. First Sentinel drew a knife and pinned one of its claws against a table. It shifted away from the stab wound, forming a sitting bear, but as soon as it had a spine, First Sentinel wrapped the fighting staff around its neck and pulled up, then pushed and twisted down. The metamorph was too slow, and the snap resonated through the room as its body went limp.

Some of the tyrants' minions could be subdued, but First Sentinel had never known a metamorph that stayed unconscious for longer than a moment.

Where's Aegis? First Sentinel had lost track of his son, and panic ripped at him for a half second as he scanned the room. Aegis was still fighting Onyx, but the fight had rampaged all the way across the room since he'd last seen the boy.

Keep going, old man. Stay mobile and get to Onyx. Use the drainer disks. A cacophony of powers and screams, grunts and blows filled the room, and as he scanned the melee, First Sentinel saw an opening.

[Push the Spark-touched away from the machine and Onyx toward it. Swinging Elbow on my mark.] First Sentinel trusted Ghost Hands to relay the message as he jumped up and then off a table to avoid the shifting and swirling battle between Sabreslate and a Spark-touched whose body was made of blades. He pushed and dodged his way through the more threatening but less trained Spark-touched guards to get into place for the Swinging Elbow maneuver.

Onyx had a hand around Sapphire's neck, using her as a shield against Aegis, who dodged around and over to get an open shot. First, First Sentinel would have to get Sapphire free. She had a gash on her side from a bone strike, an elbow or a knee.

First Sentinel holstered his fighting staff and pulled out one of his drainers as Aegis ducked under a swinging arm. First Sentinel rolled over his son's back—a move they'd practiced countless times—then dropped to the ground and slapped the drainer against Onyx's calf with a palm heel strike. He couldn't apply them more than one at a time, or the effects wouldn't compound.

With luck, Onyx wouldn't feel it right away and would take it as an ineffectual strike, giving him time to apply the second disk.

But First Sentinel didn't count on his luck for much of anything. The drainer would sap the magical energy out of anyone or anything, and First Sentinel knew from previous experience that it even worked on the Spark-touched. How many it would take to weaken Onyx enough that he could be subdued remained to be seen.

Rolling up and away, First Sentinel targeted Onyx's grip on Sapphire. She was wrestling and punching Onyx's arm, trying to free herself, but the Spark-touched Freithin's strength was legendary. His thick fingers tightened around her throat, and First Sentinel saw she was weakening. Each of her punches had a little less strength.

Stay strong, Rova. Hold on for just a second more.

Sapphire dropped all of her weight forward, pulling Onyx off his balance for a second. First Sentinel took the chance and slapped on a second drainer disk.

Onyx regained his footing and hit First Sentinel with an uppercut that sent him sprawling toward the wall. The old Shield braced for impact, already anticipating the broken bones. Instead of a painful crunch, he hit the wall as if it were a downy mattress, and slid down to the floor. First Sentinel looked up to see Ghost Hands turn back toward the rest of the room.

[Thank you,] he thought, and found his feet again, shaking off the hit. Aegis landed a solid jab to Onyx's middle, and Sapphire tore herself out of Onyx's grip, gasping. First Sentinel sprinted across the floor, pain flaring in his hip. He pulled up the pain and added it to his voice as he yelled, "Mark!"

Aegis leapt at Sapphire, who grabbed him by the arm, swung him in a circle, tightening the circle to accelerate, and then threw him directly at Onyx. Aegis straightened into a post with the shield face first, and as Onyx leaned for the impact, First Sentinel dove into a slide and scissor-kicked the Freithin's calf.

Unbalanced, Onyx toppled backward when Aegis crashed into him. The young hero brought down the shield on Onyx's windpipe as they collapsed, and First Sentinel slapped another drainer on the Spark-touched's calf. *That's all of them.*

The three Shields all jumped onto Onyx as the big man slowed. After a moment, Onyx leapt up and threw all three of them off with a scream, murder in his eyes.

So much for a quiet, efficient in and out. Recovering into a roll, First Sentinel took a second to check on the crowd. Over half the Spark-touched were already down or out. Blurred Fists cut a red swath through the room, supported by Ghost Hands' air dominance and Sabreslate's flowing stone weapons.

Despite the chaos, First Sentinel thought for a moment that they had the situation well in hand. Then a spiny Spark-touched pincushion shot a foot-long needle through Ghost Hands' side. She had strength enough to float to the ground instead of dropping, but her shields dropped, and the two Spark-touched she'd been containing took to the air.

One flew on buzzing insect wings, and the other soared on plumes of fire. First Sentinel crossed the room again, moving to Ghost Hands' side as the tide turned against them. The flame-winged Spark-touched rained fire down on Sabreslate, forcing her to duck and pull a semisphere of rock around her to block the flames.

With Sabreslate curled up under her sphere of rock, Blurred Fists was left alone with the crowd. A door swung open, and more Spark-touched poured through. *City Mother, how many of them are there?* Panic rose up again, feeding on his fatigue.

First Sentinel pulled a Spark-touched with a huge mouth and three rows of serrated teeth off Ghost Hands, dropping it with a haymaker. He turned back to the Qava, producing a bandage from his belt.

[Stay still,] he thought, and then yanked the needle out in one clean motion. He turned and impaled the needle in another charging Spark-touched. First Sentinel bound his friend's wound as best he could in a hurry.

[I'm fine. Get back to the fight,] she said in his mind, her voice strained. *She may not be fine, but she can at least keep herself out of the fight if need be.*

Ghost Hands proved her strength with the extension of an arm. First Sentinel followed her motion and saw the airborne fire-starter raining another plume of flame at Sabreslate. The Spark-touched spun in the air, losing control, then crashed into a smoldering heap. The fires subsided, and Sabreslate emerged from her dome.

After smiling to his old friend, First Sentinel rejoined the fight with Onyx, who was still trading blows with Sapphire and Aegis. He was a juggernaut, fighting on with three drainer disks sapping his strength. Onyx landed a kick to Aegis' chest, knocking the young Shield into a wall.

I don't have time for this. First Sentinel reached into a rear pouch on his belt and pulled out a sticky black marble, palming it on his left hand as he advanced. *Let's hope this works.*

The Spark-touched behemoth reached out and stopped Sapphire's punch in mid-swing, though the force of her blow pushed him back a few inches. He was fading, just not fast enough for First Sentinel's liking.

"When I present the pile of your broken bodies, the Smiling King's rewards will be limitless!" Onyx bellowed.

"You're a fool. What's to say he won't take off your head for the presumption of killing us yourself?" Aegis said, pulling himself up and back into the fight.

Good. Draw his attention. And Sapphire, keep him occupied, so I can get in. Onyx obliged, burying a knee in Sapphire's side and then turning to face Aegis. Sometimes First Sentinel didn't know which orders were being relayed by Ghost Hands and which his friends just intuited from their own skill. It seldom mattered.

"You don't know him like I do," Onyx said. "The Smiling King is not mad—he's brilliant. He has found enlightenment in the Spark."

Aegis threw a horizontal slash with the shield, but Onyx parried it down and then threw an elbow over at Sapphire. She ducked under and closed for a grapple. First Sentinel shifted around to Onyx's left, where First Sentinel had planted the first drainer.

The old Shield dodged a wide swipe from Onyx by dropping into a roll, which he regretted as pain flared across his hip again. *That was a terrible idea.*

He missed his target—right on top of the drainer—and instead slapped the marble onto the side of Onyx's foot, sticking the artifact to the ground as well. The force of the impact activated the enchantment as First Sentinel ripped his gloved hand away.

The marble started to expand, swallowing Onyx's foot and sticking it to the floor.

When faced with superior strength, mobility is the key to victory. The first Aegis had taught him that.

Onyx pulled at the expanding marble, ripping it from the floor and swinging his leg at Sapphire. She dodged away, putting space between herself and the Spark-touched. If he put his leg down, it'd stick to the ground and trap him, but without it, he had no balance.

Sapphire grabbed Onyx's wrist, and with Aegis' help they knocked him to the ground. The marble continued to grow, enveloping Onyx's knee. Sapphire and Aegis pinned his upper body as First Sentinel slammed a heel into his lower back, landing all his weight on another nerve cluster. When Onyx's bellow was that of a beast, not a man, First Sentinel knew it was over.

Sabreslate molded lengths of flexible stone rope, which Blurred Fists tied around the Spark-touched, locking them down. Sapphire and Aegis held Onyx, who was still screaming for the Shields' heads as the marble covered him entirely.

First Sentinel stepped back from the marble, drew out the small suitcase and flipped it open.

Still intact. Thank the City Mother.

"Hold the room. Ghost Hands, the dynamite."

"Everyone else, bar the entrances until we're ready."

First Sentinel pulled out his grapple gun and hooked the line to one of the bone spires.

He climbed up the undulating surface of the Rebirth Engine, getting himself into position to arrange the dynamite just so. With Ghost Hands injured, he would have to do some more of the work.

His Qava friend levitated the dynamite beside him, and First Sentinel built a small pyramid of the explosives, then wound the fuses together and trailed the cord down and off the device.

Kicking off from the fleshy side of the still-bristling Rebirth Engine, First Sentinel descended his line, recoiled the grapple, and wound the fuse out into the center of the room.

Blurred Fists would light the fuse when the group was clear, because he could run in and out in a heartbeat.

First Sentinel filled the room with his voice. "We're heading north; walls come down until we reach the last one."

"Let's go!" First Sentinel shouted. At his command, Sapphire charged the north wall. She dropped her head and slammed her full weight up through the wall, punching a gaping hole.

"Keep going!" Aegis helped Sapphire through the next one with a shoulder and shield slam. Sabreslate carried Ghost Hands along as the Qava held her side. The rest of the Shields crawled through the rough holes in the walls, and time slipped away as they broke their way out of the building.

"Faster!" First Sentinel called. He pulled a spare stick of dynamite from the crate and tossed it through the hole made by Sapphire's fist. They cleared away from the explosion and then filtered through the rubble.

They reached the last wall, which was far thicker. Aegis and Sapphire's blows barely cracked the reinforced stone.

"Find a door—now!"

Sabreslate beckoned Aegis over to help with her partner, then stepped up to the stone and concentrated. The wall rolled back from her touch, slowly but surely. For small walls, the direct way was faster, but with walls this thick, Sabreslate's talent couldn't be matched.

A ten-by-five-foot door opened, and Sabreslate dropped her arms, huffing.

Blurred Fists ran back inside to light the fuse as the Shields made their way to a safe distance.

The group found an open patch of cobblestone street. They circled up, joining hands to align with Sabreslate. The Jalvai shaped the cobblestones beneath them, and the group sank through the street to wade through the foundation, made semisolid by Sabreslate's talent.

Wrapped in the turquoise threads of her empathic tie to stone, Sabreslate pushed along a shifting pocket of air for a city block, getting them to what First Sentinel hoped was a safe distance. Sabreslate solidified the ground beneath them again and pushed the Shields back up to street level.

A glance over his shoulder showed First Sentinel the Rebirth Engine's building was a block and a half back.

Blurred Fists reappeared as a red streak, then slowed to join the group in their spectating.

"Good to go."

And then, with a flash, the building was swallowed by a smoke, the boom rumbling the street beneath them.

First Sentinel activated his shimmercrab goggles and filtered through the smoke. Where there should have been nothing but rubble, the Rebirth Engine still stood, coruscating with energy, multicolored lightning arcing up from the device into the sky above. And around the Engine, the smoke clumped into the form of gargoyles, which took to the sky, glowing red maws wide. First Sentinel could swear he heard them screaming for blood.

A few yards away, fish began falling from the smoke, and beyond that, a passing couple fell atop one another and stumbled to their feet as one person, limbs jumbled together.

"Shit," First Sentinel said. Nevri had been right, or at least partially right. All the dynamite had done was kick off another Spark-storm. "It didn't work."

He snapped open the briefcase, looking at the marble. If they left now, the Rebirth Engine would stand, the mission a failure aside from weakening the Smiling King's forces. But the only option they had left to destroy the artifact was to trust Nevri's gift and use COBALT-3's explosive.

He held the marble out. "Do we use it or not? Quickly, before the storm can spread."

"Yes," said Sabreslate.

[No,] said Ghost Hands.

"Yes," from Blurred Fists.

"No," from Sapphire.

"Yes," said Aegis. "We have to finish this. Otherwise, there's no way to use this mission to stop the summit."

Three to two. He could tie the vote, but a tie was hesitation. They had to act.

"Do it," First Sentinel said, handing the device to Blurred Fists. They'd all been briefed on Nevri's instructions, for reasons just like this.

Blurred Fists took a slow breath, nodded to the group, then disappeared into the storm.

Moments later, he returned. "All done. Now we wait, right?"

In answer, the sky split in two with thunder louder than First Sentinel had ever heard.

A cobalt-and-silver cloud of energy rose up from the Rebirth Engine like a lava plume from a volcano.

The cloud rose up and up, clawing toward the moon above. It crested, held still for a moment, shimmering in the night, and then dropped. But cloud didn't just drop; it flowed out like an immense, rippling wave from a drop in a pool. It spread from the warehouse into the surrounding streets.

Cracked open by the explosive, the wave cut through the sky, flowing out into the city like a pack of wolves. It rolled over clusters of people fleeing from the storm, and through the magnification of the shimmercrab goggles, he saw the explosive work its terrible magic.

It peeled flesh from skin, shredding victims to the bones, which shattered on the ground. And from the bones, he saw transparent shapes rising to join the wave.

City Mother, strike me blind for my hubris. That's it, isn't it. She gave us a Soulburner.

Every country on the continent had banned them over a century ago. The last one used had destroyed an entire city.

Synthesized from the essence of souls of those dying from torture, Soulburners were incredibly difficult to produce, each taking the energy of several thousand victims to fill its charge.

He'd learned about them at the academy. He'd never seen one used, but everything fit: the blue-silver energy, the cacophony of screams, the movement of the energy wave. Every soul it consumed added more fuel to the spell and would extend the wave, reaching farther and farther, like a wildfire, until all available fuel was spent. Unlike other ghosts, the spirits in a Soulburner were solid, moved like a wave. They could be contained. But they'd have to act fast.

So that's what you were up to, Nevri. Destroy the machine, us with it, and a thousand of the Smiling King's citizens in the process. When I get my hands on her . . .

First Sentinel pushed back his anger and guilt, setting his mind to the problem. There were thousands of civilians in the immediate area. *And every one of them that dies is on my head.*

"It's a Soulburner!" First Sentinel shouted to the group.

A round of cursing.

He continued. "Every person it consumes adds power to the spell! We have to cut off its power, get people out of its path. We need to go up. Far up!"

Blurred Fists strung together twelve curses in the time it would take First Sentinel to say one, and Ghost Hands floated off the ground, wavering.

Aegis took command. "Sabreslate, pull up a disk of the street. Ghost Hands, take us up above the wave. Pull as many people as you can above the cloud."

Sabreslate took a deep breath as the silver cloud spilled down the street toward them. She ran a quick circle around the

Shields, dragging her hand along the stone. She dropped to one knee and put both hands on the street, turquoise threads unfolding from her like the petals of a freshly blossomed flower. From a roof above, Ghost Hands raised her hands, and the disk shook, then broke free of the street and rose up into the air.

"Hold on, Ghost Hands! You can do it!" Aegis cried.

The silver cloud rolled toward them. "Higher!" The disk lurched, and First Sentinel hunched down for balance. The cloud of souls passed below them.

First Sentinel heard panicked voices rise up from the crowd.

"Why me?"

"Join us!"

"I didn't do anything!"

"I don't know where he is."

"Help!"

"And more."

This is my fault. Every one of them. If destroying the Rebirth Engine costs another five hundred lives, have we really helped anyone?

She'll pay for this. I swear it, so help me City Mother.

First Sentinel turned to his team. Blurred Fists was shaking. Sapphire averted her eyes. Aegis stood as still as one of Sabreslate's statues, taking it all in.

No doubt he's blaming himself every bit as much as I am.

First Sentinel looked down into the cloud, knowing he shouldn't. *They are my responsibility, and they deserve to be remembered.*

The cloud was partly translucent. A cluster of spindly arms and half-formed ghosts rent apart an old man, husked him like sweet corn and pulled his ghost up to join them as they seized upon another victim. That one was an aged Pronai who didn't have the strength to struggle as they broke, folded, and spindled his bones.

The Soulburner would fill Audec-Hal, turning the whole city-crevasse into a bowl of hunger and destruction, until there were no souls left to feed it.

Chapter Sixteen

First Sentinel

We need to stop this thing, now. Any ideas?" First Sentinel called, his voice dwarfed by the Soulburner.

[It's hard enough just keeping us aloft.]

Sabreslate said, "Even if we erect one physical barrier, the souls are coursing down every street in Audec's Bowels. This thing moves like a cloud; it will flow and fill wherever it can. The only way to stop it is to cut off its fuel supply and let the wave dissipate."

It's all slipping away, the waters are above my head, and I was an idiot to think I could swim. Now we're all going to drown in my arrogance.

"What if we just raised another wall?" Sapphire asked.

"I don't know if I could do it fast enough," Sabreslate admitted.

"Try," Aegis said. There was no room for negotiating with that tone of voice. First Sentinel recognized it as the same tone the first Aegis had used. He found himself wondering how much of each bearer stayed with the shield when they passed. Thoughts like that reminded First Sentinel how little

157

they truly knew about the Aegis. Since the first days, he'd just trusted it and its bearer.

First Sentinel sank into his stance as the disk shifted, tilting into a turn to take them ahead of the wave of souls. "I need you to gain on the wave and fly low over one of the graystones!" Sabreslate shouted, more for the other Shields' sake than for Ghost Hands, who could pick whispered thought out in a cacophony.

The disk dipped down as they passed the cloud. Sabreslate leapt off and hit the roof running. She pulled the cobblestones from the street up to make a wall as she sprinted. Building connected to building across the street as she turned the neighborhood itself into a barrier.

The Soulburner cloud crashed against her construct, the spirits crawling up the side, scrambling for more fodder. They hit an invisible wall and lost momentum. The cloud fell back toward the street as Ghost Hands called out, *[Brace yourselves].* The disk slid down into a rough landing on a roof, the sound of stone grating against stone eclipsing the hungry souls for a long moment.

First Sentinel and the Shields dropped to the ground, hanging on as the disk collapsed through a corner of the building, and then sliding down toward the street. Ghost Hands took to the sky once more and followed her wife in a quickly forming but ever widening spiral. Together, they started to contain the cloud, repeating Sabreslate's miracle several times more, until the entire neighborhood had been walled off. Along with hundreds of victims they hadn't been able to save.

Minutes later, the silver cloud receded as the fuel for its hunger burned out fast, the loss of lives contained.

Where the Rebirth Engine had been lay only rubble. At least the Soulburner had fulfilled its original purpose.

And then he saw the Spark-storm, still rolling through the neighborhood. Rays of iridescent light leapt through the sky, took impossible turns and flowed over and down. The Rebirth Engine was gone, but it had birthed one last storm.

First Sentinel looked to Aegis. The younger Shield pointed toward the storm, as if to say, "Can you see this?" First Sentinel nodded, seeing his son's chest sprout a yellow thread of fear, one to go along with the fresh-born threads in each of his friends' hearts. *We've gone from a battlefield to a deadly wave, and now we're in the midst of yet another storm. This is a nightmare.*

With Ghost Hands and Sabreslate still controlling the Soulburner, First Sentinel was left with the three other Shields to deal with the storm—and no transportation.

First Sentinel started walking toward the storm, his hip a dull roar of pain. "Split up—damage control. Only call for support in extreme circumstances."

"It's a Spark-storm. Everything's an extreme circumstance," said Blurred Fists.

"He's got a point," Sapphire said. *True enough.*

First Sentinel restrained a nervous laugh. *Keep it together, old man.* "Get to it."

He pulled the grappling gun from his belt, nodded to Aegis, who was doing the same, using one of First Sentinel's older models. They hooked their grapple lines and jumped off the roof toward a blue and white fire in the distance.

Will we ever really be done, or has the whole city gone mad? Have we cracked the lid keeping the city contained, broken the delicate balance while we were trying to tip the scales of power? City Mother, watch over us in our folly.

First Sentinel would have thought it almost a blessing that many of the people in Audec's Bowels were dead before the storm hit.

Then he saw their animated corpses shuffling down the street. Shifting, twitching masses clambered for anything, the stench of tearing flesh and seeping blood filling the air as their bodies changed under the purposeful chaos of the Spark.

They're looking for something, but what? First Sentinel had never seen the Spark animate the dead before. It had given form to ghosts, warped the minds of the living, but it had never moved the dead like this, puppets on ragged strings.

It could be some kind of synergistic relationship with the Soulburner, latching on to the remnants of the gem's energies. Or maybe it was just terrible, abominable luck.

Whatever caused it, First Sentinel, Sapphire, Aegis, and Blurred Fists faced a long street of shuttered doors and muffled screams as a hundred walking dead pounded on walls and crawled through windows.

You couldn't kill what was already dead, so the Shields cut through the horde with somber efficiency. Aegis took off heads with swipes of his shield; First Sentinel snapped necks and broke spines with swings of his fighting sticks and blows from his shock gloves, trying not to let himself think about who these people had been before. Blurred Fists pushed the crowds back from the civilians that had managed to escape the Soulburner cloud.

The sky above the neighborhood was as a painter's wheel, constantly changing from blue to midnight black, showing impossible combinations of mauve, yellow, chartreuse. The buildings on the street were melting like ice cream at noon, seeping down from the tops. In minutes they'd be misshapen piles serving as mass graves. *City Mother, preserve us.*

What was Nevri hoping to accomplish with the storm? Under-mine the Smiling King's territory? Take us out with the storm? Both options were all too plausible.

One of the Spark-touched corpses lurched across the street at First Sentinel. He jumped back, wishing any of the buildings had the strength to hold a grapple line. Instead, he circled away from the puddle and toward the next doorway on the street, where he heard banging at the walls and muted shouts from the interior.

"Let us out please! There are children!" said a woman in the hurried cadence of the Pronai.

First Sentinel hurried up the steps to the landing of the gray-stone, sweeping aside a corpse that was pounding mindlessly at the door. He twisted the doorknob. It only spun in a circle, bro-ken. He kicked the doorknob through its socket and shouted, "I'm coming in!"

First Sentinel rammed his shoulder against the door, but it didn't budge. It was sticky at the sides, the edges of the wood grown into the doorframe like roots. First Sentinel drew a knife and cut at the roots, kicking the base of the door open an inch or two. He pressed up and in, watching as a pack of Spark-touched corpses shambled up toward him, clumsy feet failing to scale the steps.

"Come on, come on!" One last lunge and the door snapped, dumping him ungracefully into the apartment building. First Sentinel tried the nearest door as he shouted up the stairs. "Everyone out—now! The building is going to collapse!"

This door was stuck as well, but it was only fused around the doorknob. He made short work of it with his knife.

First Sentinel threw open the door, and a Pronai woman sighed in relief. She scooped up her toddler and raced for the exit. Three steps into her run, her feet stuck to the ground like it was flypaper. But the rest of her kept going. Joints and muscles ripped at the knee and the femur, and she crashed to the floor at his feet, turning as she fell to protect her child. The toddler slipped out of her hands, and First Sentinel dove to catch it.

The child was screaming, redder than the fresh-spilled blood all around them.

"I've got you." The child continued to wail as he looked to the maimed woman. *I don't think she even feels the pain yet. Small blessings.* First Sentinel sat the child down on a chair for a moment and hauled the footless woman over his back in a fireman's carry. She reached out for her child, and First Sentinel retrieved the infant and hurried the three of them out of the building. Above them, the ceiling started to bubble and sag.

Time to go. He took a deep breath and pushed on, weighed down by the woman. *Come on, Wonlar, just like when you were young.*

The storm-made corpses were still trying to climb the stairs. They weren't getting anywhere, but they were still in his way. The Pronai woman's blood seeped down his leg as they left the building. She wouldn't make it.

Wounds didn't tend to close in a Spark-storm, and First Sentinel had seen the neighborhood's only doctor torn to shreds by hungry spirits just minutes before. But every life was worth saving, so First Sentinel drew his grapple gun and shot out a line, pulling them up and out of the way.

The dead moaned with a vague sadness and pawed at his feet. For a moment he smelled the blossoming of crocuses among the stink of death. *Just the storm, playing tricks with my mind.*

Another hour of chaos and the storm passed, along with the Pronai mother. She left him with a screaming child, a broken district, and his ever mounting guilt.

They'd destroyed the Rebirth Engine, and if they could get the word out to the tyrants that Nevri had betrayed them all, they might be able to stop the summit. But the cost . . .

Nevri made puppets out of us. What would we'd have let her get away with if we'd moved on her schedule? Half of him dreaded finding out, but the other half couldn't wait to know, so he wouldn't be stuck imagining the worst.

But first, they had to put the dead to rest. The Smiling King's forces were nowhere to be seen, so the Shields gathered the survivors together to burn the bodies and say prayers over the fallen. Audec's Bowels would not recover from this disaster. Within a week, it would be a ghost town, haunted by the enormous ribs that formed its skyline, seized upon by the Spark-touched and other castoffs, inhospitable to the decent poor who had been stranded here. Another territory lost in the war between the Shields and the tyrants.

Every time I try to make things better, make a decisive move to free my city, it comes back to explode in my face.

Maybe I'm just fooling myself. Maybe I learned folly from a deluded fool, and it's just taken me fifty years to realize it.

First Sentinel picked himself back up again and pushed on, his doubts swirling around him like the recently banished spirits of the dead.

Chapter Seventeen

Interlude—The Plutocrat

Nevri looked out on Audec-Hal as the smoke cleared. From her personal mansion at the Head, a building towering over the city from its place atop Audec's skull, she saw dozens of fires burning down to embers.

First Sentinel thought himself clever, striking before the appointed date.

She'd anticipated the Shields' early move, and so when her spies brought word of the chaos in the Smiling King's district, she'd sent the word to her teams.

Sixteen groups, seeded around the city, carrying passes allowing her people into the other oligarch's domains, struck all at once.

A sniff of the brandy and her mind painted a picture of the swift justice meted out by her forces:

Safehouse shelters burned to the ground; suppliers' ware-houses raided, the stores destroyed or stolen; apartments raid-ed, the traitors' allies dragged out into the street and hung from lampposts.

"Be brutal," she'd said to the assembled groups, her best covert operatives. "These traitors are to be made an example of. When they die, let their neighbors know the reason. Burn the memory into their minds."

Qazzi Fau, her most zealous lieutenant, had smiled from ear to ear as she'd given the orders. He held his polished sword like a lover, caressing it and speaking softly to the blade. He was a monster, but he was her monster. When she'd found him, Qazzi was a simple contract killer. Under her direction, he'd become an indispensable asset. He removed those that stood between her and order, and now he oversaw an entire district, his monomaniacal focus broadened to become more versatile.

Those that stood with her were showered with fortune.

And those that stood in her way were ground underfoot.

She swirled her snifter of brandy, took another exquisite sip. Each time she outsmarted the Shields or a rival, she returned to her first love, brandy, remembering the taste of the day she'd carried off her first heist: the day Nevri the Lash had been born.

This bottle was the first of the night's spoils, taken from the home of one of the rebels' so-called Shield-bearers, a Jalvai doctor who ran a clinic in COBALT-3's territory.

Another knock at the door.

"Come."

Dlella slithered in, a sheaf of papers in her hands. She looked as pleased with herself as Nevri felt.

"The final reports, Executor. Fifteen teams had total success. Only the team sent to First Sentinel's apartment reported failure. The rebel has moved, as we suspected."

Nevri took the papers and dismissed Dlella with a curt nod. Dlella was an excellent assistant, a subtle plotter, and her ambition reminded Nevri of herself at thirty, ready to burn the Senate.

But Dlella lacked the nerve to set out on her own. She still waited for her moment to strike, to overthrow Nevri.

She would be waiting a long time.

Nevri crossed to her lacquer-topped desk and set the papers down, the brandy beside it. She'd read the reports three times, committing each to memory. Then she'd composed her letter to the other oligarchs, proof of what they could accomplish through simple information sharing, the least of the planks of her agenda for the summit.

The Smiling King would be incensed, especially since she'd gone to the length of giving the Shields a Soulburner. But he was a madman on the best of days, and the others would overrule him. And if they didn't, one weakened oligarch could not stand against the other four.

She returned to the window, watching the last rays of dusk as night came to Audec-Hal. Pinpoints of light drew the line of the city like a waiting lover splayed out, waiting to be ravished. Waiting for her.

With this success, the others would have to come to the table. And when the summit was done, the Shields' fate would be sealed, and she'd have the other oligarchs right where she wanted them: close. Close enough to find out the rest of their weaknesses.

Another sip of the brandy. Hints of caramel, oak, and the sweetness of triumph.

If the Shields had the audacity to come to the final meeting, come clawing for their payoff, then she'd have a special gift to start the summit: First Sentinel's head on a pike.

Chapter Eighteen

Aegis

B oxes. His world was full of boxes. Wooden and cardboard, they stacked to the ceiling, half full, overflowing, boxes inside of boxes.

The battle for the soul of Audec-Hal was raging, and the city's mightiest hero was packing underwear. They had to repack and move all in one go to minimize chances of being found or followed. His belongings had all been moved for him when he had been a "guest" of COBALT-3, so now he had no idea where anything was.

Selweh grabbed another handful of clothes out of a box and moved them to a day bag while Wonlar shouted from across the apartment, "Where did you put my night-blooming whistal?"

Selweh stopped in place. *How would I know that?* "I don't know! Why weren't they in with the other herbs?"

"Because I asked you to take them to the planter to seed."

Aegis scratched his head, trying to remember. "I never did that. I have no idea, Dad."

Selweh heard the exasperation in his father's voice. "Do you remember what I use those to make?"

What are those for again?

Selweh tracked through his memory, the countless lessons his father had given him on artifice. He'd never taken to it, and mostly listened to the lessons out of a sense of filial duty.

"No?"

Wonlar stepped through the maze of boxes and walked into the makeshift bedroom with Selweh, rolling a tapestry in his arms. "I have to use night-blooming whistal for the solution that refreshes the ward on my longcoat. I've only got enough for two batches here. I'll have to order more. That could take all month. Dammit."

"Why do we have to move? Isn't this place fine for now?" Selweh asked, even though he knew, as he tried to deflect his father's attention away from the blame. His father could never resist a chance to explain himself.

"This safehouse is tiny. It would never do as a real apartment. We're going to the basement at Douk's. And don't complain."

After Dlella had walked in on a meeting, the Shields had just boxed everything up in a panic and thrown it in this, the nearest safehouse. It wouldn't do for a long-term apartment for the two. Douk's basement was little better, but it was close, and they needed a headquarters more than an apartment for the time being.

Their fellow Shields would do the moving part, shuttling the Ikanollos' belongings faster than Nevri could track them (Blurred Fists), through avenues where they couldn't be tracked (Sabreslate). There was the chance that they could be followed by fellow Pronai or Jalvai, but both of the Shields were trained to pick out tails.

Selweh closed the bag he'd been stuffing. "Who said I was going to complain?" He was still reeling from the evening. The mission had been going so well before it exploded in their faces. Neither of them had gotten enough sleep, and it was all he could do to keep from snapping at his father.

His father set down the tapestry and sat to one side, favoring his hip. It was Wonlar's annoyed parent stance, every bit as intimidating as the face he wore at night for the criminals and tyrants. "Selweh . . . "

The younger Shield threw his hands up and turned around, moving on to the next box. "I didn't say anything."

The Rebirth Engine mission had been a disaster at best, and the news hadn't seemed to do anything to disturb the summit.

That's what we get for counting on the Smiling King to have a reasonable response to anything, Selweh thought.

"We need to get all of this ready by tonight for the cart. Then the meeting," Wonlar said.

"You honestly think we can have all of this packed by tonight? You're mad." Aegis turned and threw his hands up in frustration. "The stress of the war has clearly shattered your mind."

"Wenlizerachi is coming over for dinner to help."

Selweh almost growled. "Then why don't we just wait and let him do everything? He packed everything from the old place, and it took what—an hour?"

"Because it'd be rude."

Selweh shrugged. "Or efficient."

"Or rude." Wonlar pushed the rolled tapestry into Selweh's hands. "Keep going. I won't have us sitting around when Wenlizerachi arrives."

Selweh picked up the tapestry and set it in a pile with the rest of the carpets and wall-hangings his father had accumulated over the years. "Shouldn't we be planning our next move, thinking about what to do with Nevri?"

"We are doing that, but we're also packing."

So he packed. Really, it was unpacking and repacking. Wenlizerachi was efficient, but the boxes were without order. It seemed that the Pronai had just packed everything in piles, going from ceiling to floor, not leaving anything behind for Nevri's thugs.

I suppose when you're evacuating a compromised position, organizing isn't exactly the first thing in your mind.

Selweh repacked more clothes, the training weapons, and stacks of beakers. He packed twenty boxes of books, using Wonlar's horrendously particular demands for cataloguing, and then he sorted out three boxes of sculptures, wrapping them in clothing and tapestries for padding.

He sat and allowed himself to mourn the old apartment. It had been his home for almost as long as he could remember. He knew the alleys and rooftops in this neighborhood like the back of his hand, from the training his father had given him from the age of four, through his time as Second Sentinel, even into his assumption of the mantle of Aegis. It was *home*, and he'd never even had the chance to say good-bye. But going back would be stupidity. Nevri would have guards posted, and having a deal wouldn't stop "unaffiliated" thugs from taking a shot at him.

When Wenlizerachi arrived, Selweh crossed the apartment to wrap him up in a big hug. "Thank you so much for coming over." Then he leaned in and whispered, "You have no idea how much this means to me."

Wenlizerachi answered in a conspiratorial tone, "You could have just left it all for me to do. I don't mind."

Selweh said, "Yeah, but don't tell Wonlar you said that."

The Pronai nodded.

"Let me show you what we're doing. And what would you like to eat? None of the dry goods are going, so I'm going to cook everything I can." The other Shields had brought everything, even the food. There was no telling what could be used in a ritual to track them down through sympathetic associations.

Wenlizerachi's eyes glimmered in a fashion usually reserved for massive brawls and all-you-can-eat buffets (the ones that didn't disallow Pronai).

"Oh, really?" he said, and Selweh smiled, the weight off his shoulders. Selweh and Wonlar explained what had to be packed where.

Before dinner was done, the whole apartment had been sorted, neat stacks of boxes in neat rows, ready to be carted away to Douk's apartments above the café.

Selweh thought it was a pity they couldn't have stayed in the old apartment, but eventually Nevri would have had the apartment raided by three hit squadrons and a unit of Qava, Pronai, and Freithin assassins.

Unless they showed up before Father had his morning tea. Then he'd kill the lot of them, and he'd be cursing while reheating the water.

Humming over the stove and stirring vigorously, Selweh stir-fried all of the remaining vegetables with the short-grain rice and a befuddlingly tasty combination of every spice left on their rack that Wonlar hadn't already packed for later use in his artificer's work. Selweh tumbled the food over and over, tossing it up and catching it with nimble motions. He added one more dash of crushed *zu* nuts and turned off the stove.

Selweh called, "Dinner" to the other room where his father and friend were packing. Wenlizerachi appeared before the word stopped echoing in Selweh's throat, holding out a plate to receive his first shares. Selweh doled out two helpings onto the plate.

"Looks great, thanks," Wenlizerachi said. Selweh blinked, and Wenlizerachi was perched on top of a crate, chopsticks shoveling food into his mouth.

Wonlar emerged from the back room, wiped sweat from his forehead, and took the plate offered him. "Thank you." Selweh nodded. *When the war is over, I will be a cook,* Selweh thought.

Even free people ruling themselves need to eat, and eat well. Food brought people together to sit at a table to share of themselves, even if for just a few minutes. And it was safe enough that his father would approve.

Wenlizerachi got up, ready for his third serving, but waited until Selweh took a plate's worth of fried green peppers, winter squash, and cabbage over sauced brown rice, before helping himself to another plate.

Wonlar clapped him on the shoulder. "Good cooking."

"Thanks. I used pretty much everything. Unless you want *Yuyu* seeds on your stir-fry." Selweh held up a glass tube of sandy-brown spicy seeds, used mostly in the Howbeh style of cooking from the far north. He was pretty sure the bottle was the same one he'd bought three years ago when he first started to pursue cooking. Even with laboratory airtight sealing, they wouldn't be worth anything.

Wonlar chuckled. "No, thank you." As a testament to his father's hunger, Wonlar finished his whole plate before starting to talk revolution. He gestured with his chopsticks to Wenlizerachi, like a teacher calling on a student. "At tonight's meeting, I want you to give us the word in the veins. We need a sense of how our public support is faring, and then we can decide how to use it."

Wenlizerachi nodded as he got up for another helping. Selweh sighed. "Let's just hope that last night gets traced back to Nevri. Then we can make something good out of that disaster."

Wonlar and Selweh knocked on the door to Bira and Sarii's loft in Viscera City.

The loft was a strangely comfortable juxtaposition of empty walls and accumulated art. Qava decorated for space and texture, not seeing as other races do. For Bira, Sarii had sculpted the whole apartment into a work of art, patterns carved into the wall, bas-relief murals on the ceiling, graystone furniture that rose up out of the floor. It was a lived-in art installation.

The others had already arrived, sitting at their places around the great stone table in the dining room.

Wonlar paced around the low table while the others sat around hand-sculpted mugs of tea and coffee. "The explosions covered up any evidence we left at the warehouse. We need to find another way to make sure the blame falls where it needs to."

Although there were couches and beds, there were no chairs in the loft. Sarii preferred the floor or floating in the air, and Bira refused to replace the chairs that had been destroyed the last time she and Sarii had a had spat. *At least, until Sarii apologizes. Therefore, never.* That's what Bira had said the last time Selweh asked, and he knew better than to interfere.

Wenlizerachi gulped down another cup of tea, then took a long breath, several pieces of paper trembling in his hands. He started to say something, then stopped.

Selweh's heart sunk, seeing the Pronai's threads twisting. Wenlizerachi tried again, then succeeded on the third try.

"It's worse. Much worse. We got played, Wonlar."

"What happened?" Rova asked.

"The Shield-bearers. Dozens of them. Safehouses, store rooms, and friends. Someone pulled off a coordinated strike. The train station hideout in Straight Knee, the Sanavero brothers at Right Shoulder, Colni and her sisters, and more."

Wonlar hurled his mug at the floor. The worn stone shattered on the wood, tea spilling out and seeping into the cracks between the aged planks. "How?" It was a demand more than a request.

Wenlizerachi offered the papers. "I don't know. These are the reports from eye-witnesses, survivors. They all struck last night while we were busy with the Soulburner. More than half of the Shield-bearers are gone."

The papers were passed around the table. Selweh sped-read the pages, taking in the locations, the tallies of the dead.

"Idiot!" Wonlar said, storming back and forth, his ears red.

"And if we go to anyone's funeral, we could be walking into another trap," Selweh said, his voice shaking.

Wonlar stopped in place and held up his shaking hands, looking at the group. The Shields grew still, and he lowered them, taking a long breath. "I have to talk about something else, or I'm going to destroy more of Sarii's artwork." He turned to the Jalvai. "I'm sorry about the mug."

"Fuck the mug, I'm about to smash something," Sarii said.

[Let's move on. We can't find justice for our friends if we stew in our rage,] Bira said, her mental voice curt where it was almost always serene. "What do we know about public response to the

174

Soulburner?" Wonlar asked, pouring himself another cup of tea in a fresh mug.

Wenlizerachi spoke again, his hands calmer. "Reports are jumbled. Very few people got out of the way in time to avoid both the Soulburner and the Spark-storm."

Wonlar stopped for a moment, hand cupping his chin as he thought. "The Smiling King will retaliate against someone, assuming Onyx survived the explosions."

Bira spoke to their minds, her voice level, calm. *[If he didn't, then who knows? This is the Smiling King after all. Logic need not apply.]* Selweh surveyed the room, watching the carefully braided threads that connected the Shields. And among them, his own tangle. Thick arcs of gold loyalty and bronze dedication connected him to the other Shields, along with the deep emerald braid that arced to his father. And tangled within them all, a weak jade thread that arced hopefully from Sapphire but became lost and knotted.

Rova was a loyal Shield, a pure soul, and a caring friend.

But Selweh had a city to save. He couldn't lose focus. It wouldn't be fair to her or the city. He'd be with her, thinking of the city, or out on patrol and distracted by wanting to speed home and see her again.

Love had nearly ripped the team apart once before, and he wouldn't risk it happening again. Selweh looked to his father, saw the gray threads of regret that he wore like a cloak. Selweh shut his eyes and tried to steady himself, to calm his heartbeat instead of gazing into the vastness of Rova's eyes.

Wonlar spoke again. "But what are those other plans? We put everything on hold for the Rebirth Engine, and it blew up in our face! The summit's in a week—that doesn't leave us much time to derail it. If any of the tyrants are making moves after the Rebirth Engine, they're playing it tight to the chest."

"So we got nothing out of it other than a massive death toll. Good job, team." Sarii said.

"If the Rebirth Engine was really the source of the surge in Spark-storms, that's certainly more than nothing," Selweh said, shooting a frown at the Jalvai.

This plan had spiraled out of control. It seemed like as soon as they got a step ahead of the tyrants, something else blindsided them and put them back on the defensive.

Sarii waved off his frown, dismissive. "There was a storm right after we destroyed the Engine. It'll take months to know if we really did any good."

"Please, stay positive," Wonlar said. "What's done is done."

Sarii twirled a stone bracelet around her finger, shaping it to slide up her hand and wrap around her wrist in soft coils. "Getting all five of them in the same room could be the catalyst to get tempers to boil over and start the war we're looking for."

Wonlar's response was curt. "That's exactly what happened twenty years ago, Sarii. If you recall, it didn't end well." Selweh saw his father glance his way, just for an instant.

I'm the legacy of that rebellion. But how different would my life have been if she had lived? I'd just have one Shield parent instead of another.

Selweh had only the vaguest memories of his mother; the rest came from the stories Wonlar told him and the pictures his father treasured above all else.

He let the memories fall back in his mind. "What I'd like to see is two or three of the tyrants ganging up on another of them. It'd be localized, on a smaller scale. Controllable."

[I don't think we can count on having that much finesse. We're trying to start a brushfire, but it could easily become an inferno.] Bira was always the note of realism.

"Wenlizerachi, give us the word from the veins," Selweh asked. *Time to get this conversation headed somewhere.*

The Pronai stood and started to walk quick circles around the table, counterclockwise to Wonlar. He stopped at the head of the table.

"Folks are confused. They are blaming the flood of souls on the Spark-storm, not the gem. They have noticed there are more storms of late, but they talk about it about the same way as when we had that drought two summers ago: Nothing to be done about it, just keep your head down and endure." As he spoke, he moved in a blur around the circle, settling into a solid stance to make specific points. "People say they want to be free, to be rid of the tyrants, but it's said with a wishful far-off look, like saying, 'I wish a bag of money fell out of the sky into my lap.'"

Wonlar faced Wenlizerachi and moved his attention between the Pronai and the seated Shields as Wenlizerachi talked. "We need to make liberation into a real possibility before they'll make a move."

It has to be within their grasp, or else things will have to get so bad that the only way for them to survive is to revolt. While Yema had control of the City Mother, she kept the populace afraid, burgundy and yellow threads hanging over everything and strangling resistance.

"We have to do something radical; it'll overcome the City Mother's power. And that means massive damage," Sarii said. *Her cynicism is at times a breath of fresh air, other times little better than a toxic wind. We need her to keep us in check, but I can't let her drag us down,* Selweh thought.

Michael R. Underwood

Wonlar shook his head, "The casualties required for that, though."

Sarii rolled her eyes as she looked up at Wonlar. "When the war comes, the veins will become rivers of blood. This will just speed the process along."

"Surely there's a difference between people dying in the revolution and deliberately worsening conditions in the city to incite a revolt," Selweh said.

[What would you want to do to make the apathy give way?] Bira asked.

Sarii held her palm open, and the stone in her hands shifted through different shapes as she spoke. "Food shortages, property damage, get the taxes raised even more. Highlight everything wrong about their reign, and remove the few necessary comforts they have—then we'll see a different side of this city."

"We should shut down the execution amphitheatre," Selweh volunteered. He'd been there, head on the block, seen normal people's threads of every color stained red with bloodlust, and his father had arrived not a minute too early. "It's a distraction; it builds hatred of those trying to change things, and lets the tyrants make the populous think they have the city's best interests at heart."

He caught Wonlar's attention, saw the flash of pain, and the emerald thread between them fluttered as the memory surfaced. "I agree that it needs to be shut down, but that's not remotely low profile."

Sarii held up her shifting stone, making it into a bouncing ball. "And if we target the entertainments and the distractions, the immediate effect on our public opinion will only be negative. If you remove a child's toys, the first thing the child will do is

178

scream and throw a fit." The ball broke into pieces and fell with hard thuds to the table below, shaking the plates and glasses.

[But we want them to throw a fit,] Ghost Hands said in their minds.

Wenlizerachi blurred over and resumed his seat. "This all depends on what the tyrants are going to do to distract people during the summit. With the right show, something their newspapers and heralds can trot out and draw attention to, the ambient distrust of the summit will get glossed over by the spectacle."

Selweh sighed. The tyrants had the city locked up, controlling information, food supplies, jobs—nearly everything. And with the City Mother's influence, it was nearly impossible to rouse the people in groups. A person here or there might be strong enough to fight against the tide, but the Shields needed a wave of their own.

Sapphire said, "More likely, they'll disrupt any protestors and distract the rest with games and executions, perhaps arrange a high-profile murder or kidnapping to be plastered on every news post and paper. One eye-catching lithograph of a pretty little girl, and suddenly people can't think straight."

"How's Fahra doing?" Sarii asked. *Not helping.*

Rova narrowed her eyes, leaning forward across the table with her broad arms. "Not the same. And she's doing fine."

"Good."

How does Wonlar keep them from killing one another? This team needs a summit of our own before doing anything.

"Let's focus here," Selweh said with his Aegis voice. Rova leaned back off the table, Wenlizerachi leaned forward, and Wonlar dropped his shoulders. When his father worried, his shoulders hunched up and in, until he looked like he had no neck.

Wonlar nodded to his son. "Thank you. What is our immediate move?"

"We spring Nevri's trap," Selweh said.

Wenlizerachi sputtered. "There's no way the money's worth that risk."

Wonlar cracked his knuckles. "Not the money. Another chance to take her out in person, do what I should have done last time. Start this revolution and let the tyrants know we're serious. You're right, Sarii. We've been wasting time. We have to force the endgame."

Selweh shot his father a look. *You could have told me about this, Dad.* Wonlar ignored him.

Sarii's stone shifted to mimic Nevri on the table, stone blood spilling from her neck. Then Dlella's form grew out of the pool, standing tall, waving a hand to command imaginary servants. "Even if we kill Nevri, someone will take her place. And then we'll have a blood hunt."

Selweh jumped in. "Unless we succeed in letting all of the tyrants know that Nevri was the mastermind behind the Rebirth Engine's destruction."

The stone in Sarii's hands shifted into a set wolf trap, jagged claws waiting for prey. It started to close and then creaked to a stop. "I still don't see how we can turn a meeting into an assassination. She has to know we'll be out for blood."

Wonlar leaned forward, conspiratorial where Rova was threatening. "That's the beauty of it. We show up, but not in the way she expects. She has patterns, and we can turn those patterns against her. We'll use the propriety of the Senator-turned-Executor to pin her up against the wall. She'll greet us in businesswoman mode and won't spring the trap until she's had time to gloat."

"You're as mad as the Smiling King if you think we can take her out when she knows we're coming." Sarii leaned back in her chair and crossed her arms.

"It can work," Rova said, anger in her eyes. "We always play it cool with Nevri. If we go for the throat, we might surprise her."

Thank you for believing, Rova. Selweh smiled at her and watched her jade thread twitch with excitement. Selweh instantly chided himself and dropped the smile. *I shouldn't have done that.*

Wonlar punched the table, shaking mugs and glasses. "It has to work." *Please let it work.*

Selweh cast his gaze around the table, looking to the others. Worry was thick in the air.

Wonlar knelt at the table, looking around with that fire in his eyes, the flame that burned with devotion, compassion, and vengeance in equal portions. The same flame Wonlar had taught Selweh to tend in his own heart.

Wonlar made a fist with one hand. "I had a chance to kill her in the subway car. I didn't take it. I'm not going to pass up another opportunity. I can't let her terrorize the city any longer."

He continued, "None of her lieutenants will be able to hold the domain together as well. The other tyrants will pick away at the successor until there are four where there were once five. And then we're one tyrant closer to freedom."

Sarii sighed. "And when the next one falls, two more pretenders will split up the territory, and it'll keep going until we do something to build up a new government to take the place of the old. We need to recruit, arm the people for when it's time to turn an insurrection into a full-blown revolution."

Nods. "No arguing there," Selweh said.

Wonlar said, "But we need to start toppling the big players before we can be ready to make the final push. I won't make the same mistakes as last time. Let's focus on Nevri."

"She'll have her best muscle and most likely an army at her back."

Wonlar's arm shot out, and then he squeezed the fist closed. "And I will have the Shields of Audec-Hal at mine. All I have to do is get within arm's reach."

Chapter Nineteen

Sapphire

It's a bad idea.
It can work.
It's a bad idea.
It has to work.
She has to pay.

Sapphire's heart and mind toggled between the extremes as she waited in her position at the Heartstown station. Traffic was lighter this time, in the hundreds instead of thousands. The flows of people were directed rivers instead of the solid sea of the pre- or post-work rushes.

Cracking varnish rippled up and down the walls. The story of the building's disrepair was told on the walls and the floors, and showed itself in the swirling eddies of trash that collected along the edges of the room, kicked up by rushing businesswomen trying to sneak around the crowd.

Sapphire watched the scene from a high landing as the river of people scaled the stairs to the Twisted Toes line, smallest in the room. The Twisted Toes line didn't get much traffic after six at night—the commute was long, and few people bothered to work a distance three-quarters of the city away from home.

The few who did always looked out of place, uncertain of themselves, as if someone would stop them and interrogate them, asking them why it was so important to work clear on the other side of the city. For some, a four-hour commute to a terrible job was their best option.

It had been easy enough to get word to Nevri to arrange the meeting, given the size of her spy network.

A nervous Ikanollo man passed by, his gaze stuck on his feet, muttering beneath his breath as he walked apart from the single-file progression of his fellow commuters.

Sapphire heard Ghost Hands' voice in her mind, calm but firm, relaying First Sentinel's orders. *[Move to position three.]*

[Moving,] she thought, and started down the stairs, three steps in a stride. These were steps built for Ikanollo or fragile Qava, so they were not quite long enough to accommodate her feet. She kept her weight back, landing on her heels as she descended with care, the toes of her corded sandals peeking over the edge each time.

Ghost Hands floated through the crowd down on the main level, and below that Sapphire could see a duo of Ikanollo descending the stairs like they were going to war. They could only be Aegis and First Sentinel. You could put the two of them side by side, wearing the exact same clothes and standing exactly the same way, and in two moments she could still tell the father from the son.

It wasn't the blood link, the feelings Sapphire felt viscerally that they experienced visually. It was a difference in carriage, the tone of voice, and the way Aegis met her gaze full on as an equal. But most of all, it was the slivers of connection she saw break through the hero façade Aegis put up.

Selweh knew how she felt, had to know the longing that overwhelmed her whenever he was in the room. But he kept her at arm's length, always hesitating, his heart swinging between interest and restraint.

When would it be right? Could she wait for the tyrants' fall? She'd heard enough stories from First Sentinel about Aria to stay her words these past years, but every day it hurt more, and her patience wore thin. It could be different with her and Selweh. *It will be.*

But first, they had to settle the score with Nevri.

She reached the main platform and cut through the river of commuters. People made way for her without thinking. Most of the time, it was far better to take a few more steps or stop for a moment rather than face the Freithin's wrath. The legendary temper of her people was all propaganda, mostly from Medai Omez. Her people were neither vengeful nor gentle by nature, no more than Ikanollo, Jalvai, or any of the other races. Most Freithin's anger at being enslaved was matched by their capacity to feel compassion deeply through the blood bond.

Still, the reputation had its uses at times.

At the front of the landing down to the Headtown line, Sapphire spotted the immaculate shine of the shoes of one of Nevri's bodyguards. Was First Sentinel really going to follow through? They'd had to kill in the name of freedom, but this was different. This time they meant to kill, no holding back.

The hate rolled off First Sentinel from twenty paces away.

Sapphire waited at the west edge of the platform, a smaller bubble around her as the citizens flowed around Nevri's Freithin roadblocks. Aegis and First Sentinel stood shoulder to shoulder at the edge of the guard's dead zone.

[I don't like the feel of this,] she thought, hoping Ghost Hands would pick it up and relay the message. Aegis' wariness was like

a boiling fire in her stomach, the mirror of the First Sentinel's coiled anticipation. She didn't doubt First Sentinel's resolve anymore. He'd do it if he got the chance. She'd do it herself if need be.

Sapphire thought back to the screams of the dead, the souls dragged into the cacophony of the Soulburner.

Nevri was a monster, and the city would be better off without her.

The sprawling red beast of a train rolled in, covered in ancient patterns that had confounded every scholar in Audec-Hal. The trains ran and didn't break down. COBALT-3 had created some small private lines in her domain, but nothing could compare to the old trains.

Sapphire thought it fitting that the Shields would make their move in a structure that predated the tyrants and would outlast all of them.

Nevri gestured to the open door. Two of her guards entered first, keeping any others from entering. Nevri went next, looking over her shoulder at the two Ikanollo. They shared a quick glance, and then Aegis looked back to Sapphire. Stepping onto the train, he flashed a reassuring smile that was laced with fear.

Sapphire took long strides across the platform and boarded the next train car, seeing that Blurred Fists was already standing inside, one hand in an overhead loop. They shared a nod, and then she took the two seats at the end of the train car, just beside the door between her car and Aegis'.

And now, the waiting.

Chapter Twenty

First Sentinel

Eighteen Years Ago

With the completion of my Intercession Engine, we were finally ready to move against Medai Omez. After Aria's death, we were joined by her successor, the fourth Aegis, Aernah, a teacher.

Aegis, Forked Lightning, Red Vixen, Ghost Hands, and I met atop the warehouse on 11th and Gray at the edge of the right leg, just a few blocks from the Freithin pens. It wasn't even six yet, but night had already fallen to give us the cover we needed. I could hear the sounds of the factory beside the pens, the pounding of machinery. I could see and smell the acrid smoke spewed forth by the soot-black stacks ahead.

Red Vixen's breath misted out of her snout as her teeth chattered. The Millrej fox-kin's fur was collecting ice crystals, her whiskers twitching in the cold as she rubbed her gloves together, red raiment looking luminescent orange in the fading lantern light.

"Always glad to have gloves on nights like this, though I can't tell you how many pairs I go through—claws and all. How often do you have to replace yours, Lightning?"

Forked Lightning had only been with us for a few months, less than a year since the Spark-storm gave him the gift to throw electricity with his hands. But in return, the Spark had taken his sense of smell, along with his hair.

He ran a hand over his hooded mask, tracing the arcs of yellow back across his scalp. "Haven't had to, not since First Sentinel made me these." The rubber gloves let him control the lightning strikes; his ability wouldn't activate unless he removed them. "Why don't you just make fingerless gloves?" he asked.

She rubbed her paws together, looking at the edge of the alley as I waited for my watch to signal six o'clock. "Defeats the point, freeze the tips of my claws off. Numb claws are no good in a fight, eh?"

"It's time," I said.

I turned to Aegis, who nodded. She'd been Aegis for two years, and she still deferred to me half the time. She'd find her confidence soon enough. The others did.

"Let's move out. Everyone, remember your tasks," Aegis said with her teacher's voice and the confidence expected of her mantle.

I pulled out my grappling gun and aimed for the corner of the building across the street. Aegis did the same, hitting the opposite corner. As we swung down, Ghost Hands floated the other two behind us.

We reached the entrance without incident. The sky above us was black on black, blocking out the stars. The outer walls were manned by three guards, easily dispatched, their keys turned against their master's use.

But from there, we had to cross the fields lit by floodlights and patrolled by bound spirits. The spectral sentries floated in unreadable paths across the grassed field between the fence and the pens themselves. That's where they let the Freithin walk, stretch their legs, and see the sky—or whatever of it they could with that smoke cloud overhead.

I wondered if some of the Freithin had ever even seen the stars. Would a race born into captivity below smog have myths of the starry sky?

Aegis led us across the fields, finding a way between the moving fields of light. The spirits were limited to their field of illumination. As long as we stayed in the dark, we were safe. And with the shimmercrab goggles, we had no need to fear the dark.

Halfway across the field, I saw Medai Omez's guards. The first, a Pronai, was leaning on a spear barely taller than she; the other was a Qava at attention. Both were dressed in the wrapped scarves and robes of Omez's western homeland. Aegis signaled me forward, along with Red Vixen. She wanted those two taken out quietly, or else she would have called Forked Lightning and Ghost Hands.

I pulled two throwing blades from my belt and took aim as Red Vixen dropped to all fours and began stalking up toward the light of the lanterns above the guards' heads.

Red Vixen crept to the edge, where her eyes would catch in the light. I threw the blades, and the lazy Pronai was caught unawares. My knives landed in her collarbone and solar plexus, and she slumped to the ground.

The Qava guard's voice filled our minds. [Intruders!] I trusted Ghost Hands' telepathy might to be able to mute the guard's telepathic projection before it could reach the others. Red Vixen jumped the Qava, claws and fangs tearing at his cloak.

Stumbling back, the guard knocked Red Vixen off her feet with a telekinetic blast. As I saw her flying back, I charged forward, knives out and flashing in the lantern light. I dodged left just before thrusting in on him. I'd guessed well, only feeling the next blast on my right half. I yielded to the pressure, spinning like a top. With the force, I planted my knife in the Qava's neck.

Both guards down, we gathered for a moment at the door, before heading in.

I looked to Aegis, who nodded and gave the orders. "We can't be certain how many of Omez's guards heard that, so from now on, we assume that we've been spotted. But don't go tromping around just because. When we get to the main chamber, we split like I said. We can't do this halfway, not something this big."

"Ready?" It was as if she were asking herself as well as the rest of us.

We nodded, and then Aegis opened the door.

Down a long hallway was another guard station. Two rows of double beds and a sitting area; a half-dozen guards were already on their feet. Forked Lightning took point, clapping his bared hands together. The room filled with thunder, the lightning forking as it crackled out. The goggles only showed shades of red, but I could have sworn the lightning came through pure white.

Half the guards were on the ground when my vision returned. Another quarter were flailing and trying to put themselves out, shedding layer after layer of wraps, Omez's required uniform becoming a restrictive burden. The other four Shields entered the room and dispatched the group quickly. If the rest hadn't heard us by then, Forked Lightning's display did it.

We fought through two more groups on the way to the main chamber, taking two sets of stairs up to the guard overlook, where they could observe the Freithin pens.

The first thing I noticed was the smell. Omez kept more than three thousand Freithin in these pens, and he apparently saw no reason to give them any help in keeping things clean. Sweat, feces, and the stench of sickened bodies suffused the room. I couldn't imagine how they could stand it, other than to realize that the lung-choking soot of the factories was no better.

The room was the size of a city block, the pens stacked four stories high at the center of the room, surrounded by guard outposts at the cardinal directions, one per level.

Narrow bridges at each corner led out to the pens. The bridges, clearly made for the guards' use, were barely wide enough for a grown Freithin to walk without turning to the side. The larger Freithin would be forced to inch sideways until they came to the wider landings.

From the plans, I knew the landings to lead out to caged-in tunnels that led to the factories, with sentry ways above. The Freithin were monitored at every point, and always caged in, kept at a disadvantage. But the guard towers at the four corners had minimal visibility to one another. The pens had become too large, and Omez was too cheap to double up on staff. His greed became their opportunity.

"Get these people out; we'll take care of the Blue Heart," Aegis said, looking to Red Vixen and me.

I nodded. "Go quickly. Moving them will be hard with the heart still active."

The Blue Heart had been created to control the Freithin, to turn their inborn empathy into a leash. Designed for hard labor, Medai Omez and his team of alchemists had created the Freithin race sixty years ago in the alchemical vats of Sa-Yungash, across the deserts to the west. Omez brought the vats here, to Audec-Hal, and used Freithin as the backbone of his industry, creating laborers who could work harder and longer than anyone else.

But without the Blue Heart, they would be free to choose their own paths. Just as the City Mother's power had been turned by Yema to subdue the citizens of Audec-Hal, the Blue Heart kept the Freithin obedient, answering only to Medai Omez.

I watched Aegis, Ghost Hands, and Forked Lightning head for the far corner. A three-story-tall tower stood in the center of the room, with open glass walls allowing them to survey the Freithin 360 degrees. In addition, there were corner stations on each floor, outside along the walls.

I turned to Red Vixen. "We're going to take these outposts one by one. Make sure they're all cleared before we start moving the people. Hopefully, Aegis and the rest of them can destroy the Blue Heart before we need to move to the center."

She nodded. "I hear you. Evacuating a mass of homicidal Freithin is near the bottom of my list of things to do."

"Mine too. This way first."

As we circled around the room, I noticed that none of the Freithin were looking at us. They were all looking at one another, as if ignoring their observers. If you knew you were being observed your whole life, I suppose there was no need to be reminded of it every time you opened your eyes.

We were relying on the guards to focus on the cages rather the other stations. If they alerted one another and descended on us all at once, we'd be sorely pressed.

Three stations fell like clockwork. Attacking one station at a time, we only had to deal with groups of three. It was easy enough to lure one out to subdue and then go two on two with the others. The close-quarters fighting favored Red Vixen's natural weaponry and my dagger-and-fist infighting over the guards' massive two-handed clubs, which were designed to subdue the Freithin. And Omez's rank and file was no match for trained warriors.

We'd cleared the top floor and were heading down the stairs when we were exposed. Four silk-wrapped guards, staying close enough to cover one another, gathered around the landing between floors.

Red Vixen looked to me for commands, but I simply reached into my pouch and tossed down a smoke pellet. To their credit, the guards didn't panic, just held their ground. Fortunately, that allowed Red Vixen to crawl down between them and hamstring two before the others could react.

Seeing clearly, thanks to the shimmercrab goggles, I jumped off the top floor landing, sprang off the near wall and then the parallel wall to clear the guard's defenses, and delivered a kick that knocked one of Omez's still standing men into another.

We cleaned up that group in time for another. And another. Twenty guards later, we were on the ground level, with a growing collection of bruises and my left hand numb due to a direct shot from a sap. With numbers and a constrained battlefield, no one was good enough to go unscathed. Maybe the first Aegis, but he was long buried, the first to be laid to rest in the Hall of Broken Shields.

"How many of these bastards are there?" Red Vixen asked when the last group went down.

"Enough to make Omez confident in housing thousands of Freithin."

"Five thousand guards won't be enough when Aegis is done with the Blue Heart," she said, grinning like she'd just found a plump chicken.

With a quick chuckle, we kept going. I only noticed the smell when I wasn't thinking about anything else. My eyes slid to the pens, pulled by something out of place.

One of them was looking at me—a woman with skin a dull shade of sapphire, standing proud despite the tattered gray sack that strained to cover her body. Her eyes were narrowed, face pressed against the edge of her cell. I stopped, as if I were a schoolboy again, caught raiding the supply cabinets at school.

"What?" asked Red Vixen, tugging at my coat. "Come on."

The woman held my gaze for another moment; then the sound of a bolt whizzing by my face snapped me out of the trance and back into the moment.

The bolt came from a group of guards on the far wall, ten at least, with more pouring out from the door. Another volley of bolts arced toward us, and we hit the iron grates of the walkway.

The walkway shook with the rhythmic pounding of boots advancing. Red Vixen looked to me over her shoulder as another volley of bolts pierced the air just above the handrails.

"What now?"

"Now, we crawl. Come up when the others are between us and the bolts. Keep your head down, and fight low."

We started to crawl. It only took a few moments before the guards came back into sight, rounding the corner. I tossed out another smoke pellet, but one of the guards managed to kick it as it exploded, spreading the smoke off to the side. They passed by and left me to draw my knives.

Red Vixen and I came up in a crouch, waiting for them to close.

These guards were smarter than most. Instead of swinging the clubs at us, they pulled out knives and closed in, trying to use their numbers to bury us.

I rolled around on the walkway, with three guards wrapped around me, vying for position to bury their curved knives into my heart. I took shots to the shoulder, thigh, and the back of my still numb left hand, but kept going on panic-driven adrenaline. I stabbed one guard in the kidneys, slit the throat of another, and got to my knees to pommel-strike the third into unconsciousness.

Red Vixen was pulling herself from a slick pile of dispatched foes, the silver walkway becoming a mottled brown from the mixed blood of the various guards.

"Keep going," I said as I limped over the bodies, trying to stay low to escape the crossbows.

"When will they be done with that heart?" she asked.

"Don't know. Just keep going." I tried not to show the pain, but I could see blood had mottled patches of her fur as well.

I saw the crossbows first and pulled out of sight, holding Red Vixen back.

"Close your eyes." I pulled a flash stone from my belt, calculated the angles, and tossed it at the wall. The stone bounced off toward the guards, and I shut my eyes. The flash went off, and I rose up, left arm on the guardrail to guide my way as the light dissipated.

I leapt feet first into the guards, knocking two of them over as they clawed at their eyes. One of the guards kept her calm, shouting, "Draw your knives—they're here!"

She was the first to go as I scrambled forward over the two downed guards to shut her up. Either she was the officer and would have the keys, or she should have been, and needed to be silenced anyway.

I shoved a tall, gangly guard into the rails to clear space. He caught a hand on the rail as he flipped over the side. Good enough. I feinted a straight thrust, provoking the guard to dodge left, and then twisted the thrust into a cut that caught her across the shoulder, the blade slicing through layers of scarves and loose-fitting clothes. I twisted the blade to slide it in below her collarbone. She slumped to the floor, and I removed my knife.

Around me, Red Vixen tore apart the other guards in a captivatingly brutal dance. She took a club blow to the back and kept going. The Millrej was favoring her right side by then, from the earlier wounds.

The gangly guard that I'd written off tried to pull himself back up over the side. I gave him a helping hand—right into the far wall—then slammed him to the ground. He had wisdom enough to pass out, or at least fake it.

I looked around, checking for other guard stations. They were all empty. I scanned the pens, and the same woman caught my eye again, looking at me expectantly.

Ghost Hands' voice filled my mind, relief heavy in her words. [The Heart is gone. We're coming to you.]

"That's our signal." I reached down and pulled another set of keys from the belt of the female leader, adding it to those I'd liberated from the other guards. "Now let's hope we can get them out without too much of a riot."

It started with an unrestrained shout, like someone out in the open after having been shut up inside for too long. Then others joined it. Shouted curses, cries of surprise, disbelief.

The leash had been cut. I strode down the walkway leading to the cages, holding up the keys, and cupped my other hand to my face, extending my voice as far as I could.

"I am First Sentinel, Shield of Audec-Hal and sworn enemy of Medai Omez, the man who made you to be slaves. He used the Blue Heart because he knew you were too strong to be controlled otherwise. We are here to help you, to free you from this monstrous captivity."

More rustling, shouts from above and all around. I reached the corner of the cages, opened the door, and walked into the narrow passageway between the pens, where the guards led the Freithin to and from their work. I handed over a batch of keys to Red Vixen and began to open cells, shouting all the while.

"We neither expect nor demand anything of you. As of this moment, each one of you is as free as my companions or me."

An older Freithin man met me at the door, two thin threads connecting with my heart—white hope and yellow fear. I wouldn't know what to think of me, had I been in his place. I unlocked the cell and moved on.

"But while the tyrants still hold the reins of power, no one in Audec-Hal is truly free. Medai Omez's factories, COBALT-2's sick experiments, the Smiling King's Spark-touched, Magister Yema's Warlock Guard, and Nevri's economic stranglehold. Each of the five tyrants tries to make slaves of the people of the city, but we will not let them. That is not how the history of this city will be written. One day, the children of this city will learn of this time as a dark moment that was swept away by righteous people of Audec-Hal."

I opened more gates, watched shaking young men pacing in their cages, seething with anger, older Freithin hunched in their cells with scars crisscrossing their backs like a dense woven net. I saw the threads in the room shifting, bright colors of hope and anger flourishing while those of fear and obedience faded.

"The Shields of Audec-Hal are working toward a future that will have no tyrants and no slaves. Instead, we will return to being a city of equals, governed by peers who make choices in the best interests of the city as a whole. We wish to see the Senate reborn, and for Audec-Hal to shake itself from this decades-long nightmare."

In another cage, there was a mother and a suckling babe. The mother stood back from the door as I opened it. I swung the door inward and extended a hand.

"Come with us and we will help you get out of this building and find safe haven to hide from Medai Omez while he rages over his loss. If we could, we would lead an uprising right now to storm Medai's castle and cast him down, but we would need your help."

The mother held her baby away from me but walked toward the door as I moved on to the next cell.

"If you come with us, we can feed and shelter you, let you gather your strength to strike back later. The choices are yours; we are only here to help, to give back the power that is rightly yours. Each of you who join will bring the reign of the tyrants that much closer to an end."

I looked inside the next cell. It was her. The one among the Freithin who had watched me before the Blue Heart was destroyed.

"Medai made you to be slaves, but you don't have to be. I've seen great courage in the eyes of Freithin, wisdom and strength. I do not accept their claim over you. Your destiny is in your hands now."

She nodded, walking toward the door as I opened it. She extended a massive hand, and we shook.

"Thank you, First Sentinel," she said. "I am Rova Remembers, and I would fight alongside you and your Shields."

I'd heard a little about Freithin naming conventions. Not allowed to take family names the way others races did—those who did were publicly beaten—the Freithin had created a tradition of taking role names, Remembers, Watches, Protects, and so on.

"Thank you, Rova Remembers." I returned the handshake and felt like a boy again, my small hand dwarfed by hers. "I would be honored if you would join the Shield-bearers, our invaluable group of supporters."

"I will bear your shield and become a Shield myself. I've looked after others since I was old enough to guard my little brother. And I have a debt to settle with Omez."

From the energy I saw in her eyes and the strong shine of her threads—emerald and brass and white, I was fairly sure that Rova would become a full Shield, not just a Shield-bearer. A full-grown

Freithin as a Shield of Audec-Hal. My mind reeled at the possibilities, already planning.

"Find me once we're out of the area, away from Omez's guards, and we can talk more."

Aegis and the others arrived in the room; I distributed the rest of the keys. We opened the cages, Red Vixen and Ghost Hands on watch for the rest of the guards. I kept moving to make sure I didn't collapse. Medai's alarms brought wave after wave of guards, but we weren't five Shields anymore. We were five amidst a sea of Freithin, their red threads lashing out for anyone bearing Medai's colors or badge.

Dozens more guards flooded the room, seeking to stem the tide of blue bodies, but we could not be stopped that night. There was no charge to Medai's palace, as much as it saddened me. Aegis had the right of it when she told us, "One victory is enough for the night, especially a victory this monumental."

That had elicited a smile from me. She was starting to get it. I just hoped she'd live long enough to come into her full potential.

By the time the night was over, the building was in ruins, the cages shattered into a surreal jungle-gym several stories tall. Thousands of Freithin had broken into smaller groups, heading out to safehouses and the homes of Shield-bearers. We'd spent months preparing the space, but it'd be months more before we could get them settled into homes in other districts, outside of Medai's domain.

We hoped that the other tyrants would rejoice at Medai's loss and refuse to help him reclaim the errant Freithin. Leaving them free would mean more heads for them to tax and cheap (but not free) labor for their industry. In this city, one thing you could always count on was the tyrants' greed.

Three thousand more taxpayers were out in the city now, and hopefully and some fraction of them would become Shield-bearers, and maybe even one or two would become Shields. The city was one step closer to being free.

Chapter Twenty-One

First Sentinel

For several moments, the steady rhythm of turning wheels was the only sound in the train. Nevri regarded the Shields with an inscrutable smile. First Sentinel was very aware of the four Freithin looming tall in the train car.

Let's see if we can't get some more information before I rid the city of the woman responsible for its fall.

According to Ghost Hands' plan, Sapphire and Blurred Fists stood ready in the car behind them. Ghost Hands herself and Sabreslate were waiting at the checkpoint ahead. *We're as prepared as we can be. It's time to see who has the better contingency plan.*

First Sentinel started in on the gangster, trying to moderate his tone. He failed. "I think you forgot to mention something about the explosive you gave us. A Soulburner?"

Her face didn't so much as twitch. "Oh, that. You're welcome. After all, it was the only thing guaranteed to destroy the Rebirth Engine. And according to my records, that neighborhood gives your group a lot of trouble. Highest rate of Spark-storms, highest incidence of Spark-touched converted to the Smiling King's army. Consider it a bonus for services rendered."

Leaning forward in his seat, First Sentinel gave her the same look that had broken the resolve of a thousand criminals. "Your 'bonus' cost hundreds of lives."

Nevri leaned back—only a finger's span—but for First Sentinel, every bit of it was delicious. He saw flecks of yellow fear appear in the coppery-red thread tying her heart to his own. *I'm getting to her.* He restrained the urge to recite the names of his dead friends, to shove the names of the dead in her face. But he had to wait just a little longer. The checkpoint was coming soon. It would have been impossible to secret all six of them into the train at once. But this way, they'd all be there to see Nevri's end.

Nevri lifted a briefcase to her lap. "Despite your refusal to follow the schedule, I intend to hold up my end of the bargain," she said, changing the subject. First Sentinel suspected that the money might be booby-trapped, but didn't care. His eyes never left the Plutocrat.

First Sentinel leaned forward, going through the motions to take the briefcase at her feet. *Not long, now.*

She held up the suitcase, her hands full and her attention down on the lock.

They weren't to the checkpoint yet. Another minute.

It has to be now. There may never be a better moment.

First Sentinel leapt across the gap and closed his hands around her throat. His face went wild, eyes burning with fury as he squeezed her windpipe closed with his shock gloves. Aegis intercepted two of the guards as they closed in on the pair. First Sentinel's bracelet glowed with alarm, and he heard the rear door break open. *That'll be Sapphire.* His backup would be in here in an instant, and then it would be four Shields against four Freithin thugs and one helpless tyrant.

First Sentinel growled, "You won't get away this time. Not like you got away with your gang's crime sprees, not like you got away with buying yourself a Senate seat, not like you got away with burning the Senate house down and seizing the city and inviting monsters into my home.

"Not. This. Time."

And then, a dozen illusions dropped at once. The train car filled with bodyguards of all races.

Still not enough. City Mother, give me the strength to destroy the woman who corrupted your legacy. Let me avenge you, even if it is the last thing I do.

A thick hand grabbed First Sentinel's arm, ripping him away from Nevri. First Sentinel lashed out with his foot, aiming for his assailant's knee. The kneecap shattered, and First Sentinel reasserted his hold, pressing harder. Nevri tore at his grip, but she'd never been a physical contender. She had *people* for that.

First Sentinel rocked forward into a head butt, ramming his forehead into Nevri's nose. Dazed, her pawing stopped for a moment. He glanced side to side to read the scene.

A Qava raised a hand toward him. First Sentinel pulled the stunned Nevri off her seat, and they dropped to the floor. He felt her still breathing, but barely.

The telekinetic blast went over his head, ripping the train-car door off its hinges. There was a cry of pain from outside, and then the door disappeared to one side as Sapphire finished squeezing her way into the car. Air rushed in, pulling at his coat.

Sapphire grabbed the kneecapped attacker and threw him head first through the rear wall of the train car. She was a whirlwind of destruction let loose on the subway. First Sentinel crawled toward the Freithin, still holding his grip on the gangster-tyrant, who had started fighting again, kicking out at him with stiletto heels. He crawled to Sapphire's feet as she jumped over him, tackling two of Nevri's Freithin bodyguards. Aegis was being buried beneath a pile of bodyguards, but he kept them off First Sentinel and his objective.

Just a little longer, he pleaded. He could feel Sabreslate and Ghost Hands with them too, and Blurred Fists' hands hammering away somewhere behind him. They were all here, all witness to her end.

Sapphire caught a sprinting Pronai across the neck with a clothesline, sending him spinning up and into a vertical pole. She hit a Qava over the head with an elbow, and First Sentinel heard something crack.

Blurred Fists had already snuck his way in, dodging between the bodies until he was intercepted by two other Pronai. The three chased one another around the train car through the small spaces not occupied by fighting bodies. The train car went red from spattered blood and blurred motion.

First Sentinel took several stray shots to the head, ribs, and hips, several incidental and one heavy. One of Nevri's guards stomped down on his right heel, and he felt the ligaments tear and snap as his foot hyperextended.

He screamed the names of dead friends, letting out the rage and the pain. He curled his foot up instinctively but kept squeezing, continuing his litany, citing all the lives Nevri had snuffed out to get to him.

Nevri was out, but not gone.

Hold on, old man. Don't stop now.

Another shot to the head, and his vision exploded. But he didn't have to see, just feel. He didn't need to see to know his knuckles had gone white. They twitched, the muscles spasming and threatening to give way, to quit before the job was done.

A dull blow to the shoulder sent him end over end, and First Sentinel and Nevri slammed into the base of a seat. But First Sentinel didn't let go, not until someone kicked him in the solar plexus with a steel-tipped boot.

He sprawled, gasping. *Damnable. Weak old man, can't even do this one thing.* Through strained eyes, First Sentinel saw a blue fist coming at him. Decades-trained reflexes pulled him to the side, and the fist glanced off his temple. First Sentinel raised his arms to defend, keeping his hip braced against Nevri for reference. He tried to sit up, but pain in his hip dropped him to the ground.

First Sentinel was two men at once as he fought. One was Wonlar Gonyu Pacsa, the beaten and broken old man, barely able to move; the other was First Sentinel, the veteran hero, acting on trained reflexes and refined instinct. The part of him that was First Sentinel kept Old Man Wonlar alive, and he continued fighting. *End this now.*

First Sentinel grabbed the boot as it came down again, and twisted, pulling the attacker off their feet. The booted attacker and the Shield were a jumble, scrambling on the train-car floor. First Sentinel held up one hand with a shock glove to defend, while the other slipped into a leather pouch.

His voice called out, "White on one!" First Sentinel popped the flash stone a moment later, hoping his team had reacted fast enough. He closed his eyes but was still blinded by the point-blank visual overload.

Satisfied that the flash stone would incapacitate the booted guard, First Sentinel flipped around on his side, landing on his bad hip and screaming as he searched for Nevri's neck. *Seat, wall, shoulder, there.* His hands found purchase, but he didn't feel a pulse. *Nothing.* He held his hands in place for another half minute, continuing pressure, but there was no pulse against his hand.

It's done. The first tyrant to rise is the first to fall, and it's all worth it. He could die now and go happily to the arms of the City Mother.

First Sentinel's sight returned. Nevri's lifeless body slumped in the corner of the train car as the train rolled on somewhere south of Collar's Corner. Before he could stand, he took another shot to the ribs, and pain broke his reverie. The veteran part of him kept fighting, lashing out with his good foot and pushing the assailant back.

"Fade!" First Sentinel croaked, giving the order to retreat. The train car emptied in an instant. Blurred Fists was gone as soon as he spoke. Sapphire grabbed two Freithin guards, kicked open a door, and dragged the three of them out of the train car into the open air above the city.

First Sentinel pulled himself to the open doorway, looking to the skyline outside. He had strength enough left to bring up the grappling gun and land a line. Then Aegis was with him, wrapping his arms around the old Shield. The two of them rolled off the side of the narrow platform, between the train-cars, and dropped to the end of the rope as gracefully as a toddler falling on his face.

First Sentinel wrestled with his son to be on the bottom, and his legs dragged on the street as they landed, tearing his pants and painting the streets with streaks of orange blood.

He recalled the grappling line and rolled a dozen times across the street, losing hold of Aegis.

Pain swallowed him as he stopped, overwhelming the push adrenaline had given him. He lay on the street, a broken pile of bone and muscle. The gray sky darkened to black, and he felt the end coming on.

It was worth it.

City Mother, watch over my son, and he will watch over You.

Chapter Twenty-Two

Interlude—The Madman

It was dark in his room, the way he liked it during day-time, when he slept and plotted and played. There was one red-tinted light in the corner, by the door, where they came and told him things, where they brought the new playthings and took them away when he was done with them, bored or satisfied.

The Smiling King looked over to the bed, where the new play-things were struggling against their bonds. He'd had them bring two after the beautiful machine was destroyed.

Those monsters, inhuman, foolish, and near-sighted, why didn't they understand what he was trying to do? To free them all from the limitations of the flesh, let their spirits erupt from their bodies and dance with the beautiful storms.

The storms. He wanted a storm, yearned for it, to feel the change lick at his skin like the tides, to be caressed like a lover. Before the beautiful machine, the storms came to him so rarely, so few chances to add to the family. *And now they've taken it from me, those monsters!* He'd string them up in his tapestry, make them eager participants in his art.

They squirmed again. The playthings, not the criminals. They were not playthings yet, not this kind, just the playmates that sometimes cheated and broke the rules and broke his heart and left him to cry for days and days in the room, when he sent them all away, and the playthings too.

But today, today he wouldn't let them ruin his joy, his art. These two were beautiful, a brother and sister, plucked from a brothel. The boy's wide eyes were like caramel, his skin like a blooming flower, soft but supple, and they struggled in the ropes like they were a summer wind. And she was like a little doll, sharp features and raven-dark hair. Clumps of that gorgeous hair were spread across the bed, the scissors from his last game set on the bedside table. She was crying—they were both crying, their mouths bound.

They're so close, almost ready. Ready for Rebirth. "Now, my dears, it's time for another game. The winner will be the first to be Reborn. A new life and new joys, a part of my grand cast of players."

He strolled over to the bed, jumped on top and bounced before reaching over to their gags. The boy turned his head. *He's shy, the poor thing. Not for much longer.*

The Smiling King removed the cloth from the girl, tapped her button nose with his finger, and then turned to caress the boy's beautiful jawline while he twitched. *Still shy.* He removed the boy's gag, and the plaything started to plead.

"Just let us go, please let us go—we didn't do anything wrong."

The Smiling King dug his fingers into the boy, strong but supple flesh yielding to his touch. "We have a winner." He felt the change ripple through him, tickling him up and down. The

Smiling King squirmed and laughed, letting the change flow out into his new friend. The boy's skin darkened from yellow to dark, dark blue, midnight blue like bonnets in the nighttime, friends of the moon with its silver light, and his eyes turned silver too, little moons, wide.

He's still afraid, poor thing. "Don't be scared. Let yourself be Reborn." The boy's skin hardened, then cracked, patterns spreading across his skin like the dirt of a desert thirsty for rain. His bonds broke with his newfound strength, and the boy fell forward into the Smiling King's embrace.

He held the boy close, cooed to him and stroked his hair as the Rebirth continued. The boy's nose ballooned and popped, revealing a bare nasal cavity. His sister was screaming too, a discordant harmony between them separated by octaves and the Smiling King reminded himself to keep them together. *They make such wondrous music together.* The boy's screams modulated, shifted in pitch and tone, from fear and horror to exultation.

The Smiling King burst with excitement. "Yes, yes, yes! That's it! Embrace it!" The boy's skin shifted color again, turned white by the ivory sheets, yellow by the Smiling King's skin. The boy wasn't resisting anymore, his hands clutched to the Smiling King like a needy baby. He was Reborn into his new life, a blank canvas waiting to be turned into a part of the great tapestry. The Smiling King smothered the boy with a sloppy kiss and then whispered in his ear.

"Welcome to my family." He left his newborn child squirming with joy on the bed, and turned to the girl, her face stained with tears, screaming her brother's old name.

"Please don't! Let me go—I don't want to change!"

The Smiling King brought a finger to her lips, silencing her screams. He reached inside himself and brought up the rush of the change, reaching out with both hands for her pretty doll face.

"Hush. It's your turn now."

Chapter Twenty-Three

Aegis

They waited in the safehouse for two days. Two days of surgery and pacing and hushed talking. Two days of uproar and chaos on the streets. Aegis was nowhere to be found in the city during the chaos, because Selweh spent every waking moment at his father's side.

He'd studied every inch of the safehouse's four walls over the hours, committed it to memory alongside blueprints of warehouses and the indelible memory of his old home.

The safehouse was somewhere between the size of a large closet and a small apartment. It had one room and a beaten old bed that had smelled like a grandmother and had started to smell like near-dead Ikanollo, stained with sweat and blood and fading hope. There were no windows, no decorations but the bare wooden walls that splintered every few inches.

He stood in the same place he'd stood for the majority of two days, at the foot of the bed, looking at the sleeping form of his bandaged and beaten father.

Wake up, Dad. You're not done here. I need you, he repeated for the thousandth time, willing his father to recover, to wake up and lead the fight.

He kept hoping that Wonlar would wake up, emerge from the sleep that scared Selweh more with each passing hour. He whispered the hundredth prayer of the day and then began changing his father's bandages, starting from the broken ankle and working his way up to the probable concussion. Finally, Selweh wrapped another length of gauze around his father's shaved head.

Don't you leave me. Not now, not ever.

There was a knock at the door, and Selweh perked up, his hand finding the club he'd stuck into his belt. Then the knock finished—three quick raps and then one hollow pound. *It's Rova.*

Selweh set down the club, laid his father's head on the soaked pillow, and walked to the door. *Remember to get ask Mehgi for another pillow, or at least a clean set of sheets.* The apartment was hers, because she was the Shield-bearer nearest to the street where they'd crashed after the fight in the train-car.

They were lucky she had a spare room set aside for emergencies. His father had lost a lot of blood, and they'd been able to get Dr. Acci over within half an hour. *Father's web of contingency plans comes through again.*

Selweh saw Rova only as a silhouette, backlit by the naked bulb hanging from the hall ceiling. But the shining jade thread winding hopefully toward him couldn't be mistaken. The constant reminder of her feelings, the feelings he couldn't return, not yet. The mission needed all of his attention if the city was to be free in time to save his father from a bloody grave.

"Come in," he said, stepping aside as she ducked sideways under the lip of the doorway.

"Any change?" She put a hand on the foot post of the bed. Next to her it looked like a child's bed or a toy.

"No." The two stood side by side, a river of unspoken words crossing between them, until Selweh cleared his throat. "I need some fresh air. I'll be back in a minute."

She nodded. "Of course. Take as long as you need." Sapphire pulled up the armless chair from the corner of the room and set her weight on the edge, legs wide to support some of her weight. *I'll see if Mehgi has a stronger chair—something Rova can actually use without having to squat.*

Selweh waited at the door and watched his father for just a second more, then descended the stairs two at a time and walked out to the front stoop.

Out on the street, traffic was light, even at two before the academies let out. Mothers or fathers strolled up and down the street with small children; merchants pushed rickety carts along cobblestones and barked their fresh wares; there were few buggies and motor trikes. The air was sticky, an unseasonable rash of heat that had carried on for three days.

It wasn't the welcome heat of a warm spring, but the sticky heat of deep summer, the kind that made people shower three times a day and go running for the shade. His father would call it a symbol of the Shields' imminent victory, the coming summer after the long winter of the tyrants' rule, but that poetic idea was hard to swallow just right then.

Selweh fanned himself with a hand and took a seat on the stoop. His feet dangled over the edge like he'd done since he was a little boy. He watched the people pass him as just another Ikanollo, distinguishable only by the threads that bound him. Wonlar had given him a brass ring with inlaid emerald that provided the same thread-masking as the amulets the others used. *It used to be Aria's, he said.*

He sat there for several minutes, enjoying the slow flow of traffic and the slightly more fresh air. He hopped off the stoop to street level and started a circuit around the block. Selweh lost himself for a while in the rhythm of his steps, the heel of his shoes on the street. He listened to the sounds of the merchants' calls and babies' gurgling cries, the pedicabs whirring by, and took in the smell of smoke from the belching motor trikes.

In these simple moments, he could nearly trick himself into thinking that all was right with the world, that he lived in the version of the city that his father had told him about, the city he'd fought to restore, instead of a city enslaved. He saw the city the way he dreamed it would be once the war was over and justice restored.

As usual, the vision lasted only a moment. A half-dozen red-clad neighborhood guards walked around a corner, clubs in hands, scanning the street. Coppery threads of malice flailed about them, searching for an outlet. A baker saw the group and turned his cart to cross the street. His axle threw a wheel, and the cart toppled, spilling loaves of bread in the middle of the street. *That's going to be a situation in about three seconds.*

He counted in his mind as he walked toward the cart, non-chalant.

Just after he reached three, one of the guards blew her whistle. "You there! You're blocking traffic." The goons were Nevri's, at the bottom of the heap in her corporation. *Take a vacuum of power above them, add conflicting orders from all sides, and you have a great recipe for uncontrolled aggression. Simmer with heat until boiling.* Selweh bet they were just spoiling for a chance to lash out.

Thank you, City Mother. Something I can actually do something about.

The guards encircled the baker and his cart. Selweh didn't have his raiment, or the Aegis. *I won't need much to send these cowards running. They're as scared as the baker. Just better armed and more poorly mannered.*

"Let me help you pick up, sir," Selweh said to the baker, ignoring the guards. He picked up the wooden wheel and walked toward the group, coming up behind two of the red-clad thugs.

"Stay out of this," said an Ikanollo guard, tapping his club in hand.

Selweh raised his hands to his shoulders as the guard approached. "I'm just trying to help."

"We've got it taken care of," the Ikanollo said, swallowing the ends of his words, vein in his neck pulsing.

Aegis walked past the guard and lifted the cart enough to refit the wheel. Without the Aegis in hand, he had only a fraction of his strength, but it was enough for this small feat.

"How'd you . . . ?" the female guard asked, trailing off as she watched Selweh's Goddess-blessed strength. *That's right, I'm not just another Ikanollo. Why don't you leave?* he thought, half-wishing they had a Qava to get the clue.

Selweh knelt again to pick up a loaf with a hard crust, never taking his eyes from the crowd. Behind him, the baker quaked with fear. "I can help with the spill, officers. I'm sure you're very busy." *If you take the easy way out, I don't have to get my hands dirty or endanger the civilians. Or you can be dumb and start something.*

Your choice.

They decided on option two. The guard who'd called out the baker took an overhand swing at Selweh. He sidestepped and pulled the guard over his waiting foot, sending her to the street. Two more guards rushed him.

Selweh slid between one guard and the cart, pushing the first guard into the other. He kept going, pressing the next guard. They outnumbered him and had weapons, so they were able to land a few glancing blows. But in less than a minute, the thugs were splayed out on the cobblestones around the baker's cart, clutching nerve clusters and cracked bones. Selweh finished helping the man gather his wares. The guards had the sense to leave rather than try again. He bet that they'd be back in minutes with backup, but he'd be far gone by then, and the baker too, if he took Selweh's advice.

Selweh walked back to the apartment building holding a bag of still warm loaves of bread. The baker had insisted on giving Selweh a reward, and they'd spent more time arguing the point than it had taken Selweh to down the guards.

He knocked his code at the door, and after a moment, Sapphire let him in.

"Bread?" he asked, shaking a loaf beside his head, a smile on his face.

"What happened out there? I felt your adrenaline rush." She took the loaf and broke it. Sweet-smelling steam licked out of the loaf, and Selweh reached out to tear off a piece for himself.

"It was nothing. I met a very kind baker by the name of Bau. He runs Bau's Breads, two veins over."

Rova chuckled as she took a bite from her half of the loaf. Selweh set the bag down at the foot of the bed.

"Any change?"

Rova's silence was answer enough.

Wake up, Father. We need you.

"When is Dr. Acci coming back?" Rova asked a minute later, breaking Selweh from his repeated entreaties. "Tomorrow. If he doesn't wake up in the next day and a half, Acci says he may not wake at all." Acci had survived Nevri's purge, one of the few Shield-bearers who hadn't been targeted, which made him the Shield's last and only doctor.

Her heartbeat jumped. "I'll have Bira come by again. Maybe she can reach him this time . . . "

They were all grasping for hope, but if they give up on Wonlar . . . they might as well give up entirely.

Selweh lied. "That's a good idea."

The air was thick with silence and sweat for another minute, and Selweh went back to the door.

"I'm going to get something to go with this bread."

Rova waved him out of the room. "You've been cooped up here too long. Go take a real break, at least an hour. You're wound tighter than a grapple gun." She tapped the bracelet on her left arm. "And this time, call if you decide to make some new friends." She sent him off with a smile, showing that she didn't take it too seriously. Selweh picked up a bag from the corner, containing his raiment and, more importantly, the Aegis.

"And leave that here," she called after him. He didn't listen to her. The shield helped him think. His mind worked better with it in his grip. He couldn't say if it was the voices of the past bearers or just the comfort of habit, but it worked.

Nearly an hour after leaving the safehouse, Selweh was very happy he'd insisted on bringing the Aegis. At the north end of Collar's Crook, he heard the sounds of someone trying to batter down a door.

"Open in the name of the Executor!" someone shouted in a booming basso voice.

And which Executor do they mean? Selweh asked himself as he ducked into the nearest alley. He was met by a fifteen-foot-wide pool of sewage-covered concrete. Selweh took three dashing steps and vaulted over the pool, then hid behind a pile of trash. He set the groceries aside and pulled out his raiment. He donned the mask and exchanged his everyday tan shirt and worn black pants for the warded green-and-white tunic and leggings. Lastly, he drew the shining Aegis and ran his left arm into the loops, grabbing the polished handle. Aegis felt the shield's power wrap around him like the memories of his mother's embrace. *Now let's see what you're up to.*

Aegis took two steps back toward the street and leapt over the pool. He turned the corner and bellowed with the titan's voice, "Let these people be!"

He heard his father's voice in his mind again, an old lesson from when he was still Second Sentinel. *"Draw the public's attention, make it known that we are here for them, that we accept the responsibility and will not stand by while they are terrorized."*

Part of the crowd was arranged on the stairs leading up to the graystone while, the rest milled about on the street. They'd already taken down the door, so he couldn't tell how many were already inside.

Aegis activated his bracelet, hoping that Rova would be happy, or at least satisfied. Emergency alarms didn't tend to make anyone happy. *Except maybe Father when he's grumpy.*

Long strides carried him down the block as the former Plutocrat's thugs squared off. There were twenty of them all together, ten at the base of the two sets of stairs leading up to graystone apartments, the rest trailing up the stairs and into the buildings. Aegis raised his shield and barreled into the crowd, sending guards tumbling like pins of a game from someone else's childhood. *This is more like it.*

Selweh's games as a boy had been "I Spy a Clue" and "Tail the Grocer." Aegis had gotten into many fights as a boy, standing up for the Shields, so he knew well how to fight a crowd. Even so, twenty was a lot. If they actually knew how to use their numbers, this would go poorly for him.

Aegis swung the shield left and kicked out to the right, catching the chest of a surprised Ikanollo guard. The guard flew up and back into the stairs. Aegis heard bones crack as he spun the shield in a horizontal swipe, catching another guard across the temple. He leaned into the swing of a club and grabbed the offending arm, stripping the club and breaking it across the guard's knee. He took the opening and barreled out of the crowd, getting himself space again, never letting the group envelop him.

Aegis spent twenty seconds clearing them out, dancing between half-trained guards, grappling and throwing them around like rag dolls. When half their number lay on the street, the group broke and scattered, deserting their comrades inside the building. He didn't know what was happening in the rest of Nevri's district, but if it was as chaotic as what he was facing here, there would be far worse things happening that night than a simple break-in.

Aegis bound up the stairs into one of the graystones. He heard his father's voice in his head, saying, *"Bad move, son. Unfamiliar territory, quite possibly a trap. Don't go charging in. Check the doors; always keep an eye on the exits."*

Aegis grabbed the doorway and slowed himself just inside the landing. *What did they want in here?* he wondered. *Random chaos, some vandalism, and intimidation, or were they sent by someone?*

The old wood under his feet creaked as he looked down the hall. Nothing. He took a breath, listening to his senses and his intuition. The doorknob to the first floor apartment was over-turned—probably being held by one guard, with another two flanking with close-range weapons. He didn't see any other entrances to the first-floor apartment.

There was no way to be sure how many had gotten inside. Nevri's guards didn't operate in groups that large, but everything was off program, off pattern. None of the thugs below were lead-ing, which meant the leader was in there somewhere. Or maybe they didn't even have a leader.

Well, you have to start somewhere. Aegis kicked down the door and dove inside end over end, coming up to face the guards he was satisfied, but not pleased, to see. There were three of them, all Ikanollo. Two men held foot-long daggers toward Ae-gis as a female guard in the middle reached up to draw a long-sword from a back-slung scabbard. *Why did people insist on back scabbards?* They were uselessly awkward unless you had time to spare.

Aegis smiled. "I'll let you surrender if you tell me Nevri's latest orders." The information they had was worth more than the satisfaction he'd get by leaving three thugs sprawled on the floor.

They did not oblige. The woman brought the longsword for-ward in a powerful cut, her whole body moving with the blade.

Good form, he thought, raising the shield at an angle. Her strike was deflected and slid off to his left, the broadsword lodging in the wooden floor. *Too much follow-through, though.*

He lashed out with a right cross to the face, and the woman dodged back to take it on the chin instead of the temple. He pressed again and slammed her into the door as the other two closed.

He spun, putting his back to the door, and faced the two men. Aegis took in the room behind them.

Bare walls and three rough-carved chairs around a wrought-iron table. No sign of the inhabitants. Absent or hostage? Aegis reminded himself to check once he was done with the trio.

The two with knives had enough sense to come at him at once, but not nearly enough skill to capitalize on their advantage. Aegis sidestepped to the left, out of the arc of one knife. He knocked aside the other with his shield.

Aegis pivoted back toward the guards, lunging to hit one with a shield strike between the ribs. Then he pulled that guard off balance and sent them tumbling into the knife of the other, spilling orange blood across the bare floor.

Aegis backhanded the unimpaled guard with the shield and dropped the two to the ground. The swordswoman had picked up one of the knives and came at him again. But she held the knife like a sword, tried to cut him at distance.

"You can still yield and talk," he said, covering himself with the shield as she circled.

The guard remembered herself and lowered the blade, then came in with a brutal underhand stab. Aegis tucked the shield down, leading her blow to slide off the side. He entered behind the shield and hit her with a body blow, then grabbed her dagger arm and tossed her over his shoulder, laying her out on the floor. He stripped the knife and made sure she stayed down. She obliged.

With the guards all dispatched, Aegis paced through the bare rooms, looking for inhabitants.

The washroom and bedroom were equally empty, painting a picture of an office worker—or other single soul fortunate enough to occupy Audec-Hal's ever shrinking middle class—with a narrow unmade bed, a half-full bookshelf, and the bedroom dusted in a coat of dirty laundry.

Out of the thoroughness instilled by his father, he walked over to check the bedroom closet and was rewarded by muffled whimpers from inside. *There you are.* Aegis threw open the lock and door to reveal a middle-aged Pronai in a rumpled suit. The man dropped to the floor, hands and feet bound.

He squirmed on the floor at a panicked, comedic pace as Aegis dropped to a knee. "Calm down. I'm going to untie you."

Aegis pulled the sock out of the man's mouth, which let loose a flood of speech.

"By the City Mother, you're Aegis—never thought I'd meet you—thank you—wow."

Aegis continued untying the man's bindings. "Hello."

The Pronai sat up, wringing his wrists in a quick pattern as he continued. "They said they were looking for the Shield-bearers, and I said I didn't know, and—and then they tossed me in here and how long has it been—it feels like forever."

"What's your name, sir?"

"Farenkaonali," the man said as one syllable.

"Mister Farenkaonali, I need you to calm down. Talk slowly, if you can."

The Pronai took a breath and narrowed his eyes in focus. "Have they found him yet? First Sentinel? They kept on talking about First Sentinel, finding him, getting him."

Oh no. "What?"

"They said he was injured. They found out, wanted to get revenge for Nevri."

Please don't let them have found the safehouse. Or at least let Rova have fended them off.

Now they're going to hear I'm in the neighborhood and send more.

Sapphire's alarm gem was flashing along with his. He toggled his alarm off, so the others wouldn't split up. "I'm sorry, sir, I have to go. Are you hurt?"

The man shook his head. "Just banged up a bit. I'll be fine." Aegis scanned the apartment quickly, to make sure he hadn't missed anything, and then raced for the door. He called back to the Pronai man, "Thank you for the information. City Mother be with you."

Please let me be in time.

The door to Mehgi's building hung ajar, holding on by splinters to the doorway.

Sapphire, I hope you heard them coming.

Selweh scaled the stairs three at a time, a solid rhythm betraying his arrival to anyone with half an ear to listen, but he didn't care.

At the top of the three flights, he saw through an open door into the small room. A body was splayed across the threshold, one limp hand trailing over the lip of the stairs.

"Hello?" he called, holding the Aegis high without obscuring his vision.

"In here," Sapphire said as she crossed into sight. Aegis breathed out, relieved, stepping over the body to check on his father. Wonlar was still in bed, unmoving and undisturbed, Sapphire standing above him. The floor was covered by a half-dozen bodies of the Plutocrat's guard, broken and mangled.

"How did they find us?" she asked. "Did they follow me?"

Aegis shook his head. "It was probably me. We need to move him immediately," Aegis said, gathering up the bags, one eye on the door.

Sapphire nodded. "I was waiting for you to come back. Or for more of them." She gestured at the unconscious thugs.

"Get him out of here as soon as you can." Aegis held up the bracelet, tapping on Rova's glowing gem. "Ghost Hands should be here soon; then the two of us will find you, and we can get him to another safehouse. I'll clean this place out before we leave, for Mehgi's sake."

Rova scooped First Sentinel up, one arm around his shoulders and the other under his knees. In her arms, he looked like a sleeping child nestled against its mother's breast.

Sapphire took a breath. Something on the tip of her tongue tried to get out, but then she swallowed it. A beat later she said, "Take care of yourself. I'll see you soon." He knew what she wanted to say, and it was enough. The threads between them were woven by years of words unsaid, feelings buried for prudence's sake.

Aegis gave her a smile. "Go."

A nimble duck under the doorway, and she was gone. Aegis wrapped the guard's bodies in the linens and stacked them in the corner behind the bed, then arranged the trash and other supplies.

The room now as clean as he could manage without supplies or storage, he took a seat on the foot of the bed and waited. *Come on, Ghost Hands. Anytime now.*

Ghost Hands' voice in his head. *[You've been busy. Where's Sapphire?]*

"I'll explain while we get rid of these bodies."

[Lovely.]

City Mother, protect her. And my father too.

Chapter Twenty-Four

Sapphire

Douk was an excellent host, but he made an abysmal nurse. Rova had kept him out of the room, tending to Wonlar herself until Dr. Acci arrived. Wonlar's fever had settled a bit when she got him set in the bed. She had even managed to slip some more water down his throat.

It had taken her more than an hour to get through both Nevri and the Smiling King's domains, dodging patrols and roving bands of guards. She'd had to bribe three sets of border guards to get to Douk's Daily and safety, where she hoped Wonlar wouldn't have to be moved again until he was well.

Come back to us. We need you. Selweh needs you, and this city needs you. If you die now, your spirit will linger, and the last thing I want to do is burn your body in a bed of sea salt and force you to pass along.

As Sapphire sat in the café basement, watching over Wonlar, she heard bells ringing in the distance.

They'd have to be the size of a Freithin or two Ikanollo stand-ing back to back to be heard from the street. What would call for bells that loud?

The ringing grew louder, joined by muffled voices that Rova couldn't quite pick out. Unwilling to leave her post and risk an altercation or discovery, she waited. *Come on, Douk. Of course I need him now, after I've sent him away.*

Soon enough, she heard clumsy steps down the stairs and then a knocking code. Sapphire opened the door, and a flushed Douk launched into rapid speech, almost as fast as an agitated Pronai.

"The summit! It's starting tomorrow! The four tyrants are meeting, but they didn't mention anything about Nevri or some-one from her domain. They passed by with giant bells and a mass of troops wheeling a cart, with a Freithin herald bellowing the news. What are you going to do?"

Douk's expression, though interested, was not so much that of concern as excitable curiosity.

Sapphire looked to the unconscious First Sentinel, and then turned back to Douk. "First, we have to call a meeting."

Douk nodded and left. Rova sighed, rubbing her temples with both hands. This was First Sentinel's role, or Aegis. The responsibility felt uncomfortable; it weighed on her, gripping tight around her throat, trying to take her breath.

"Aegis should be here soon anyway. Send him down when he arrives, and we'll talk it over. Just make sure they all know about the summit."

Killing Nevri was supposed to stop the summit. *Now Dlella and Yema have united to ensure it comes to pass. The tyrants will band together and scour the city.* If Nevri's domain was representa-tive, they might have already started.

And our leader is still on death's door with a rapidly approaching appointment.

Sapphire returned to the bed and knelt, praying to the City Mother that she might look after Wonlar, after Aegis, after them all.

Chapter Twenty-Five

First Sentinel

When Wonlar woke, each tiny motion took an act of will.

He felt like he'd hit himself with a dozen drainer disks. *Lucky old man, you should be dead. Then the two carryovers from the past could be buried side by side.*

Instead, he was surrounded by his friends in the basement of Douk's coffeeshop. His bed had also become a desk, with maps and charts piled on the sheets. Selweh and Rova fussed over Wonlar like the caring couple they should be, doting on an invalid father. Douk brought *dounmo* tea, somehow just freshly steeped and perfectly hot, as if he knew when Wonlar was going to awaken. *Truly a miracle worker.*

Wonlar gritted his teeth and stretched out his leg. Over the course of several minutes, he moved, winced, collapsed, and then moved again, until he had pulled himself up to a sitting position, propped up against a shelf with a sack of flour as his pillow. He looked down, and there was a kingly meal on his lap—roasted chicken, root vegetables, and *yomu*-shell pasta with a red-pepper sauce.

"Douk, you should have been a chef."

Douk smiled. "Actually, Selweh made this. It was the only way I could get him to take a break from watching you."

"Tell me everything." Wonlar took a bite of the pasta and listened.

They told him about the fights in the street, the succession conflict, and the summit's beginning. He'd been out for a week. *I almost missed it all, and now I don't have time to plan.*

Wonlar blinked his eyes and focused on the scrawled schedule Selweh had put together for the summit. "We have to do something tonight, during their opening ceremonies. The tyrants will be together for the first time in years."

Bira spoke in his mind. *[And they'll be more heavily protected than ever.]*

She's right.

He thought back to the early days, when the Shields were just a handful of upstart kids and one hero. *Go where they aren't.*

"And that's why our target tonight isn't the summit." Even grinning hurt, but he didn't care. This was their chance.

"What, then?" Sarii asked, elbows forward on the bed.

Wonlar smiled as broadly as he did when he was surrounded by laughing children. "The Tower. Tonight, we free the City Mother."

Sarii threw her hand up in frustration. Bira asked, *[What?]* in an incredulous tone, and Wenlizerachi's eyes crossed. Selweh was still, his brow furrowed in thought. Rova leaned back, hand going to her chin.

"Even with most of the troops pulled from each domain, the Tower is guarded by all five of their forces," Selweh said.

Sarii shook her head. "None of them wants to leave the City Mother's temple unattended."

Yes, yes. I didn't say it'd be easy.

"But they won't expect it. The tyrants' best will be with them, Nevri's succession is still unclear. The cover of chaos is our best asset right now."

Selweh said, "But we'll be going in a man down, and you're the only person who has a chance of breaking the bindings."

"I'm going," Wonlar said.

"Don't be stupid!" Sarii slapped his leg through the covers. Wonlar bit down on his tongue rather than wince.

"She's right. You can't be serious about going on a mission," Selweh said.

Wonlar grunted. *Broken old man. If I had a new body, I'd storm the tower right now.* "How else do you intend to free City Mother when you get past the guards?"

"We should just wait until you're healthy. There are plenty of things we can do to interrupt the summit," Selweh said.

Wonlar took a breath, then a bite of food. He resettled and another wave of pain dropped him flat on the bed. Maps and plates toppled off, clattering to the floor.

"See?" Sabreslate said. *Damn her, she's right.*

"All right. Aegis, what are the other options?"

The flour pillow propped his head up enough to see the group, but he sat himself up again, despite the fresh pain. He took Rova's offered hand, going slower this time.

Selweh stood and started pacing. "We can hit the meeting place or make smaller strikes against holdings across the city to divert their attention. The longer they concentrate their forces, the more attacks we can make on their infrastructure."

"Omez's slave pens," Rova said. "He's built his numbers back up, to almost as many as when you broke me out."

Wonlar nodded. "Good. More."

"COBALT-3's laboratory," Selweh said, flexing his left hand. "Outside of her direct command range, the automata's AI will be weaker."

"Even better. What else?"

Rova glanced at Selweh, her gold thread of partnership dominant, keeping the jade in check. "With the right catalyst, we can start a riot in Nevri's domain. Her lieutenants and thugs have been pushing people to the limit. It wouldn't take much to tip them over the edge."

"And rightly so," Selweh said.

"What's the catalyst, then?" Wonlar asked.

Aegis stopped in place. "I am. It's been a while since I stirred up a good riot."

[Where do we direct the mob?] Bira asked.

"Nevri's security compound," Wonlar said.

"So, what? They can give the guards crossbow practice?" asked Sarii.

"If we're going to mobilize that many people, it has to accomplish something," Selweh said. *Of course. But the compound means casualties. Lots of casualties.*

"What else could we do with the mob?" Wonlar asked. "We do need to put the mob to some use, but can't we send them after something less dangerous?"

Sarii sculpted a bland office building with a scrap of stone, holding it in her hand. "Central corporate offices?"

Selweh snapped, a thought striking him. "That or the Plutocrat's bank."

Wenlizerachi said, "The bank is protected as well, but it has more of a draw. If we did it, we could give people back decades of taxes."

Wonlar set his empty plate aside. He barely remembered eating it. But hunger was good. Hunger meant he was healing, that he'd be able to rejoin the fight faster and end the war. Selweh took the plate and offered to get more. Wonlar waved him off. "Just tea."

Back to business, Wonlar thought, already feeling stronger. "Five Shields and a mob against the Plutocrat's bank. You'll need tools to get into the vault unless you get enough Qava and Freithin in your crowd."

Rova stepped back and walked around the bed. "We can handle the vault door. I'm more worried about their response team. Within half an hour we'll have the whole security division on top of the bank anyway, and then the casualties will be massive."

It's a better plan than my suicide run on the tower. The tower can wait for when I'm better and we've whittled down their forces.

"It's violent, it's dynamic, and it necessitates a response. We're striking in a weakened domain. We go tonight unless someone has a better plan," Wonlar said.

"I still think we're overextending ourselves," Sarii said.

She may be right, but we've come too far for caution. "You're the one who wanted us to do more, take risks. We don't have the breathing room to play small anymore. Without the tyrants' infighting, they'll come down on us with everything they can muster, and we'll constantly be on the run. Let's at least make it a running battle instead of a Dead Woman's Chase."

After a few more minutes of details, they were agreed. *Tonight the war goes to a new level, and I'll be stuck in bed.* Wonlar sipped his tea and asked for the newspapers and reports. He had to catch up—and fast. They'd put the tyrants on the defensive. Time was always the ally of the establishment, and Wonlar was tired of waiting.

Chapter Twenty-Six

Interlude—The Sorcerer

The halls of the Audec Academy of Artifice were ornate, carved graystone laid down centuries ago, maintained by frequent treatments. First-year students learned to make the unguent of preservation, and only those who succeeded were allowed to move on to the greater mysteries. Yema had been one of them, a lifetime ago.

Magister Yema ran a hand along the wall, felt the grooves of the mural that told the story of the fall of Audec, the founding of the city, and the birth of the City Mother.

Yema had left this place behind years ago, when mere science could no longer hold his attention. *Artifice was so limited, merely pushing the elements to their limits, instead of shaking the foundations of the world itself.*

He heard shuffling in the room ahead, the flapping of wings, sycophantic birds hopping about, courting favor with the other oligarchs. This one sent his assistant to talk to that one's assistant; talking circles around one another, always angling toward another agenda. They built tentative alliances with whispers and baseless promises behind doors that had survived the tide of years.

He cast open the doors, and heads turned toward him.

The newest oligarch was the first to respond. Dlella, would-be heir apparent to Nevri's corporation, sat forward on her tail, arms crossed. Her eyes locked on Yema, and then she nodded. She seemed to have learned Nevri's lessons well, but she was untested. Her territory was across the city from his, so he would neither be threatened directly if she succeeded, nor would he be in a position to attack her if she failed. *Still, best to watch her closely.*

Yema looked to the Smiling King. The madman's head was lolled to the side, twenty colors spilled over one another like his face was a canvas. The Smiling King chanted a nursery rhyme and stroked one of the seven hands belonging to his deformed assistant. The seven-handed man leaned into his master and cooed, three other hands scribbling away on separate sheaves of parchment. *Disgusting.*

The little birds flapped their way out of Yema's path as he took his seat and threw back his cowl to display the tattoos that adorned his head, proof of the pacts he had made, the power he held. Yema turned to Medai Omez, nodding to the slaver in his shifts and wraps in bright yellow and green. Medai was backed by his four cowled bodyguards, tall blades slung over their shoulders. The merchant smiled with golden teeth, then resumed turning a pair of blue cloisonné balls in his palm.

Ever since he'd lost control of his blue beasts, Omez had been cautious, weak. But the merchant-king had a talent for making a mask of his intentions, and even Yema's spies had failed to discover if the scarf-clad slaver would ever again wield power the way he had in the first years since the Senate's fall. He still had slaves, yes, but his new crop of Freithin could not compare to the herd he had lost.

Yema turned at last to his left, where COBALT-3 stood—never sat—at the far side of the table. Her chrome plates shone from polishing so diligent it couldn't be the work of mortals.

Magister Yema had preferred her father: less attached, more clear in his focus. His peer, ally, and rival to the south had inherited her grand-maker's preoccupation with the mysteries of organic life, but she paid handsomely for additional test subjects. And Yema was always happy to take a rival's money.

"Shall we resume?" Yema asked. Today he officiated, set the agenda, and controlled the flow of the summit. After Nevri's death, it had been Yema who took the reins, insisting that the summit continue. Dlella backed his assertion, trying to claim Nevri's seat before it was even cold, but her boldness served his purposes.

In taking control of the summit, he'd accepted the responsibility that came with it, the corralling, the appeasing. He'd had to force the Smiling King to stay on task and keep Dlella's dagger eyes from provoking COBALT-3 to pull out the Millrej's forked tongue.

Children, all of them.

Medai pulled his chair in, making more noise than needed. "Yes, let's."

Yema looked to the Smiling King, who had ceased the rhyme and looked at Yema with rare clarity.

"We were discussing the matter of the insurrectionists' boltholes." Yema waved his hand, and a map of Audec-Hal appeared on the blank yellow wall behind him. "Nevri succeeded in razing and destroying over a dozen, but we've identified more, locations that were kept back from Nevri's original effort. I understand the need for our caution, especially given the late Plutocrat's recent demise."

Medai shifted in his seat, nervous. The Smiling King collapsed into a fit of profanities, clawing at the air.

"But if we are to end the threat of the Shields for good, we'll need to be more trusting with information before we begin our assaults. Ideally, we will be able to attack each one at the same time, to catch the Shields by surprise."

The Smiling King slapped the table. "Flies! Damn flies!" Then he licked his hands, sucking in a broken carapace and cracked wings.

Ycma continued, ignoring the madman. "I propose that we each make a list of known and suspected hideouts in our own domains, then coordinate our strikes."

"Agreed," said Medai Omez.

Dlella nodded. "Yes."

"Affirmative," said COBALT-3.

The Smiling King smiled. "Damn flies, squash them all, flies. Tasty with bacon and chives. Chives and flies."

Yema cut the Smiling King off before he could get too far from the topic. "Moving on, I'd like to talk about security rotations for the district gates. The Shields have been able to move between districts too easily. I'd like to propose more restrictions on movement between districts."

"I respectfully disagree," said Dlella. "It will not be sufficient to stifle the Shields' activities, and it will hamper trade. We've known for years that they use Audec's bone hollows when we crack down on intracity travel."

COBALT-3 turned to Yema, catching his eye. Yema nodded, and COBALT-3 spoke. "Agreement: The Magister is correct. Assertion: Restricting passage will limit their activities and reduce the difficulty of maintaining surveillance on their operating areas."

Dlella hissed. COBALT-3 and she locked gazes, eye to sensor.

The Millrej rose, scaled tail looping around her chair. "And it will slow trade between domains, reducing our revenues. That in turn reduces the number of soldiers we can pay to search for the Shields. Then they will merely steamroll our forces and escape. Again."

"Erroneous assumption. Fact: Approved mercantile shipments and movement can be granted high priority to enable uninterrupted trade."

Yema stepped in. "Does anyone else have a comment on the proposal?"

Medai Omez stood. "I would like to hear more specifics before moving to a vote. What kind of additional measures are we suggesting?"

Clarification, specifics. *I carved out my territory in this city to rule, to leverage power into more power. Not to debate specifics with a quartet of psychotics and dull-witted amateurs, Yema thought.*

He sighed. One day, he'd be rid of them all, and there would be peace. The summit would let him crush the Shields, and then he could rub out his competitors, one by one.

Then the city would be peaceful again. No Shields, no oligarchs—just his firm hand controlling the future of Audec-Hal. The thought focused him as he jumped in to move things forward once again.

Chapter Twenty-Seven

Aegis

Wonlar had always told him that the war had begun at the Republic Bell. It was only fitting that the war's ending start there as well. The bell itself was eight feet tall and half that wide, old copper long since gone to verdigris. Aegis wondered if it could even be polished back to its original shine, or if it had been too long left.

He looked around the four entrances to the plaza. The bell was surrounded on all sides by government buildings. They'd never been officially claimed by Nevri, so they'd been hollowed out and turned into a market. Anyone could sell there, as long as they paid Nevri her thirty-five percent.

Ghost Hands spoke in his mind. *[We're in place.]* The late-afternoon crowd was thick, not as thick as he'd like, but it would have to do. *Momentum builds quickly, but I have to get it started.*

Aegis ripped off the gray cloak he'd used to hide his raiment and leapt up onto the platform that housed the Republic Bell. He raised the Aegis high and rang the bell loud enough for the whole district to hear. Once, twice, three times. Before the tyrants, three bells had called for a public assembly. Only the older citizens would even remember the significance, but his father had insisted.

All eyes in the square moved to Aegis. His emerald, white, and silver raiment caught the fading sunlight, making him into a shimmering jewel.

His voiced filled the plaza, clear and compelling. His father has always been a wise man, a powerful man, but no other man or woman in Audec-Hal had the presence of Aegis.

"People of Audec-Hal, listen. We stand on the edge of liberation."

"Nevri the Plutocrat is dead by the hand of First Sentinel, Shield of Audec-Hal. I stand before you to say that the future of the city is in your hands. The Shields alone cannot free this city. We are your champions, but six women and men alone cannot turn the tide. Only you, the people, can truly pull Audec-Hal out of the nightmare it has endured these last fifty years."

The people shuffled, murmuring. It was the same anytime he spoke. *They want it, but so few are willing to risk themselves, their families.* He saw the burgundy threads hold fast, strangle out the nascent emotions he'd stirred up. *But now I add the incentive.*

"For years Nevri and her associates have taken the spoils of your labor, taxes for everything imaginable. Extortion without reason, tax without recompense. And where does it go? To Nevri's corporate bank, not five blocks from here."

Aegis paced around the bell, drawing people in from all directions. He glanced up to see Ghost Hands and Sabreslate quietly subduing the few tyrants' guards in the area, and hoped they had yet to signal an alarm.

"How would you like to reclaim that which is rightly yours? Take back decades of taxes and forced bribes? The tyrants and their finest guards are half a city away right now, plotting how to better oppress the city. Join us and we will storm the corporate bank, throw open the vaults, and you can retrieve what is rightly yours."

Some nodded, and a few even cheered. *Now more.* He had to control the passion, shape it to the city's need, make an army and not just a mob.

"Do not take more than your claim; we have to share with one another. Divisiveness, jealousy, and infighting are their tools, not ours. This city is one of cooperation, equality, and fairness. We offer you a chance to right the balances. And tonight is only the first step. Spread the word, for by this summer's end, the tyrants will be driven from the tower of The Crown. The republic of Audec-Hal will be restored. All of this is within our grasp!"

The crowd was energized, freshly formed purple threads of earned authority streaming out to Aegis' heart. "Now come with me, and we will take back our city!"

The crowd started to shift, ripples of motion gaining momentum.

And now we move.

Aegis pulled out his father's grappling gun and fired toward the north entrance. The rope carried him up and over, depositing him at the head of the crowd. He nodded to Sapphire, and then turned to the people.

This could go poorly so fast. City Mother, guide us.

"People of Audec-Hal, this way!"

They followed. Slow at first, as the crowd jumbled, not yet moving together. After years of decrees prohibiting the assembly of unrelated adults, decades of living with one eye on the lookout for the guards, the people of Audec-Hal didn't quite know how to be a group anymore.

In another generation, the city might be too far gone. Parents could tell stories of how the city used to be, but few children would take up the banner as fervently as he or Blurred Fists had. *Revolution was in our blood; it's not in theirs.*

They moved toward the bank, slow and deliberate. People leaned out windows and doorways, pulled by curiosity, and Aegis drew them in with snippets of his speech. He held the shield high for all to see, and the crowd grew, drawn to the last symbol of the City Mother's benevolence.

He trusted in the others to help keep the group in order and avoid attrition from those whose nerve broke before the fight. He wouldn't push, wouldn't coerce. He could call to each man and woman's patriotism. *And to their greed, really, but is it greed to desire the money you've earned with your own labor?*

They crossed out of the residential district of office workers into the financial district. Aegis crested a hill, and the bank rose into view.

The guards had mobilized, as Aegis expected. He counted several dozen armed soldiers in the street, and guessed there would be twice as many inside.

He lifted his voice to project over the crowd. The mob trailed for blocks behind him, a sea of heads and shoulders. "There it is!" Aegis pressed the gem on his bracelet to call the team forward. "Shields on me! Citizens, follow us when we've taken care of these guards!"

Aegis bounded forward to the head of the crowd. A volley of magical blasts fired off from the guards' assorted artifacts, but he held the Aegis out ahead, and nothing connected.

He couldn't risk the glance over his shoulder to make sure the crowd wasn't hit, but he didn't hear any cries of pain, and hoped for the best. *Focus, Selweh. Break them fast. We can't hold this crowd together for long.* He charged into the mass of guards, sweeping the Aegis to bowl over three waiting Ikanollo.

No turning back. Forward, on until the tyrants are deposed or the last Shield is buried. No more waiting, no more skulking in shadows. *Finally.*

Aegis joy and excitement exploded in a rallying shout, "For Audec-Hal!" and the battle was joined.

The street had become a meat grinder of chaos and stampedes, flashing blades and pressing crowds. The Shields and their crowd had the guards outnumbered ten to one, but the guards were better armed, and Aegis spent most of his time keeping the citizens rallied.

A large Millrej bear-kin guard with jet-black fur and a pronounced snout had forced five citizens back against the wall of the bank. The bear-man spun a thick quarterstaff, administering blows like a cruel master-at-arms punishing his problem students.

Aegis shouldered another guard out of the way and leapt to their aid. He deflected the quarterstaff up and away and pushed the bear-kin onto his back.

He took the five under his wing. Three men and two women, all in their twenties it seemed, outclassed but earnest. Earnest was good. Will could make up for many deficits, if properly prompted and guided. He just had to keep them alive.

"Attack two or three at once, vary high and low strikes, and watch both sides of that staff." The bear-kin crawled to all-fours and roared.

We need to get a foothold inside the bank if this is going to work. Aegis pulsed in with a feint, drawing a bite from the guard. Back-pedaling, Aegis grabbed the Millrej's snout-mouth and wrapped his right arm around his jaws. *Got you.*

Aegis called, "Attack!" The group of five swarmed the guard. They picked away at him with their small weapons, knives and trowels and clubs. The Qava woman buried her fire poker into the guard's side, no doubt pushed by her telekinesis. The bear-kin growled in pain through its closed snout.

The Millrej reared back, pulling Aegis off the ground. Aegis released his shield hand and hammered the Aegis down onto the bear's head while his team picked away at the bear-kin's sides. A paw struck the Qava woman on the side, knocking her down.

"Get clear!" Aegis called, driving the shield into the Millrej's head again. The Millrej cried out in pain and collapsed into a hirsute mass.

Aegis shouted, "Form on me and press inside!" Then he spoke in his mind, hoping Bira would hear him. *[Ghost Hands, blow the doors, now!]*

He turned back to his unremarkable squadron and drew them forward. One of the men was a Pronai. He'd be able to move between targets quickly.

"Stay close to me. Keep them off my back, and attack with me or one another. Never fight alone. Call out if you're in trouble. The most important thing you can do is communicate."

The doors were covered by a pair of Freithin; a Millrej wolf-kin wielding a case of rapiers; and a Jalvai, who stood horizontally out of the wall. The Jalvai had raised a half-circle barrier up out of the street to bar any intruders.

Aegis called in the wreckers. *[Ghost Hands and Sabreslate, doors on three.]*

He crumpled a passing guard with a roundhouse kick, then pulled back and spread his arms to steady the squad. "Wait for my mark."

Ghost Hands swooped over the crowd, raising both hands. Several bolts and arrows shot up at her and were waved away; their angles tweaked just enough to fly wide.

[Two. One. Mark.] At the mark, Sabreslate widened her stance, sinking several inches into the cobblestones. Aegis saw and remembered the ordeal she'd put herself through the night they'd destroyed the Rebirth Engine. But she didn't show any signs of slowing down.

At the same time that Sabreslate sank into the ground, Ghost Hands gestured toward the wall. The Jalvai construct cracked, and the guards behind it lost their footing, falling against the doors. Metal bent with a pained groan, and the struts strained. Despite the women's efforts, the reinforced steel of the doors held fast.

The Jalvai guard scrambled to repair the wall, but Sabreslate emerged beside her and grabbed the woman, leaving the semi-circle only two feet high. The two of them disappeared into the stone wall in a jumble of kicks, punches, and grapples.

Another wave of force cracked the wall and pulled one of the steel doors off its hinges. "More!" Aegis called, scanning the Shields' forces, taking count and making calculations of what to do when they'd breached the doorway.

Ghost Hands shot out another wave, sending guards diving for safety. One of the Freithin guards jumped out of the way, avoiding the blast by diving into the surrounding citizens, fighting with power, but not control. If they couldn't hold from the door, then they'd make a perimeter. But that would mean they were more spread out. And that gave him an opening.

"Sapphire, form on me! Ghost Hands, push the left flank!"

Aegis called his squadron forward, along with another dozen citizens. They were bound to one another by a thin band of dull green of casual partnership, but were joined to him by strong purple threads of loyalty, tinged with silver adoration. They'd fight for Aegis, but not one another. He would rather have it the other way around.

Selweh had borne the mantle for three years, carrying on a tradition decades in the making, goaded on by the ghost of the four patriots who had given their lives for the city. The people followed the ghosts, the shield, and the concept of Aegis more than the man or woman who bore the title. *Do I really deserve that loyalty? The only way to be sure is to keep earning it.*

A crossbow bolt shot toward his face, and his training took over. He ducked, and the bolt whistled overhead. He heard the version of Wonlar in his mind again, instructive more than chiding. *Stay in the present. Contemplate later.*

"I'm here, Aegis." Sapphire filled the space behind him, and he formed a huddle, looking to his fellow Shield and the nearby citizens.

"We're taking the door. Sapphire, move right and engage the Freithin. I'm taking my squad up the middle. We need to take the door so everyone can get inside. I'm leading them in; can you hold the door?"

"Your squad?" The question had a touch of doubt.

Aegis smiled and looked around, clapping the shoulders of the citizens to his right and left. "Yes, my squad. Can you hold the door?"

"Of course."

"For Audec-Hal."

"For Audec-Hal," was the muddled response. *We'll have to work on battle cries.*

Sapphire led a group off to the right, engaging the rampaging Freithin and the remaining guards hunkered behind the short wall. Overhead, Ghost Hands was slowly ripping the door out, the sound of tearing metal a slow constant in the background.

He addressed his squad. "We're going to break through the middle. Stay with me, and don't stop." They were all surrounded by yellow bands of fear flapping in the wind, entangling the purple and silver, threatening to shear the newer threads.

"You can do this. Trust me and trust one another." The yellow in the bands dimmed as the purple and silver lines broke free, then braided themselves around the fear and squeezed.

A dozen bloodied bodies were strewn about the street the attack already taking its toll on their mob. Weblike rivulets of blood filled the mortar hollows between the cobblestones. The crowd was still massed, and they were fighting hard, overwhelming the guards, but at great cost. *And we haven't even made it inside yet. We have to move faster or give up.*

The door fell free and crashed to the ground, sending up a cloud of dust.

Aegis looked up, raised his shield and his voice.

"People of Audec-Hal, charge!"

He led the surge himself, adopted honor guard at his heels and a motley host in tow. On the right, Sapphire plowed through a trio of guards and tackled the wild Freithin, clearing the path to the door.

On the left flank, Ghost Hands had most of the guards pinned against the wall, assaulting them with stray weapons and debris. A large Millrej guard fired crossbow bolts as fast as she could, but did little to waylay the Qava.

The rank-and-file guards on the door had spread out to cover the left flank. Aegis hit them with a wave of bodies and overwhelmed the guards, pressing inside the bank.

His eyes adjusted to the lower light, but it was his ears that cued him in as taut strings snapped loose. "Down!" he called, leaning forward behind the Aegis. A half-dozen bolts glanced off the shield, but he heard even more find deadly purchase elsewhere.

"Close the distance; don't let them pick you off!"

Aegis charged into the crossbowmen, bounding over a long counter filled with blank deposit slips. Ten in the middle of the rank dropped their crossbows and went for their swords. "Close!" he called again as the room filled with his army.

There were another fifty guards inside, most posted in the center crossbow line. Behind them, another ten stood around the vault door. The last group was back and to the side, flanking the guards at the vault. Reserves. They'd press when he most needed them not to.

At the vault door, a serpentine Millrej reared up on her tail and laughed. "I had hoped you'd survive long enough for this. I wanted your head for my own, the first prize to mount on my desk as Executor Dlella."

He wasn't surprised that Dlella had made a power play for the position of Executor. Hold the bank and you held the domain's power. And if she could repel their attack, she'd cement her spot among the oligarchs.

The four can't be allowed to become five again.

"Don't clear your desk too soon, Dlella. Or have you not noticed the hundreds at my back?" He raised his shield and a cheer erupted, more people spilling through the doors every moment. His host numbered the better part of two hundred, and by the time they engaged, it could be as many as three.

The nearest reinforcements would be a district away. And by then, the people would be entrenched; they'd be doing the defending while he and a select few looted the bank to get the money to distribute.

Aegis thought loudly, counting on Ghost Hands to keep her attention up. *[Put Sabreslate and Blurred Fists on the door, and watch for more guards. Dlella's in here with some of them. Keep the reinforcements out of the bank, and we can continue as planned. Alert me when they arrive.]*

Aegis advanced slowly, the shield forward to protect against the crossbows. "You can back down, Dlella, keep your forces intact. I'm sure you aren't stupid enough to leave all your cash in the primary bank, are you? Not a smart move if you're bankrolling a coup." The crowd behind him shuffled in place, nerves and fatigue tearing at their energy.

Have to make it sound good, rally their spirits.

Dlella hissed. "I'm not going anywhere, Aegis. Bring your common horde; throw away lives like chips in a game. Every heart that stops beating is a tally in my ledger. And when I have your head on my desk, their will to fight will evaporate."

Aegis scanned the crowd, re-evaluated his numbers. *It'll have to do.* "Take the vault, and watch the left flank!" he shouted, and pushed forward into another charge.

Dlella's guards unleashed a volley of crossbow bolts. Most shattered on an invisible sphere of Ghost Hands' making. Aegis and his forces crossed fifty feet of finely tiled floor and took another crossbow volley before reaching the vault. A red blur emerged from the crowd, with steel-gray streaks following it.

Aegis brought up his shield as the blur approached, and a blade skittered off the side, forming sparks in its trail. *Pronai bladesman. No, woman.* That would be Red Whirlwind, another of Nevri's heavies. If she had already thrown in with Dlella, then the Millrej was already well positioned to succeed Nevri as the Executor. *Not good.* He had hoped for more infighting, less unification.

"Get Blurred Fists in here now!" Aegis shouted, hoping they could spare him on the outside. Aegis scanned the room for Red Whirlwind, expecting another pass. He caught her too late, a painting of blurred gray lines and spouts of blood appearing to his left.

She's eviscerating their entire left flank, softening it up for the reserve group. Aegis kicked an Ikanollo guard in the gut, pushed off, and turned, trying to catch up to the Pronai slaughterer.

Aegis cried out above the din of battle. "Why don't you stop dulling your blades on them and face a real challenge, Whirlwind?"

The woman's answer came in the ringing of steel on steel as a sword glanced off the Aegis. He felt a sting along his thigh, then saw the line of orange through the cut in his raiment. *Better me than any of them.*

"Fists!" Aegis tracked the lines, anticipating the next strike as it came overhead, then sidestepped to the right, keeping the shield up and reaching out with his leg to trip the Pronai.

His interior First Sentinel voice spoke again as Aegis closed the distance: "*The more you can tie her up, the less she can use her speed. Turn it into a brawl and you'll have her on muscle. Make your opponents' strengths their weaknesses.*"

She lashed out with a thrust to the chest. He dodged to the side, but his body void wasn't fast enough, and he felt the sword slice him below the nipple before the Aegis stopped the swing. The sword stopped by his shield. Aegis grabbed Red Whirlwind's wrist and squeezed. *Got you.*

He channeled the pain into his grip. Aegis felt a crack but couldn't hear it over the melee. Her sword clattered to the floor, and Aegis brought her in as close as a lover.

The Shield reached around with his left hand and forced the other blade out of her grip. He pulled Red Whirlwind off the floor and slammed both of them into the tile, the Pronai on the bottom. He heard more cracking, and then she vanished from his sight. A hunched red river poured through the crowd and streaked out the door.

That will do for now. Aegis stumbled to the side and then picked himself up. *That cut needs a bandage immediately.*

"Rally to the vault!" Aegis shouted to the crowd inside, his voice strained. He reached out to Ghost Hands, calling, *[I need Ghost Hands or Sapphire to the vault door immediately. Red Whirlwind just vanished. She's wounded but might re-engage. Keep your eyes open, Fists.]*

In front of the vault door, Dlella drew a slight Qava woman up in her tail and sank her fangs into the woman's neck. The Qava's brown skin paled, veins running blue with poison, and Dlella dropped her to the floor, spasming. The snake-woman then wrapped her tail around an Ikanollo man in a threadbare suit.

As she pulled him in, Aegis jumped between them and filled her mouth with the shield. Dlella distended her jaw, opening wide to dislodge the Aegis. He let the shield drop free and flipped around the Millrej to grab her around the neck, just below the opening of her hood. Aegis wrapped his legs tight around her core and squeezed. *Let's see how you like being constricted.* His strength was diminished without a direct connection to the shield, but it was still enough for the task.

Dlella flailed and writhed, rearing up to her full height. Aegis was level with the top of the vault door as he rained punches down on the back of her head. He spotted Sapphire wading through the crowd in the middle of the room. He punctuated his thoughts with blows to her head. *Between the two of us, we should be able to force the vault door.*

The Millrej bashed Aegis against the vault, trying to shake him off. They traded blows as Sapphire approached. He tasted copper on his lips and felt blood dripping down his shirt. His grip slipped when Sapphire pulled on Dlella's tail. The two of them dropped toward the tile. Aegis pulled on Dlella, maneuvering around to land on her rather than the ground. The air went out of his lungs when they hit, but Dlella was limp below him, coiled on the floor.

"Thank you," he said after catching his breath.

Sapphire beamed, her jade thread shining from his praise. "Shall we?"

Aegis nodded. He looked down to grab Dlella and hand her off to someone as a hostage.

She was gone. He scanned the room, trying to pick out her scales. Aegis bit back a curse and reached out with his mind to draw Ghost Hands' attention.

[Dlella's gone. I think Red Whirlwind pulled her out. Keep your eyes open.]

"Let's get the door," Aegis said to Sapphire.

He turned to several loose clusters of citizens, bruised but determined. "You, empty the drawers behind there. Spread the money around, and get it out of the building immediately!" The groups pushed toward the teller's area. A Freithin woman wrenched open the door, making way for her smaller companions.

Sapphire wrapped her hands around the brass wheel while Aegis retrieved the shield and moved to the hinges. He brought down the Aegis on the joints as Sapphire forced the wheel. The metal warped in her grip but it turned, even while groaning in protest.

A few seconds more, and the vault door snapped off the lower joint. Guards were swarming the door, but they were held at bay by the citizen army. The citizen army wouldn't last long under the pressure, not without the Shields leading them directly.

"Faster!" Aegis turned and took control of his forces. "Hold the line! Stay together, and defend your neighbor!" The vault continued to groan and creak. *Come on, Sapphire.*

Off to one side, the group he'd sent off passed bags of marks through the crowd, each person taking a handful of bills. If nothing else, they'd given people a taste of victory. The money could pay for a long overdue doctor's visit or put food on the table for a hungry family.

"Almost there," she shouted through grunts of exertion.

Aegis swatted away a pike aimed for a Jalvai's head. "Push them back, and prepare to move inside the vault. This is a choke-point—the advantage is ours."

Risking a glance over his shoulder, Aegis saw the vault door jutting out toward the bottom. Sapphire bent over and tried to rip it out of the upper joint. She pulled clockwise, then counterclockwise, straining and stretching the metal. *It won't be long now.*

He held the line against another wave of guards, pushing forward to lead from the front, a kick here and a swing of the shield there. With Audec-Hal's greatest warrior at their fore, the people were brave, sharp, and powerful. Their threads of gold and red shone brighter than he'd ever seen from anyone but a Shield or Shield-bearer.

Is the City Mother with us somehow, working against Yema's corruption of her power?

Most likely, it was just the strength of the citizens, stirred up enough to overcome the threads of control. *The strength is their own; all we're doing is letting it show.*

Aegis heard a creak, then a tear. He dropped a Jalvai with a roundhouse kick and scanned the door as he turned through the kick. Sapphire threw the vault door open.

"Twenty of you—inside with me. Sapphire, hold the door, and then follow us in!"

Aegis dropped back, handing over control of the bank door to Blurred Fists. Aegis' squad and more followed him through the vault door, into the tall room with shelves running all the way to the ceiling, numbered and ordered bags and boxes—and guards.

Lots of guards. Instead of having most of the security outside the bank to dissuade them, or even inside to keep them from the vault, Dlella had arrayed the majority of her guards inside the vault itself. Nearly every inch of the floor was filled with the boots of her forces. The dozen felled by the door left enough space to charge in, but Aegis backpedaled as he saw the overwhelming numbers.

He thought loudly once more, so Ghost Hands could relay the situation. *[I see the better part of a hundred guards inside the vault. We'll need everyone inside now if we're going to go through with this; otherwise, we pull back now. What's the situation outside?]*

He listened, but there was no response. Aegis hoped the message had gotten through via Ghost Hands. There were so many people in the fight, so many thoughts to sort through. He kept his squadron close, and they held the opening to the vault. If nothing else, he could keep the guards inside from getting out into the main floor of the bank.

Ghost Hands' voice filled his head. *[We're going to be swamped in about half a minute. Reinforcements coming from both sides of the street. I was just about to bring everyone inside and move to a siege defense.]*

Aegis threw his frustration into a punch that lifted a Pronai guard off the ground and crashing into his comrades, sending all five of them tumbling to the ground. *[No good. We'd be surrounded in a vulnerable position.]*

Scenarios and possibilities played out in his mind. None ended well. *[We can't do it. Sound the retreat. I need a new door out the south side of the building in less than a minute. We get the citizens out first. Dlella's guards will stick with us.]*

[All of this for nothing?] asked Sabreslate through the mental link.

[Not nothing. Several thousand marks in bills are already making their way into the crowd]. But it should have been hundreds of thousands.

Aegis yanked a guard's halberd out of his grip, sent them down with a kick, then handed the weapon to a citizen on his right. "Keep them at bay; use the reach it gives you."

[Plus, we stirred up enough anger and courage to start a focused riot. I wouldn't call that nothing,] Aegis responded.

Sabreslate said, *[A couple thousand marks won't go very far in a crowd this size. This momentum will vanish as quickly as you were able to muster it.]*

[And if we stay, those people who might fight for us again will all be dead, and us with them,] Sapphire said.

[We can argue later. Get people out safely, now.]

First, he had to control the group in the vault. He pulled out a fire grenade that contained magic bound to an explosive core, and tossed it all the way into the back of the vault. It landed clattering among the stacks of gold and platinum.

The explosion filled the vault with dust and smoke and shouts. If Aegis was lucky, it'd ruin tens of thousands of marks of currency and would keep the mass of guards confounded until they could stumble over one another and out of the vault.

Then he called for a controlled retreat, consolidating their forces. He threw the vault door closed again and locked the spindle wheel handle in place with another guard's halberd. *[It's decided. We're leaving. Someone make me a new door on the south side of the building.]*

[I'm on it.] Sapphire jumped fifty feet over the crowd and landed by the south wall. She hammered on the wall, forming dents with each blow.

Aegis shouted to the crowd at the top of his lungs. "We cannot take the vault, and there are more guards coming. We have to leave—now!"

Shouts of disappointment and anger rolled across the crowds, threads twisted and turned ugly, gold and purple threads fading. *And just like that, we lose them.* Some would remember the money, the thrill of momentary success, but most would just return to their lives, this day forgotten.

The haft of the halberd cracked, and the vault door swung open. Guards poured through the door, pushing Aegis troops back. They filled the room around the citizen's army and pressed the flanks.

[We're getting heavy pressure from the vault. Tell the citizens outside to scatter and fade, head to the back alleys. They can't chase

everyone. Sapphire, get that door as fast as you can.] Hoping to give Dlella's forces something else to worry about, he took out his father's flame wand and shot a few gouts at the tables, chairs, and nearby wall.

"Grab as many wounded as you can!" Aegis shouted as he led the retreat from the vault door and Sapphire's position at the south side of the building. He searched the crowd for Dlella, hoping she'd retaken the field, but the Millrej was still missing. *Damn.* He picked up a wounded Ikanollo and a limp Pronai and hauled them over his shoulders.

As he approached the side wall, Sapphire's bone-shattering roundhouses tore out chunks of brick. *That's enough.* "Out the hole, now. Scatter ranks! Keep yourselves out of the guards' hands. Live today, fight tomorrow. This is just an early blow for the revolution, many more will follow. You are all heroes. Remember this day!"

Aegis continued to encourage the people even as he urged them to run, passing wounded through the hole while holding off the massing guards.

[Hole's open on the south side, vault guards closing in. Update from the outside?]

[We're caught in a crossfire. Dozens have broken and are running through the back ways. We can't hold for long.]

Aegis heard Sabreslate snicker through the telepathic connection. *[Won't need to. Meet me outside the bank door, and I'll get us out of here.]*

The moments stretched long as Aegis ushered the rest of his people out through the hole, fighting off three or more guards at once to cover their retreat. The Executor's forces grew more bold, feeling the tide turn in their favor.

Aegis swatted spears and swords away, always in motion. But the more he had to fight, the less he could lead.

Sapphire held out a hand as the guards closed in. "Grab hold—
it'll be faster." Aegis tore a glaive out of a guard's hands and swept
four more guards' weapons with it, his swing ending a thrust to
an Ikanollo's collarbone. He jumped back and reached out with
his right hand as Sapphire wrapped her huge hand around his
wrist. He grabbed with his shield hand to protect his shoulder,
and Sapphire leapt high over the melee, taking the smaller Shield
with her.

Crossbow bolts followed them as they arced through the
air, but the shots went wide. They landed by the door, beside
Sabreslate and a hovering Ghost Hands. Outside, Dlella's forces
had merged and surrounded the door.

Ghost Hands maintained a force field by the door, keeping
the exterior forces at bay. *[Go ahead. I'll hold them off and take the
high road out.]*

Blurred Fists appeared out of nowhere, and they were all
assembled.

"This was just the beginning! The days of the tyrants are near
an end!" he shouted toward the crowd. The crowd was a mob no
longer, just dozens of scared and wounded people running for
their lives. *I failed them today.*

Sabreslate called for the Shields to circle up. They joined
hands inside the shrinking bubble of protection. As one, they
sank into the ground, the cobblestones rushing up to greet them.
Aegis wished the stones could wash away the sting of failure.
They'd done so much, assembled a force of hundreds, with so
little to show for it.

Chapter Twenty-Eight

First Sentinel

*I*f it weren't for Douk, I'd drown in boredom. I'd also be down fifteen pounds from the recovery. Instead, Wonlar was well fed by
constant servings of gossip and an endless supply of tea, pastries,
and salads.

It had been three days since the failed bank attack. The
Shields were licking their wounds and waiting for another opportunity. *I'm going on the next mission, no matter what Selweh
or anyone says.*

The summit was fully underway, and Wonlar could sometimes see a hammer floating overhead, waiting to drop.

Wonlar had full reign of the basement, a kingdom made of
crates and towering piles of coffee beans. Douk had brought down
more furniture, all from the Post-Republic art movement. They
were harsh, soulless, all hard lines and cold metallic hues. In one
corner, Douk had brought out the seasonal supplies, preparing
the multicolored flags of Midsummer's March, the fifteen icons of
the story of the plummet, and more. Each day Wonlar discovered
some new knickknack stored away in a corner. Xera was a pack-

rat, and there were supplies left over from parties ten years gone. She called it being prepared. Wonlar approved.

He spent the morning organizing stacks of Douk's paperwork so he could have a proper desk, when a familiar voice broke his silent calm.

"My friend, I have something you simply must hear!" Douk tromped down the stairs again, opening the conversation as he'd opened the last twenty. *Everything he tells me is "critical" or "amazing." City Mother bless him for his enthusiasm.*

"What's happened this time, Douk?" Wonlar asked.

The flush and sweat of excitement played out on Douk's face as he talked. "I just saw people taken away in a wagon, right in front of my own café! Just five ordinary people, chatting on the corner. I think they were deciding on what to order when they came in, but that's just me. After all, why stand on the corner outside my café if not to come in and enjoy my fresh-roasted coffee, the camaraderie, and the wonderful food?"

Douk could ramble for the better part of an hour, given the slightest prompting. Wonlar found him most useful when guided. "The wagon, Douk."

"Of course. It's about as wide as the street and twice as long, painted in a garish green color that hasn't been in fashion since the fall of Audec."

"Why did they take them?"

"Some horrid made-up reason, said that the people were suspects in the attempted bank robbery."

"But that wasn't even in this domain." *Is this one of the results of the summit?* If the tyrants were pooling their resources on law enforcement, extraditing across domain lines . . .

"I know! The leader of the guards doing the roundup was a top-heavy Freithin woman. Her shoulders were covered in spikes and wider than a double door. She said that they were working in collaboration with Executor Dlella's forces."

If the Smiling King has recognized Dlella, Wonlar guessed the others had too. *We need to break up those meetings, keep the tyrants from cohering into a lasting partnership.*

"Anything else?"

"I saw inside the wagon. There were more than thirty people in there. They kept going down the street, picking up people at random. I heard patrons say they'd seen other wagons the last couple of days. How many do you think there are?"

Wonlar answered Douk's question with another. "And where are they being taken?"

Douk glanced to each corner and then shrugged guiltily, as if his ignorance were a failure. *You can't know everything, my friend.* "I'll ask people what they've heard, but I don't imagine anyone who comes to my café would know something like that. I can go out right away and speak to some of my acquaintances in the corporation."

Wonlar shook his head. "Don't put yourself out for this. It just means we have to track one of the wagons back to their holding location. Get a message out to Blurred Fists and see what he can do."

"Of course! We can't allow this to continue. And by we, I mean you, but really we, the city and its people. Can I bring you anything?"

"A new pen, more paper, and more tea. I need to think."

Wonlar pulled out a map and tried to decide where this wave of kidnapped citizens could be taken. Candidates for the Warlock Guard, subjects for COBALT-3's experiments, wage slaves for Dlella, or new subjects for the Smiling King?

Douk nodded at Wonlar's comment and then scaled the stairs, reinvigorated by his continued involvement. One of these days his support was going to get him killed, and there wouldn't be any more pastries, no more protracted meetings over the smell of his Yehbu Grey roast. One fewer flower left to bloom when spring came again.

Chapter Twenty-Nine

Interlude—The Successor

T he newly self-minted Executor slithered across the floor, deepening the sand mounds formed over weeks and weeks of nervous slithering. Dlella had claimed Nevri's title, but not her actual office, not yet. Soon she would fully slide into the power gap left by Nevri's timely passing.

One by one, the Lieutenants will swear to me, and I will take the corporation to places Nevri even dreamed of. Expand abroad to consolidate Ibje refinement, streamline supply chains, and crush the Shields for good.

Dlella's office had marbled walls and no furniture save for a pile of pillows in one corner where she could recline. A broad window draped the room in sunlight for her afternoon naps, where she soaked up the warmth to stay energized.

The bank robbery had been thwarted, though not without losses. Consolidation was the current order of business. The summit was an excellent chance to forestall hostilities from the other oligarchs, take time to breathe, get the loyalty of Nevri's other lieutenants. Backing Yema's play to continue the summit gave her cache with him and let her show her savvy to the others. She'd learned long ago from Nevri that although money solved most problems, only reputation could solve the rest.

She'd pushed back the Shields' mob, but her work was not yet done. Not all of her former peers had come to their senses and sworn to her as the new Executor.

Qazzi Fau was due presently, and her head was still dull from Aegis' hammering fists, three days after the fact. She picked up the wide cup of medicinal tincture and took another sip, swirling the hot liquid around her forked tongue and letting it cool slightly before swallowing. The warmth coated her throat, and she felt pain leech out of her body as the hot liquid ran down her throat. Weakness was a luxury she could not afford. This she also learned from Nevri, one of a thousand lessons Dlella was putting to use as the late Executor's successor.

There was a knock at the door, and Dlella beckoned in her twitchy Pronai secretary. His shaking hands held a notebook and a pen.

"Qazzi Fau is here to see you, Executor."

Dlella continued her slithering route, feeling the sand give way to her tail. "Wait here for a minute, and then send him in."

She would let him know she was in control. She needed his support, but as a subordinate, not as the peer he used to be. Qazzi would bring with him the forces of the northwestern territory under his supervision, control of the Right Shoulder gate and the entrance taxes and tariffs that went with it. If he broke faith with the corporation, there would be a civil war in her territory. *That cannot be allowed. He will swear to me or die.*

Another knock, and Dlella said, "Enter."

The governor of Right Shoulder entered the room, one hand hanging on his sword belt. His Spark-touched eyes appeared as blank white orbs, but they could see color and texture perfectly well, along with the threads as any Ikanollo. His eyes saw one other thing as well—the future: possibilities and likelihoods. That power made him a useful ally and a deadly opponent. He used it mostly in combat, but Dlella wasn't sure if it extended outside of the martial arena.

Does he know how this meeting is going to pan out already, or is he uncertain as well? Dlella hid her pain, hid her nerves. She put up the perfect façade of an Executor, unquestionable and all knowing. They'd been equals, rivals, for years, but that ended today.

"Welcome. Please, take a seat." Dlella opened her arms wide, and then settled back on her coils.

Qazzi took a place in front of her desk, assuming a wide stance, arms crossed. "I don't want to squander resources on a succession war, so I've come to make a bargain."

To the point. She'd always appreciated that about him. "Tea?" she asked, continuing the niceties she knew he didn't care for. But insisting allowed her to keep the conversation under her control and avoid his overbearing momentum.

"No."

"Very well." Dlella snapped twice and a rodent-kin boy rushed in with a pot of tea and two cups. The boy poured her a fresh cup and left the other cup empty at Qazzi's side. "I will require the support of your security forces, full cooperation on administration and logistics, and forty percent of the transit taxes and tithes from the Right Shoulder Gate. You will accompany me to the summit and show your support. When they know you are under my protection, you will be able to continue your hunt for First Sentinel."

Qazzi didn't move, didn't blink. He was nearly impossible to read. He let her words die out, waited a moment. He responded in a flat voice. "Twenty percent, and I will have full jurisdiction on hunting down the Shields. And I want governorship over Cane's Collar."

Twenty? Dlella swayed behind the desk and took a sip of her tea. Qazzi didn't move.

"Thirty. You'll have jurisdiction inside my domain, but the hunt for the Shields is an all-city matter. I am cooperating with the other oligarchs. We are pooling resources so we can wipe them out before they regroup. Nevri underestimated First Sentinel, and she died for her weakness. I will not be that foolish, and neither will you." She tried to leave no room for disagreement in the tight cadence of her words. But would he fall into line?

Qazzi drew his sword and held it up, caressing the blade with his free hand. "Twenty-five, and you will make it clear to the Oligarchs that it is my blade that will take First Sentinel's heart."

He wasn't threatening her. Or so she hoped. Qazzi regarded First Sentinel as the last great prey, the only one who had escaped him. He'd already killed one of the Aegises, but he'd never been able to keep the Shields' aged leader in his grasp. First Sentinel was a reminder that Qazzi could fail. For such a cunning warrior, Qazzi exposed some weakness quite easily.

"Done. I'll have the paperwork for the particulars sent to your office." She imagined that if she made him do the busywork himself he'd likely just stab it and send it back in pieces. He was a warrior, not a bureaucrat. But he was a leader and had some of the city's finest killers on his payroll. And if she was going to be the Executor, she needed to follow the proper channels, so the foreign trade partners would acknowledge her. There'd be time to reshape the corporation soon enough.

"Watch your back, Dlella. Their desperation gives them strength. We will not play like Nevri did. This is war, and we will leave no survivors." Qazzi sheathed his blade, then turned and walked out the door.

Former rivals for subordinates, former enemies for allies, and former annoyances for arch-enemies. Dlella's had become an interesting life. She resumed her slithering route with a smile.

Chapter Thirty

First Sentinel

L ife in wartime meant the Shields had to be even more cautious. The daytime patrols were doubled, night patrols tripled. The strain would eventually wear on the guards' combat readiness, but the summit and its resolutions had slowed the Shields' movements to a crawl, even after Nevri's death.

If they had to take four detours around closed districts every time there was a meeting, they weren't going to be able to respond to anything. The tyrants had fully leveraged their control over the city, but trade had dried up. By Wonlar's calculations, the tyrants couldn't keep the restrictions up for more than a week without seriously undermining their bottom line, but that would be enough time to complete their summit and finish whatever resolutions they were debating. Assuming the tyrants were motivated enough by Nevri's death to come together and put aside their decades-old grudges.

They're playing to their strengths, so we have to play to ours.

The first night of increased patrols, Selweh led a raid to torch one of Yema's barracks in the middle of the night. The next morning, the Shields robbed several tax offices and distributed the money among the districts surrounding the failed bank attack, building on the seed of goodwill in that area. Every day brought two, three, even four missions. Three days into the lockdown, the Shields' time frame had grown very short. Missions were born, planned, and executed in hours rather than days or weeks.

Strange that we're at war and I'm bored out of mind. The others are running themselves ragged, and all I get to do is wander around in Douk's coffeehouse and listen to everything secondhand.

The idleness eroded his patience like rain on the cliffs of the city. He was involved in planning most of the missions, but the closest to action he'd gotten since Nevri's death was watching a few brawls outside of the coffeehouse and seething that he couldn't intervene.

But it couldn't be helped—his leg still refused to accept his weight. He'd tried to walk without a cane that morning and had dropped to the floor like a sack of three-grain flour.

Selweh stepped down from the kitchen and gave him the smile that he'd had since he called his father "Wonner." "Good news. The proceedings for the day were cut short. Smiling King assaulted Dlella, and Yema stormed out."

Wonlar scaled the stairs oh so slowly and hobbled out into the back room. Douk's back room ("the party room," he liked to call it) had abstract paintings titled *Revolution* and *Renewal*, several early sculptures from Sarii before she stopped taking commissions, and a circular glass table with seats for three.

Wonlar lowered his voice and took the nearest seat, setting his cane against the table. "The fire?"

Selweh nodded, continuing to pace. "Yema got into his carriage in a huff at noon and hasn't been seen back since."

"Excellent. The more we can get them worried about their individual problems, the less they'll think about pulling together."

Aegis pursed his lips, thinking or gathering courage, then said, "I want to go back to COBALT-3's laboratory, the one where they held me."

Selweh stopped and shuddered, no doubt remembering the cold tables and the meticulously brutal experiments. Then his son smiled wide and said, "If we wait much longer, all of the intelligence I gathered while escaping will be useless. There are probably eigthty citizens in there, and I can't let them suffer."

Wonlar nodded. "It will raise our profile, showing we can still fight even when the tyrants are at the ready. Good. Tell Bira I'm coming along this time."

Selweh crossed his arms, his eyes narrowed. "Do you really think we'll let you?"

"No, but eventually you'll give in. We need everyone on this."

Selweh put a hand on his father's shoulder and cracked a smile. "Even the broken-down crotchety ones?"

Wonlar laughed. *How is it he always knows how to make me smile?* Wonlar stood, wavered for a moment, then placed a hand on Selweh's and sank back to his chair. "Especially those. I'm going with you." *I'd go mad if I spent another night in here, useless.*

Selweh hugged his father and left for the front room. Wonlar was alone again. Just a broken old soldier whose war was passing him by. All this for the death of one woman. Their gambit to end a war was merely sending the city careening out of control. *Good job, old man. You caused this, so you have to fix it.*

He set aside his cane and pushed down on the sides of his chair. Pain exploded in his leg, but he growled, straightening on his strong foot. He wavered, put a hand to the chair, and then let go, standing on his own. He laughed again, grabbing the cane and setting about his preparations. This was going to take a lot of tea.

Chapter Thirty-One

Aegis

The sun was already a memory by eight, hidden beyond the cliff above the resting bones of the titan's foot. The bones were stacked against the canyon wall, the ends covered by the accumulation of soil. In one of the stories he told to the children in Bluetown, Wonlar said that Audec's skeleton was merely slumbering all these millennia. And one day he'd wake up and obliterate the troublesome city that had grown up around him like industrious carrion. *If he hasn't woken to crush the tyrants, I don't think he ever will. It's up to us.*

Selweh watched the street traffic from the corner outside Douk's coffeehouse, leaning against the wall as the moon took to the sky. Three patrols had passed in the half hour, each from different directions, and not a one went by without stopping to hassle someone every block, asking for papers, warning that there was a curfew, or demanding a toll. He wanted nothing more than to stop them, but making a scene would expose their position.

Selweh ducked back inside of the coffeeshop and saw his companions at rest. Bira and Sarii played a round of "Titan's

Bones" while Rova and Fahra played their tenth game of checkers at one of the high tables. Rova sat on a low chair and faced Fahra, who dangled her feet off one of Douk's tall bar stools. The arrangement necessary to put them on the same level brought a smile to Selweh's lips. He grabbed hold of that smile, wrote the memory into his mind, adding it to the memories of being young with his father, of nights spent curled up with books, and the joys of discovering the wonderful alchemy of food. They were armor as much as the reinforced cloth of his raiment, especially in the past week when missions and planning crowded out sleep.

His father still hadn't emerged from the basement, and it was past the time they'd set to leave.

Selweh saw Wenlizerachi blur through the kitchen, pursued by Xera, who wielded a stale loaf of bread, laughing. Audec-Hal's champion wove his way around the mock conflict and down the stairs to the basement.

"Father?"

Selweh heard a sharp exhalation of breath, then, "Hold on." He took two more steps down the stairs and saw his father straining with the tall boots of his raiment.

"Are you all right?"

Wonlar grabbed the boot and shoved his foot inside, eliciting a popping sound and another wince. Wonlar reached to his side where three mugs steamed with liquid—*dounmo* and his elixirs.

"You don't have to come along tonight," Selweh said.

Wonlar finished off the mugs in quick succession and stood, trying to hide the pain. "None of us have to do this, son. We do it because we push ourselves, because we can't wait for someone else to do it for us. Now give me a hand with the coat."

Selweh helped his father into the rest of his raiment, watching Wonlar gather his strength. His father put aside the shroud of illness that had wreathed him since Nevri's death and rebuilt the mask of First Sentinel, just as Selweh had learned to put on the face of Aegis when the shield found him. Eyebrows narrow, lips tight, shoulders back, and chin up, whole body at the ready. *Make everything about you say, "I am in charge; you do not want to get in my way."*

His father was nearly seventy years old, and the man put on the face better than anyone Selweh had ever seen.

"Bring them down. It's time."

Chapter Thirty-Two

First Sentinel

Everyone knew that Audec's bones were hollow. Children in every district were raised on the stories of the shardlings and the other horrors that dwell in the bone pathways. Most people were smart enough not to use them. *Often times, we don't have that luxury. This is one of those times.* In order to bypass the district-by-district lockdown, the Shields took a route through Audec's right hip to get into COBALT-3's domain.

Shimmercrab goggles showed him the vast interior of Audec's hip in red-scale, the steep drop-off to his left below the stable pathway. He'd walked that path a half-dozen times before, and the safest route was also the highest up, near the front of Audec's hip. The six Shields walked in a tight formation. Ghost Hands hovered above the group, keeping her attention open for any of the denizens of the hollows.

[Anything?] First Sentinel asked in his mind for Ghost Hands to hear.

[Not yet,] was her response.

Blurred Fists scouted forward again. He'd run ahead a hundred yards, then sped back to rejoin the group and report.

"This place always makes my blood cold," he said.

"I know," Sapphire jerked her head around to look over her shoulder. "Did you hear something?"

First Sentinel shook his head.

[I felt nothing,] Ghost Hands said.

He resumed walking, leaning on the cane for as long as he could before pushing himself in the real fight. "Keep going. I want to get to the laboratory in the blue time so we can be out by dawn."

First Sentinel heard the sound as Ghost Hands spoke in his mind.

[There's something ahead.]

Skittering. The sound of bone on bone.

"Sounds like shardlings," Blurred Fists said.

"Ghost Hands, cover us from the air, Sapphire and Aegis to the front. Blurred Fists, watch our flank. Sabreslate and I are on support."

The Shields took their positions as the skittering sound intensified, rolling over and redoubling itself again and again.

"Ghost Hands, barrier please." He felt the wave of her assent in his mind. She levitated higher, robes flowing in the chill winds that ran through the hollows.

A wall of barely visible energy appeared around them. The surface shifted like a soap bubble, swirls stretching and overlapping as the group moved forward.

After a few steps more, First Sentinel saw the shardlings. There were three, each a collection of more than a hundred arm-length slivers of bleached-white bone. They moved like a continual spill, collecting into a mound and then springing forward, leap-frogging over themselves again and again.

When the shardlings hit Ghost Hands' wall, the sound reverberated through the cavern. They probed again and again, jagged
bones reaching out like tendrils to test the barrier.

"We have to keep moving. Ghost Hands, push them back,"
First Sentinel said, continuing to walk forward.

The wall pressed forward as the shardlings continued to attack. One skittered to the drop-off and disappeared out of sight.
It's not gone; it's flanking. Several times before, he'd seen shardlings
climb straight up the walls of the bone pathways to attack them,
and he expected no less.

"Blurred Fists, pick that one up when it comes back. Ghost
Hands, can you make a full demisphere?"

"Not for long. I can't maintain it all the way and have any
energy left for the fight."

So we have to pick a front and then go. Or we can be smart.

"Ghost Hands, on my mark, I want you sweep those two off
the edge. Then we all run and get them behind us. Blurred Fists,
I want you to run interference. Don't get pinned down, but see if
you can slow them."

The group all nodded, and they prepared for the charge.

First Sentinel watched the shardlings' pattern of attack, and
waited until they'd disengaged a few feet from the barrier.

"Go!"

Ghost Hands swept the remaining shardlings off the edge,
and the Shields started sprinting. First Sentinel downed an
elixir that reduced his weight to nothing and had Ghost Hands
push him along so he didn't have to aggravate his leg. There
were still several miles to go, but if they could get enough of a
lead on the shardlings, First Sentinel bet that they could keep
the creatures at bay with Blurred Fists' speed and Ghost Hands'
shields.

After a few hundred feet, the elixir's effect expired, and he had to run on his own. First Sentinel's bones creaked, and sharp pain tore at his side. *Not enough painkillers.* He grabbed a couple of pills out of a pouch and dry-swallowed them, then felt the tendrils of relief stretch down his body. *Thank the City Mother I made them so fast acting.*

First Sentinel looked over his shoulder and saw Blurred Fists behind them, jogging in reverse as the shards emerged from the cliff, closing with alarming speed. Blurred Fists cracked their bones with the set of crusher gloves First Sentinel had made him. He allowed himself a little drop of pride in their craftsmanship. Then he reached to his pouch again and produced a small explosive.

He raised his voice, calling, "Blurred Fists, bomb in my left hand!" He held out the explosive as he ran, and within a second, it was gone.

The boom came mere moments later. First Sentinel had never figured out how to make longer-fused versions small enough to carry in pouches. *My to-do list would never run out even if I were designing full-time.*

The bomb had pulverized two of the shardlings, leaving just one on their trail. *One, we can take.*

"Just one left. Stand ground!"

The Shields stopped and turned to face the creature. Ghost Hands stayed aloft, and Sapphire moved to the high end of the path, next to the wall.

Sabreslate shifted her cloak into a pair of razor-tipped maces and armor, and First Sentinel cracked his knuckles, activating his shock gloves. The remaining shardling charged right down the center, making its way toward First Sentinel. Aegis stepped in front of his father and leaned into his shield to brace for the attack.

Sapphire shaved sideways to hit the creature at the flank. She grabbed handfuls of bone shards and snapped them in her grip while the rest of the beast lashed out at her and Aegis both. Aegis covered her with the shield, and they pushed the construct back. Blurred Fists made several passes, and Sabreslate joined the melee with stone maces. Between the four of them, they pulverized the beast until what remained stopped moving, reduced to a pile of inanimate bone.

First Sentinel kicked at the pile, satisfied. "Alright, now double-time it to the exit. Our window is closing."

They entered the compound without a hitch, dropping five guards by the gate and three more in the interior corridor. Sapphire mangled COBALT-3's automata like they were paper, and First Sentinel nourished fledgling hope about their chances for the first time since he'd woken up from his injuries. First Sentinel kept moving, cane clicking quickly on the tile so he could avoid thinking about what a bad idea it was for him to be there on the mission.

He'd taken enough painkillers to put a grown Freithin under and balanced it with a full pot of spiced tea. *It's amazing I'm not buzzing as fast as Wenlizerachi.*

The ceiling was lined with electric runner lights, which led the Shields on the path toward the laboratories. Aegis took point, telling them about the patrols through Bira's telepathic link.

[There should be a larger automata guarding the juncture up ahead. Sapphire and Blurred Fists, flank left; Ghost Hands and Sabreslate, go right. First Sentinel and I will go up the center. Keep out of those hands if you value your lungs. If COBALT-3

shows up, get her to First Sentinel and me. We've got a present for her.]

A dull green light shone through the blurry glass windows in the double doors as Aegis led the Shields with hand signals, counting down. He closed his last finger into a fist as he stepped up to a door and kicked it open.

The room was mostly bare, with laboratory supplies stacked along the walls beside large boxes filled with paper. As Aegis had warned, a twenty-foot-tall automaton sat in the middle of the room, illuminated eyes and rotating head scanning the room.

"Go!" Aegis shouted, not bothering with telepathy now that the automata had seen them. Aegis and First Sentinel charged up the middle to draw the automata's attention.

First Sentinel primed his shock gloves and reached for a knife. As they charged, First Sentinel scanned the automata for a good handhold to climb up toward the power station on its back.

Aegis dove under a massive mechanical hand and used the shield to shear the automata's armored belly. Sapphire tackled the thresher from the side, and Ghost Hands used her telekinesis to immobilize its left hand. First Sentinel scrambled up and around the left side toward the power plant and slashed the power cables, glad that he had thought to insulate the gauntlets.

With their concentrated fire and the thorough application of explosives, the Shields brought the automata down with a loud crash.

But that just cost us whatever surprise we had left. Aegis took them to the doors of the laboratory subjects' wing by the time more forces arrived. They squared off against a dozen Ikanollo-scale automata wielding charged-tip pikes. The automata had turned a four-way hallway into a chokepoint, pikes out and buzzing. *COBALT-3 doesn't appear to be in residence tonight. She's probably quartered somewhere closer to the summit. Luck is with us.* Though he was curious to see if the scrambler he'd finalized would work.

Ghost Hands knocked the electrified pikes up into the ceiling and the combined charge of Sapphire of Blurred Fists broke the automata's line. After that, they made short work of the machines. Aegis dove into the fight, grace and power incarnate. *He's using the rage well. Keeping it contained, using it without being blinded by it. Maybe I should be learning from him now.*

The laboratory wing was a litany of sins, spelled out in the smell of feces and vomit, the constant moans of the inmates, and walls with stained with dried-blood spatters in orange, red, blue, and black.

Ghost Hands relayed Aegis' orders once more. *[We need to find the keys for the doors to break out the subjects. Ghost Hands, Blurred Fists, and Sabreslate, head through the north corridor. The rest of us will go south and meet at the other entrance. Don't break anyone out yet, we need to do it all at once so we can handle the crowd. Be on the lookout for gurneys or other ways to transport the heavily wounded.]*

[Go, now.] The group split again, and First Sentinel waited for Aegis to give the order for the two of them to move down the south corridor. *He's keeping an eye on me,* First Sentinel realized. *It's what I would do.*

Aegis nodded and spoke in a low voice, leading First Sentinel and Sapphire down the hallway. "The guard with the keys should be roving the corridors with an escort of two or three others, checking on subjects. It's a more advanced model, better programming. Let me take it and just mind the escorts. The key-carrier has an alarm system, so we need to be fast."

A light fixture blinked ahead, casting the hallway in a slow strobe of periodic illumination. Aegis walked low, hunched over but eyes forward. First Sentinel listened to the slow drip of water from a crack in the ceiling and the gentle buzz of electricity. The Shields moved quietly, waiting for the telltale clicking of metal on tile.

There it is. Forward and to the left, around the corner. Aegis heard it as well, holing up a closed fist. Aegis waved Sapphire and First Sentinel to the wall behind him. *[Good, keep it quiet and avoid the other guards for as long as we can.]*

Aegis peeked around the corner, then turned back and gave another countdown.

[Four. Three. Two. One more.]

"Go." Aegis took two quick steps out from the wall and turned, swinging the shield around to sever the cables and cords in the guard's neck joint, popping the head clean off. Aegis snatched the head out of the air with his free hand and grabbed the construct, lowering it silently to the ground. Sapphire carried the lifeless machine over to one of the empty cells and hid it. *She didn't even ask me to help. Have to keep my eyes open, protect my team however I can.*

They crossed two hallways and turned another corner before First Sentinel heard the triple staccato of the key holder and its escort. He placed them at nineteen paces down the hall.

Aegis leaned over to First Sentinel and whispered, "Do you have any charge left on the ruby breath?"

First Sentinel nodded, holding up two fingers for two charges. Aegis nodded and pointed around the corner. "Ten paces."

First Sentinel drew a foot-long bone from his belt, looked to Aegis, then popped out from the corner to face the automata. He waited a half-second until they stepped into range and twisted a segment of the bone. A red-and-orange gout burst from the bone and rushed down the hallway, swallowing the trio. Aegis leapt into the hall, grabbed two overhead pipes, then started to swing forward like an ape in the jungle. He swung down into a pair of the automata, kicking with fire-retardant boots.

Sapphire threw one of the charged pikes, which embedded itself in the chest of the third, dropping it in a burst of electricity. First Sentinel pressed up the middle, moving as fast as he could manage while keeping steady. His staves flashed against the key holder's guard, luring it into creating an opening.

The key holder's metallic voice filled the halls. "Intruder Alert. Laboratory Hallway B-3-7. Intruder Alert." Klaxons picked up the call, orange lights flashing. *Damn. Our timeline just cut in half.*

Blows flew as the key holder swung its glaive at inhuman speed, pressing Aegis back against the wall with a barely blocked strike. The staves let him defend against the glaive, but when he closed, his blows barely dented the automata's armor. *Gloves only, then.*

"Press!" Aegis called, and the Shields converged on the key holder. Aegis swung the shield high, First Sentinel ducked to sweep with the staves, and Sapphire knelt to deliver a cross to its midsection. The key holder's glaive blocked the trip and deflected the shield, but it couldn't stop Sapphire's body blow. The construct crumbled in half and folded to the floor. Aegis dropped a shield smash onto the automata to finish it, and snatched up its keys once it was down.

Aegis looked at the keys, sorting them as best he could, thankful for COBALT-3's obsessive organization. "We have to get the prisoners out as quick as possible," Aegis said as he slipped some keys off the wide ring. "Split up—we'll each take one section."

First Sentinel reached out with his mind. *[Ghost Hands, do you hear me? We have the keys. Converge on my position as soon as you can.]*

[Loud and clear. En route now.] A few moments later, Blurred Fists appeared and took over half the keys, then vanished out of sight. Sapphire took a handful and Aegis handed First Sentinel an even smaller portion. *Time to prove I can pull my weight on this mission, injured or not.* First Sentinel pushed his gait faster as he walked down the hallway, barely leaning on the cane as adrenaline ran hot.

Chapter Thirty-Three

Aegis

Aegis heard a soft grunt as his father took a turn just a bit too fast. *He's not really healed yet. If we get into a protracted fight, he could become a liability. Now it's my turn to keep him safe.*

Just halfway down the hallway of COBALT-3's prisoners, Ghost Hands, Sapphire, and Sabreslate arrived from around the corner with four guards on their heels. The automata went down fast when the Shields stood their ground, but the guards continued to pour down the hallways, slowing their rescue efforts to a crawl.

Ghost Hands relayed Aegis' orders as he struggled to turn a key in the rusted tumbler before him. *[Regroup at the south entrance for the exit push. Make it fast.]*

As quick as anyone can be trailing a crowd of tortured citizens, half of whom can't stand on their own. This had sounded like a much better idea yesterday.

Aegis opened the door to a cell, letting the red-tinted light of the hall seep into the small room.

"Who is it?" asked a small voice. A male ermine-kin Millrej blinked at Aegis through the light passing by his upheld hand.

"It's Aegis and the Shields of Audec-Hal. We're here to stop COBALT-3's experiments and get you out of here."

The ermine-kin snapped up to his full height and then almost tipped over. He looked painfully malnourished, ribs prominent through his thin shirt. "City Mother be praised!" He wobbled to the side, and Aegis steadied him with a hand. Aegis walked the man out into the hall, and the Millrej gained the strength to walk on his own.

"Head down this hall and meet the rest of my team at the double doors. If you see a patrol, shout for help."

"Bless you, Aegis."

Aegis smiled. *This is why we fight.* "You're welcome. Now go, quickly." The ermine-kin plodded along the hall, head down, whiskers out.

Opening three more cells only yielded two more prisoners. The other cell held an emaciated Pronai man, dead on his bunk. Aegis paused long enough to close the man's eyes, wishing he had the time to gather the dead and give them a proper burial with the rites of the City Mother.

Aegis exhausted his supply of keys, and then led the prisoners down the hall toward the south entrance. He paused for a moment at the cell where he had been kept, looking into the empty room. He mouthed a few silent curses before moving on.

Never again. No more playthings, COBALT-3.

Aegis and the survivors he'd freed rounded a corner to find a crowd of fifty patients and the other Shields. Sapphire had a tiny Qava on her back, and Sabreslate held a shaped-stone sledge for a man with a broken leg.

"That everyone?" he asked.

"Everyone that's still living and could be moved," Sabreslate said.

"Sapphire, let Sabreslate take that woman there. I want you on point. Wedge formation, civilians in back. Sabreslate, you're on rear guard with the sledge."

The Jalvai nodded, but she didn't look happy about it. *We can't all get the glorious jobs all the time.* She and Ghost Hands could protect a crowd better than anyone, while still attacking their enemies. And they'd have to exploit every Shield's capabilities if they were going to escape with the prisoners.

Aegis stepped into place just behind Sapphire. He hurried forward to help with the double doors, but they swung open without being touched. He'd thought Ghost Hands had helped them out. Then he saw three thresher units and COBALT-3 standing between them.

"Greetings: Welcome back."

Crap.

The room was as empty of threads as it was of everything else: no adornment, no furniture.

Aegis relayed orders as he stepped forward, walking straight at COBALT-3. *[Sabreslate, keep the civilians on this side of the doors. First Sentinel and Blurred Fists, hook left and right toward COBALT-3 on my mark. Sapphire and Ghost Hands, take the automata.]*

COBALT-3 continued, walking forward into the cold blue light of one of her electric lamps. "Assertion: Your return was expected. Explication: Received alarm and returned for confrontation. Assertion: You will not escape this time; experiments will resume."

Aegis laughed. "Request: Shut the hell up and fight." *[Mark!]*

He launched forward and threw a left hook with the shield. This needed to end quickly, before his father got tired, before they were surrounded, before the civilians could panic or collapse.

So, fast.

The room exploded into action. Variables and possibilities danced in Aegis' mind as he dodged COBALT-3's punch. The automata creaked and groaned; sounds mixing with the screams of the tyrant's former subjects; sparks flew and mixed with the plumes of magic from First Sentinel's wands.

Aegis jumped back away from a kick and risked a quick look over his shoulder to check on the civilians. A thick mesh wall of stone had formed over the door, Sabreslate's work.

He looked back to find a metallic fist colliding with his face. Aegis rolled with the impact as his blood splattered on the tile. Hurtling back, his eyes tore and his vision blurred. He brought the Aegis up to cover his face as his back cracked against a wall. Pain danced up his spine as he pulled himself up to a shaky fighting stance.

Standing, he saw First Sentinel fighting COBALT-3, a whirlwind of knives and articulated limbs. But his father was still weak and slow. He took a roundhouse kick on the side, up and under his protective longcoat. His father doubled over, and COBALT-3 raised a foot to stomp down on the fallen hero.

Oh no you don't.

Aegis tackled the mechanical tyrant, knocking her several steps back and away from First Sentinel. Aegis took an elbow to the collarbone and hoped he was just imagining the cracking sound. He recovered, raising the Aegis to block the line to his collar. With those serpentine limbs, COBALT-3 could attack on any line from any position. But she was still a machine; she had patterns, and they could be exploited.

"Eagle's wing on three!" Aegis called, watching red streaks pound into COBALT-3's carapace armor.

"One!"

Still huffing, First Sentinel broke left, taking Aegis' position, while Blurred Fists kept COBALT-3 occupied by filling her vision with harmless but distracting strikes. The machine tyrant struck back with powerful swipes, but Blurred Fists was never there.

"Two!"

Aegis wheeled around, feeling out the proper hinge point as he considered the civilians. Another wave of guards would be arriving any moment, and Sabreslate couldn't hold them off forever. Not while keeping the group calm.

"Three!"

Blurred Fists feinted to the side and turned up the speed of attacks, drawing COBALT-3's attention away from First Sentinel. First Sentinel braced, and Aegis planted his feet on his father's shoulders. He sprang up, flipped twice in the air, and brought the Aegis down directly on the back of COBALT-3's head. Aegis didn't feel the metal give beneath the shield, and he saw that his blow had barely scratched as he landed from the strike.

"Datum: Recent upgrades to my armor's tensile strength exceed your maximum force-generation capacity."

Thank the City Mother for blunt machines. "Thank you. Sapphire, in here, now!"

Chapter Thirty-Four

First Sentinel

Coming!" Sapphire yelled in response to Aegis' call.

She dodged under a lumbering metallic limb and stood with a leap, throwing an uppercut at COBALT-3. The machine ruler blocked with crossed arms. But not without cost. The Shields saw her armor give, and rallied. "Press!" Aegis called, and threw a heavy blow to COBALT-3's midsection, not intending to do any damage, just trying to unbalance her while Sapphire continued to attack.

The Shields surrounded COBALT-3, overloaded the inputs, and split her attention so that the Freithin could break her down.

First Sentinel reached into a back pocket to make sure that the scrambler was still there, and Blurred Fists continued to press the tyrant, this time at her flank. The scrambler should deactivate COBALT-3, but only if he could attach it directly to her power source. *And you're not exactly on your form tonight, old man.*

"Condescension: Previous evidence displays your team unable to overcome a standstill. Assertion: Surrender is appropriate at this juncture."

First Sentinel laughed and then tried to draw her attention as he closed. "Haven't you heard? We're crazed insurrectionists. Sense went out the window when your predecessor and your peers took this city away from the people and started playing god."

COBALT-3 deflected Sapphire's jabbing knee, knocking her away with a blow to the Freithin's hip.

No longer pressed from all sides, her serpentine hands reached back and over herself to grab Blurred Fists' hands. The tyrant pulled them up over his head as he squirmed faster than First Sentinel's eyes could follow. A bright yellow band of fear sprouted from the Pronai's chest, twisting like another flailing limb.

First Sentinel was frozen in place, trying to get his body to move. Pain from his leg smothered his attempts, leaving him prisoner to his own vision.

Sapphire leapt at the tyrant again, but COBALT-3 caught her with another brutal kick, sending Sapphire to the ground.

Within an instant, First Sentinel saw the fight slip away from them. The action slowed to accentuate his paralysis. Fear, doubt, and pain locked him in place, helpless.

Move, dammit!

With a scream, he shook off the fear and advanced. With his original cane lost on the other side of the room, First Sentinel leaned on a fighting stick, hobbling his way toward the fight.

Aegis swiped at COBALT-3 and Blurred Fists, desperately trying to help as COBALT-3 pulled at both ends of the Pronai like a doll.

An acrid spray of blood filled the air as the Pronai's hip tore, fabric and flesh ripping as Wenlizerachi's right leg went one way and the rest of him the other. Blood flowed up his torso and dripped from the Pronai's face. Blurred Fists screamed paragraphs of pain in agonized Pronai.

"Get him free, now!" Aegis yelled, his voice breaking as he climbed up COBALT-3 and pulled at her grip. COBALT-3 clubbed Aegis with Blurred Fists' leg, splattering his mask with blood. First Sentinel dragged one foot in front of another, finally in range to throw a gauntleted roundhouse at COBALT-3. She slapped it away, but rage at his friend's injury had flushed the pain away. One hand went to his belt and found the scrambler.

This ends now. We have to get him to a doctor immediately.

The scrambler was gray and black; the reduced vicite core attached to a charged battery and set to neutralize the robot tyrant. The device was built with a stolen power core from COBALT-2, so First Sentinel hadn't been sure it would even work, or how well, until COBALT-3 had confirmed that her core used the same multiband vicite design when they'd rescued Aegis. COBALT-3 constantly modified herself, improving on her creator's design. But he hoped the cores were close enough that his alchemical process would let the scrambler's core cancel out the power from COBALT-3's core.

The Shields massed on COBALT-3 while Blurred Fists cried one long-drawn-out meaningless word. First Sentinel's thumb found the blue button on the scrambler.

City Mother, guide my hand.

COBALT-3 tossed Blurred Fists at Sapphire. In the same moment, First Sentinel dropped under the swinging arm to plant the scrambler on the underside of the tyrant's power unit. The scrambler whirred to life and flashed bright blue. A sucking sound reverberated off the walls and COBALT-3 froze in place, head quirked to the side in surprise.

Aegis called the retreat, his voice pained. "Sabreslate, get them out of here, now. Sapphire, Ghost Hands, keep the big ones away from the civilians. First Sentinel, escort on the civilians. I'll get Blurred Fists."

First Sentinel crossed the room, watching over his shoulder. COBALT-3 could snap back to life at any moment. The Shields could get the subjects out, their objective achieved, but it might cost them one of their lives.

Aegis draped Blurred Fists over his shoulders and made for the door. First Sentinel picked up the detached leg and carried it out. His own leg screamed in solidarity with Blurred Fists, fear overriding the adrenaline and inviting the pain back in. As they reach the door, COBALT-3 started to twitch back to life.

Sapphire held the rear, occupying another giant automata, and First Sentinel ducked around the corner to another hallway. The Shields rushed down the hall, pushing the civilians through the rest of the building. Even while holding Blurred Fists, Aegis annihilated the confused guards they met along the way. A black thread of guilt was wrapped tight around his heart, extending to the fading Pronai. The thread matched First Sentinel's own, just as strong.

A minute later, the Shields broke the threshold of the building and reached the street.

Aegis huffed as he gave orders. "Ghost Hands, Sabreslate, and First Sentinel, take the civilians to a safe distance. Sapphire and I will get Blurred Fists to a doctor. Scatter—now!"

First Sentinel squeezed Sapphire's arm, furious he wasn't in any condition to go with them. "City Mother be with you."

Sapphire nodded and then started into a flat run.

I won't sleep, not tonight. I'm not sure any of us will. Except for the one of us who might never wake up.

Chapter Thirty-Five

Sapphire

Sapphire tore down the streets, each bound the size of three Ikanollo paces. Dr. Acci was miles away, and Blurred Fists was losing blood fast. *He doesn't have much time,* Sapphire admitted, her heart aching with her friend's pain.

Blurred Fists had collapsed from the shock. *It'll be a miracle if he's still alive when we reach the doctor.*

Sapphire and Aegis stopped in an alley where Sapphire tore the leg off her raiment to make a tourniquet. It would only do so much good with the artery bleeding out at Pronai speed.

Aegis looked up to Sapphire, tears welling in his eyes. "Take him and run as fast as you can. I'll try to keep up. Don't stop for anyone or anything. Just get him to Dr. Acci."

Sapphire nodded and took Blurred Fists up in her arms again. Head down, she kicked off, sprinting down the street.

The streets were nearly empty, a local curfew keeping people in their homes. The streetlamps rushed by on both sides, shadows moving from every direction, but Sapphire didn't stop. She was throwing his life and hers up the air because there could be patrols around any corner between here and Hook's Hole. Ghost Hands or Sabreslate might be able to move faster, but either would have to soar through the open sky and be even more exposed to COBALT-3's flying automata sentries or Yema's Bull Mosquitos. And going through the ground with Sabreslate was out, due to the strain it put on the body.

Which means it comes down to me. The tourniquet seeped onto her raiment, all the jostling and motion exacerbating his condition.

He wouldn't make it all the way to Acci's. *Is there somewhere closer, a hospital or clinic?* She wracked her brain as she ran, trying to jog her memory by looking at the store signs and street posts. The nearest hospital not run wholly by COBALT-3 was fifty blocks east, and even their local security was in COBALT-3's pocket. The free clinic on 111th and Heart Meridian had closed down two months ago, when Dr. Ustin was arrested for practicing without "official sanction," having refused to pay the bribes.

Nothing. She kept running; saw a gang down the block huddled under a lamp with a broken glass case. She dashed right by them and hoped they don't pursue. Even if they did, they'd meet Aegis first, and City Mother protect them if that happened.

The tourniquet had soaked through already, and Blurred Fists' body was getting rigid. *Not enough time, there just isn't enough time. If it were anyone else, maybe.* But now the fastest Pronai the city has ever seen was dying just as quickly.

Sapphire stopped, planted both feet in the cobblestone street, and filled her lungs. "I need a doctor! The Shields of Audec-Hal need your help! Can anyone hear me, I need a doctor!"

Windows were closed, doors shut, and the only reaction she got was an odd stare from a homeless man pushing a cart filled with mottled bags.

She started running again, continuing her call. "Doctor, I need a doctor! Help, anyone!" Every block, she shouted again, desperation giving way to futile obstinacy as Blurred Fists' life slipped away.

Three blocks later, she felt the echo in her heart that came from his closeness vanish. The sinking feeling in her gut that she had been sharing disappeared, leaving a gaping emptiness. *Please, no.*

Wenlizerachi was gone, his life given for the dream of a free city he'd never known and would never get to see.

Aegis caught up with her, tears in his eyes. Just as she felt him with her birthright, he could see the Pronai with his own, watch Blurred Fists' threads cut. Aegis put an arm on her shoulder and embraced the lifeless form of their friend.

Years of memories washed over her in an icy wave of loss. She remembered meeting a young Wenlizerachi as she helped run errands for his mother Zeraneyachi. She remembered when Zeraneyachi had died and her son took up the mantle. She remembered hundreds of battles and meetings and his ready smile and easy laugh. All of it gone in an instant.

Sapphire dropped to the cobblestones, Aegis with her. For a minute, they were a shrunken island of grief in the gargantuan city. Between choked-back tears, Aegis said, "We need to get off the street. Before the guards come."

Six Shields had gone out that night, but only five would see the dawn.

Chapter Thirty-Six

First Sentinel

Wonlar chewed up the floor at Douk's, strides too long for his still tender leg as his cane clicked on the ground, but he didn't stop, pushing through on anger and grief. He walked as though maybe if he paced fast enough, Wenlizerachi wouldn't be dead.

He wouldn't have another life on his conscience, another friend to bury, another victim in the war that had swallowed Wonlar's whole life for so long that he barely remembered what it was like to just be a person.

The only two lights on in the basement were the lamps hung at head level on either side of the stairway door. First Sentinel pulled the shadows along with him, silhouettes pacing the room just ahead and behind. They matched his worry, but he didn't care for their company.

I should be sleeping, resting my wounds and making sure I'm functional in the morning. He tried several times, lying down on the cot that was almost his death bed and had been a prison for longer than he usually spent making a new piece of armor.

The sounds of creaking wood told him that he was not alone. The low pitch of the creaks told him it was Rova. *Either that or I'm in for a fight.*

Rova's knock settled the uncertainty. A blue hand pushed back the door. She was dressed in a plain gray tunic and leggings. Night clothes from the look of them, the rumple, and the worn thread.

"I heard you tromping around down here. Why are you still awake?"

Wonlar raised an eyebrow. He didn't think that Freithin empathy would pull her out of bed by the force of his worry.

She continued. "This close, I can't help but feel it."

"Sorry." *I can't get anything right today. Maybe this is it: I've finally lost my edge. The time's come to put away the raiment or pass it on to someone else. Hell of a time for it.*

Wonlar shook his head and then looked up to Rova. She was strong as ever, but tired, the fatigue gaining ground at the corner of her eyes. *We can't keep going like this. I'm still thinking too small.*

They were tired, beaten, and bereaved, and the tyrants were on the verge of consolidating. He needed the others to step up, more than they already had. They had to carry him now.

First Sentinel stood up straight, pushing into the ground with his cane. *That's it.*

"We might never get another moment to strike. Nevri's dead, Dlella hasn't fully settled in, and their forces will be out of position. Rova, at tomorrow's meeting, I want to hear ideas about how to pull forces from the temple tower." A thin thread of white hope sprang from her chest, tentative, like a mouse peeking its nose out into the room checking for danger.

"The tower? That again?" It all came back to the City Mother, captive soul of the city.

Wonlar returned to pacing, his mind turning. "Yes. The six . . . five of us can't change the fate of a whole city by ourselves. I've been trying to win the war by skirmishing for fifty years, step by step, and it costs every step of the way. We owe it to Wenlizerachi and the others to bring this to an end."

Rova took a seat on a packed crate of coffee beans, one of the only things in the basement stable enough to support her.

"To win, we need the people on our side, and that means breaking the hold on the City Mother." Wonlar stopped beside Rova, put a hand to her knee. "Go back to bed; I need you rested and ready."

She placed a hand over his and gave a gentle squeeze. Wonlar slid to the side and made room for Rova to hop off the crate and work her way to the stairs.

The aging Shield paced a bit longer before settling down to sleep, stirring the soup of thoughts before letting his mind simmer overnight. Planning kept the ghosts at bay, ensuring the voices in his mind offered suggestions instead of tearing him apart with guilt.

At my age, there are enough ghosts in my mind that I need them helping me almost as much as I need Selweh by my side.

Finally, morning came. *Dounmo* tea in hand, Wonlar greeted the sun as it spilled its light down the cliff's edge and into the city. The smell of darkside mint mixed with baking dough, and Wonlar soaked up the moment.

This was the calm before the end, with all the clarity that brought with it. No matter how long and hard the night, the dawn would always come to wash away the darkness.

Selweh joined him in watching the sunrise. They talked as father and son, talked about the people passing by, how Selweh missed their old apartment, where he had gathered the neighborhood children to play Shields and tyrants in the street and then they'd all eat Douk's sweets afterward. They talked about everything but Wenlizerachi, but everything ended up being about him anyway. *He wants to claim the guilt because it was his mission, but I could have stopped her. I was right there.*

The Shields took the back room after Xera finished the breads. They made war plans over fresh bread and jams. Sweet smells and sumptuous tastes balanced the grim severity of their mission. But even the tyrants couldn't sour the taste of a piping hot loaf.

"I want to reopen discussion of taking the tower," Wonlar said to start the meeting. He saw no need to talk about what had happened last night. He knew they'd fight over the blame, tear at one another and get themselves knotted up in their threads.

Sarii rolled her eyes, and her stone plaything took the form of a bored cat, pacing in a circle and lying down. "We're not in a position to take the tower, especially not after last night."

We have to grieve on our own time, Sarii. "No, this is exactly the time. The tyrants are cracking down, but the summit shows how desperate they are. With Nevri dead and the Rebirth Engine gone, two of the five tyrants have been shaken, even with Dlella as Executor. They all have their honor guards with them at the summit. That means the tower must be relatively unprotected. And if we occupy the forces that are left elsewhere, the force at the tower will be able to finish the task and turn the tide."

"What target is big enough to pull all of the forces from the tower?" Selweh asked.

Wonlar shook his head. "Two targets."

"How are we going to cover three missions with five Shields?" Rova asked. "We'd have to send one person each to the distractions, and that only leaves three of us for the tower."

Wonlar shook his head. "I'm going alone. Two for each distraction strike. We'll need at least that many to draw their reinforcements. I want to hear suggestions for targets." He left no room for disagreement, tried to stare down Sarii as she moved to object. He felt the gold bands binding each of them to his heart tug as he tried to drag them along with his idea. "We have to do this, now. It's our only chance."

Aegis set down his mug of tea. "That's idiotic. You need as many people on the tower as you can. Let us make the distractions first, then regroup and go for the tower." First Sentinel flinched at the word "idiotic," his nostrils flaring. He tried to calm himself, thinking, *He doesn't want to lose me, and I can't blame him. I may not be that lucky again.*

Sabreslate's stone became a miniature First Sentinel, pincushioned with bolts and arrows and blades. "You're talking about a suicide run. What's that going to get us?"

Wonlar ignored the question. "Where could two of us with Shield-bearer backup cause enough trouble to draw forces from the tower?"

Rova knocked on the table, inspiration striking. "The mint in Heartstown."

Wonlar cocked his head, considering. "It's close, and important enough to be a real target. We'll need explosives, and we'd have to form a perimeter so we could maintain the position, which will take either Ghost Hands or Sabreslate. And then we'll need someone to hold the line, Sapphire or Aegis or me. We couldn't do it with just one." No one argued. "We can use the explosive I've got stocked in Lower Ribs. But that's the last of it."

Sarii huffed. "This isn't what we need to be doing right now."

Selweh said, "We can't do anything less. As long as the tyrants have control of the City Mother, nothing we do will be able to stir the people to revolution. The mob at the bank was motivated by greed more than anything, and they broke under pressure too quickly. But we did get some money, and Aegis destroyed much of the metal reserves. They'll need to mint new bills soon."

"And if we destroy the mint . . .," Aegis said.

Sarii crossed her arms and her stone shifted back into the cat, which made another circle in place before settling down again. "Just wait until this explodes in your face and none of us are here to save you."

She's in.

"It's too soon for you to go out alone," Selweh said. *Now who's the overprotective father?*

Wonlar smiled, try to show confidence. Selweh was probably right. But who else could free the City Mother? "I've fought through worse. And no one knows the layout of the tower like I do; none of the rest of you have been in the City Mother's presence before—I have the best chance of getting through to her. I can move faster by myself, get to the top in time for you all to make your escape. And if we free the City Mother, everything changes. Instead of her power being used to suppress the citizens, she will empower them, bring them together in trust. We can start riots like the bank every week, build guerilla armies inside the city, and finally turn the tide.

Wonlar waited a beat for their answers. Rova perked up, almost ready to say something, but then stopped. Sarii leaned back to play with her stone, head inclined toward Bira. Doubtless they were talking mind to mind. Aegis looked to Wonlar, his eyes racing. *City Mother, give us the wisdom to choose the right path.*

Bira broke the silence without making a sound. *[The other target should form a rough equilateral triangle with the mint and the tower. What is in that area?]*

Wonlar pulled a roll from the seat beside him and spread out a crinkled and faded lambskin map from the Republic era, written over in charcoal and ink. *If the tyrants took the time to communicate, they could guess our game. But even if they didn't, they're not going to just let us get away with these strikes.*

Wonlar looked at the map and extrapolated the triangle in his mind. *Headtown.* Headtown was the site of luxurious homes owned by the richest collaborators, extensive parks with immaculately kept shrubbery, and countless office buildings sculpted by the finest Jalvai architects on the payroll of the tyrants.

"Hit any of the big office buildings, and they'll come running," Selweh said, then shook his head. "But we can do better." *Keep thinking out loud. We need to make five minds into one.* Bira used to link their minds at meetings, but it hadn't been worth the effort to sort out the jumble and the stray inklings from the conscious thoughts.

Wonlar nodded. "We can. The Headtown barracks is too hot for anything but a hit-and-run strike, but that will draw emergency units, not guards. Hostage situation?" he asked.

Bira considered his question. "Protracted, guaranteed to draw interested parties. We'd have to time it just right, though, since when they get enough backup they'll go straight for the kill."

Wonlar stood and then returned to his roll of maps. "Good. Let's look at the floor plans from Naako, and we'll pick the best target. If possible, I'd like to have you give our regards to Dr. Herron."

Naako had designed half of the newer houses in Headtown and grown rich off it. A few years ago, after her cousin was disappeared by Nevri's goons, she'd had a change of heart. Douk got wind of her efforts to contact the Shields and arranged a meeting. She'd pledged an impressive amount of money and even better, her records. Wonlar had floor plans of every house she'd built, secret passageways and all.

"You'll keep out of the line of fire, several rooms inside, with one Shield holding the hostages, the other keeping an eye on the perimeter." *Now, for the assignments.*

"Aegis, I want you and Sabreslate to take the hostages. Sabreslate, you'll be able to modify the house to help keep yourselves secure, and Aegis will watch the perimeter and make the demands. We'll need to bring in some Shield-bearers for extra hands."

Wonlar turned to Rova and Bira. "That puts you two at the mint. I'll provide the explosives. Get in and blow the door behind you; that'll slow them down. Then get into the mint, and be sure you locate the plates. Even if I fail, I want at least one mission to succeed."

Selweh nodded. He was as good a son and soldier as anyone could ask for. Maybe one day, he'd have the chance to just be a good man. Have children of his own. Wonlar saw the jade thread that hung from Rova's heart and draped across the floor toward Aegis, obscured by his tightly woven threads in gold and bronze. *And maybe they can even do something about that.*

"We'll strike tomorrow, before they can get too far done with the summit. Word has it they're still quibbling over some tariff rates. Until their security forces get integrated, they'll fight each other for the honor of killing us."

Wonlar saw the nods of assent and the chiseled disapproval on Sabreslate's face. *She'll do her part; she always has. Chip away the blocks of cynicism and antagonism, and there was a patriot* inside that woman. The rest was just armor to protect the artist's heart.

Wonlar took a deep breath, and his eyes slid to a blanket in the corner, draped over a motionless form.

"Now it's time to pay our respects."

The Shields took the rest of the day dodging patrols and working around border guards to reach the stake purchased by the first Aegis at the edge of Hook's Hole.

As soon as they'd passed the first switchback, the Shields stopped and unrolled the bundle they'd snuck through the city. Sabreslate went to the wall and rolled out a large boulder, shaping it into a coffin, with patterns of the Pronai's Great Wheel and a perfect likeness of Wenlizerachi in his Shield's raiment.

When she was done, Rova and Selweh picked up the stone coffin, and Wonlar led the way with a lantern. They had never bothered to leave any lights in the hall, each time hoping they'd never have to go back to fill another berth.

Their steps rang hollow in the gray-brown tunnel as they left Audec-Hal proper, making their way into the cliffs between the legs.

It had been three years since they'd buried Aernah, the last Aegis. Back when Selweh was Second Sentinel. Blurred Fists had only been a Shield for two years.

They passed the hall of Aegis, four coffins side by side. The name of each who had carried the mantle was inscribed on the side of their coffin, testament to their memory and their service.

Wonlar lingered for a moment at Aria's tomb, third in the row, and laid two freshly bloomed crocuses on the coffin, one for Selweh and one for himself. The group moved to the far end of the room, leaving him alone with the coffin. The inscription showed her first Shield name, Valence; and the date when she'd first used her Spark-touched ability, as well as her time as the fourth Aegis, after their marriage and their love were torn apart by his power.

Wonlar knelt, hands folded over the stone hands carved in her likeness. *Selweh is still safe. It'll be over soon. I'm sorry for what I did, for not making amends before it was too late. I love you and I miss you.*

After a minute of silence, he stood and turned from her coffin. For a moment, the shadows played a trick on him, and he thought he saw a fifth coffin in the hall, Selweh's name beside the others.

The light moved and it was gone.

The Shields passed three more rooms to reach the first open space just beyond Qojimata's coffin, laid in six years ago. They'd lost eighteen Shields in total over the fifty years. In terms of a war, it wasn't many compared to the thousands of citizens who had perished under the tyrant's reign, but every one of them was a dear friend.

Wonlar break the silence. "Here." Sabreslate stepped up in her woven-stone raiment and raised her hands to the cavern wall. Turquoise lines of empathy extended from her hands and burrowed their way into the wall. The stone shifted out of the way, forming a smooth room just tall enough for Sapphire to pass her head underneath. Sabreslate left an elevated platform, and Sapphire lifted the coffin up onto the corner. Aegis lifted up his side, and the two strongest Shields slid the coffin into place.

Sabreslate knelt next to the coffin and traced Wenlizerachi's name by hand, then his Shield-name, Blurred Fists. She stood and turned to face the other four in the circle.

The service was Wonlar's duty, his burden. He'd spoken sixteen of them, taking over after the two done by the original Aegis.

"We gather today in the Hall of Broken Shields to remember our comrade Blurred Fists."

The voices of the other Shields' echoed in the cavern and in his mind. "Blurred Fists." *[Blurred Fists.]*

Wonlar put a hand on the coffin. "Born Wenlizerachi, of the Pronai, he gave five years of service to Audec-Hal and would have given more had he been able. His speed saved many lives, including my own and those of his fellow Shields. He will not be forgotten."

"He will not be forgotten." *[He will not be forgotten.]*

Wonlar set a morning lily on the coffin, just bloomed that day, that would fold back up again by night. The Pronai had chosen it as their flower to remind them of the beauty of a brief life.

"His shield is broken now, his service at an end. And so we commit his body to the stone beside the great city of Audec-Hal, that he might return again to race the Everlasting Race."

Wonlar continued. "Rest now, brother. You will not be forgotten."

The Shields echoed him again. "You will not be forgotten." *[You will not be forgotten.]*

Sapphire stood over the coffin, drew two fingers to her lips, and then rested them on the carving of Wenlizerachi's face. She stepped back, and Aegis approached, repeating the gesture. Sabreslate went third. Ghost Hands bowed her head beside the coffin and then stepped back. Wonlar was last as he was first, letting the tears come freely in this private moment. He touched fingers to his lips and then rested those fingers on his friend's coffin. Wenlizerachi was the fourth member of the family he'd buried here. There were none from the house of Chi left to take up the name.

Wonlar spoke in a whisper too soft for any to hear except the ghosts that inhabited the hall. "I'm sorry."

The Shields stood silent in the chamber for a half hour, each saying their personal good-byes. Their respects paid, the Shields departed, each knowing that the next mission might be the last for one or more of them.

Ghost Hands lingered behind, asking to catch up with Sabreslate so they could seal the hall once she was done. First Sentinel walked around a corner in the hall, leaving his old friend to her thoughts.

Chapter Thirty-Seven

Ghost Hands

Thirty Years Ago

*W*e'd heard that Nevri was moving several caravans of people for "questioning," but that was all. Not much to go on, but Valence was itching for something to do.

It was the first three of us: First Sentinel, myself, and Valence. We traveled along the rooftops, floating and swinging and doing our best to avoid notice. Most people don't look up, save the tyrants' guards.

The patrol was ten strong, mostly Ikanollo, with one Freithin, two Pronai, and a Qava. A well-rounded group, with versatility. We kept our distance rather than moving to engage. First Sentinel and Valence bantered, trading boasts, joking barbs, and loving words as they steeled themselves for the coming fight.

In the field, they had the blessing and the terror of risking their lives alongside their spouses. I had to say farewell every morning or night, watch as Sarii's eyebrows narrowed. I had to pull myself out of her tight embrace, the worry pouring forth from her mind like a waterfall.

The warlocks stopped at a crosswalk, and First Sentinel held up a hand to stop us. I hovered in place, listening to the warlock's thoughts as best I could.

Qava philosophy speaks of each person's mind as a house, filled with rooms. Each room is decorated and furnished with a person's memories, their emotions, and their perspectives. When I saw into the minds of one of Yema's warlocks, I felt a cold lifeless shack with Yema's thoughts echoed. Little desires and instincts skittered in the corners, afraid to show themselves.

I reached out and spoke in the minds of my companions.

[Yema is giving new orders. They're supposed to break up a demonstration on East Vein and Wexlay.]

First Sentinel responded in a voice just loud enough to carry to the three of us. "Then we head east once they round the corner."

That took us across the vein, a divide wide enough that Valence had to shift to become as wind as First Sentinel swung almost all the way to the street, swooping close enough to people to take off a few caps, protecting heads from the winter's chill. We raced over the rooftops to cut off the warlock patrol before they could reach Wexlay.

First Sentinel called a halt at the edge of the roof of an apartment building. They had a clear view of the intersection of East Vein and Wexlay. I felt the minds and bodies of the demonstrators, a tightly-packed mass of frustration and fear. Citizens with enough drive and will to overcome City Mother's influence were very rare, and seemed to be getting rarer every year.

And halfway down the block, the Warlock Guard. First Sentinel called my name with his mind, and I relayed his message. [Go on three; keep the protestors safe.] *First Sentinel counted with fingers as he thought the numbers.*

One. Valence crouched and switched to mimicking the strong graystone bricks of the lip of the roof.

Two. First Sentinel leveled the grapple gun at the corner of the roof across the street.

Three. I quieted my mind and made ready.

"Go!" First Sentinel fired his grappling gun and dove off the roof. Valence stepped off the roof and let her weight carry her down. I soared above and threw a wave of force at the Warlock Guard. They scattered, some knocked back and over, others dodging out of the way. The guards lifted wands and staves, vessels for channeling the magical power that Yema had invested in each of them.

Valence's landing cracked the cobblestones of the road. She rose immediately and charged the guards. First Sentinel swung down onto a windowsill and started throwing knives.

Several guards with long blades moved to surround Valence. I picked one of them off the ground and held him in the air out of reach. He flailed with the knife, only succeeding in spinning himself head over heels in place.

Steel rained down on the guards, who stuck to cover and returned fire with magical blasts in gold and green and red. Several blasts rose up toward me, and I floated out of their way. But not fast enough. A red orb seared my right knee, and I lost my concentration, tumbling toward the ground.

My fall was interrupted when First Sentinel wrapped his arms around me. Rather than landing in the middle of the melee, we crashed into the steps of the apartment building on the near side of the street.

[Are you alright?] he asked hurriedly in his mind, and I raised a hand to satisfy him. I didn't know at the time that two of my ribs were broken, just that the pain was overwhelming.

[Help her, I'll be fine.]

First Sentinel turned toward Valence, who was being mobbed by warlocks. He drew another pair of daggers. For her, he'd tear down the tower of the City Mother herself.

I watched them from the stoop, struggling to stay conscious and using what strength I had to keep warlocks away from me. With the strength and toughness of graystone, Valence could stalemate four warlocks, maybe five. But not eight or nine, even with First Sentinel distracting several with swipes of his knives.

The fight went on like that for nearly a minute, with Valence taking a beating, only able to drop two of the warlocks with her heavy strokes. First Sentinel fought a losing battle, crowded by five of the guards. I pushed a guard at a time away, all the while feeling as if my middle were about to collapse.

My senses faded to nothing more than the fight before me, the flashes of anger from the guards as they approached, and the desperate thoughts of my friends too far away to help. There were no thoughts from civilians watching from the windows, no birds overhead. Just the battle, and even that began to grow dim.

The record of what happened next was patched together from my memory and what little First Sentinel would tell.

A warlock's staff-swing connected with the back of First Sentinel's head, dropping him to a knee. The others had driven Valence to the ground, blasts of magic crashing in waves over her back in sickly hues.

The warlock above First Sentinel raised a curved dagger, and I felt First Sentinel's mind snap. He reached out, and the warlocks stopped. Not just the one above him, all of them. Their minds went silent, no longer even filled with the echoes of their master. *The skittering thoughts were gone too. Nothing was left to them; nothing was left of them. They were as the dead, but still living.*

I don't read the threads, but Valence told me that in that instant, the burgundy strands of control that tied the warlocks to Yema as puppets were shredded. They were cut off from their master, no longer slaves but still not free, each of their hearts locked away in Yema's vault.

But their other threads had been shorn too, the dull remnants of their former lives, all gone. They were left with nothing, no connections, no emotions tying them to anything or anyone. The houses of their minds were empty, no lights, no furniture, nothing.

First Sentinel and Valence pulled me up after the warlocks' strings had been cut, and carried me to safety.

We did not see Aria for a week after the fight with the warlocks. Wonlar and I went to her apartment over a dozen times, but she would not open the door. I felt her mind through the doorway, reached out to touch it.

After that fight, it was as if a tornado had run through the house of Aria's mind, damaging memories and staining emotions.

Aria's voice carried through the door. "Go away, both of you. I need to be by myself." I sorted through the pieces in her mind, looked at the breaks at the edge of her memories, and felt the signature of First Sentinel's power. She had been in the middle of the crowd of warlocks when First Sentinel had lashed out.

I heard Wonlar's voice, muted but tender.

"Please, love, let us in. We're worried about you. Whatever's happened, we're here for you."

Nothing. Aria appeared above me in her mindscape, arms crossed. [Get out of my head.]

I withdrew my presence, returned my attention to my surroundings. Wonlar was still pounding on her door, tears at the corner of his eyes. I reached out and touched him on the shoulder, spoke in his mind.

[We need to go. She doesn't want us here.]

"*I don't care. She needs us—we can make it better. I can repair the threads, and you can fix her memories.*"

[No. It is not our place to do those things without her leave.]

I pulled Wonlar away from the door, and he struggled against my power.

"*Aria, please.*" *His voice was softer, almost resigned.*

"*Go away. Please. Leave me alone.*"

[Wonlar,] *I said again in his mind.*

He was kneeling then, hands stretched out to the door. "*I'm sorry, love. I was trying to protect you.*"

[She knows that, First Sentinel. Of course she knows.]

His voice grew loud in my mind. [Then why won't she let us in?]

[She has suffered a great wound. When she wants help, she will reach out. Have faith.]

[City Mother, please look after your daughter . . .] *Wonlar began to pray as he stood, and I led him away from Aria's apartment.*

We returned home, and First Sentinel locked himself up in his laboratory. I felt the rooms of his mind fall to shambles, wracked by grief and guilt as he tried to lose himself in work.

I will go to ask Aegis for counsel, for I am at a loss with them. May the City Mother guide Aria, Wonlar, and all of us. I pray that this is not the end of the Shields, torn apart from the inside by one grand misfortune. I fear that if Wonlar does not forgive himself, he will carry this guilt diligently to his grave.

Chapter Thirty-Eight

Sapphire

R ova returned to Bluetown for the first time in the better part of a month. Between Wonlar's injury and the summit, she hadn't gotten east of Lower Rib. Story time was on an indefinite hiatus.

The Ikanollo guards at the edge of the district took one look at her skin and waved her through. Getting in to Bluetown wasn't the problem for Freithin—it was getting back out once they were done. Omez had no objection to letting Freithin live together, as long as they stayed in the ghetto they claimed for themselves after the Unchaining. Some Freithin had moved to neighborhoods outside of Omez's domain, but most had never left Bluetown. Cheap labor wasn't as good as free labor, but for Omez it was far better than letting any of the other tyrants have their strength.

Across the threshold, the buildings grew half again as tall in an instant, as well as doors and roads, steps and bicycles. The whole neighborhood was Freithin-scaled, rebuilt after the Unchaining. Stocky blue children tussled in the street, chased after balls the size of a grown Ikanollo's torso. Sweet scents rose on the steam from rolling carts. One by one, she picked them out by the seasoning: *flehchi*, blue soup, Miller's meal, the half-dozen Freithin dishes she'd grown up on in Omez's cages and the work houses. Most of it was horrible, but familiarity was comforting at times.

Rova stopped to sample some of the *flehchi* and nibbled on the packed cake, crumbs spilling down in a sporadic trail behind her. She let the sights and smells surround and suffuse her, breathed them in so she could store them away in her mind. *Who knows when I'll be able to come back?*

Rova had more than just family bringing her to Bluetown that visit. The Shields needed extra hands, and there were still many Freithin in Bluetown who owed their freedom to First Sentinel and the Shields. The time had come to repay that debt.

She turned left by the open-air market, where dozens of merchants bellowed the praises of their wares at full voice. Another two blocks of rolling carts and scrambling children later, she reached a wide house with a circular orange door and a white knob.

None of the houses in Bluetown had exterior stairs or porches. Her people made their houses wide and flat, with broad doors and horizontal windows that still looked to her like prison bars. She felt the life inside this house, two hearts she'd known for a long time and another, young and rapidly growing.

The door opened as she approached, revealing her brother Zong in a gray tunic and white trousers held up by brown suspenders. He let the door open wide and beckoned her in with a toothy smile. Rova wrapped her arms around her brother in a powerful hug.

Zong said, "I was wondering when you'd come back."

She shook her head. "There's been so much to do, I've barely been sleeping."

"Nor eating, from the looks of it. Get inside and we'll fill you up." Zong stepped back out of the doorway, and Rova stepped inside the house that had been her family's for years.

Much of it was the same as it had been when they moved in. It had the same bright orange walls and blue trim, the same L-shaped couches facing the fireplace. Paintings and sculptures lined the mantle, including the portrait of Zong, Rova, and Nai.

Nai Watches appeared from around the corner, holding a squirming toddler dressed in yellow clothes. Nai's face filled with a smile as she said, "Greetings, sister. Your nephew has been asking about you." Dom Watches-and-Remembers turned in his mother's embrace and squealed Rova's name.

Rova collapsed onto the old couch, shedding her worry like a coat. There would be time to talk war, but it could wait a while.

She asked after Zong's business, and Nai shared details of Dom's milestones. The toddler climbed up into Rova's arms and collapsed into a big yellow sack of dead weight and gentle breathing. After some time, she gently passed Dom back to his mother and stood. *I can't put this off.*

"Zong, I need to find some extra hands for a very important mission."

He nodded. "Do I want to know what it is?"

"Not really," Rova said. "If the tyrants ever find out who I am, you don't want to know any details."

Zong sighed, but didn't repeat what he'd said before. Zong would join the Shields himself if not for his family, both his wife and son here, and the fact that Rova had forbidden it. She'd made him swear that he would never endanger himself that way. *Except now I'm doing it for him.*

"How many will you need?" Nai asked while Dom happily bashed blocks against one another on the floor.

"At least a dozen, but not more than twenty. We can't let the group get too big, and I only want the ones you know can be trusted." *Some of us have never really gotten over being servants. We went from being slaves to sergeants, hired goons, or bodyguards. Not many—but enough.*

Rova was a Shield on her own terms, and she followed orders because she believed in Aegis and First Sentinel. And now, after all the time she and Wonlar had spent with the children, Rova had to ask their parents and siblings to put their lives on the line.

Zong pulled her from self-doubt as he counted off names. "Gau for sure, Yuu, Oa, and Ken as well. Nai, what do you think?"

Nai looked up to the corner, thinking. "You'd have to swear them to secrecy, but you can probably get Xej, Li, and the whole Guards family."

Zong nodded. "That's ten. I bet we can drum up a few more. When do you need them?"

"Tonight. I have the instructions here. Be sure to give them the passphrase." Rova pulled out a short pile of handwritten instructions on pulp paper. "It's more important to have a small number that can be trusted than a larger number that you aren't sure about. If you can't find twelve, then send every one you can. I need you to be very clear in letting them know that they're taking their lives into their own hands by joining us. I can't guarantee everyone will come back."

She felt the worry clench Zong and Nai's hearts without even having to read it on their face. She continued, hoping to allay their fears. "Everything before this has been a move to win a battle. This time, we will turn the tide of the whole war."

Zong nodded. "You'll have your people, Rova. We remember what the Shields did for us, and if I can't find enough, I'll join you myself."

Nai's nostrils flared. "Zong, don't you dare."

Rova looked to Nai and then turned to Zong. "You belong here. If you show up, I'll knock you out myself and have you dragged home in a cart."

Zong sighed. "I'll help as much as I can. Please, eat with us before you leave. You've earned the rest, and your nephew misses you. He needs something to remember you by." *In case I don't come back, you mean.*

She stayed, talked with Nai, and played with Dom while her brother went out to find soldiers for the battle ahead.

A lingering winter wind howled through the alley as Sapphire waited for the rest of the Freithin to arrive. The light from the street ended an arm span into the alley. Inches into the darkness, Sapphire stood watch at the door of their staging position. Just after nine o'clock, the sixth volunteer approached.

"When the light is sparse, how do you see?" Sapphire asked.

The Freithin's eyes looked up as he tried to recall the passphrase. "Bring a lantern and light your own path."

She nodded and opened the door. Sapphire looked to the end of the alley, out to the street. There was no sign of black on black, no movement, no stirring of shadows. And so she ushered the Freithin into the room and closed the door.

The room was dimly lit by a handful of lanterns; some hung on the walls and two were on the table, which was just three crates pushed together and covered with a cheap tablecloth. Around the table, Ghost Hands had positioned eight crates in a circle, as chairs. The walls of the warehouse were blank slate, coaxed or carved out of the cliff wall hundreds of years ago. Sapphire took a position at one end of the table as the Freithin chatted, nervous.

Ghost Hands sat opposite her, still and silent atop a smaller crate. The perched Freithin around her would make Ghost Hands look like a child pretending to play with the adults, but for her poise and her contemplative silence.

Sapphire raised a hand, and the nervous chatter dropped off.

"Thank you for coming. For those of you who don't know, I am Sapphire, Shield of Audec-Hal." She gestured across the table. "This is my comrade, Ghost Hands."

The Freithin made their greetings. When they'd settled, Sapphire continued. "The Shields of Audec-Hal have fought for fifty years to free this city. Years ago, First Sentinel and the Shields shattered the Blue Heart and freed our people."

She took a moment; let a breath pass without words. The Freithin were nodding along, agreeing but not truly excited.

Sapphire punched a fist into her waiting hand. "Tonight, we do for the whole city what the Shields did for the Freithin."

A wave of emotions crashed across their faces. Surprise, disbelief, faintest hope.

A younger male in dockworkers' clothes raised his hand. "How can we do that?" His voice was earnest, eager. *Confidence, good.*

"What is your name, cousin?" Sapphire asked. Using their names frequently would tie them to one another, help them to trust one another.

He pulled himself up as tall as he could. He was young yet, barely over six feet tall. "I am Jeku Sees, cousin Shield."

"I am honored, Jeku Sees. Our task is a distraction to make room for another mission, but we have an objective of our own." Sapphire pulled out a map and opened it on the table. The map displayed the three square blocks around the mint, with their target circled in the center.

"Tonight, we will shatter the tyrant's sham of an economy." She took out a knife and slammed it into the name of the mint on the map. The knife dug down into the crate, not deep enough to disturb its contents. *Those are for later.*

Several of the more nervous Freithin jumped back at her violent motion. *Not a good sign. Are they really right for this? Even if they're prepared to give their lives, there's more to this than a suicide mission.*

"The mint?" asked one. He looked to be the youngest of the group, no work lines around his eyes or wrinkles on his brow. No tattoo on his wrist—he'd been born after the Unchaining.

Another Freithin answered before she could, a woman older than Rova. "If the tyrants can't print any more money, everything freezes, especially trade between Audec-Hal and other cities."

Rova nodded. "Please give your names the first time you speak, cousins. I cannot ask you to risk your lives if I don't even know your names."

The unmarked youth said, "Igaz Plays." Family names like Plays hadn't appeared until after the liberation. *He might be the first child born into the name.* Sapphire hoped Igaz lived long enough to pass the name on to his own children.

The woman nodded to Sapphire. "Duma Speaks." The softness around her jowls and arms dusted with flour to the elbows marked her as a baker. Rova recognized the woman from the storytime meetings; her daughter, Yara, always had an answer to Wonlar's questions.

Sapphire looked to both of them in turn, attached the names to the faces, hoping she wouldn't have to find their families and sing *kesh* with them at the funerals while Yara cried.

A woman with a yellow and silver headscarf leaned forward to ask a question. "My name is Weja Drives." Rova recognized that name as well. Her son Arno had started coming for the stories last month. A kind boy, already tall. "If we succeed, what will happen to everyone here trying to make a living?" The jeweled rings on her fingers and gems in her scarf showed that she had done well for herself. She had more to lose than the rest. But she came of her own will, ready to fight.

[This is a revolution. No one said it was going to be easy or that there wouldn't be losses.] Ghost Hands' voice echoed in their minds. Weja frowned.

Sapphire continued, making eye contact with each of the six in turn. "There are two other missions tonight, and each team relies on the other two. The three groups will spread the tyrants' forces thin, making all of us more likely to succeed."

Igaz shifted on the crate. "How are we going to take out the mint, though? Are we supposed to break the plates by hand?"

She chuckled. "Ghost Hands, please show them." Sapphire plucked the lanterns off the table and stood back.

The tablecloth shifted at the edges, then folded up onto itself and floated off to the side. The lids of the three crates slid off, clattering to the floor. The Freithin volunteers stood to look as Sapphire held the lantern high to shed light on the contents: dozens of boxes in gray and black and silver, metallic and stone alike. The boxes held fuses and power cells, switches and panels, a collection of explosives sufficient to demolish a city block.

They'd spent Nevri's blood money on weapons, supplementing years of hoarding. This mission would tap them out completely.

"Oh," said Igaz.

There was a knock on the door. Three fast, two slow, then five short knocks that trailed down the door. It was First Sentinel's signal.

Sapphire looked to Ghost Hands, who nodded. The door unlocked without being touched. First Sentinel walked in, guiding Fahra inside. She pulled down her leg wrap and waved at Sapphire, then rummaged through her bag.

Sapphire smiled. "Cousins, I'd like you to meet my friend Fahra. She's going to do something that will help keep us safe on our mission."

Fahra returned Sapphire's smile, then started walking through the room, her charcoal moving across the page with the grace and skill a far older woman would show.

Jeku furrowed his brow. "How will this keep us safe?"

Sapphire looked to First Sentinel, who said, "That's up to you, Sapphire. This is your team."

If I tell them about Fahra's talent, it could compromise her if they're captured. But if they're going to trust me . . .

"Fahra has a Spark-granted power. Anything she draws or paints becomes immune to the Spark."

Jeku's head quirked to one side. Several of the other Freithin gasped. Bluetown had seen more than its share of Spark-storms, but they'd always rebuilt.

Sapphire continued. "We're having her draw neighborhoods and people as fast as we can, but we can't take up all her time. If you'll let her sketch you, you'll never have to worry about Spark-storms again."

There were a few excited murmurs, and the Freithin pulled themselves together to pose. Fahra wove through the crowd for a moment, studying faces in that over-exaggerated focus of youth. In mere minutes, she produced a detailed sketch of the scene. Freithin huddled, hopeful smiles on their faces.

Fahra showed the drawing to Sapphire, who drew the girl up in a hug. "Well done."

First Sentinel raised an eyebrow at the two of them. *Alright, now the next step.* She gave him the signal. Then First Sentinel pulled off his mask, revealing his face. He assumed the tired carriage he used in his storyteller guise.

"Some of you know me as Wonlar Pacsa. For the last few years, I've come to Bluetown to tell stories so that your children might know our history. Tonight, we make a new story, one that will be remembered for generations. I put my trust in you, and I know that you will do your children proud."

After a couple of surprised gasps, several Freithin nodded in recognition. Two walked over to shake First Sentinel's hand. To the children in Bluetown, Old Man Wonlar was nearly as much of a hero as First Sentinel—one more immediate to their lives, not just another of the Shields.

Sapphire waited for them to make the rounds, and then asked, "Have you been to Aegis' group yet?"

"We're headed there now," he said, fitting his mask back on.

Sapphire ruffled Fahra's hair and then said, "Make sure you get home in time to sleep for school tomorrow. I'll . . . I'll come by when I can."

If I survive. If I don't, City Mother, watch over her.

First Sentinel wrapped the Millrej girl up again and the two of them left, well-wishes going with them from the new Shield-bearers.

"Alright. Now the fun part." A smile appeared on her face, as she opened another crate. This one contained blades, clubs, and a whole assortment of Freithin-scale armaments. Most were as long as an Ikanollo was tall. They'd been made to order over the years, in private, and at great risk to the craftsmen and women. "There are enough for everyone in these boxes."

The Freithin sorted through the weapons to make their choices. Most of them were simple, since the only people who got weapons training since the ban were guards and soldiers.

And Shields. Sapphire hefted a double-bladed axe that must have weighed ten pounds. She pricked her thumb on the tip of one axe-head and held up the bleeding finger. "I would share my blood and my heart with you all. I can do no less than to call you brothers and sisters, since you are risking your lives for my mission."

The other Freithin echoed Sapphire's gesture, and they joined hands. Their blood mixed, completing the Freithin blood-bond and linking their feelings as tightly as chainmail.

Sapphire nodded to the group. *I hope they're ready.* "We leave at the strike of ten."

Chapter Thirty-Nine

Aegis

Aegis held up a fist to halt his team so he could scan the street.

Headtown was the richest district in the city, and Dr. Herron lived in its most secure neighborhood. The Shields and their Freithin Shield-bearers had already left behind three squadrons of unconscious guards as they worked their way through the district. Someone in the local guard would notice the missing patrols soon, and Aegis hurried the group to their destination so that they could strike before the tyrant's thugs could respond.

The group passed huge estates with well-kept gardens, catching the rays of the sun through the great eye sockets in Audec's Skull. The inside of the skull was lined with great alchemical lamps so the residents could have extended daytime during the winter or show off their jewel-encrusted palaces for the seasonal fetes. *We're lucky; most of them don't bother to post guards at their front gates since they installed the Brilliant Guard mercenary company for security.*

Aegis looked over his shoulder at the six Freithin and Sabreslate. The Freithin were all dressed in working clothes, carrying weapons scaled for their massive frames: axes, swords, clubs, and shields. By day they were chauffeurs and dishwashers, dockworkers and construction workers, but tonight they were a small army.

Sabreslate walked half-melded into a nearby wall, her slate-woven raiment all but indistinguishable from the surrounding stone. They'd spent three hours walking through stone of the streets, using Sabreslate's power to avoid detection before getting to the right neighborhood. *I hope it doesn't tire her out too much before we even begin.*

Aegis checked the street signs. They were one block away from Dr. Herron's mansion. Aegis held up his hand and signaled the group forward, taking long strides to keep up with the others. A formal prayer filled his mind as they crossed the last block on the way to their target.

City Mother, keep my friends in your heart, and protect my father as he seeks to cut the bindings that have enslaved you. Audec-Hal needs you; needs you free, needs your help to fight against those that would continue to destroy the name of your city.

I will do my best to make you proud.

Behind the tall, iron gate and a sumptuous garden with brilliant flowers and herbs stood a great white rotunda— Dr. Herron's mansion. The full-length windows revealed an intricate glass chandelier in the foyer. The front door was wood, painted in burgundy and lined with brass. It was made for display, not security. There was a lot of glass in the front of the house, it'll be hard to hold as is. He'd need Sabreslate to rework the house for defense as soon as the guards were neutralized.

Aegis spotted a guard walking by and kept the team down behind the hedges until they passed out of sight.

Sabreslate slid forward in the street and shaped a key from her raiment. She worked the lock for a few seconds, ducking down when Aegis signaled. *Stay quiet, please. We can't lose surprise until we're at the door.*

The lock clicked and Sabreslate swung it open a half-inch.

Aegis spoke in a quiet voice. "Follow me. I've got the door." Sabreslate pushed the gate open, then Aegis set off in a dead run, kicking up well-organized gravel into heaping clouds as he crossed the yard in mere seconds. He jumped over the stairs to the patio and kicked the door off its hinges, the rest of the team following him, heavy feet pounding. *Let's hope this is worth it, Father.*

The door flew through the foyer and destroyed an ornate black table and an expensive floral arrangement. Polished crystal shattered on the ground, spilling soil and flowers onto the waxed tile at the feet of the three guards. Their eyes widened as they saw Aegis, then reached for their weapons. "Intruders!"

Aegis bellowed orders as he tore into the guards, hoping to coordinate the team and terrify the guards at once. "Fan out, take the guards. Don't let anyone out! Sabreslate, get the exits!"

He met the first guard shield-to-sword, circled the guard's blade over and off, and then laid him out with a right hook. The second guard stepped past his fallen comrade and swung a halberd down toward Aegis head. One of the Freithin Shield-bearers swatted the halberd away with a massive club, and the blade came down heavy on the tile.

"Thank you," Aegis said as he dodged to the opposite side as the Freithin, a woman named Sei Walks. Sei pressed the guard, sweeping his feet with her club. Aegis heard bones crack as the guard landed hard on his hip. The third guard raised a bow and shot point-blank, but a whipping stone tendril swatted it away, then receded back into Sabreslate's raiment. Aegis jumped the guard before he could pull another arrow from the quiver, dropping him with a knee to the solar plexus.

The foyer was clear.

Dr. Ovarei Herron, the owner of the house and patriarch of the collaborating Herron family, turned the corner on a circular stairway and called down to Aegis from behind another pair of guards, "What are you doing?"

And there's our hostage. Ovarei was an elder Ikanollo, firm features upturned in surprise and disgust. He was draped in expensive silks imported from halfway around the world.

Aegis scaled the stairs in an instant, sizing up the guards. The first prepared for a shield strike, so Aegis just grabbed the man's belt and tossed him over the banister. Next, Aegis lashed out with a kick to the second guard's knee. She doubled over and Aegis pulled her past him to tumble down the stairs. *I expected better. Please don't be a trap.*

Aegis seized Dr. Herron by the hand and wrenched the man's wrist up against his back, forcing him down with pain. Aegis applied more pressure. "Tell your guards to stand down," he said, whispering in the man's ear.

Dr. Herron stood up on his toes to release the pressure.

The doctor kept his composure while wincing at the joint lock. "There will be a hundred more swarming this place within minutes, you do realize that. The Brilliant Guard will tear you to ribbons." He held up his other hand and the glowing ruby inlaid to a golden ring, glowing like the Shields' own alarm bracelets.

Aegis contained a smile. *City Mother be praised for the predictable paranoia of the rich.* "We're counting on it. Now order your guards to stand down."

One of the Freithin (*Hebi, was it?—he's the dockworker*) set his crate dead-center in the foyer, where the table and flowers once were, then joined his partner. Sapphire's six recruits filled the foyer and spread out through the house in three pairs. *Good, just as I said. Let's hope they keep with it.*

Sabreslate was buried up to her elbows in the wall, turquoise lines of empathy spreading throughout the foyer as the stone shifted at her command. *By the time those guards arrive, we'll have a fortress.*

"You won't harm me, I'm too valuable." The doctor was saying all the right words to sound brave, but his voice and shaking hands said fear just as clearly as his quivering yellow thread. He didn't struggle as Aegis walked the two of them down the stairs toward the crate.

"Are you sure we won't kill you? First Sentinel killed Nevri not a month ago, and we've left a trail of bodies before. Besides, if I just break your fingers, you'll live, but you'll never be able to operate again." Take the bluff. *It's a big, scary bluff. And we have explosives.* "Take a look inside that crate, will you?" Aegis asked, holding both of the doctor's arms behind his back.

The doctor got an eyeful of the explosives in the crate, and craned his head around to address Aegis, panic creeping into his voice. "Are you going to blow up the entire street?"

Aegis heard the words resonate in his throat as he responded, but the voice was cold, detached, like his father's. "If it comes to that." The act was getting uncomfortable for Aegis.

This is something they do, not us. But this is for the city. And Dr. Herron has done far worse to other people. Torture, forced surgery, and modifications to Nevri's elites had paid for the doctor's mansion, and he'd been well-protected in case his services were needed again.

Aegis turned slightly to address Sabreslate. "I'm moving into the sitting room to secure him. Let me know when they arrive."

Sabreslate looked up and down the resealed walls of the foyer, running her hands along the stone. "Understood."

Thanks to Naako, they had the mansion's floor plans. She had designed Dr. Herron's home and every other one on the block. Each one of those plans was burned into Aegis' mind, down to the sewer passageways and sewer access.

"Team one, report!" he called down the hall. Team one was Cao and Sei Walks, brother and sister who worked construction. They were already used to working together, and Aegis prayed that teamwork would keep them safe.

The response came a moment later. "We're clear!" Aegis led Dr. Herron down the hall, and turned left into the sitting room where team two was waiting.

It was only ten paces across on both sides, but there was more money poured into that small room than in ten square blocks of Hook's Hole. Rows of bookshelves climbed to the ceiling on all four walls, each filled with aged hardbacks in neat rows. Antique chairs with velour seats circled an imported black-lacquered folding table. The table was covered by cranes in flight over an abstract mountain landscape. Properly fenced, any item in this room would feed a family for a year.

Team one flanked the only other doorway out of the sitting room, standing over another pair of formerly armed guards. One of the Freithin held a small gash on his left arm, red blood dripping between his fingers. *That's Nore Crafts, he drives armored carts in Medai's domain. His partner Aung Asks is a bodyguard for a Bluetown community leader.*

Aegis repeated the Shield-bearers' names to himself. He had met most of them only that evening, and if he faltered for even a sliver of a second in calling their names or assigning tasks, it could cost their lives.

Aegis shut the door behind them and said, "Take him; I need to see to that wound." Aung took the doctor and pressed him face-down into the expensive table, mimicking Aegis' hold by pressing the man's wrists up against the back of his ribcage. The edge of Aegis' mouth quirked up in a half-grin. *He knows that one already.*

The Shield pulled a bandage from his belt and asked the Nore to kneel. "We can't have that bleeding out when the fighting restarts."

"I thought we were supposed to be secure?" Nore asked as he knelt.

"We should be." Aegis gestured with his head toward the doctor. "And don't talk about the plan while he can hear us."

The young man blushed, cheek flushed purple for a moment. "Sorry."

"It's all right. I did worse on my first mission. Now take off your hand and stand still." Aegis wiped away the blood with a sterilized cloth, and then applies gauze to bind up the wound. "It's not bad, but it will keep bleeding. Watch that arm. If you take another hit there, it could reopen. Stay to your opponents' right side; keep your wounded arm out of the way. Do you understand?"

"Yes." Nore's voice was uncertain, but his threads were strong: purple connecting him to Aegis and thin but bright gold arcing over to Aung.

"Good. I don't want to lose anyone tonight. We're going to fortify this room." He stood up and pointed at the shelves. "Let's move some of these and brace them against the door."

Sabreslate's voice carried through the door once Aegis' voice faded. " . . . at the outer wall, twenty in the first batch and another thirty behind them?"

"Stay here, and watch him. Don't let anyone in without the passphrase." Aung and Nore nodded, and he dashed out of the room.

"That's twenty and then thirty?" Aegis asked as he hurried down the hallway. The reinforced walls were more than a foot thick, but thanks to her people's gift, Sabreslate could see through it as if it were standing water, as long as she was in contact with the stone.

"Yes," she said.

Aegis shouted, "Team one, are you in position?"

"Not yet!" came the response from ahead.

Dammit. "What do they have to break the wall?"

"Nothing that I can see, but who knows?"

A moment later, Aegis heard the stone walls crack. *It couldn't be that easy, son,* rang Wonlar's voice in his mind. Aegis reached the crate in the foyer and helped the Freithin sort out their supplies for the siege.

This is going to be a long night.

Chapter Forty

First Sentinel

*H*alf a century after Nevri's coup, here we are. Three missions, five Shields, and one goal we've been pursuing the entire time.

Perched atop the crown of Audec's skull, The tower of the City Mother scaled so high that it hurt First Sentinel's neck to scan all the way up to see the top. He dragged the fourth and last of the door guards onto his pile and went to the door. Clearing out the guards had taken one of his last flash stones, but he knew that time was of the essence. Both of the other teams were already in play, which is why he only had to deal with four guards on the door instead of a whole squadron on alert.

Time will tell how much they've committed, how much of an errand I've set for myself. First Sentinel pulled the heavy golden key from the guard's belt and opened the ancient doors.

There were ten guards scattered around the room between him and the door to the stairs up. Three were huddled around a table, playing cards, another four paced the room, and the last three stood by the far door. First Sentinel dropped the key to the tower as the guards at the table turned and stood to alert. First Sentinel drew his fighting staves, spinning quick defensive patterns as he walked into the tower. *Here goes everything.*

"Surrender now and this won't hurt," First Sentinel said. There was no response. *I don't begrudge them the choice. I need the warm-up.* The first guard swung a blackjack toward First Sentinel's head, but the Shield raised a staff to spoil the shot and snapped the other one against the guard's ribs. First Sentinel slipped a staff under the guard's arm. He tossed the guard to the floor. The other two flanked out, each holding out swords.

The four pacing guards were closing fast. *Not much time. Keep to the wall, don't get surrounded. Fight smart, old man.*

He pounced on the guard by the near wall. First Sentinel beat his sword against the stone and rolled toward his off-hand side, smacking the guard across the face. The guard dropped his sword and First Sentinel put him out with a short jab with a staff. He faced the third guard as another four closed to within ten paces. The last guard was more cautious than the others; he stood at a wide distance and waited for backup.

Have to keep momentum, no stopping until I've reached the top. Drawing a vial from his belt, First Sentinel took three quick steps forward and leapt into the air, downing another elixir. The alchemical worked, ending his fall and suspending him in the air. First Sentinel put his staves away, drawing a handful of throwing blades.

Two guards stood aghast for a moment, but the other three raised crossbows. First Sentinel spun around to a three-quarters position, as if prone to their perspective, and tossed the first two blades at the nearest crossbow-carrying guard. One blade struck deep into the unpolished wooden stock of the crossbow, the other clipped his collarbone. The guard dropped to a knee and his bolt flew wide and ricocheted off the wall. Another bolt came within a hand span of First Sentinel's leg. The third punched a hole in his longcoat. *That didn't take long.*

First Sentinel tossed two more blades at the next guard, a tall Pronai woman with arms nearly as long as her legs. She ducked and bobbed out of their way. First Sentinel heard a volley of twanging crossbows and he twisted in the air to dodge.

Not enough. He felt the bolt glance off a rib and thanked the City Mother he hadn't been a half-turn to either side, which would have left him with a foot-long metal rod through his gut. He tried to ignore the wound and reached for another set of blades. This pair sailed toward the third crossbowman, a Millrej canine-kin, with the elongated black nose but not the Full-blood traits. The Millrej failed to dodge, catching a blade in the chest.

Two down, that's all I need. As expected, the elixir's effect wore off, and First Sentinel flipped over, falling. He dropped knees first onto a guard with a sword, catching the Ikanollo by surprise. The Shield drew one fighting staff and a fighting knife, his most versatile arrangement for combat with armed foes.

He lashed out with the staff to knock aside another guard's sword blow. Two of the guards lunged in on him at once, and the trio toppled to the ground. First Sentinel scrambled to protect himself from their blades as he tried to find his footing. While dodging a knife strike to the heart, he caught a knee to the ribs just below where the bolt had glanced off.

He curled his arm in front of his chest and took a knife cut along the outside of his arm, mostly blunted by the reinforced coat. *Not good; move it or they'll have you trussed up and sent off to the tyrants for dinner.* He had to break free, reclaim control of the fight.

First Sentinel squirmed free and rolled backward, finding his feet and leaving his knife in one of the guards' backs. The other guard stood slowly, forming a circle with the rest. He was surrounded.

This is supposed to be the warmup, old man. You'll never make it to the City Mother with this slop. You're embarrassing yourself. Get up.

And he did.

Chapter Forty-One

Sapphire

Sapphire's team was down by two Shield-bearers before they reached the exterior of the mint's vault. The first one, Fuhn Jumps, took a crossbow bolt through the eye when they took the door. The second fell under a hail of knife blows from a Pronai guard in the halls leading to the vault room. *His name was Ove Questions.*

Sapphire repeated their names as a mantra and kept her team close. She assigned Ghost Hands to scanning more actively for thought patterns, so they wouldn't be surprised again. *Please let the list stop at two.* Singing *kesh* for two blood-kin she had barely begun to know was more than enough.

The halls were almost painfully well lit, electric lights in sconces on both sides of the wall, every five paces. The whole place smelled like burnt ozone. Sapphire took the lead, advancing along the wall in a moving crouch.

According to the Shields' plan, both of the other teams should already be in place, and judging by the alarms sounding throughout the halls, Sapphire's team was doing their part in pulling forces from the tower for First Sentinel. *He still should have let us send backup*, she thought, praying the wounded veteran could scale all seventy floors of the tower and liberate the City Mother.

[Incoming. Two more, from the left turn ahead,] Ghost Hands said in Sapphire's mind.

Sapphire halted and stood at the ready. The four remaining Freithin set down the crates and stepped out into the center of the corridor.

"Use your numbers and your size. They won't be used to fighting this many of us at once," Sapphire said by way of encouragement.

Two Ikanollo rounded the corner, leading with their spears. "There they are!" one shouted as he lunged at Sapphire. She wrapped her hand around the top of the haft and yanked forward, pulling the guard off balance into her fist. The second turned and stabbed inward, but Sapphire swung the first guard around to take the blow for her.

The rest of Sapphire's squad closed and pummeled the woman into unconsciousness. They left her tied to her spear and buried the blade in the top of the wooden frame of a doorway, leaving her hanging. The ease of their progress inside the mint left her worried. Where was the real security? Had the tyrants really left it with a skeleton crew?

"Keep up the pace," she said. "We want to make our stand inside the vault, and the reinforcements will already be on their way." *They may just flood the halls with numbers, try to overrun us. Either that or send in the elites. It's what I'd do.*

Sapphire ducked around a corner to scout and saw the vault filling the whole end of the hall. A full squadron of guards stood at the vault door, half of them armed with crossbows, the others carrying halberds. Several of them were looking down the hallway and locked eyes on her. *And there we are. But they won't leave their posts, in case we flank.* She ducked back out of the corridor and waved her unit back.

"Is there another way to the vault?" Sapphire whispered to Ghost Hands.

[Not that I remember.]

She considered for a moment, looked down to the crates her fellow Freithin were carrying, and smiled. *They won't expect this.*

"How fast can you throw one of these bombs, Ghost Hands?"

Sapphire felt as much as heard Ghost Hands' chuckle in her mind. *[Fast enough. Pick the right one, and the blast radius should cover half the hallway. Leave yourself some room for the shrapnel.]*

She motioned the team back around the end of the corridor and pulled a box the size of her head from one of the crates. "This should do."

"Follow two paces behind me," she said to her Shield-bearer cousins. Ghost Hands extended a hand, and the box floated out of Sapphire's grip.

Sapphire watched around the corner as the switches flipped. The bombs shot down the hallway as fast as a crossbow bolt. Sapphire judged the explosive's velocity against her own running speed, waited a few seconds, then started running.

"Go!" she said. The guards dove to the floor as the explosive detonated against the vault door, consuming the far end of the hall. The concussive blast muted her hearing, but she kept running. Sapphire reached the far end of the hall as shrapnel clattered to the ground at her feet. She took a quick look over her shoulder and saw her team a few paces back.

Ghost Hands wiped the smoke away to reveal a hole the size of a dinner table in the vault door. The handful of guards that hadn't been killed or incapacitated by the blast went down quickly, and Sapphire took stock of the room. It was thirty feet long and twenty feet wide, with room on each side of the vault door. Plates and tools and dyes lined the walls, each in their own lock box. *All I have to do is break the plates, but if we take the whole room when we go, all the better.*

"Set the perimeter, and prepare for siege. Ghost Hands, you're in command of the door, I'll take any who get inside. Shield-bearers, two on each side of the door. Space yourselves out at arm's length to protect against bolts and blasts, but always support your partner. I'll take care of the plates."

The team took their places as Sapphire confirmed that all of the plates were present and accounted for.

She hoped Aegis' team and First Sentinel were faring this well. *And with fewer casualties, City Mother permit.*

Chapter Forty-Two

Aegis

The Brilliant Guard had broken through the walls three times, and Sabreslate was running out of material to use in shoring it up. Much more, and she'd risk bringing the rest of the house down. The soldiers hauled away as many of the chunks as they could each time, depleting her supply. Every bit of stone drawn from another wall made the other entrances that much easier to penetrate. It was a game of attrition, and not one that favored the Shields.

We've had one bout of luck, if you could call it that. After the third breakthrough, when forty of Nevri's thugs were swarming the courtyard, a Spark-storm tore through the neighborhood. The storm hailed knives that cut into the guards, and where they were cut, the blood turned into coils that swallowed the soldiers.

Moments later, the soldiers were Reborn out of the blood into dark-red insectoid creatures that tore into their former fellows. The Brilliant Guard now fought itself, and in the chaos, Sabreslate had the opportunity to shore up the defenses, pulling out the cobblestones in the street to remake the front wall.

Aegis and a couple of the Freithin took cuts from the hail of knives, but their blood flowed as normal, sparing them the choking coils. *I think we can call that a successful test. City Mother be praised for Fahra's gift.*

But the respite didn't last. Another thirty soldiers arrived, carrying a battering ram.

"We can't keep going like this," Aegis said. "We need to consolidate, give ground, and reinforce our position." He dispatched the last few guards from the most recent wave to flood through the broken doorway.

"To the waiting room, then? What's our exit route?" Sabreslate asked. Nore and Aung pulled the bodies aside and stuffed them into the foyer closet, then replaced the heavy desk to brace it closed.

Aegis recalled the floor plan and said, "There should be a sewer access from the back door, where they dump the garbage. Leave the walls around the sitting room, the back hallway, and the door. We should be able to hold that a bit longer."

"Right." She took a deep breath, mustering her strength. The effort was taking its toll.

I can't ask her to do much more of this, Aegis realized. "How thick will the wall have to be to stop that battering ram?"

"Thick enough that I'd only be able to cover the waiting room—and then we wouldn't have any way to breathe."

Aegis thought out loud. "Nine people in a room that size. No good. Give me the hallway and the back entrance." He raised his voice to carry through the building.

"Team one, hold position! Teams two and three on me! Form up! We're retracting the walls! Move, move!" he shouted.

"They're readying another volley," Sabreslate said. "This is going to hurt."

"Start pulling in the walls."

Sabreslate nodded, retreating down the hall to take her new position. Another explosion shook the building. Spider-webbed cracks spread all the way up the two-story foyer.

Move quickly, Father. I'm not sure how long we can hold here.

Chapter Forty-Three

First Sentinel

The third floor was segmented by long, narrow hallways, much easier for stealth. First Sentinel walked them like a ghost, picking off the guards one by one on his way to the next stairwell. Each level, the stairs rotated between the west, east, north, and south sides of the tower. Originally, it was supposed to have been a part of the priests' prayers, walking the paths of the four directions in an intricate pattern as worship to the City Mother. *I remember taking the whole day when we came here on a trip for my school, all those years ago.*

For First Sentinel, it meant the ascent might take the better part of the night. Every step he took could cost his friends' lives.

Climbing along the outside was out of the question—the exterior of the tower was impregnable and smooth, no gaps or holds for climbing gear. Ghost Hands might have been able to fly up the side, but the lack of windows meant she'd still have to break in somewhere. *And she's fantastic at crowd control when supporting a group, but not on her own.*

And this is my battle now.

Checking around the corner, First Sentinel saw another pair of guards, forty paces away. The old wooden floor creaked, but the ceilings were low enough that he wouldn't be able to sneak up on anyone by floating along the ceiling.

So I bring them to me. First Sentinel cupped his hands and shouted down the hallway. "Hey you, which way to the stairs?"

They turned and called the alarm. One waved down the T-crossing hall. The other, an armed Freithin male, started toward the Shield. His greatsword was as tall as First Sentinel.

Thank you for splitting off from your partner. The long hallway gave him the time to put on a shock glove and then draw a knife. The guard had range to spare, but moving as fast as he was, it would be good for one swing and then First Sentinel could go in for the grapple. *Grappling a Freithin is a fool's errand . . . unless you have tricks.*

First Sentinel rolled a smoke pellet between his fingers as the Freithin shouted a battle cry.

Intimidation, really? I wrote that book before you were born.

The Freithin stepped within ten paces, and First Sentinel smashed the smoke pellet on the floor. The shimmercrab goggles kept the smoke out of his eyes and registered the guard's heat amidst the gray cloud. First Sentinel ducked and rolled beneath the wild swing and severed the Freithin's right hamstring with a passing slice. The guard dropped to a knee, and First Sentinel buried the knife in the guard's kidney. He jumped up to grab the Freithin around the neck with the shock glove, sending electricity racing through the big man's body.

But he was a Freithin, so that only made him mad. The sentry reached up and grabbed First Sentinel's arm, then pushed off with his good foot and smashed the two against the wall.

First Sentinel tucked his neck to avoid cracking his skull, but as his back hit, something twinged in his ribs where he'd taken the glancing shot earlier. First Sentinel reached down to pull his blade out with a twist and stab again, closer to the Freithin's spine. The tangy smell of blood tinted the air, and the Freithin fell against the wall again. First Sentinel swung around the Freithin, avoiding the crush. The Freithin's legs were useless, so First Sentinel brought the knife up to slit the guard's throat, putting him out of his misery. *I'm sorry.*

First Sentinel looked up to see three more guards fill his vision. The first one thrusted for his face with a spear, and First Sentinel dropped a knee to duck under the shot. He reached up and grabbed the spear's haft, then wrapped his around it and pulled himself up toward the guard, stabbing up into his armpit.

First Sentinel felt a dull impact against his side as the protection in his shirt kept a mace from caving in his ribcage. First Sentinel swung the handle end of the spear around at the mace-holder, who ducked under his swing and circled away.

First Sentinel stabbed the staff back behind him in a blind shot, hoping it bought enough time to get out of the pinch.

Breaking loose, First Sentinel lashed out with his knife. The second guard's mace swung around to strike First Sentinel's hand as he attacked, so the Shield changed the arc of his cut to avoid the strike and cut across the guard's collarbone. *And that's why I use knives.*

Turning with the strike, First Sentinel knocked the second guard over with a kick and saw an overhead strike coming in from the third guard's longsword.

He didn't have time to block, even if he could count on his knife to stop the swing. Instead, First Sentinel dropped straight down as he raised the knife, praying he was right in judging the arc of his strike.

The cut sailed through empty air and connected with the wall inches above First Sentinel's face. The guard's strike skidded along the tile wall with a horrible sound. First Sentinel stood up into a tackle, taking the guard while he recovered.

You better stop counting on your luck, old man, or it'll run out just in time to get yourself killed.

First Sentinel clocked the guard with the pommel of his knife and felt the man go limp. The Shield's ribs sang a discordant song of agony as he stood up, and before he could catch his breath, a giant hand curled around his foot and brought him right back to the floor. First Sentinel scrambled around to his back, feeling the twisting pull in his ankle, his foot still held in a vise like grip.

The Freithin guard stared at him through bloodshot eyes, crawling along the floor with a trail of red behind him. *No time to stop and wonder how he's still alive—I need to get him off my foot.* First Sentinel stabbed at his hand while he reached for another smoke pellet.

"You're not getting away, Sentinel," he said, blood filling his mouth. *Damned fool is killing himself faster by trying to talk.*

So First Sentinel goaded him on. "None of you are going to stop me. Not Yema or COBALT-3, and definitely not you." First Sentinel cracked the smoke pellet in his hand, reversed the knife grip, and brought the blade down toward the Freithin's head.

Through the smoke, he saw the red-tinted signature of the guard's hand come up to block, but the Freithin couldn't see the strike. First Sentinel took off the better part of the Freithin's thumb before the knife stuck through the top of his skull. The grip on his foot went limp, and First Sentinel shook his leg free. First Sentinel collapsed backward on the floor, feeling the warm puddle beneath his longcoat.

He took a few long breaths, assessing his injuries. *At this rate, I'm not going to be able to reach the top in one piece. Something in my plan needs to change, and I'm not sure what other tricks I have left to spare.*

An old voice spoke up in his head with a temptation, and he brushed it away. *No, never again.*

Chapter Forty-Four

Sapphire

An hour into the mission, the real threats showed themselves. Sapphire and the rest of her team were positioned to hold the gap left by the blown vault door. The five Freithin marked out a concave semicircle kill pocket inside the vault, daring anyone to close to within melee range of the group. All the while, Ghost Hands deflected the projectile fire, protecting the Freithin's formation. They'd felled thirty guards around them with this technique, though they had also spent a full crate of explosives scattering groups along the way.

First came the Stalker Model II automata. The Stalker IIs were deadly melee combatants designed by COBALT-3, with flexible coiled bodies, modular weapons, and an insectoid aesthetic—antennae, armored carapace, and six legs. They were only as tall as an Ikanollo, but bristled with weapons and were as fast as a Pronai. *Thank the City Mother there's only two of them.*

Sapphire leaned over to dodge under a whirling blade-chain and continued hammering away at the carapace armor with her hand axe. It wouldn't give, even to the alchemically sharpened edge. She left the axe stuck between flexible joints and engaged the Stalker hand to blade. *Maybe I can just dent the slippery thing until it can't move.*

Ghost Hands was busy holding off the latest squadron of guards and their crossbow fire, leaving the other Stalker automata to her Freithin Shield-bearers. Sapphire kicked the Stalker back to the wall and went on the defensive for a moment to watch her kin. The Freithin were strong, capable, but the Stalkers were designed to kill Shields, and their programming for fighting Sapphire was close enough that it kept the four Freithin on the ropes by itself.

The other Stalker spun its upper body and pushed the Shield-bearers back outside the reach of its blade, then pressed toward Duma and caught her across the inside of her wrist, deep enough that she'd probably never use the hand again. *What good was a one-handed baker?*

Duma stepped back, and Weja dropped out of the line as well, pulling off one of her scarves to make a tourniquet. Red blood stained Weja's brightly colored scarves, ruining the sheer material.

[Ghost Hands?] Sapphire called in her own mind while fighting the Stalker automata. She hoped her teammate could pick through the psychic static of the guards down the hall and the four desperate Shield-bearers.

[Yes?] came the response, uncertain.

Sapphire connected with a right hook to the automata's face, knocking it back a step. *[I have to take out these Stalkers, or they're going to tear our people apart. On my mark, I want you to encase the Stalker I'm fighting inside a force sphere, to contain an explosion. Got it?]* Sapphire backed up toward one of the crates, giving ground. The Stalker advanced, tracing intricate patterns with its blades that left no openings.

[The other field will have to come down for me to be able to do that,] Ghost Hands conveyed by thought.

[I know. I'll call the order to hit the ground, and you switch the fields.] Sapphire cartwheeled over the crate, retrieving a small explosive that came with an adhesive patch, one of First Sentinel's designs.

The Stalker automata cut Sapphire along the leg as she flipped, then slid around the side of the crate to press her. She landed on her good foot and stuck the explosive to the automata as it attacked. Sapphire dropped onto her back and tossed the stalker over her head toward its metallic twin.

"Hit the ground!" she shouted, and saw the shimmer of Ghost Hands' field switch to a sphere around the two automata.

[Can you hold in both?] Rova asked.

[We'll see.] The automata picked at the explosive with mandibles and blades, confused. But the adhesive stuck, and the shimmering sphere filled with fire and shrapnel, contained.

Crossbow bolts flew through the air where the field had been, but most went far too high, aimed for Freithin hearts and heads. One of the shots struck home, and Sapphire saw a bolt take Jeku through the collarbone. Sympathetic pain exploded in her head, and she rolled on the floor for a few moments, oblivious to everything but the pain of a blood-bonded kinsman's life being snuffed out not ten feet from her side.

Half of them gone: Jeku, Fuhn, and Ove. Wonlar, I hope you make this worth their sacrifice. From Wonlar, her thoughts went to Aegis. He was only two districts away, at the doctor's estate. But he might as well be across the continent. If he was hurt, there would be nothing she could do.

The five of them got to their feet. One-half of one automaton remained, twitching and flailing blades with its quickly fading energy supply. Sapphire kicked the broken machine out of the vault toward the surprised guards.

A new shape appeared behind the guards, a shifting mass that undulated over and through the group to cohere momentarily in front. *Protean*, Sapphire thought, recognizing the Smiling King's quicksilver killer, the most dangerous of his Spark-touched army. They'd faced a metamorph when they destroyed the Rebirth Engine, but Protean had more power, more mass, and more experience.

Sapphire would not let that thing take any more of her people from her.

The thing's features shifted constantly as it talked, one voice bleeding into the next. "Come peacefully, and you will be granted the bliss of Rebirth at the hands of the Smiling King. Resist, and the ending of your story will be written in blood on the walls of this mint."

"Nice to see you too, Protean," Sapphire said, then turned to her Shield-bearer kin. "Stay close, and always pay attention. Protean can transform into practically anything, but it has to maintain its mass. Any of you still outweigh it, so use your size and don't let it scare you."

Her words rang hollow as the Spark-touched drew itself up, becoming tall but gaunt. Its fingers elongated into claws, its teeth multiplied into a jagged maw. It let loose a scream that wavered between three octaves.

"Close with it, get in under its reach," she said, taking position at the head of the remaining three Freithin Shield-bearers.

The guard's commander shouted an order, "Advance!" as Protean lunged forward.

[*Ghost Hands, keep them out of the vault!*] Sapphire shouted in her head, barreling forward into Protean's attenuated form to wrap her arms around the narrowed torso. Talons dug into her back, but she kept her momentum, driving the two of them into the wall.

"Go for its arms!" Her back was ablaze with pain. Igaz, Duma, and Weja joined the melee, bracing Protean's arms against the wall while Sapphire worked its belly with quick jabs. Then Protean shrank, arms withdrawing from the Freithins' grip and sprouting from lower in the Spark-touched's torso, reforming as four squat arms with large hands. Its belly sprouted sharp spines and Sapphire let go, stepping back to assess the situation while Protean grappled with her Shield-bearers.

She felt Ghost Hands' desperation. The Qava was straining to maintain the force field as the guards tested its strength with hammering blows.

Move fast, Wonlar. We can't last forever.

Chapter Forty-Five

First Sentinel

*B*ecause *what I really need right now is a good bout of running for my life. I must have missed that appointment on my calendar.*

First Sentinel pivoted off a handhold on a corner and swung himself around into the next hallway, eleven guards on his tail. First Sentinel discovered, to his chagrin, that the junior priests' quarters had been converted into a barracks. Not wanting another delay, he opted for stealth.

It half-worked, and he'd made it almost two-thirds of the way up the tower. But now he had a tail that stretched down a full level. The blue-tile walls painted with centuries-old murals of Audec history raced by as he ran. *These halls were meant for reverent pacing and walking meditation, not cat-and-mouse games.*

Crossbow bolts soared over his head and within an arm span of his back, ricocheting off the ceiling and the walls nearby as the Shield ducked and weaved. First Sentinel worried how long his painkillers would last. He had dry-swallowed another set of pills halfway up the tower, but when the gashes and flesh wounds from tonight caught up with him, his half-ruined leg and the endless weeks that had lead up to the mission would probably be the end of him. *If I slow down now, it's all over.*

First Sentinel tossed his second-to-last flash-bang behind him at the next T-juncture, and poured on the speed to clear the hallway by the time the guards regained their vision. First Sentinel had avoided the direct way to the next level, instead circling around through the washroom and its two entrances, one of them by the next set of stairs. *It may mean I end up with a few of them in front of me, but it'll be better than facing the lot all at once.*

Adrenaline and fatigue played a wrestling match, urging him onward and dragging him down as he turned the corner into the sparsely appointed washroom. The junior priests were given little more than chamber pots and simple sinks, and the tyrants had neglected to improve upon those amenities.

First Sentinel looked both ways as the washroom emptied out into the hallway, and saw a clump of six guards halfway down the hall.

"There he is!" one said. *Damn.*

First Sentinel tossed out a handful of caltrops to bar their way, before bounding up the stairs two at a time. It wouldn't slow them by much, but if luck stayed with him, he could lose them on the next level. If memory served, there were only two levels left; then he would reach the hall of the City Mother, which took up the top third of the Tower.

First Sentinel kept ahead of his tail all the way through the lower ritual rooms and the senior priests' quarters. *Where are the priests, if not here?*

Yema had replaced most of the real priests a long time ago with his Warlock Guard, and from what First Sentinel could tell, those warlocks were all going to be in the hall itself. *Another hurdle before I can do what I've actually come for.*

The spiral stairs around the curved edge of the tower gave way to thirty-foot-tall double doors, painted in the brightest emerald green and inlaid with silver. The doors were thrown wide open, letting First Sentinel see into the hall. Most things looked larger when you were a child, a simple difference in scale. This place looked just as big as it had decades ago.

Stretching up into the starry sky, the hall took up the entire width of the tower, with wooden rafters winding up the side, mixed in with old stone abutments and pathways. They'd been replaced and renovated countless times over the years, constantly under repair.

At the center of the room, atop a graystone platform circumscribed by golden runes, sat the largest emerald in the world, perfectly cut to twelve sides. Just over a yard wide, the jewel was the vessel of the City Mother, guardian goddess of Audec-Hal.

Countless burgundy threads spread from the City Mother, the power that had kept the city docile for decades. One thread was the strongest of them all, wrapped a dozen times around the emerald, smothering its natural emerald light. This one thread had controlled the City Mother since shortly after the destruction of the Senate building. Wrapped taut, the other end of the thread arced through the air to the heart of a solitary figure.

The figure was cloaked, the cloth darker than midnight on a moonless night. The hood of his midnight cloak was pulled back, revealing a bald skull with tattoos inked in every color.

No. Not him.

Magister Yema, holder of the thousand captive hearts of the Warlock Guard, master of the sorcerous arts, and controller of the City Mother. He was wreathed in burgundy threads, wearing his braided threads of power like a crown.

Nevri had ended the rule of the Senate, but it was Yema who had robbed the city of hope, taking the City Mother under his control and turning her connection to the populace into his greatest weapon.

Around him were fully a hundred of his Warlock Guard, each bound to give their life for his.

They were waiting for him.

And on the other side there's me. No allies at his back, his belt of tricks all but exhausted. *And I'm likely to pass out any minute.*

He had to get close enough and try to break through to her, hope that his decades of resistance and devotion have made him strong enough for the task. That maybe, just maybe, he'd hear her. With Yema so close to match his power, freeing the City Mother might be impossible.

But if he ran, the warlocks and the other guards would catch up to him. And even if they didn't, the forces returning from the other missions would. The distraction missions were not designed to be stable on their own.

Yema started laughing, and the Warlock Guard circled in, brandishing wicked knives and glowing wands.

His only choice was to make his final stand and free the City Mother, even if it killed him. Hopefully it'd kill Yema too.

Aria, I'll be seeing you soon.

Chapter Forty-Six

Aegis

Things would have been fine if Qazzi Fau hadn't shown up and brought ten of his top assassins. First, they shattered Sabreslate's reconstituted wall. Then the black-clad killers filled the sitting room, taking Aegis' team apart with the death of a thousand cuts.

Qazzi taunted Aegis as they fought, trying to bait the younger fighter into a mistake. "Where's that decrepit old man you call your leader? Still nursing his wounds, or is he off slinking in the shadows somewhere, playing the hero?"

Aegis took the insults and threw them back, the repartee just another part of the battle. If he just brushed them off, it could dishearten the Shield-bearers. He had to fight back with words as well as steel.

"The 'old man' has survived everything the tyrants have thrown at him for fifty years. You'd be lucky to have his longevity, but I don't see that happening, given your choice of allies." His shield slashed and parried, the steel sometimes seeming to move of its own accord.

Aegis kept Qazzi away from the rest, but in doing so, he couldn't split focus to command his team. Aegis heard Sabreslate's raiment lash out at the killers, smelled the sourness of spilled blood. But whenever he tried to look sideways to check on Nore or Aung, Qazzi was on him instantly, spinning his twin sabers in blinding patterns. The assault was already tiring Aegis' shield arm, countless shocks turning his muscles into jelly.

His father's voice in his ear: "*Stay strong, Selweh. Move your body, not the shield.*"

Qazzi continued. "Oh, I intend to live long past the time they burn your ashes and pour them into the river, Aegis. And long enough to kill the next idiot who takes up the name, and the next, until the only people left are smart enough to know their place."

"Everyone is born free." Aegis cleared Qazzi's swords with the shield and threw a kick to the man's groin.

Qazzi knocked the blow aside with his knee. "Not in Audec-Hal."

"Especially in Audec-Hal." Aegis followed the kick with a right cross that caught Qazzi square on the jaw.

At the same time, Aegis took a roundhouse kick to the ribs. Both men stumbled back, recovering. When Aegis caught his balance, he was out of Qazzi's range. He took the respite to step back and flick his gaze over to the rest of the room.

Both Aung and Nore were still standing, Nore favoring his right side. They were each fighting two of the killers, blood staining their sleeves and pants. *They can take a beating, but not for much longer.* The Walks siblings were fighting side by side near the entrance, but their teamwork couldn't compensate for the clumsiness of their strikes. They were being picked apart by Qazzi's better-trained killers.

Sabreslate fought in a corner, squared off against three of the assassins. She whipped flexible stone tendrils to keep them from attacking all at once, using her position to protect her flanks. But the tendrils were moving slower than normal, and Aegis could see her mask was drenched with sweat.

When Qazzi's team struck, Dr. Herron had run for the door, trying for the hole in the wall, but Aegis had caught the man with a clothesline. The hostage was unconscious on the threshold. He'd served his purpose. It didn't matter if they got out with him, as long as he didn't enlist any more help.

"Don't mind them, my people are taking care of your people nicely," Qazzi said as he closed again. He swung low from the left with one blade and swept down from the top right with the other, trying to drive Aegis back so he could pull his killers and flank.

It's what I'd do if I were in his position.

Instead, Aegis dove over Qazzi's lower blade and into the pocket left by the downward slash, covering his back with the shield. Rolling back to his feet, he lashed out with a sweeping kick to take Qazzi Fau off his feet. The blow didn't land, but the killer had given ground, returning the pair to the center of the room.

Aegis continued the banter. "Your people look like they're dressed for bed, not fighting. Or can't you afford to buy them more than one outfit with that measly tax share I hear Dlella's given you?"

From his new vantage point, Aegis got another glimpse of the fights. Sabreslate's left arm hung limp, black blood coating her raiment, and Rova's kinsmen were backed up against the wall, flailing at the killers' blades. Cao took a sword up under the ribcage and dropped to the floor. Sei screamed in sympathetic pain and Qazzi's men leapt on her as well.

You're done, Aegis. Get what's left of your team out alive.

"Retreat!" he shouted, too loud for the walled-in room. Aegis wheeled around toward Sabreslate, putting himself between Sabreslate and the assassin.

Sabreslate took the opportunity and bolted for the door, her legs still strong. Aung tried to push past the killers, and impaled himself on two of their blades, but kept moving. Nore was wiser, jumping over the downed killers and then bolting through the middle of the room toward the sewer exit in the back.

Qazzi backpedaled to cut Nore off, but Aegis gave chase, shooting out a leg. Qazzi had to jump into the crate of explosives to avoid the shot. Dlella's new right-hand man planted a foot on the edge of the crate and bounded back off. Aegis ran by the crate, snatched up an explosive and set the timer to fifteen seconds.

This was one of his father's. It would set off all the rest and level what remained of the building.

Aegis tossed the explosive back into the crate and jumped to tackle Qazzi. The assassin dodged to the left, but Aegis managed to bring the shield down on the tendons above his opponent's heel. Aegis rolled out of the dive to his feet, satisfied by the sound of Qazzi's scream. Aegis ran out the room and down the hall to the back room. Sabreslate stood over the sewer entrance, grimacing.

Aung disappeared down the hole, and Sabreslate waved him over with her good arm. "Get in so I can seal it behind us!"

"Big boom in five," Aegis said. He dropped into the sewers, landing in a crouch that covered him in slime to the waist.

Sabreslate dropped down behind him, hanging onto the edge of the floor with her empathic bond, starting to seal the floor behind her. Qazzi leapt down on her through the small hole, and the two of them crashed into the running current of the sewer floor.

Aegis felt the bass of the detonation and heard the sounds of stone walls crumbling. A fireball passed overhead, only a few licks spilling down into the sewer.

"Form up!" Aegis dove onto the shifting pile, trying to pull his teammate away from Qazzi. The killer had jettisoned his sabers and was stabbing at Sabreslate with his treasured straight sword.

Aegis pushed Qazzi back and filled the sewer pathway between him and Sabreslate. "Get back. I'm point, you're mark."

"Got it." Qazzi regained his feet while Aegis spoke, and charged forward again. His sword searched for a way around Aegis' shield, but the Shield's defense held.

Nore and Aung joined the melee, coming in on Aegis' left. *They should split up and help me flank him, but I can work with this*, Aegis thought, as he shifted right to circle around Qazzi.

"Press!" Aegis said, and the four of them struck in near unison. The assassin leapt back in the small pocket remaining, dodging out of the way of Aung's long arms and Aegis' shield swipe. He did not, however, dodge the strips of stone Sabreslate had pulled from the ceiling and shaped into swinging tentacles. The stone tentacle knocked him from the air, and the Shields pounced again.

Qazzi was prepared for them this time, though, blade out like a pike set against a cavalry charge. Aegis slid down the blade, using his shield, but the killer twisted the guard, and the tip dug into Nore's ribcage. The man's howl filled the whole sewer pathway. Qazzi pushed Nore toward Aung while Aegis jockeyed for position to grapple.

But Aegis couldn't get a grip, not while Qazzi sliced and stabbed in the tight quarters, making space where there was none and keeping them at bay. The city's premier killer slipped out from under the group with strength belying his build. Aegis clambered to his feet and caught a glance at Nore. Nore's threads disintegrated to nothing as the Freithin's blood drained down the sewer pathway in the already cloudy current.

Now we are three. Qazzi moved like he hadn't even taken the shot to the heel, so Aegis knew they couldn't all outrun him. *Maybe one of us, even two, but he'd hunt down the last one until that Shield a stain on Qazzi's sword to be wiped off on the person's own clothes.*

Qazzi spun his blade in a defensive pattern and resumed baiting Aegis. "What now, hero? You've only got one little lamb left, and then I get to go to work on the two of you. Yema has no doubt dispatched your fool of a leader by now, and I hear that Protean has been dispatched to deal with your team at the mint." His smile was ugly, the grin of merciless arrogance. "If you surrender, I might even let the others go."

Yema is in the tower? Dammit. They were all supposed to be in Heartstown for the summit. If he was telling the truth, there was no way any of them could get to the tower in time to help, not even Ghost Hands by air or Sabreslate by stone.

Qazzi lunged, catching Aegis in a thought. The young Shield reacted on instinct, sloshing backward to bring the Aegis into line to deflect the blow.

Aung jumped at Qazzi, who produced a dagger from his hip and stabbed through the Freithin's palm, ripping up and out through the webbing of the man's fingers. Aung fell as his screams ricocheted off the walls.

Qazzi raised both blades, the bloodied tip pointing at Aegis' throat. "Ready to give up, hero? Or do I get to make this one sing a symphony of pain? I think I'll go for the toes next."

I can't beat him, even with Sabreslate and Aung. Someone has to hold him off. Aegis dove forward again, slammed Qazzi against the wall with a satisfying thud . . . as the sword punched straight through his gut.

His vision blurred, and he doubled over. Through the pain, Aegis managed to yell, "Run!"

Chapter Forty-Seven

First Sentinel

The Hall of the City Mother was large enough to fit a congregation of three hundred, with fifty priests and another hundred acolytes in the rafters.

When he was a child, he'd come to take part in an homage service. *I felt something change there, felt Her presence in my heart.* He'd watched the thread of devotion wind up from his heart and toward the giant gem, matched by an emerald thread from the City Mother Herself.

This time, instead of a congregation, priests, and acolytes, First Sentinel was alone with Magister Yema and his Warlock Guard. Yema snapped twice, and the warlocks formed into two ranks, between the Magister and the Shield.

"I didn't believe the rumors when they said you'd be here—not at first. I just decided to reschedule my monthly visit, on the happy chance that I could rip out your heart. Thank you so much for being obliging."

"No, thank you, Yema, for obliging me. This will be infinitely easier with you here."

Now it might even work. But I can't do it with all these guards running around.

First Sentinel's mind spun, trying to plan how to fight a hundred guards while being assaulted by the Magister's sorcery. *And with my bag of tricks running on empty.*

Yema gave the order to attack, and the first rank charged while the second rank fired over their backs. *Think fast, old man. Or it all comes crashing down.* The Shields couldn't risk climbing the tower just to claim his body for the Hall of Broken Shields. Aegis would try, and they'd have to hold him down until he came to his senses.

First Sentinel's hand dropped to his belt and drew the grappling gun from its holster. He shuffled back and fired the hook into the rafters. The hook landed on target, and he pushed the button that whipped him up to the side of the tower and into the intricate rafters.

Yema bellowed at his warlocks as First Sentinel soared out of range. "After him! If you let him escape, I'll feed your hearts to the sewer rats!" They scrambled for the ladders, and the handful of warlocks already in the rafters started to converge.

First Sentinel pulled himself up onto the walkway. It was wide enough for two to walk shoulder to shoulder, but only just. It would limit their numbers in any one position, giving First Sentinel a chance to deal with them one or two at a time. The old Shield rushed the nearest guard, who couldn't quite keep his footing on the shaky planks. The warlock attacked with a knife coated by crackling energy. First Sentinel parried the blow with a shock glove, sending the knife spiraling out toward the center of the room. First Sentinel grabbed the warlock's arm and threw the man off the side. He screamed all the way down as First Sentinel continued on toward the next ladder.

Five layers above, there was a winch with hundreds of feet of rope, positioned directly above the emerald. *If I can get up there, then maybe I can even the odds.*

The air around him was thin, smelling of sawdust and unfinished wood. First Sentinel stepped onto an abutment that jutted out toward the center of the room, forming a quarter-circle with the pathway leading to another set of rafters.

At the corner was a trio of Yema's Warlock Guard, holding a tight formation. At top, a tall Pronai held a spear at the ready, standing over a waiting Ikanollo woman who held a femur wand and a crouched, Full-blood hedgehog-kin Millrej, bristling with blades as well as spines. Behind them were another few guards scattered along the far side of the rafter.

First Sentinel checked the struts under the far part of the rafter and, fingering an explosive, wondered if it would stay up with the corner blown out. First Sentinel decided against it, slipping the small bomb back into its pouch. The warlocks from the ground level were working their way up, cutting off his retreat.

The corner was his best path up. *Unless I want to try the grappling gun again and risk the guards at the far side cutting my line before I can scale up to the platform.*

No, it had to be straight through or not at all. No time to go around. But explosives weren't his only tool. He drew one of his fighting staves and the last flash stone. First Sentinel palmed the stone as he charged the trio of warlocks, spinning the fighting staff to draw their attention.

The Ikanollo let loose with her wand, shooting yellow bolts that matched the threads of fear that sprouted from the trio's chests. Yema's control kept them loyal, made them stand their ground, but it couldn't keep them from fearing First Sentinel, the unkillable rebel. *Reputation has its rewards.*

First Sentinel ducked and rolled under the blasts, feeling the rafters wobble and creak beneath him as he came back up to his feet and tossed the stone. He covered his eyes, waiting for the flash.

The Pronai called, "Flash!" but the stone went off before First Sentinel could see how the others reacted. First Sentinel removed his hand just after the flash, watching through his shimmercrab goggles. He'd gotten in range of the spear wielder. The warlock had one hand on the end of the haft and the second hand a foot higher for balance. With his grip back that far, he had little tip control and less leverage. First Sentinel beat the blade aside with his staff and closed in. The Pronai had protected his eyes, but the Millrej hedgehog-kin was scratching at his eyes with a moan.

First Sentinel waved the fighting staff in front of him in a defensive pattern to ward off the spear as he kicked the Millrej in the face. The hedgehog guard fell halfway off the platform, his upper body dangling from the side. He flailed, toe claws digging into the planks for stability.

The Ikanollo fired another blast from the femur wand, catching First Sentinel in the leg. The magic tore away his leggings and the top of his boots, searing flesh just inches below the still healing wound from his fall after killing Nevri.

The pain dropped First Sentinel to a knee, then to his belly as he forced himself down to keep from falling off the platform. He pushed back up and spun on his back, holding on with one hand as he tripped the Ikanollo.

The Pronai warlock dropped the spear and pulled a knife. The Pronai cut down toward the Shield's neck, but the distance was long enough that First Sentinel leaned away to dodge the strike. He put the Ikanollo warlock between himself and the Pronai. *One at a time, thank you.*

She scrambled back to her feet and got in the Ikanollo's way while First Sentinel found his footing. The platform bobbed up and down as the blows and crashes stressed the rope supports.

Faster, now, they're catching up to you. First Sentinel stood as far up as he could without leaning on his wounded leg, whipped the fighting staff into the Ikanollo's side, then pushed her at the Pronai again.

There's no way I can make it the rest of the way, crawling. Get up, old man. Keep going.

First Sentinel pivoted on his good leg, grabbing for the Pronai's wrist as he caught the first twitch of the blow. The Pronai was fast, and the two fell into a clinch. The Pronai flailed, and they both started wobbling.

First Sentinel wrapped the Pronai in an arm bar, then dropped him to his knees with the pressure from the grapple. First Sentinel pushed and dropped the Pronai off the platform. *Two down, keep going.* First Sentinel fell on the Ikanollo again with the butt of his fighting staff, cracking her sternum.

First Sentinel stood with a grimace and moved along the other side of the platform. He clashed with the next handful of guards while the Warlocks closed the distance behind him. His left leg was dead weight, so he fought dragging it.

What I'd give to have Aegis here, or Sapphire.

Chapter Forty-Eight

Sapphire

A t the lip of Ghost Hands' weakening force field, Protean rolled off from the inside wall of the vault and slammed Weja to the ground. It morphed its fingers into claws and dug them into Duma's side. Sapphire heard the cracking of bones, and then Duma gasped her last breath as her ribcage cracked open like a book. For a moment, grief overcame Sapphire as she felt her blood-bound sister's pain, and all she could think about was having to explain to Yara that her mother was dead.

Weja cried out in wordless sorrow, diving on top of Protean and punching with incoherent rage, channeling the anger and pain of loss. *Animalistic fury is good against Protean, but when three Freithin can't hold the shapeshifting beast, how can two?* The Freithin tumbled on the floor, trying to get a grip on the ever shifting Spark-touched.

If she had the rest of the team, she'd try to bring a building down on Protean, or trick it into becoming small enough to enclose in a magically reinforced container enchanted by First Sentinel—any of the things they'd done to stop it in the past.

But she had only Ghost Hands and Weja by her side, and no free escape routes. Blunt fingers shifted into claws as Protean pressed Sapphire, cutting a gash through her ear. She kept punching, kicking, trying to bruise Protean's mass into immobility and fatigue, the only tactic she saw left to her, save for bringing the whole city block down on their heads. *Not my idea of a good end to the evening.*

A crossbow bolt clattered off the far wall of the vault, inside Ghost Hands' field. Then another. One caught Protean in the back, and yet another punched a hole in Ghost Hands' cloak before the rest of the volley was knocked aside.

The Qava's voice rang in her mind, strained and tired. *[I can't hold on much longer. We need to get out.]*

Sapphire landed a punch square between Protean's two bulbous eyes and the slits left for breathing. *[You're right. I'm going to toss another batch of the explosives onto the guards. We duck behind the vault opening, then make a break—right turn out of the vault. Relay the order to Weja.]*

Ghost Hands responded, *[Of course. On your mark.]* Sapphire saw Weja narrow her eyes, no doubt listening to the voice in her head. She threw a kick to Protean's shifting center of mass, and then pushed off. Sapphire reached into the crate and plucked out two mid-sized explosives. She set one timer to two minutes, the other to five seconds.

[Mark.] Sapphire pulled out the shorter explosive, tapped the silver button, then hauled back and tossed it overhand into the ranks of guards. She dove to the side, watching the explosive bounce. The boom echoed around the corner of the vault wall, and Sapphire was back up, shouting, "Go!" as she tackled Protean, pulling him off Weja. Ghost Hands flew above and to her right, and Weja scrambled out of the vault, breath heaving with effort.

Protean speared a sharpened pseudopod through Sapphire's gut. Sapphire grit her teeth as she pulled herself off the protrusion to flee with her teammates. The handful of survivors from the guard squadron were scrambling to their feet.

Ignore the pain. Just run.

She broke into a full sprint, cracking the tiles with her heavy strides as she raced down the halls to catch up to Weja and the flying Ghost Hands. Rapid padding footfalls followed her, maybe two seconds behind. Sapphire reached into her belt and tossed a flash stone behind her. She saw the light bounce off the walls, and the rapid footfalls slowed, a pace or two farther back.

Sapphire shouted in her mind. *[Protean's right on my tail. We'll need a quick fade once we get free of the building, or it'll tail us all the way back to the safehouse.]*

Ghost Hands' response was strained, as if out of breath, though Qava didn't breathe. *[I don't think I have enough in me to do anything drastic.]*

[You're far too skinny to make a good meal, it's true.]

Ghost Hands chuckled. *[I bet my brain is juicy.]*

Sapphire caught a claw across the calf, but didn't break stride. *[Can we concentrate on getting out alive?]*

[Just saying. You're going to have to catch me, all right?]

[What?]

Ghost Hands turned, hovered in the air, and two slabs ripped off from the wall, smashing Protean between them. The mass toppled to the ground, and Ghost Hands dropped out of the air like a sack of coffee beans. Sapphire slid to a stop to catch the falling Qava. She was as limp as the stuffed doll Sapphire's brother had made out of scraps back when they were in the pens.

Sapphire and Weja ran for the entrance, broke open the door, and ran out into the lamp-lit evening.

"Safehouse—now," Sapphire said, and they bolted down the street toward the alley that led to their rendezvous point. She tried to rouse Ghost Hands, but the Qava woman was out cold, her mind silent.

We made it. Some of us. I wonder if Aegis did. Or First Sentinel. It's in their hands now.

As Sapphire turned the corner toward the alley, the mint went up in a cacophony of explosions, red and yellow plumes blossoming up into the sky. The trio disappeared into the corner and sought refuge from the watchful eyes of the city.

Chapter Forty-Nine

First Sentinel

First Sentinel had scaled three levels of rafters, followed by a long stream of warlocks behind him and with several groups ahead. The winch was still two stories up. *One level up, and I can make a jump for the end of the rope and the crane.*

Magister Yema was a bald yellow spot down below, waving his arms, the burgundy strand between him and the emerald contorting and twisting. The threads smothered the City Mother's brilliant light, but First Sentinel could see cracks through the ribbons. If he could just get an unimpeded shot at the emerald, he might be able to end this whole thing. *I bet Yema would bring the rafters down if it wouldn't mean risking damage to the emerald.*

First Sentinel reached another group. He baited a warlock holding a sickle, stepping into her range just long enough for her to take a swing. First Sentinel dropped back and let the warlock follow through, sending her off balance. The warlock stumbled forward to regain her balance, and First Sentinel leaned back in and cracked her across the jaw. Warlock and sickle fell from the platform.

The other two lunged forward, determined not to be picked off. One wielded a sword, and the other reached out with hands that sucked away the light from the air around them.

I don't want to find out what that does firsthand. First Sentinel stepped sideways, away from the dark hands, and when the swordswoman reached out, he swung into her blow, sending the blade across to block her compatriot.

First Sentinel shuffled forward and pulled the swordswoman by her cloak, sending her tumbling into Dark Hands. He watched the warmth drain out of the woman's face, paralyzed by pain. She didn't even have the energy to cry out, as her life was drained away in an instant. Dark Hands was lost in ecstasy, his face flush.

Not wanting to risk suffering Dark Hands' power, First Sentinel pushed past the two of them and kept going. *Just a little farther.* He jumped and climbed up another ladder, seeing the blades thrusting down the hole at the bottom of the next level. *This'll be interesting.*

Yema's voice rang clear through the wide expanse of the room, and a shiver rushed all the way down First Sentinel's body. *Not good.*

His vision blurred into a mass of red, and the ladder crumbled in his grip. First Sentinel fell, spinning, the emerald rushing up toward him like a long-forgotten lover.

Don't die yet, old man.

First Sentinel shook off the daze and reached for his grappling gun as his longcoat whipped around him, threatening to tie him up into a straightjacketed corpse-in-waiting.

Fifty feet above the emerald, then forty, thirty. The gun came up, and First Sentinel fired at the far side of the ramparts, praying for his luck to hold. The hook found purchase, though First

Sentinel's arm threatened to stay behind as his trajectory curved down and away from the emerald.

Not fast enough. The rope tore, or was cut. First Sentinel didn't know, couldn't tell. He fell again, but instead of the gem, the ground reached out to catch him, and he collapsed in a cracking, crashing roll.

First Sentinel snapped his head up, even though his vision was still shaking, his head pounding. He thought he'd sprained his ankle, maybe fractured something in his once good leg. His grappling gun had clattered to the floor out of reach, his legs were useless, and the warlocks were right there, Yema laughing behind them.

The warlocks closed, but Yema called them off. They formed a circle, surrounded the two men with a wall of steel and magic. Yema strode through the crowd and stepped into the circle.

"If only the rest of them could see you like this. Broken, beaten, useless." Yema smiled again, revealing ivory-white teeth with sharpened canines. "Well, perhaps not useless." He reached into his cloak and pulled out a jewel-encrusted dagger with permanent bloodstains in all colors marbled up the edge of the blade. The pommel was ruby, carved into the shape of a heart.

He's not just going to kill me. He'll take my heart and use me against the other Shields, a puppet, a powerless witness to the betrayal he'll force upon me.

A burgundy thread unfolded from Yema's cloak, reaching out for the Shield, trying to slip through the weave of his threads: gold threads for his brother and sister Shields; a broad thread of brass reaching out toward the City Mother; supplicant, dimming strands of hope flailing for anything to hold onto.

First Sentinel's mind raced as his heart screamed in fear, feeling the thread of domination reaching out.

I can't. I won't. Not them, not my friends. Not my son. Not Selweh.

The guilt of Aria's death and his folly weighed on him, threatening to flatten him with its weight as the burgundy thread fought its way through the weave of his emotions, seeking purchase.

I'm sorry, Aria. I've held onto this guilt like a drowning man holds to his last broken plank. I couldn't help you without breaking us, and then I failed you again. But if I die here, Aegis and all of the others will be next.

I promised, and I won't fail you again.

First Sentinel sloughed off the guilt like a snakes' skin, felt it fall away from him, freeing his hand and his heart.

He reached out for the burgundy thread, tore it from Yema's chest, and tossed it aside to wither and die. Yema recoiled, clutching his chest.

"What? I thought you . . . "

It had been nearly thirty years since the last time he'd used his powers to save Aria. To lose Aria. His heart raced, blood pumping so fast he feared he would burst. He'd inadvertently pulled out several other threads as well, and saw them squirm on the floor, shriveling up like sun-bleached grubs. *It still works, but I've as little control as ever. Focus, old man.*

Yema cried out in wordless rage and then reached forward for the Shield again, stabbing the dagger at First Sentinel's throat. They tumbled to the floor.

We're just two puppet masters vying for control of the soul of a city. Two sorcerers, two leaders. Two stubborn old men, refusing to give up, incapable of yielding.

They struggled over the dagger with wordless snarls and grunts. As First Sentinel grabbed hold, he pushed the dagger toward the thick braid of threads linking Yema to the distant building where the Warlock Guard's hearts were kept. First Sentinel pushed their hands, using the dagger as a focus to saw through the threads binding the warlocks to Yema's control, drawing again on the power he'd forbidden himself out of guilt and fear.

Threads tore by the thousands. They frayed, strained, and then snapped free, flying around the room, searching for a heart to cling to. The thickest threads were red rage to First Sentinel and the burgundy control to the City Mother. First Sentinel hacked at the burgundy thread and watched it snap along with the others. There was no going back. Not after Blurred Fists, after the Shield-bearers, after Nevri, after the Soulburner.

This has to end now.

The shifting, shouting, waiting crowd of Warlock Guards went still, enraptured. The only sounds in the room were the two men's struggle, each scrambling for control. Yema regained the dagger and found his feet, wobbling to a shaky stand. The magister backed away and started to chant a spell. Behind him, the black-cloaked crowds murmured, some still dazed, some panicking, others yawning as if waking from a long sleep.

"Please, help me!" First Sentinel shouted. *Please, snap out of it.* He tried to find his footing, and then fell flat on the ground as the fracture deepened and his ankle gave way. First Sentinel reached for his belt, but Yema pounced again. He twisted away from the blade, so instead of the heart, Yema stabbed through First Sentinel's shoulder, the edge sliding across his clavicle.

All he could do was scream. First Sentinel curled up, trying to protect his vitals, but Yema was on him, stabbing again.

City Mother, help me. This is your true son, Wonlar Gonyu Pacsa, Shield of Audec-Hal. Can you hear me? This man has held you captive for fifty years, used your power against your children. I will die here today, but don't let him keep on controlling you. For the sake of my son, I cannot let guilt stay my hand. Yema and the others are strangling the life from this city, bit by bit.

First Sentinel opened his eyes, reaching out for the City Mother. He took a deep breath and pulled with all of his being.

He pulled himself along the brass thread he'd kept and tended for fifty years. He pulled with fifty years of fighting, hoping, and planning, his thread tended diligently and tirelessly, like the crocuses Aria held dear. Every battle, every meeting, every invention, and every impassioned speech had brought him to that point, made the thread wide, the weave strong and tight.

The burgundy thread frayed an inch at a time, then faster, and faster, unraveling Yema's power. First Sentinel hauled at the thread, and it tore. He pulled once more, ignoring the pain from Yema's dagger, ignoring his screams of rage, and just pulling. He saw through the burgundy to the brilliant facets of Her emerald. He stretched out and pulled with his last breath.

And something reached back. First Sentinel heard a voice in his head, cool but heartening, old but ageless.

[I see you, my son. Finally, I see you. You and your people have removed the veils from my eyes, layer by layer, over the years. Today I can see clearly. Now it is my turn to help you.]

Yema reared up for the kill, once-ivory teeth stained with blood. First Sentinel was frozen on the floor, looking up at him and at the emerald beyond, which glowed as bright as it had when he was a child. The anchorless mass of burgundy threads shifted colors, lightened. Burgundy was replaced by deep emerald, arcing out across the whole city.

I've done it. She's free.

The dagger came down, but Yema's hand was stayed by a waifish Pronai woman in a black cloak. She twisted the blade out of his hands, and she was not alone. The circle shifted, closing around Yema, and a mass of black-cloaked figures fell upon the sorcerer like a pack of wild animals, stabbing, slashing, biting, screaming their vengeance and retribution.

The frenzy continued, stretching out as First Sentinel saw the red threads of hatred twirl from the distant tower, intermixed with the emerald that bound every citizen to the City Mother, no longer choked out by the burgundy.

When they were done, the former warlocks cast aside their cloaks, piling them atop Yema's lifeless form. They gathered around First Sentinel, dressed only in tunics and undergarments. The former warlocks helped him up, and the whole group walked to the emerald.

The City Mother spoke to First Sentinel again, her presence in his mind as comforting as trace memories of the womb. *[Yema will never take another heart, my son. But there are others who still hold the reins of control over my children.]*

First Sentinel coughed, tasting blood in his mouth. "I know. They're next. The Smiling King, COBALT-3, Omez. I won't stop until they're all gone and your Senate is restored."

[But first, you need to rest. Start now. Your friends are coming for you.]

The world went dark, but it was the comforting dark of sleep, of rest, of the last dark before the dawn. As sleep took him, he smelled crocuses, freshly bloomed.

Chapter Fifty

Aegis

The sewer passageway was coated in blood, but Aegis saw the world only in shades of red through his goggles. Blood seeped down his side from the stab wound to the gut, but he wasn't alone in his pain. Aung was fighting on through a hundred cuts and stabs. Qazzi was a juggernaut, always pressing, always attacking. He turned the smallest advantage into the room needed to land another blow, even as the Shields laid into him again and again. Aegis' friends had ignored his call to run, and he didn't have the strength to protect them.

A kick to the sternum knocked Aegis onto his back, leaving him to stare up at a manhole. Aegis weighed the options. He considered the time of night, the neighborhood they'd emerge into, likelihood of patrols, and availability of escape paths. It was worth the risk.

Qazzi tried to pin Aegis to the ground with a blade through the gut, but Aegis rolled out of the way to catch the shot across his back.

"Up the manhole!" Aegis called as the blade tore through his raiment. He lashed out with a kick, then rolled up to a crouch, shield out to protect him self once more. He pressed Qazzi, going on the offensive despite flagging strength and mounting wounds. He swung the shield in too slow arcs, launching strike after strike.

Qazzi dodged a shield strike and countered with a lunge to Aegis' face. Aegis swatted the blade away, trying to hold his ground. He gave an inch at a time, blood running down his raiment in growing streams. Without attention, he knew he'd go into deep shock soon.

Sabreslate called, "Come on!" from the manhole opening, and Aegis hopped back, bending back in a body void to dodge a slash coming in under the shield. Instead of opening his intestines, there was a sharp pinch as his clothes tore and the blade grazed his abdomen.

Something loose passed over his back. He glanced up to see a gray rope hanging from Sabreslate's animate cloak, the two above holding on. "Grab it!" she said, and Aegis reached up, wrapping his right hand around the rope.

They pulled and he shot upward, clearing the manhole and spreading his feet to land on both sides of the top. Aegis stepped back, and Aung slid the manhole cover back. The Freithin collapsed onto the manhole cover, his whole weight keeping it closed.

Aegis stepped back to look around in the night, seeing the street in red-scale. The streets were bare, the aristocracy tucked away inside their fenced and locked doors, three houses to a block. *No patrols in sight. Small blessings.*

Aegis heard a dull pounding from below, and the manhole cover shifted.

"This won't hold once we leave," Aung said.

Aegis sighed, catching his breath. "I know. And if we wait here, guards will come, or he'll come out the next closest one."

"What do we do, then?" Sabreslate clutched the wound on her arm, gathering her raiment back up from a rope into a cloak.

"You go. I'll hold Qazzi off and fade back to the alley." Aegis wavered, the world bobbing without moving.

"He'll kill you before you can fade," Sabreslate said.

"Maybe. But you'll get away, and the Aegis will find another guardian."

Sabreslate shook her head. "I can't do that. Your father would kill me."

Aegis growled. "If you don't leave, I'll beat him to it."

Sabreslate managed a laugh. "Never."

Aegis stoked the fire in his heart, showed its flame through his eyes, a mottled gray thread of frustration wrapping tight around the shining gold between them. "Go," he yelled. "We can't stop him; we can barely contain him. If you stay, we all die!" Hot tears slid down his face.

Sabreslate's nostrils flared, and he saw her start to argue, but she sighed, shoulders slumping with fatigue and resignation. She stepped back and nodded to Aung.

Aegis stopped onto the manhole cover, knelt down, and looked to the last of his Freithin Shield-bearers. "You've done more than enough. Go home and tell the tale of the bravery of your kin. The Freithin have repaid their debt to the Shields twice over. Call on us, and we will answer."

Aung tugged on Sabreslate's arm, and after another moment, they left. Aegis waited on the street, holding back the manhole cover against the scrapes and thuds.

A minute later, the sounds stopped. Aegis lifted his eyes and looked around street, waiting for Qazzi to reappear.

Aegis stood in the middle of the street, throwing open his arms. "Come out, Qazzi. Let's get this over with."

And he waited. Countless moments passed as he scanned up and down the street, looking for patrols and wishing his friends the greatest of haste.

He turned over his shoulder just in time to see Qazzi diving down from a nearby roof, blade first. *No time to bring up the shield, no time to do anything but die.* Time slowed to a crawl as Aegis struggled to lift the shield. Far in the distance, a column of light erupted from the Tower of the Crown, climbing higher than his eyes could see.

Father. You did it.

The world around him continued to move at a crawl, but suddenly, Aegis was free. A brilliant emerald thread stretched down to him from the Tower. *She is with me.* Boundless energy filled Aegis' veins. He rose up to meet Qazzi's blade, and a mighty fist followed it, arcing up and connecting with the assassin.

The blow hurled Qazzi back twenty feet. The assassin broke down the wrought-iron fence of an aristocrat's yard as he fell. Aegis had never been this strong, stronger than Sapphire even.

But now the City Mother was free, and Aegis was Her champion.

Aegis heard a cool voice in his mind. It reminded him of his mother's voice.

["Selweh Aria Pacsa. I am with you, my champion. Come to the tower; your father needs you."]

Aegis looked over to the broken fence. Where Qazzi should have been be, there was only the marred garden smashed between the bars. *He's gone.* Aegis turned toward the tower and broke into to a run, faster than he'd ever run before. *If you die on me, Father, I'll never forgive you. You have to live to see the city reborn.*

Epilogue

First Sentinel

When First Sentinel awoke, the Shields were gathered around him, with a pair of the Freithin Shield-bearers, all of them bloodied and beaten. The hall of the City Mother was still streaked with the signs of battle, white and emerald tiles stained and marred. There were bodies scattered around the room and the rafters.

But the tyrant's minions were nowhere in sight. With the City Mother's power returned, the sanctity of the tower was restored, as it was before the fall of the Senate. Only those with Her blessing could enter, and none who bore ill intent would be able to cross any threshold of the tower.

We have a fortress, now. We'll be under constant siege, engines brought in from all around the world, bought with Nevri and Medai's money, designed to crack even the titanbone.

"Report," First Sentinel croaked.

"The mint is gone," Sapphire said.

Aegis said, "As is the doctor's house, but he escaped."

First Sentinel nodded. "Doesn't matter. Where's Yema?"

Aegis shook his head. "He was dead by the time I got here. And everyone else was gone, save for the priestesses."

First Sentinel nodded, weak. Every inch of his body was sore or stinging—bloodied, beaten, or both. *I ought to be dead, in truth. Broken ribs, twisted ankle, fractured leg, probably more. If I hadn't freed the City Mother, I doubtless would be. Instead, the old man lives long enough to see the beginning of the next chapter in the history of Audec-Hal.*

"Take me to a window. I want to see the city."

Aegis and Sapphire lifted him up, walked him down two flights of stairs through almost empty hallways. Sapphire's jade thread curved around him toward Aegis, braided with a white strand of hope. And in Aegis' thread to Sapphire, several strands in the thread were lighter, a shade closer to evergreen.

First Sentinel's smile widened as they walked out onto the level below. He saw a priestess of the City Mother at the far end of the hall, bright emerald cloak catching the lantern light as she stopped and bowed. *Did Yema have them locked up somewhere? A question for another time.*

They stopped in front of a full-length mirror and set First Sentinel down. The priestess chanted, and the mirror changed, revealing a view of the city. The Shields looked out to the top of Headtown and down the neck to the whole city.

It was nearly light as dawn spread a long shadow from the tower and the northern cliffs down on the city. The shadow of the tower stretched all the way down past Hook's Hole, and for a moment First Sentinel thought he could see the veranda of his old apartment, where he'd stood each morning, looking up to the tower and waiting for this day to come.

The fifty-year winter has ended. Spring is here. And Audec-Hal will know summer once again.

"Take me back up. And put on some tea. We have work to do."

Aegis lifted First Sentinel and then spoke. "They're preparing for another healing, Father. You've been badly hurt." Another priestess approached, carrying a basin of water, towels piled over her arm.

"I'll be fine now. I don't plan on dying until our job is done."

The seasons would not change on their own, nor quickly. It would take a great many storms to bring on the summer. Thunder, lightning, storms, and floods—the path wouldn't be easy.

First Sentinel looked around to the Shields, battered and bloodied. *Ghost Hands, my oldest friend. Sabreslate, both supporter and critic. Sapphire with her great strength and boundless heart. And Aegis, my son, greatest of us all.*

He remembered the ones who had passed, Blurred Fists and Aria and all of the rest. They all had brought the Shields to this moment. *With the City Mother supporting us, Her tower our sanctuary and headquarters, we will finish this war.*

Then the city would be free again. Selweh could have a real life, and First Sentinel could retire. *I'll hang up my raiment and belt and spend my days telling stories to children, all the children of the city, not just a handful of Freithin in Rova's living room. I'll drink endless cups of tea and bask in their smiles.*

He couldn't dream of anything better.

Glossary

Acci, Dr.: A Shield-bearer. A Jalvai doctor who mends the wounds of the Shields.

Aegis: A Shield of Audec-Hal. There have been five bearers of the Aegis. The first was the founder of the Shields of Audec-Hal, though his true name remains a mystery. Other bearers include Zenari, Aria Enyahi Gara, Aernah, and Selweh Aria Pacsa.

Aegis, the: An enchanted heater shield, the emblem of the Shields of Audec-Hal. Grants its bearer a connection to the power of the City Mother, including incredible strength, agility, and stamina. Cannot be wielded by any but its chosen. When an Aegis dies, the shield finds its way to a new bearer.

Aernah: Also known as Aegis. The fourth bearer of the Aegis, a former school teacher. Deceased.

Aria Enyahi Gara: Also called Valence. Shield of Audec-Hal, and the fourth Aegis. Married to and then estranged from Wonlar Pacsa. Mother of Selweh Aria Pacsa. Deceased.

Audec: One of the titans who fell to the earth in the first age and died upon impact, creating a crevasse in the shape of his body. Today, only his bones remain, serving as the building blocks of the city of Audec-Hal.

Audec-Hal: A city built in the crevasse formed by the fall of the titan Audec. Formerly ruled by a Senate, Audec-Hal is currently controlled by a loose alliance of five leaders: Nevri, COBALT-3, Magister Yema, Medai Omez, and the Smiling King.

Bira Qano: Also known as Ghost Hands. One of the original Shields of Audec-Hal. A Qava of considerable telekinetic talent. Married to Sarii Gebb.

Blue Heart, the: An alchemical artifact used by Medai Omez to control his Freithin slaves. Destroyed by the Shields of Audec-Hal.

Bluetown: The self-imposed ghetto of the Freithin. Located in Medai Omez's domain.

Blurred Fists: One of the Shields of Audec-Hal. There have been four Blurred Fists, the mantle handed down within one family. The mantle of Blurred Fists is currently held by the Pronai messenger Wenlizerachi, the great-grandson of the original Blurred Fists.

City Mother, the: Patron goddess of the city of Audec-Hal. The City Mother once protected the city, binding its people together with Her compassion and strength. Controlled by Magister Yema, She currently uses Her power to keep the people of the city submissive and afraid.

COBALT: One of the original rulers to seize territory in Audec-Hal after the fall of the Senate. COBALT was an android obsessed with understanding biological life.

COBALT-2: Created by COBALT, and creator of COBALT-3.

COBALT-3: One of the rulers of Audec-Hal. COBALT-3 shares her grand-creator's obsession with biological life. COBALT-3's domain is the city's right leg and part of the trunk.

District: Name for a neighborhood of the city of Audec-Hal.

Dom Watches-and-Remembers: Son of Nai Watches and Zong Remembers.

Domain: The area controlled by one of the five rulers of Audec-Hal.

Dlella: A Full-blood serpentine Millrej lieutenant of Nevri's.

Douk Tager: An Ikanollo Shield-bearer. Owner of Douk's Daily, a pro-Shield coffeeshop. Well-connected in the circles of the Audec elite. Married to Xera Tager.

Dounmo: A blend of highly caffeinated tea. Known to have pain-relieving properties.

First Sentinel: One of the first Shields of Audec-Hal. Also known as Wonlar Gonyu Pacsa. Ikanollo alchemist and gadgeteer of the Shields. Adoptive father of Selweh Aria Pacsa, the fifth Aegis.

Forked Lightning: Former Shield of Audec-Hal. A Spark-touched Ikanollo with the ability to create lightning bolts. Deceased.

Freithin: One of the races of Audec-Hal. Originally created by alchemical processes for the slave pens of Medai Omez. Blue-skinned, they are large in stature and never stop growing. Due to their size, they are incredibly strong and tough.

Ghost Hands: One of the first Shields of Audec-Hal. Also known as Bira Qano. A powerful Qava telepath and telekinetic.

Ikanollo: One of the races of Audec-Hal. By far the most common race in the city, Ikanollo are yellow-skinned and brown-haired, to a one. Once they reach majority, all Ikanollo men are identical, and all women are identical. Ikanollo differentiate one another through their ability to see the threads of emotional connection between people.

Jalvai: One of the races of Audec-Hal. They have gray skin the color of stone. All Jalvai are born with the ability to control and shape stone, making them champion artisans, architects, and builders.

Kesh: A Freithin song of mourning sung over the deceased by their family.

Medai Omez: One of the rulers of Audec-Hal. Also called The Slaver, Medai was the one to bring Freithin to the city. His domain is composed of part of the trunk of the city, as well as the left arm.

Millrej: One of the races of Audec-Hal. Each family of Millrej takes after their animal patron, with physical characteristics such as fur, scales, or horns. In puberty, some Millrej are revealed as Full-bloods, growing into full anthropomorphic hybrids.

Nai Watches: Married to Zong Remembers. Mother of Dom Watches-and-Remembers.

Nevri: Also called Nevri the Lash, Executor Nevri, or The Gangster. A former member of the Viscera City Slicers and former member of the Senate of Audec-Hal. Now one of the five rulers of the city, controlling the territory of Audec's head and the right arm.

Qazzi Fau: A Spark-touched Ikanollo Lieutenant of Nevri. Formerly a contract killer, Qazzi maintains a group of assassins who help execute Nevri's will.

Qojimata: Former Shield of Audec-Hal. Deceased.

Oligarchs, the: Another name for the current rulers of Audec-Hal. One of the acceptable terms for public discourse.

Onyx: A Spark-touched Freithin Lieutenant of the Smiling King. Incredibly strong and seemingly inexhaustible.

Pronai: One of the races of Audec-Hal. Red-skinned, everything about Pronai is fast. They mature, think, move, and age far faster than the other races. Most die of old age by thirty.

Qava: One of the races of Audec-Hal. Born without sensory organs, their faces flat, Qava perceive the world through telepathy and telekinesis, subsisting on the thoughts of other races.

Raiment: The clothing and equipment of a Shield of Audec-Hal. Used both to conceal their identities and to make themselves symbols of freedom and resistance.

Red Vixen: A former Shield of Audec-Hal. A Full-blood fox-kin Millrej. Deceased.

Rova Remembers: Also known as Sapphire. A Shield of Audec-Hal. A Freithin, born in Medai Omez's slave pens, Rova joined the Shields when her people were freed.

Sabreslate: One of the Shields of Audec-Hal. Also known as Sarii Gebb. A Jalvai mistress of stone. Able to shape her stone raiment into weapons, shields, and more.

Sapphire: One of the Shields of Audec-Hal. Also known as Rova Remembers. A freed Freithin who joined the Shields shortly after the Unchaining. One of the largest and strongest Freithin in Audec-Hal.

Sarii Gebb: Also known as Sabreslate. One of the Shields of Audec-Hal. An older Javlai. A former sculptor. Married to Bira Qano.

Selweh Aria Pacsa: Also known as Aegis. Born Selweh Aria Gara. Formerly Second Sentinel. One of the Shields of Audec-Hal. The fifth bearer of the Aegis, and son of Aria Enyahi Gara. Adopted son of Wonlar Gonyu Pacsa.

Shields of Audec-Hal, the: A group of rebels fighting to overthrow the rule of the tyrants. Founded by the first Aegis shortly after the Senate fire.

Shield-bearer: One of the civilian supporters of the Shields of Audec-Hal, who provide shelter, supplies, information, and more.

Smiling King: One of the rulers of Audec-Hal. Also called The Madman. Suspected of being connected to the Spark-storms, the Smiling King's forces are mostly composed of Spark-touched who have been brainwashed and whom the King regards as his family.

Spark-storms: Supernatural storms that plague the city of Audec-Hal. Spark-storms permanently and inexplicably transform animate and inanimate matter, change the laws of physics within an area, or create other inexplicable changes.

Spark-touched: Those changed by Spark-storms. Some are physically transformed; others are granted strange abilities. No two people change in the same way.

Threads: Colored bands of emotional connection that tie people together. All Ikanollo can see the threads tied between the people they connect.

Tyrants, the: Another name for the current rulers of Audec-Hal. Officially forbidden in public discourse.

Unchaining, the: The raid conducted by the Shields of Audec-Hal that destroyed the Blue Heart and freed thousands of Freithin slaves controlled by Medai Omez.

Valence: One of the first Shields of Audec-Hal. Also known as Aria Enyahi Gara. Her Spark-touched ability allowed her to change her physical form to match something she touched (water, air, steel).

Veins, the: Slang for the streets of Audec-Hal, as if they were the titan's veins.

Warlock Guard, the: A group of Yema's servants whose hearts have been removed in a magical ritual, allowing Yema to control their actions.

Wenlizerachi: Also known as Blurred Fists. One of the Shields of Audec-Hal. The fourth Pronai to bear the mantle of Blurred Fists. A part-time courier.

Wonlar Gonyu Pacsa: Also known as First Sentinel. One of the founding Shields of Audec-Hal. Has the Spark-touched ability to control the emotional threads that connect people. Estranged husband of Aria Genyahi Gara. Adoptive father of Selweh Aria Pacsa.

Xera Tager: A Shield-bearer. Co-owner of Douk's Daily. Married to Douk Tager.

Yema: One of the rulers of Audec-Hal. Also called Magister Yema or The Sorcerer. Yema's domain is composed of the city's left leg and part of the trunk, and he controls the Warlock Guard as well as the City Mother.

Zenari: Former Shield of Audec-Hal. An office worker chosen as the second bearer of the Aegis. Deceased.

Zeraneyachi: Former Shield of Audec-Hal. The third to bear the mantle of Blurred Fists. Mother of Wenlizerachi. Deceased.

Zong Remembers: Brother to Rova Remembers. Married to Nai Watches. Father of Dom Watches-and-Remembers.

Thread Color Key

Beige – curiosity
Black – guilt
Brass – devotion
Burgundy – tyranny/control
Coppery red – malice
Dull green – casual partnership
Emerald – familial love
Evergreen – romantic love
Flushed pink – lust
Gold – comradeship
Gray – frustration
Jade – unrequited love
Light pink – embarrassment
Navy blue – sorrow
Orange – greed
Purple – authority/command
Red – hatred
Silver – adoration
Turquoise – empathy
Yellow – fear
White – hope

Acknowledgments

Shield and Crocus can be traced back directly to a conversation with my classmate Jon Christian Allison in the dining room at the Clarion West Writers Workshop in 2007. That day, I'd read an awesomely gut-wrenching story of Jon's, and I was inspired by his story to try my hand at a New Weird short for the following week. That story (which fit into a short story about as well as an Olympic-sized swimming pool fits into a shot glass) would go onto become the first version of *Shield and Crocus*.

This novel has come a long way from that original short fiction piece, and it would not have been possible without the assistance and support of a metric ton of wonderful people. A shorter version of these acknowledgments would just be to thank every person I talked with for any length of time between mid-2007 and today. *Shield* was the work that took me from aspirant to neo-pro, as I learned revision, submission protocol, and how to take rejection.

Lots of rejection.

But like the Shields, I took those setbacks and got back up to try again.

I want to start by thanking Jon Christian Allison for his story and that conversation, which set me on the path. I also want to thank the teachers, students, and staff members of the 2007 Clarion West Workshop, especially Graham Joyce, the resident instructor the week we workshopped "Shield & Crocus." At the end of the round of critiques for my story, Graham charged me with expanding the short piece into a novel.

This novel wouldn't exist without the inspiration of the works of China Mieville, Jeff VanderMeer, KJ Bishop, and others who contributed to the New Weird movement. To those who came before, I tip my hat, honored to be able to carry on the genre conversation that you all started.

Huge thanks are also due to Scat Hardcore, my first writing group, some of whom have probably read this novel five or more times across its different incarnations. Massive llamas of thanks to Marie Brennan, Siobhan Carroll, Alyc Helms, and Darja Malcolm-Clarke.

Big thanks to my Muse Brother Bryan Roberts for help in banging out the plot for this and nearly all of my other novels.

Massive high-fives to the many, many friends who helped as beta readers and proofreaders, helping me get earlier versions of the novel ready for submission: Daniel McDeavitt, Nicole Kaplan, Melissa Kocias, Élan Matlovsky, Rick Novy, Mary Rodgers, Tina Wallace, Kate Walton, and Adam Zabell.

Thanks to Kari Stevenson and Meredith Levine for their crucial support in the down times.

And to Gina Wachtel, the publishing fairy godmother who made it all possible.

A father–son high-five to my father, David Underwood, who opened the door.

Thanks again and again to Meg for every single day.

A hearty woot of thanks to my Agent of Awesomeness, Sara Megibow, for agreeing to take up the banner and give the novel one more shot at the Big Show.

The team at 47North have been amazing—passionate, professional, and responsive. David Pomerico, Alex Carr, Fleetwood

Robbins, Justin Golenbock, Britt Rogers, and the others: You are awesome, and I'm honored to be on the list.

Lastly, and perhaps mostly, my boundless thanks to David Pomerico, my editor—who always believed in First Sentinel and the Shields—for providing the comments that would put me on the right path and for coming back with the vision and passion to bring this book to readers everywhere.

Thanks to each one of you, the Shield-bearers who made this book happen.

Michael R. Underwood
Baltimore, Maryland
February 2014

About the Author

 Michael R. Underwood is the author of the Ree Reyes series (*Geekomancy*, *Celebromancy*, *Attack the Geek* [novella]) as well as the forthcoming Younger Gods series. By day, he's the North American Sales & Marketing Manager for Angry Robot Books. Mike grew up devouring stories in all forms, from comics to video games, to tabletop RPGs, movies, and books. Always books.

Mike lives in Baltimore with his fiancée, an ever growing library, and a super-team of dinosaur figurines and stuffed animals. In his rapidly vanishing free time, he studies historical martial arts and makes pizzas from scratch.